ISBN #   9798696998732

Contact Information:
KBA Publications
P.O. Box 2863
Phenix City, AL 36868

Printed in the USA.

Dedication

I dedicate this novel to my daughter, Keiara, and granddaughter, Ja'myra, and my host of nieces. I also would like to sincerely apologize for my absence, but please take into account, we can't be divided mentally. Fathers, if we don't play our important role in our precious young ladies' lives, there's a great possibility they'll be led astray.

<u>Prelude</u>

December the 23rd, 1994. Darrel Donnell and Ebony Smith decided to go out into the Kansas City winter, trying to catch the holiday spirit. Ebony loved the small gathering at Big Johnny's place. That club could hold up to a full one hundred people maximum. Yet on any given night, you probably wouldn't find that many people under his roof at one time. That's what was so thrilling to Ebony. She could always count on enjoying herself there. Basically, there were plenty of middle-aged couples; sometimes there were single guys and single females, joining the party, too. There were no inappropriate activities occurring either, because everyone was over thirty-five and as peaceful as could be.

There was only one altercation that Ebony could recall; Ms. Matty Mae Strong's oldest son Junior got sloppy drunk at the bar. That night it was obvious that all of his gentleman characteristics abandoned him. He started making small conversation with every female that crossed his path.

Junior made his first mistake when he put his hands on someone else's woman. Big Johnny didn't play that mess. This was his place of business, so he would always immediately handle his business. Nothing disturbed Big Johnny like someone who could not control their liquor.

"Come here woman," Junior said, dragging on each word, locking his strong fingers around Sallygean's wrist. *"You like ole' Junior, don't you."*

"Mister! You don't have to put your hands on me to talk to me," she politely said, aware that her boyfriend wouldn't like that.

"You want ole' Junior to show you a good time, don't you?"

"Man please," Sallygean paused. *"Now will you please free my wrist?"*

Junior had a mouth and mind full of disgusting things to say, but Big Johnny stepped in and put to rest his thoughts.

"Junior, why you have your filthy hands on the young lady?"

Sallygean's body felt a big relief, all the tension escaped her body. She felt more at peace with Big Johnny coming to her rescue instead of her boyfriend, Willie Mack. Willie was a hot-head and very, very jealous. He was the type that wanted to know the reason a male was all up in his woman's grill. So to avoid as much drama as possible, he didn't allow guys to be in his woman's presence without him being present.

"BJ mind ya business," Junior addressed Big Johnny.

"This is my business," Big Johnny growled, looking Junior into his bloodshot eyes. *"Now I'mma ask you son for the final time to take your greasy paws offa the lovely young lady."*

By Big Johnny's tone, Junior knew the giant was dead serious. He looked down at his mechanic's hands, oil and dirt caked up under his fingernails, and stared back at him. Junior released.

"Thank you BJ," Sallygean whispered.

"I'm the one you should be givin all the thanks to," Junior said, smiling.

Sallygean rolled her eyes., *"You the one who should be thankful that my man Willie didn't catch your dirty ass doubting me, cause it woulda been some serious ass kickin for real,"* she thought.

"Sallygean, I apologize for this," Big Johnny began, *"I'll bring you and Willie a couple of drinks over and they'll be on the house. I want y'all to finish enjoying the night while it's still young."*

"OK." she whispered, distancing and dismissing herself from the company of Junior. She also pondered the idea of enlightening her man on the situation, but quickly thought it was best not to. Besides, there was no damage done nor did she feel any danger. Sallygean surrendered to Big Johnny's suggestion; this allowed Willie and her to finish enjoying the rest of the night.

"Can I get a drink or two on the house too, BJ?" Junior breathed. His heavily scented breath was evidence that he had one drink too

many.

"*No! You don't deserve one,*" Big Johnny replied.

"*Come on, BJ,*" Junior begged.

"*If you start anymo trouble round here, I'mma give you one across the lips,*" Big Johnny promised as he shook his huge fist in Junior's face.

"*I'm talkin 'bout a drink, not a knuckle sandwich,*" Junior friendly replied, trying to deceive Big Johnny into thinking that he didn't possess a dangerous bone in his body.

"*I got customers to attend to, I don't have time to attend to jackasses,*" Big Johnny locked eyes with Junior. "*It would be a better idea if you go home and slept off your troubles Buddy! Cause there won't be another drink being served here to you tonight.*"

"*You throwin' me out?*"

"*If I was,*" Big Johnny made two fists, "*You'd be picking yourself up from the concrete.*"

Coming back to reality, Ebony leaned over to Darrel, She wanted him to clearly hear her.

"Baby what's the most people you seen in here?"

"That's a good question," Darrel responded, giving the question some thought as he patted his right knee and hummed to the group Emotions. Ebony spent a good ten minutes looking around the small club. The bar held fifteen stools and all fifteen were occupied. There were at least twelve tables and eight booths. This was the most people she'd seen in here. Her mind was mentally trying to calculate the crowd. Darrel smiled into her brown eyes as if he could read her pretty little mind.

"Baby come to think of it, it is a pretty good crowd in here tonight. I'd estimate it's about seventy-five or maybe eighty people."

Ebony smiled, "I'd say bout eighty."

Darrel rubbed her stomach, "I'd say eighty-one, counting my lil man."

"You know that would mean I put in all the work."

Darrel palmed her stomach, "Then you'll give me a princess. Daddy's very own little girl."

"Now that's better," Ebony agreed, taking a sip of her *cherry seven-up.*

She wanted to season her soda with gin, but Darrel wasn't going for it. He feared that even the smallest amount of alcohol could cause damage to their first unborn. Upon learning about his wife's pregnancy, Darrel became more cautious of her and his child's health. Ebony couldn't lift over ten pounds in his presence; he also banned her from carrying grocery sacks from the car. Ebony was only allowed to carry a sack if he inspected it first. If Darrel even thought the sack would be over eight pounds, he'd remove the heaviest items, and then give it back to her. Ebony was not even allowed to move furniture around.

"That's a man's job," he clarified *"No straining or struggling whatsoever."* She stopped smoking, because Darrel ruled against it. They were teammates and Ebony respected Darrel speaking out for the concern of their creation.

"We'll have a healthy child."

"Thank you my love," Darrel kissed Ebony on the cheek.

"The lips would've been better."

"How was that?" He asked, complying with Ebony's wish.

"Better, much better."

Darrel watched the people on the dance floor. Mr. Cain, a short stocky brother with no neck had the time of his life.

"Baby, look at your Uncle Bubbu go. Cut up Unk."

Ebony focused on Mr. Cain. The guy was doing the Mashed Potato. She got in a good laugh, once he started doing the Cabbage Patch. While Darrel choked with laughter, tears of joy slipped down her face. Mr. Cain was determined to be the best dancer that night. Without cracking a smile, he started doing the Running Man and Cabbage Patch in unison and in reverse.

He took his dancing very serious. As sweat covered his face, a slim female danced with Mr. Cain. She did the *Melanie Cool* dance and laughed her tail off. She enjoyed dancing, and because this guy was dancing by himself, which he always did.

"Oh God, oh God," Ebony laughed. "Lord please make Darrel's Uncle Leroy stop." She joked with her husband. "Darrel, he got my stomach hurting," Ebony confessed.

Once the song was over, Mr. Cain walked by their table.

"Playa, playa," Darrel hollered, catching Mr. Cain's attention. "Bru, you won the trophy for tonight."

Mr. Cain bowed twice, giving the room a second view of his bald spot. Anxious to finish his duty by shaking his booty, he made his way to the bar to wash down a couple more cheap drinks. Mr. Cain was very consistent about entertaining the people—he enjoyed it more than they did. This was his workout, Mr. Cain's exercise, guaranteed to shake off a couple pounds. Big Johnny looked forward to his company.
Every time they crossed paths in the street, Big Johnny would ask, *"Mr. Cain, will you be joining us tonight?"*
Mr. Cain always replied, *"If the Lord don't call me home first."*

Big Johnny knew Mr. Cain was not going to pass up the free bottle of Wild Irish Rose; especially after their first day of meeting. That's the day he had Mr. Cain unload two truckloads of beer for the reward of a single bottle.

Darrel noticed Betty and her common-law husband heading in their direction, "Look what the wind done blew in."
"What? What?" Ebony asked, looking at the dance floor. "Not over there Sweetheart. Look at the door."
Seeing her best friend Betty gave Ebony a reason to giggle. She couldn't wait to share the news with her about Disco Dynamite a.k.a., Mr. Cain and his dancing. That was some information that was guaranteed to uplift Betty's spirits. Not to mention that Mr. Cain always brought happiness to so many with his joy and energy. It was as if he had cancer, and was trying to infect the crowd by spreading his peace around.
"Hey Baby Momma, and how are you Baby Daddy?" Betty greeted, placing her purse on the table, as she sat down.
"Please forgive me for not congratulating you both sooner," Silk stated, collecting the seat next to Betty.
"Brotha you cool cause we still have seven more months to go," Darrel revealed. "I look forward to the opportunity to return the congratulations."
"We working on it, okay—okay," Betty spat with laughter. As
Mr. Cain bypassed their table, Darrel saluted him with his beer bottle.

"Uncle Bubbu ready for round two. Playa, playa, show the good people how to do the Robot, you dancing machine."

"Darrel, what you just say?" Betty asked, knowing he'd just pinned Ebony's uncle's name on this stranger. However, she was accustomed to Uncle Bubbu, because he kept everyone rolling with laughter. He'd put people in the mind of Leroy Brown by his style of clothing as well as by his conversation. The thought alone put tears of joy in Betty's eyes.

"Oooonoooo not anotha Uncle Bubbu Leroy Brown," she managed to blurt out in laughter.

"Ebony baby, do your Auntie know your Unk out here getting his shine on?" Darrel teased, watching Mr. Cain on stage, doing the moon walk backwards. When he started doing it forward, the crowd gave him the complete dance floor. He moon walked and began doing the prep with a hand clap. In between sections, he would pause, placing his hands on his hips and nod. The crowd clapped and cheered him on. They all knew a party was not a party without Mr. Cain, and he was definitely a party animal.

"Baby, I'll be back, I'm going to run to the car and get Betty's present right quick," Ebony whispered in Darrel's ear.

"I'll go get it outta the glove compartment for you," Darrel offered. "Besides, I need to get me a fresh pack of cigarettes anyway," he said, remembering there was only one cigarette left in his pack, and Darrel didn't like being on his last leg.

"Enjoy your Uncle's show, I'll be back in a flash. You won't miss me." Before Darrel could get in another word, Ebony was dashing towards the door; she didn't want to tongue wrestle with him any further.

***

"Yeah, I'll fix you 'bout gettin' sassy and 'bout meddling in grow folks business," Junior murmured, crawling underneath Big Johnny's truck. Once locating the brake line, he cut clean through it with his Rambo hunting knife. Brake fluid spilled all over Junior's chest. "Shit, I'll be damned if I don't move fast enough," he grinned.

While snaking from underneath the truck, Junior massaged the green, warm liquid in his chest, giving his chest hair a thorough bath. Taking another large swallow of the Thunder Bird caused him to choke. Junior would choke to death before he'd spilled a drop of cheap wine. After getting another mouth full, he oscillated it around as if it were mouthwash before swallowing.

"Now, that's much better."

The cold temperature caused thick white smoke to race from Junior's nose and mouth. Blowing into his hands, he tried to produce heat to them, but to no avail. The way his lungs were on fire gave Junior the foolish misconception that his breath would bring forth heat. He laughed at the thought. Junior wanted to go into the club, but knew he could not. Five days earlier, Big Johnny had barred him for two weeks, so he still had 9 days left. Junior wanted to interact with people other than the hobos, but there were no other hangout spots left for him to go. Not being able to control his liquor seemed to always get him into trouble, which is why he also couldn't be around his mother while intoxicated. She was like most mothers, and he didn't like hearing her mouth. Ms. Matty Mae Strong didn't like the things that came from her son's mouth, and she didn't have a problem letting him know it.

Junior frequently allowed alcohol to get the best of him. He also made the mistake of letting his liquor do most of his speaking. His mother, often displeased with the things he said, strongly suggested he wash his mouth out with soap. Junior spit back without a bit of hesitation.

"Just because you recommended I eat a bowl of shit doesn't mean that I'll do it." His comment got him thrown slap out of the house for a couple of days.

"Boy! *Until* you learn some manners, don't step a foot back into my house," Ms. Matty Mae Strong stated.

Since Junior had those two run-ins on the same night, he slept in alleys and under bridges. As Junior staggered through the dirt paved parking lot, the club music grew louder.

"Here's the season to be jolly, but how can I when I don't have no one?"

He stopped in his tracks. Seeing Ebony's slim feminine figure speed-walk through the lot immediately caught Junior's attention. He could hear her humming Toni Braxton's song, *I Love Me Some Him*. His antennas quickly went up. He cried out with a wolf noise as he held his head towards the sky. Sniffing through the air, her perfume exuded, causing Junior's eyes to race across the parking lot. The inside light from her car revealed his target. He moved in on his prey like the predator he really was. Soon as Ebony exited the passenger seat, she came face to face with Junior. He scared the living daylights out of her, Ebony grabbed her chest. It was almost in a manner that would allow her to stop the fast pace of her heartbeat, or even as if she was trying to stop her heart from jumping out of her chest period.

Junior pointed to her occupied hand.

"Is that for me?"

Ebony looked down at her right hand. It appeared as if she'd forgotten that she was palming Betty's gift and Darrel's pack of Newport's. Junior closed in their gap some. As he walked forward, she could smell the fresh brake fluid and cheap wine on him. Each step Junior took forward, the more steps she took backwards. Finally, he had her pinned up against the car. After pocketing Ebony's possessions, Junior collected his knife once again. He put the cold, iron metal up against Ebony's throat. Slowly racking the blade over her flesh, it was obvious that there was not a hint of sympathy in Junior's body. His mind had been called to the test. It appears as though he was ready and willing to answer. He licked Ebony's side burns.

"Please no! Please don't do that." She whined, as tears slid down her face.

"You wanna die?" Junior asked. "*Because* with you dead or alive, I'm going to have me some fun. So do I have to slice your pretty little throat first?" he asked, leaving a trail of saliva from her face down to her throat.

"Oh God. I don't want to die," Ebony cried.

"Then you better act right," Junior heavily breathed. The strong alcohol breath invaded her nostrils. "You gonna act right?"

"Yes," Ebony whispered.

"You gonna cooperate?" Junior asked, licking her tears.

"Yesss," she nervously cried.

Junior could barely hear Ebony this time. He'd put so much fear in Ebony, her eyes were closed. As tears repeatedly raced over her lips, Junior licked them. He was confused because he didn't know which turned him on more, her fear or her lips. Ebony was afraid to breath.

"Open your legs." Junior's demanded. "That's right Baby Girl, submit and bow down to a force that's greater than yours." Junior added. As Ebony obeyed his every command, Junior dug in the crotch of her pants. "You're hairy and wet. You want some of Junior, don't you? You need Big Daddy to bury himself in you, don't you?" As tears skittered and raced down Ebony's face, she stood there helpless, fearing for her life. She silently prayed that she'd be rescued, prayed that this was only a bad dream, and hoped when she opened her eyes, it would be Darrel's face she saw. She desperately prayed that it would be Darrel's four fingers clawing in and out of her flesh.

* * *

Darrel was so in tune with Mr. Cain's entertainment, that he didn't miss Ebony, until Silk finally spoke for the first time.

"Say D, what your 'ole lady gone to do, make the pack of cigarettes?"

Darrel examined Big Johnny's wall clock, the big hand was on the twelve, while the little hand rested on the eight.

"It was twenty minutes before eight before she left," he stated.

"How you know?" Betty inquired.

"Because that big ass clock Big Johnny haves sitting over the bar told me so," Darrel answered slipping out of his seat.

"Big Johnny got everything big," Silk joked, "Big money, big clock and a big woman."

"Cassandra's not fat, she's just big boned," Betty said, taking up for Cassandra, because she wasn't present to represent for herself. "Darrel where you going?" she asked.

"Where you think I'm going? I'm going to check on my baby," Darrel responded with a worried look in his face. Darrel's chest presented the heartbeat of a male who was moments away from winning a twenty-one lap marathon. While heading for the exit, someone shouted out his name.

"Hey Darrel."

"Not right now," he barked, continuing towards the front door like it was the finish line. Darrel burst through the door as if he were throwing a block for a quarterback. Once he stepped out of the door, he began to lightly jog. The cold air converted the exhaled air coming from his nostrils to smoke. Darrel heard some small crying; he stopped breathing and focused more on the noise. Darrel knew that moaning from anyone. Suddenly, his jogging turned into a springing motion.

"Ebony? Ebony? Where are you?" he yelled with panic in his voice. "Ebony where are you?" he screamed much louder.

Ebony's body clenched as Junior rammed his manhood in and out of her in a rapid pace. The more Darrel's voice echoed, the faster Junior thrust. The more he needed to satisfy the cravings of his body, it was a certain that sex and alcohol was always beyond his control. Realizing that he was on borrowed time, Junior reached his goal.

"I-I-I-I." he muttered. "Damn girl, you were good." By the time Junior threw his penis back into his pants, Darrel was there. He could not believe what he saw. Ebony blouse was ripped, both of her firm breasts were out in the open, her pants and panties babysat her ankles, and Darrel saw nothing other than death.

"You want some of 'ole Junior, Boy?"

Darrel's body was so full of rage, his anger made it impossible for him to comprehend.

"Darrel, he got a knife." He did not hear Ebony's warning. Without hesitation, he charged Junior with the strength of a bull. Junior was lowering the knife towards Darrel's head when suddenly his hand was blocked and pulled behind his back. Darrel punched him in the Adam's apple; and like the speed of lightning, he swung Junior's head into the back window of their car. He repeated his assault once again, but this time Junior's head hit the driver's side window. Totally furious, Darrel twisted Junior's arm until he were able to pry the weapon free of his grip. Darrel stabbed Junior in the stomach and rode his body to the ground. Finally, he hammered the knife home right inside of Junior's chest. Suddenly, Silk grabbed Darrel's arm, before he could deliver an additional puncture.

"Bru! Bru! The man gone now. He can't be saved."

Darrel crawled off Junior's dead body. As he fought to catch his breath, Ebony walked towards him. He rose to his feet, and Ebony walked into his arms. They held onto one another tightly. It was as if both of their lives depended on it.

Now aware of all the commotion, Betty walked up on the incident. Once she noticed Junior's lifeless body, she covered her mouth. As she gave his corpse a second glance, she saw that his chest was gutted open. To her it looked like someone had gutted a fish. Silk walked over and embrace Betty, trying to block her view. His intent was to try to shield her from also carrying this nightmare.

In the past few years that Silk had known Darrel and Ebony, he could not ever recall a time when Darrel was ever a violent person. He knew that what he saw was not Darrel's doing. Silk knew that this situation had to have been forced upon him.

"D, we gotta get you a good lawyer. I don't know what happened, but we should be able to beat this case on self defense."

"Bru, there's no such thing as a self defense law in our state," Darrel said, holding Ebony even tighter.

***

Six Months Later

Everyone waited patiently, so they could be dealt with for been disobedient. Consequence had to be paid for unacceptable behavior. As a result of different foolish and ridiculous adventures, Judge Sayso was now given a justifiable reason and opportunity to put some discipline in their life. Today's menu in his courtroom promised to fill plates with a full course meal that consisted of jail time, prison time, probation, community services and fines.

The people were ready to get this tragedy behind them. They so desperately wanted to move forward. Some would capitalize from their bad experiences, while others couldn't help but become repeat offenders. The judge guaranteed that he would draw them all one of his famous invisible straight lines, and as a result of that, they all would certainly hold hostage or make a mental note of his rulings.

"You break the law you will be punished."

No civilian could get comfortable, and butterflies were in each one of their stomachs. Worry covered their faces like makeup. Every time the attorney's were in process of announcing their next defender, the people would all hold their breath. It seemed like the stress one might experience if they were at the last step of a cliff.

Some of the victims thought logically while others continued to think rebellious. Lunatics act like Looney Toones. Their minds were made up of ridiculous ideas, and they had similarities to morons. Abnormal activities were their logical way of life; destination the penitentiary or somebody's graveyard, no education led to incarceration, and this first young male was a product of his environment.

Judge Sayso studied the seventeen-year-old Caucasian boy's criminal history, knowing damn well he was unfit for society. He truly wanted to throw the book at this insane individual, lock him up and throw away the key; toss him sixty years, almost as if it was only a vacation. However, since he was dealing with one of his own people, there was only going to be a slap on the wrist. Later that day, Judge Sayso would be having lunch with the boy's grandfather to discuss the child; behavior.

"Driving under the influence of alcohol, driving without a license, no proof of insurance, crashing into three college students, killing one, while leaving the other two in critical condition and leaving the crime scene." Judge Sayso paused his reading to steal another look at the defender. The boy stood before him smiling. He was unmoved by the material the judge was reading, and acting like he didn't have a care in the world. Sayso's face became red as fire.

You little shit, I know better! I know I'm supposed to throw your ass in prison. Yes, feed you to the wolves, and allow the system to suck all the youth out of your wicked body, he thought. Yet, instead he addressed the lawyer.

"Counselor how does your client plead?"

"Sir, guilty to count one, guilty to count two, guilty to count three," the lawyer immediately replied, without meeting eyes with the *judge*.

"Counselor what about count four, you failed to mention a plea on that charge?" *the judge* asked with dismay in his voice.

"Oh yeah, sorry Your Honor. My client also pleads guilty to involuntary manslaughter, Sir."

Judge Sayso stared into the lawyer's pale face. He knew he had no choice but to depart from the court guidelines. While everyone else in his premises waited for the mercy of the court as well.

"Counselor, I'm going to go against my better judgment, know that I should not because a long prison term would do your client some justice and give him some sense of direction. And just maybe he could return back to our society as a complete human being."

The client gave Judge Sayso an evil look while his conscience said some of the most ungrateful words.

"Counselor, does your client have anything he would like to say before I sentence him?"

"Nothing other than he sincerely apologizes for his wrong doing, Sir."

"Very well," Judge Sayso gave the defendant the meanest, mean-mug he could produce. "Son, the court sentences you to the state penitentiary for sixty months. During your incarceration, the courts recommend that you get your GED, complete the five-hundred-hour drug class, and also enroll in AA classes upon your release. You'll be on a ten-year supervision release."

"Ten years' supervision release," the lawyer huffed. "Now, Your Honor, don't you think you're going a little overboard here?"

"Oh hell naw!" The defendant became light-headed, finding it difficult to breathe, yet that did not affect his comment. *He looked at the judge crazy, and* immediately turned to face his attorney and continued. "Mothafucka, you told me if I plead out to this bullshit, I'd only get five years! Son-of-a-bitch! That ain't no five years. That shit sounds like more than five mothafuckin' years to me."

"Bang, bang, bang," the Judge hammered his gavel on the surface. "Order in the courtroom! Order in the courtroom!"

Others waiting to be sentenced became ill. Clearly their bellies produced more than butterflies, thanks to this uneducated idiot. The room was filled with laughter and whispers immediately followed. Once Judge Sayso was victorious of regaining full control of his courtroom, he spoke once again.

"Son, due to your lack of education, you weren't competent enough to distinguish five years between sixty months. Young man they both are no different than a five-dollar bill or five single one dollar bills," The Judge further informed him.

"You fuckin' asshole," the defendant mumbled under his breathed.

Judge Sayso shook his head at this sadness, at this madness. He bangs the gavel once again, "Court is now in session," his voice rang out.

"Dumb lawyer, dumb client. This here is a circus and the Judge is the clown," someone whispered, causing laughter to once again escalate.

"If another outburst erupts in this court, someone will be fined, given seven full days in the county jail, and two hundred long hours of community service," the judge threatened. "And if there's anything else I can add, I promise, it will be added too." He glanced around the courtroom, trying to see if there was another idiot willing to call his bluff. "Now that's better."

Determined not to allow the courtroom activity to interfere with their discussion or thoughts, Darrel and his lawyer leaned closer to one another. Lance Coon, the attorney made the strong suggestion to Darrel that Ebony should testify.

"No, no, no," Darrel growled. "I will not allow you to take my wife through this again. She's eight months pregnant, and there's been enough pressure on her."

"She was the victim. She..." The lawyer's paused, due to Darrel cutting him off.

"Hey, hey," he frowned, "I said no, and no means no."

"Mr. Donnell this is your life! This here is your freedom at stake buddy, not mines. Your ass is on the line here," Lance exhaled. "Pal, as your representative, I put myself in your shoes. So please don't think I don't understand your situation. However, by me being your appointed attorney, I am out to give you my best advice. I feel your concerns," the lawyer sympathized. "But trust me. It would benefit us both if Ebony testified. Did you just see how the judge gave that idiot a break?"

"He was white, I'm black."

"Color has nothing to do with this case. But, since you mentioned it, there's a great possibility that the courts just might be in your favor." Lance took a deep breath. "You never been in trouble with the law before and the guy you killed in self-defense has a rap sheet stacked up higher than the Empire State building. We have some pointers in our corner. I mean, we might not get the slap on the wrist, but if it was up to me, you should not have seen the inside of a courtroom to start with. But there's a pretty good chance the judge will consider your infraction to be no different than any other civilized human being. I would have murdered the bastard and eaten his heart and lungs after I ripped them out had he raped my wife."

Darrel exhaled, leaning back in the Oakwood chair. Every time he looked at his palms, he envisioned Junior's blood. Trying to clear his head of such a horrible memory, Darrel thought about how he scrubbed his hands raw, because his mind often played tricks on him.

Finally, there were several bangs followed by the announcing of his name.

"Darrel Donnell! Will you and your counselor please rise?" ordered Judge Sayso.

"Well this is what we're here for," Lance said, hopping to his feet.

The 43-year-old, pale faced lawyer stood 5'8", presented the frame of a small child, but could pass for a teenager. He appeared to wear a size seven shoe, and was serious about giving his clients the best. He had taken an oath to fight hard for his clients, and clearly was not one who helped only for the pay check, but more so to seek judicial victories over the courts. When Lance and Darrel first met, he told Darrel he became a lawyer because he felt the need to assist people who were not so fortunate. Twenty-three years earlier, he too stood helpless as he witnessed the court give his best friend's son an unjust thirty years.

"Mr. Lance, good to see you again," Judge Sayso greeted. He knew he was in for a trial, because he'd grown accustomed to Lance advising his clients not to take plea bargains. He understood Lance's motto, fight for further relief. "Counselor will you please approach the bench?"

Before stepping forward, Lance adjusted his yellow tie. Judge Sayso wasted no time.

"I see you have a very interesting case here. I respect that you're not the kind of lawyer to consider copping out, but under these circumstances have you even considered taking a plea?" Sayso whispered. Before Lance could speak the judge continued, "I gave your case some great thought. I invested some serious hours in reviewing it. I've analyzed your client's situation from many angles. Why? I don't know. That was an answer I could not produce for myself. So Counselor, please don't ask me to produce one for you. I'm willing to make you an offer. One I think you and the courts will be pleased with."

"What offer is that Sir? And please know I cannot accept anything without consulting with my client first."

"I understand Counselor," Judge Sayso agreed, looking down at the intelligent little guy he'd grown to respect.

Lance bucked the system and had avoided becoming a part of the circle. He had become popular for being an attorney who would decline on every deal thrown his way. Lance stayed loyal to his clients. Selling them out wasn't part of his vocabulary.

"Counselor, what if I were able to convert the murder to involuntary manslaughter and give your client twenty-five years instead of life without parole. Let's say I break the quarter into two pieces," Sayso asked, displaying two fingers. ". fifteen and ten. Once your client completes the first fifteen years, he can do the other dime on probation. Counselor, this is possibly the best offer I can make. And please do take into account that I don't have to do not one day of this time with the individual. I feel the need to be able to rest good tonight, knowing I did the right thing."

"Would you please excuse me? I need to discuss your terms with Mr. Donnell?"

Judge Sayso nodded, "Counselor, don't fail to mention to him this is his best interest, not mine."

"Will do, Sir," Lance replied, turning on his heels, imitating an ROTC step. He approached Darrel and spent the next fifteen minutes relaying and explaining this delicate situation to him. Lance wanted to know what Darrel thought about Judge Sayso's offer. Darrel felt comfortable with the outcome, and so did Lance, but he was the type that never showed any facial expression or gave much body language of any kind. Lance was very pleased with the judge's offer, but if Darrel didn't agree, he would have immediately told Judge Sayso. They were ready to pick twelve, cause the case would definitely be going to trial.

The jury would have to find his client guilty or insane without reasonable doubt, but they didn't want to take any chances. After Darrel was sentenced, Lance talked Judge Sayso into allowing Ebony to have a thirty-minute visit. Both were pleased with that decision. When Darrel walked out, his excessive weight loss was concealed by his orange jumpsuit. While awaiting trial in jail, Darrel worried so much about Ebony. He was concerned about their unborn child and how she was managing without his helping hand. As a result of his stress, he shed over twenty-five pounds, and his wife gained double that amount.

"Your stomach has gotten big, Ma," Darrel said, rubbing her stomach.

"Silly man, I'm eight months. My stomach's supposed to be big," Ebony explained, guiding Darrel's hand into the designated area. "Now feel your daughter kickin'. She won't let me rest for nothing in the world. She kicks when she's hungry, kicks when she sleeps and is tossing and turning right now. Darrel, when I was into my fourth month, I went to get my ultrasound and this child had the nerve to keep her knees crossed, so they couldn't see her private parts. I didn't know what we were gonna have. But I really didn't care; I just wanted a healthy baby. The sonographer told me that they would be able to tell me the sex of the baby around the fifth month, so since your child wouldn't cooperate, they rescheduled me."

"You oughta be proud, she knew that early to cover herself," Darrel yawned.

He'd been awake since 2AM that morning, waiting to get this court thing behind him. He was ready to move on with his life, and now that he'd been sentenced, he actually felt better. A burden had been lifted. Now his only concern was his family. The thought of them living without him, was giving him gray hairs, and way before he was old enough to have them. Lance entered the room, disturbing their privacy.

"Knock, knock, knock," he playfully hit the air, pretending he was knocking on a door.

"Ms. Smith, are you sure you're not carrying twins?" Ebony rearranged herself in Darrel's lap.

"I hope to God we're not cause this one child will be more than a handful." she admitted.

"Congratulations to you both on parenthood. I just needed to run in to inform your husband that once I finish up here, I'll be stopping by the jail later this evening. I have another case, so I must get back in the courtroom," Lance sighed.

"Ok Mr. Lance," Darrel responded. "Thanks for everything." Lance gave Ebony a smile.

"Ms. Smith what are you having?"

"A girl," Ebony reported.

"I have four daughters and another one on the way myself," Lance revealed. "Now I have a question for the both of you and I'll give y'all three wild guesses."

"Shoot your question," Darrel insisted.

"What sound is this? Whine, whine, whine..." Lance sounded off.

"That's easy, real easy," Ebony smiled. "A baby."

"Yeah, Mr. Lance that's the sound of a baby crying," Darrel agreed.

"You both are 100% correct concerning the baby part, but you both fail to specifically state the sex of the child," Lance smiled. "The sound I made was 'A daughter's cry'," he confirmed, rushing out to get back to the courtroom.

"A daughter's cry," Darrel repeated.

Chapter 1

Ebony tossed and turned two hours straight; the baby refused to allow her to rest, and she wrestled from side to side trying to find a comfortable position. She turned on her right side, but that didn't work because the baby was kicking as if it was performing leg exercise. Ebony changed to the opposite side to accommodate the child, but her daughter continued to put up a fight. So she immediately rolled flat on her back. That's when the struggle increased, and that's when Ebony began to feel warm fluid wash down her legs.

Yep! Seventeen days' shy of the 40-week prenatal cycle, Ebony had gone into labor. Her water had officially broken at 4A.M., and she panicked.

"Betty! Betty! Silk," she screamed and banged on her bedroom wall.

Considering the time of day, she was certain that she was breaking into her neighbor's tranquility, but it was perfectly okay because that's exactly what her best friend and husband instructed her to do. Betty banged back and responded.

"Hold on girl, we're on the way."

She and Silk stayed true to their word, because they rushed to her rescue in under five minutes flat. Upon their arrival, Ebony was spread out on the delivery table at the birthing center with three nurses giving her their undivided attention. There were two female nurses who patiently stood on each side of her; one religiously kept her face free of sweat and was coaching her through her breathing techniques, while the other monitored her and her daughter's vitals. The third nurse was a male. He counseled and assisted Ebony with her pushing. She found herself in another very, very uncomfortable position. Her legs were wide open with both thighs propped up in stirrups. The male nurse slowly pushed and eased her shoulders forward, encouraging her through the birthing process.

"Push, Ms. Smith, push," he instructed.

"Come on, Ms. Smith, I know it hurts, but it won't be for long," the nurse expressed, patting Ebony's forehead with the cool cloth.

"She's coming, the baby's moving right along," the nurse publicized who was monitoring the baby. While watching the ultrasound belt, which was attached across Ebony's stomach, the nurse kept noticing the repeated shifting of the belt.

"Come on Ms. Smith! You're doing a good job," the doctor praised, looking far up and in-between her legs. "Now here we go," he added, seeing the infants head present at the base of her vagina.

As she pushed, tears fell from Ebony's eyes. *This here is extremely too much pain for one female to bear*, she thought, chasing her breath.

"O God! It feels like my whole insides are comin' outta me," she exhaled.

As she pushed, Ebony continued to fight for air. She inhaled, she exhaled and continued to follow the instructions given to her. "It hurts! O God it hurts!" She repeatedly cried out.

"We know, Ms. Smith, we know," the doctor comforted Ebony. Though he sympathized, he wanted her to know that she wasn't the first female to report pains, nor would she be the last. "Ms. Smith, you'll make my sixty-seventh delivery this year," Doc revealed, making Ebony aware of the fact that this was not his first rodeo. "Forty-two boys and twenty-five girls."

"Push, Ms. Smith, push. We're almost there," the monitoring nurse reported. And though it wasn't said, that's what the nurse thought the delivery doctor should have been saying in the first place.

"Continue pushing, Ms. Smith. Come on now, let's push a little harder, but take your time. We don't want you to rip," the male nurse advised on the lead of the monitoring nurse's actions.

"Come on, little baby, come see the doctor," the doctor jovially said, carefully assisting the infant out of her mother's womb. "Ms. Smith," Doc began, as fluid and afterbirth freely flowed. "When a father watches the delivery of his child, he'll become over-protective of their mother."

"How we looking, Doc?" the male nurse questioned?

"We're almost there, son," Doc responded to his child.

Once the infants upper body was in the doctor's palms, the child kicked the rest of her way out of the darkness.

"Paddle, paddle. Swim your way into the light," Doc teased, using the same famous words he'd stated while previously performing other deliveries. "Now this is what I call God's creation," he added, passing the infant to the nurse.

The nurse who had been pampering Ebony, would now tend to the needs of her child. While she tested the baby's vitals and bathed her, Doc checked Ebony out for tears and ensured that all the afterbirth was out. He wanted to keep her infection free.

"Ms. Smith, you have a beautiful, seven-and-a-half-pound healthy daughter," the nurse reported. "Congratulations, Mama."

"Thank you," Ebony cried out in pain and joy.

"Now you have to give her a brother or sister," the male nurse joked.

"I don't know about that," she slightly laughed, touching her stomach.

"Feels like you lost a hundred pounds – doesn't it?" the monitor nurse asked.

"Um huh," Ebony grunted.

"My last child was eight pounds, nine ounces. Can you imagine that?"

"Yes, I can. I thought my daughter would weigh more than what she did," Ebony said, feeling lighter than a feather.

No more back pains, no more eating for two. Thank you Lord, she thought to herself, staring into the bright super large lights, hanging over the delivery table. Her stomach was almost back to normal and so was her breathing.

***

As Ebony gazed around the room, she noticed that the hospital room was so fresh and so clean. There was a television set mounted on the center wall, but Ebony did not see any use for it, especially at the present moment. She knew her friends and family would keep her company and make her feel loved and comfortable.

Ebony took a sip of her orange juice because the doctor said she needed to rebuild her immune system as soon as possible. And fluids would put electrolytes back into her body and help with nourishments necessary for breast feeding. As she delicately rose up to drink, Betty sat on the bed beside Ebony, giving her the moral support she needed.

Betty and Ebony had been friends for a little over six years. They had met at the bowling alley, and after discovering they were also neighbors the rest was history. Big Johnny peeled off two one hundred dollar bills and pressed them into Ebony's cold palms.

"Young lady, buy your baby girl something nice, and if there's anything else I can do, please don't hesitate to ask."

"BJ, you really don't have to do this," Ebony replied. Big Johnny squeezed Ebony's palm closed.

"This is something I want to do," he confessed, backing away from her to collect his seat. Ebony observed his steps and mumbled two words.

"Thank you."

"You're more than welcome," Big Johnny nodded.

Ms. Matty Mae Strong walked over to Ebony's bedside. She eased Ebony's hand in hers.

"Ebony, I'm sorry for everything. Until the Lord calls me back home, I plan to spend the rest of my days on earth with you and your daughter. I'm ashamed of what Junior has done, and I hope to God that you don't hold it against me." Tears fell from both of their eyes.

"Everything's going to be just fine."

Ms. Matty Mae Strong dabbed her cheeks, and then gave Ebony a hug. Big Johnny wanted to shed a few tears of his own, but he went another route. Instead, he took a swig from his half pint bottle of Jack Daniels. He made an old ugly whisky face, then held the bottle in Silk's direction.

"What the hell! I might as well," Silk accepted his offer. "Big Johnny, I can use a celebration drink," Silk added. After taking a swallow, he examined the bottle, and there was still a couple of swigs left. Big Johnny was done, so he gave him a wave.

"Knock yourself out."

"You sure?" Silk questioned, ready to pass the bottle back.

"The less fire-water for me the better," Big Johnny replied. As he stretched, the back of his right palm struck the TV, giving him another reason to exercise his voice. "What good is it to have a TV and not use it? It's 'bout time for George and Weezie."

"BJ, you like the *Jefferson's*?" Silk smiled.

"Love 'em. Love 'em to death. That's my program. I don't watch nothing but the news and the *Jefferson's*," Big Johnny grinned, turning straight to the exact channel. "Oh, I forgot to mention *The Price is Right*." Big Johnny paused, trying to collect his best Bob Barker voice, "Come on down! You're the next contestant," he smiled.

"Alright, Bob Barker," Silk echoed, enjoying the entertainment.

Neither Ebony nor Betty had ever heard Big Johnny talk so much, nor had they witnessed him in any other environment than in his club. It did not go unnoticed that he was a little tipsy, because he smiled more and became extra friendly. Originally it was not Big Johnny's intention to be in the hospital that long. Initially, he'd planned to run in, see the baby, give Ebony a few dollars, and then head straight back to his club to catch the day time traffic.

"When is the baby coming?" Ms. Matty Mae Strong inquired.

"Good question," Big Johnny yawned, crossing his legs but never taking his eyes off of the tube.

"Y'all guess is good as mine," Ebony volunteered, thinking the question was addressed to her.

"Silk, ain't you tired of standing?" Betty asked her husband. Silk motioned no and continued enjoying the sour liquor taste on his tongue.

"A great king once said, why stand when you can sit? And why sit when you can lay?" Big Johnny wailed, smiling at everyone.

Seconds later, when the room door opened, Silk took a couple of steps backwards, taking more room than needed as he saw Doc bringing in the infant.

"Bout time," Silk teased.

Doc came in, examining his surroundings. His eyes swung from Silk to Big Johnny and back to Silk. Big Johnny looked rough, while Silk wore a clean shave, low hair cut, and his white t-shirt, blue blazer, black slacks. A pair of low-cut black gators added a slightly casual/preppy dress code to his presence.

"Are you the father?" he asked Silk, because he looked like more of a concerned family man or father than Big Johnny did. And without either man ever really speaking, Doc based his assumption off of their physical appearance.

Confused about Docs question, Silk threw Ebony this puzzled facial expression like, *"What should I do?"* She nodded at him like they both were telepathic. Silk cleared his throat and then gave Doc an answer.

"Yes Sir that would be me."

"Congratulations. You have yourself one healthy child here," Doc eased the baby over towards him. Silk accepted the infant with caution, and waited until Doc exited the room. Once Doc was gone, Silk made his way over towards Ebony and doted over the baby.

"Baby girl, you're beautiful like your mother," Silk teased as Big Johnny cut into his path. His interference was almost as if he thought Silk needed a second opinion. He gazed over towards Ebony.

"May I?" he asked.

"Yes you may," Ebony replied, watching Big Johnny lift the child. "Hey, little Momma. My name is Big Johnny, but everybody calls me BJ," he introduced himself. "Now what's your name?"

Ebony held her stomach while laughing at Big Johnny, because he was trying to talk in baby language.

"Girl, what's the baby's name?" Betty bumped Ebony, waiting for a response. She wasn't by herself, because everyone in the room wanted to know the child's name too.

"Nakeita," Ebony noted. "Nakeita Renay Smith."

"Ain't that sweet? Nakeita is a pretty little name for a pretty little baby," Big Johnny said, finally allowing Ebony the opportunity to hold her daughter for the very first time.

Betty leaned in, putting her face closer to the baby.

"Ooh, Ebony. Ooh, Ebony girl."

"What? What?" Ebony grunted, feeling a sharp pain in her stomach. "I feel like I'm about to birth a storm of cramps. Now Betty what are you doing all that uhhh-ing for?"

"That girl looks like Darrel from head to toe," Betty claim.

"You ain't even seen my baby's toes yet, o' crazy lady," Ebony grinned. Betty uncovered the baby's feet.

"Just like I said - she even has her daddy's toes."

"Girl, get outta the way before my baby catch pneumonia fooling with you," Ebony said, rewrapping her daughter.

"Betty, how you know what Darrel's toes look like?" Silk teased, giving Ebony a wink.

"Umm, hum. Get her, Silk," Ebony cheered. Ms. Matty Mae Strong pranced her way over to Ebony.

"Let Mama hold that little sweet thing?" Once she locked her arms around the newborn, the real baby language began. "Hey sugar foot," Ms. Matty Mae Strong sweetly cooed. "Give Mama some of that nasty, nasty sugar." She kissed the child's fingers "Yeah, umm hum, I got me some of the nasty, nasty sugar. I'mma teach you how to make pumpkin pies, pecan pies, red velvet cakes, lemon cakes, sweet potato pies, that's right, you name it, I'm gone teach you. We gonna make everything from scratch too..."

"No wonder your cornbread always be sweet," Big Johnny intruded in on Ms. Matty Mae Strong's conversation.

"She be putting a little cake mix in it, BJ?" Silk joked.

"Yup," Big Johnny laughed. "And she can cook some collard greens too." Ms. Matty Mae Strong quickly shifted her attention to Big Johnny.

"BJ that's because I be puttin' my whole foot in 'em," she teased, letting them all know she had jokes of her own.

That afternoon everyone enjoyed each other's company. Ebony took time out to thank each individual for taking time out for her and her daughter. They all assured her that her and beautiful Nakeita were family. Ebony cried along with her daughter, because this was the kind of love she didn't know about. Betty tried to put her sneering to rest, so she whispered in her ear.
"Girl, you know damn well you always have been like a sista to me."
"Let me hold my God-baby again," Silk demanded, scooping Nakeita out of Ebony's embrace.

Ebony freed up her grip, because she remembered Betty could not have any kids. Her body was all out of commission. Most people knew Betty had experienced three abortions long before she ever turned twenty-one. Her first abortion occurred when she was in high school, after she was raped. She was forced to have the second one, because her boyfriend received a college scholarship and confessed he wasn't ready for a family yet. He thought they were both too young and a baby was going to be way too much for him to handle at the time.
Though Betty wanted to go through her third pregnancy, once she enlightened her new boyfriend of her pregnancy, he got ghost on her. She desperately wanted to tough it out with the child, but the thought of being a single parent overwhelmed her, so she went on with the abortion. Sadly, at the time it seemed like the best thing for her to do.

Chapter 2

Fifteen Years Later

Ebony worked her fingers to the bone, trying to support her daughter and husband. Now she was married to her two jobs. Playing secretary from 6AM to 1PM was no strain to her - yet standing on her feet from 2PM to 10PM for Wal-Mart could be hectic sometimes. To Ebony, it seemed like the flow of customer traffic never lightened up. It would only tighten up. The place stayed busy from the moment she reached her cash register, until the minute she was relieved from her shift.

Ebony looked forward to her two days off and enjoyed her vacations when the time came. Taking care of Nakeita's wants and needs really wasn't a problem, because she always sacrificed herself for her daughter. Ebony gave of herself without hesitation too, because she knew that's what her mother had done for her. Nakeita was into the latest fashion. And one thing for certain, she was a child that tried to run neck and neck with the Jones. And to no one's surprise, Ebony broke her neck supplying the expensive name brand clothing, because her baby stayed on the A/B Honor Roll. Nakeita had been making all A's and B's since head-start. Now, she whined about how hard school work was for her as a tenth-grader. Ebony understood her challenge, but encouraged her to buckle down and work harder.

On this particular day, Ebony walked through her front door to Nakeita blasting music, as she vacuumed the living room floor. Ebony couldn't understand how youngsters today understood one word of what the latest artist were saying or singing, loud as the music was. Nakeita turned the vacuum off with her feet, and rushed to free Ebony's hands of groceries.

"What's in the bags, Ma?"

"Girl, please cut down all that loud music, before you make me go deaf," Ebony said, covering her ears. *Shawty, I'm only gonna tell you this once, you're the Illest,* Nicki Minaj sprang from the speakers,

"Baby, you're the illest," Nakeita sang, dancing and snapping her fingers around Ebony, who walked over and cut the stereo off herself.

"Nakeita, what I tell you about wearing them skimpy pants?" Ebony scolded, with her hands on her hips, realizing how much her fifteen-year-old daughter had developed into a full grown woman. "Keita, Baby, these grown guys won't be looking at you like the child you are. You're going to have to stop wearing tight-ass clothes."

"What you want me to do, Ma? Wear my pants saggy and baggy like I'ma boy?"

"Don't play with me, girl!" Ebony warned, unloading their night's meal on the counter. She stopped to rub her temples. "Nakeita, I told you a million times to throw away those skimpy pants and you haven't done it yet. So will you please go into your room and put on something more suitable. And please bring them pants back with you," she said in a calm and gentle voice.

Nakeita stared at her mother; she understood that she was only being hostile for her own benefit. A few years earlier, Ebony was complaining about Nakeita's clothes one day. Betty told her bits and pieces of a story about her mother being raped. As Nakeita headed to her room to change, she remembered the day she'd learned of her mother's abuse. Angry, she'd fled to her bedroom crying, and to add insult to injury, she slammed the door behind her. She thought Ebony was picking on her, so Betty took off behind her. Once inside the room, Betty rocked the then thirteen-year-old Nakeita as if she were an infant. Once she explained Ebony's situation, Nakeita eventually grew accustomed to not getting angry at her mom and just went along with her mother like children are supposed to.

Nakeita without further argument went to her room and returned to Ebony with the shorts in her hand. Without one word, she dropped them into the trash herself, and then she walked over to her mother and gave her a kiss on the cheek.

"Ma, I'm sorry if I upset you. It won't happen again. We'll start getting my pants a size or two bigger, so I can make you proud of me." Ebony hugged her daughter.

"You're my child. I'll always be proud of you," she stated, stroking Nakeita's natural jet black, silky long hair.

"Ma, I seen this Louis Vuitton purse... I gotta have it," Nakeita said.

"Lil girl, you always seeing something that you gotta have."

"Oh, yeah. I need the shoes to match."

"Girl, you're always spendin' my check before I could even make it," Ebony smiled.

"Ma, please," Nakeita put her hands together in a praying position.

"Now did you hear me say no?" Ebony laughed out loud.

"Thank you Ma, you're the best mother in the whole wide world," Nakeita hugged her.

"Yeah right! You'll say anything to get what you want."

"No, Mama, that's not true," Nakeita replied, looking into her mother's eyes. "How daddy say it? No exaggeration."

The mention of Darrel always put sorrow in Ebony's eyes. She often wondered what it would be like to have him home. Would their daughter take him through the changes concerning the clothing issues? Would Nakeita take more interest in the kitchen? Would Nakeita communicate more with him than she did with her? Would Darrel be quick to spoil their daughter as well? Every time Ebony had too much free time on her hands, she would always spend the day asking herself questions concerning Darrel and Nakeita. It never failed, that's why it was best for her to stay busy: stay occupied with something to keep her mind from wandering off to a place where she didn't need to be, because if she wasn't careful, it would corrupt her day and have her looking sad and feeling depressed. Days like that often forced her to her bedroom, where she was in a slump and didn't want to be bothered with anyone. When she got like that, Ebony felt the need to be alone. She wouldn't eat or sleep, and she would spend almost twenty-four hours balled up in her bed, staring at the white wall or her snow-white ceiling. Nakeita noticed when this mental heaviness occurred; she would respect her mother's privacy and take advantage of being authority free.

"Lil girl, come on over here. We gonna enjoy this day," Ebony said with a serious facial expression. "Huff," she barked, intimidating Rozay.

"Ma, how you know about all that music?" Nakeita gave Ebony a curious look.

"Child, I'm not deaf. That's all I hear on the radio, twenty-four-seven, day in and day out," Ebony went on and on with her conversation.

Nakeita loved when her mother got into this mood; she'd run off at the mouth and do all the work. The plan was to clean and fry chicken, smother the cabbage, make baked beans, macaroni and cheese, and candied yams. But Nakeita fell off in a chair and kept her mother motivated by lending her an ear. Nakeita never tried to get a word in, she just smiled and laughed, until her mother came to her senses—which she always did. And like always, when Ebony's talking spells would come into play, by the time she finished, all the work would be done.

"Girl, I thought you were going to help me cook?" Ebony questioned, grabbing a seat across from her. "We were going to cook this meal together, remember?"

"Ma, I would've been in your way. Holding you up, I would've helped you and you know it, but you looked like you didn't need any help to me."

"How do people look when they don't need any help?" Ebony questioned, smiling.

"I tell you what, next time you sit back and kick your feet up and watch me do all the work," Nakeita cut her mother off to challenge the comment she was about to make.

"I know that's a lie," Ebony pointed at Nakeita. "You do all the work? All by your lonesome? My Nakeita Renay Smith?"

"Yup. All by my lonesome," Nakeita nodded.

"Now that's a day I need to hurry up and see," Ebony exhaled, regaining her breath. "So when will all this happen? Please let me know, so I can mark it on my calendar. Will it be this year or next year?"

"On your next day off," Nakeita said.

Ebony frowned, looking puzzled, trying to calculate her next two days.

"On Saturday or Sunday?"

"Hold up na! We ain't said nothing 'bout your secretary job, we talkin bout on your Wal-Mart job," Nakeita immediately corrected.

"Come to think of it, when is my next two days off?" Ebony questioned herself. Looking over her stove, "When am I off again," she mumbled. "Aw shit, child, I'm sittin' here losin' my mind. I'm off every two weeks."

"Ma, smells like something's burning," Nakeita sniffed into the air.

Ebony hopped out of her chair, rushed to check on her smothered cabbage, and as she started stirring them she became talkative. *You go motor mouth,* Nakeita thought to herself, because her plan never failed. Once her mother got occupied, she'd become carefree, all her burdens would be lifted, and she'd just get lost in conversation.

"Ma?"

"What child?" Ebony sternly replied, because she didn't like to be cut off.

"How long will it be before you finish cooking?"

"Why?"

"Cause I just wanna know."

"You got somewhere to go?"

"Yes."

"Where?"

"I wanna run down to Grandma's house right quick to get us a sweet potato pie and a red velvet cake."

"Now that would be a great idea," Ebony said, placing the candied yams lid back over the skillet. "I shouldn't cook these candied yams."

"I love candied yams."

"Me too. That's why I cook them," Ebony faced Nakeita with her hand propped on her arm,

"Tell your grandmother I'll bring her a plate once I finish cooking. And by the time you come back, I'll be finished making the potato salad." Ebony peeked over in the potato pot — they were boiling good and steam filled the air.

Nakeita started making her way to the living room, dancing and singing.

"I whip my hair back and forth, I whip my hair back and forth, I whip my hair back and forth," she triple sized.

"Who sang that song?"

"Willow Smith."

"Then let Jade and Will Smith's lil daughter sing her own songs," Ebony said, laughing deep from her stomach to show she had a good sense of humor.

***

Big Johnny sat at the wooden picnic table stuffing his mouth with a plate of smothered greens, yellow rice, pig tails loaded with salty onions and a super large piece of Ms. Matty Mae Strong's sweet cornbread. The side bowl of black-eyed peas laced with okra caused him to send Ms. Matty Mae Strong on a mission to fetch him another piece of cake bread, which was his name for her cornbread.

"You have yourself quite a large piece of land here," he said, once she returned with the other slice of bread.

Big Johnny wasted no time with crumbing the bread into his bowl of peas and okra. While giving the cornbread time to suck up all the juice, he thought about how she came into the land. Wichita was a small city and everybody knew about everybody's business. Ms. Matty Mae Strong had a husband named Carlos, but everyone called him Country Boy, and it didn't bother him one bit. Carlos became so used to the name that he started introducing himself by that name. Carlos couldn't read or write very well, but he could build some houses. Ms. Matty Mae Strong loved the ol' country boy to death. She'd birthed fourteen of his seeds, nine girls and five boys. The kids took after both parents, the daughters were scattered out in other branches of Kansas, running successful catering businesses, baker's cafes, doing different cooking events. As a matter a fact, anything that involved cooking, you could count them in.

Four of the boys took over their father's business after he died. Some years earlier, Carlos had fallen from a roof. Before going on to glory, he added landscaping to the family occupation. Their fifth son, Junior on the other hand, felt the need to be the black sheep of the family. He took after Carlos on the educational side. He knew machine work like the back of his hand, and could strip out a transmission quicker than most people could fix themselves a cup of coffee.

Big Johnny wiped the smile clean off his face.

"Ms. Matty Mae Strong," he chuckled, at his own country accent, "You know us country folks is the only people who call people by their whole name."

"Then your country self needs to stop," She teased, placing a large lemon ice tea in front of him. "A leader leads by example."

"Yeah, while the young buck's stuck on monkey see, monkey do."

"And that's why monkey stuff always happens, cause they're always monkeying around." Big Johnny unscrewed the top of his gin bottle and spiced up his tea. "Here, get you a little taste to get the cobwebs outta your system." To his surprise, she finally accepted his offer. Ms. Matty Mae Strong swallowed the fifty-cent shot in one motion and back tracked with two large glasses of cold, icy water.

"Ms. Matty Mae Strong, one thing I can't figure out."

"Have you ever taken time out to think about the fact that everything ain't meant to be figured out? Sometimes some things have to remain a mystery." Big Johnny nodded to concur, poking out his bottom lip.

"I agree, but to kill my curiosity, why are you around here selling plates for two to five dollars and selling cakes and pies?"

"It gives me something to do. I enjoy feeding the people. This is my calling. I'm a certified caterer. I feed the homeless people every day, and daily they look forward to my meals."

"And you work the shit outta 'em, too."

Big Johnny acknowledged, laying his fork down and picking up a napkin to free his mouth from crumbs. Before he could finish speaking, a young guy in his mid-twenties walked up.

"Big J, what's the business?" he addressed Big Johnny as he sat at the table with him.

"Bell, where you been, son? I haven't seen you around in this neck of the woods in some time now." Big Johnny asked.

"Ahhh! You know me Mr. J, I'll wander off from time to time."

Ms. Matty Mae Strong ducked off into the house for a split second and reappeared with another plate of food stimulating to Big Johnny. Bell nodded in approval.

"Thanks," he muttered.

"All this land with no man. Mum, mum, mum," Big Johnny mumbled with a mouth full of food.

"I'm a blessed widow as the Lord planned. Mum, mum, mum," Ms. Matty Mae Strong replied.

"Mr. J, she got you then. That was cold. That was cold, Mr. J," Bell said, making a closed fist by his mouth while he spoke. He was practicing good manners, because he did not want any food to fly out.

Big Johnny marked Bell's words verbatim, but in a female voice, and added a little authority.

"Son, mind your business."

As Nakeita was making her way down the trail, Ms. Matty Mae Strong was the first to spot her.

"There comes my baby, there comes Mama's grandbaby. Nakeita where have you been! I ain't seen you in two whole days...?"

"School, Grandma, school. The people keep me piled up with homework. I'm beginning to think my teachers don't have a life of their own outside the schoolhouse," Nakeita explained. She turned her attention to Big Johnny. "Whassup, Uncle J?"

"I'm good and full now so I can't make no complaints. So how's your mother?" Big Johnny asked out of sincere concern.

"Mom's good."

Big Johnny went into his pocket and came back out with a ten-dollar bill. "Here you go, Nakeita."

"Preciate ya, Unk."

"Now you got you a few dollars for school money. What grade you in now?" he asked, slipping to his feet. He was finished eating and there was no specific reason for him to continue keeping the seat occupied.

"Tenth."

"You're working your way up the ladder. Now you have only two more years to go. You going to college for a few years to further your education. Ain't cha?" That was Big Johnny's sly way of encouraging her.

"I might, but first I gotta graduate."

"Young lady, you know it's very important to get your education," Big Johnny advised, pulling out a cigar. He was all ready to feed his lungs, after feeding his belly. It was a habit he had for years.

"I know cause my Mama stays on me about it."

Big Johnny nodded, putting fire to the cigar. He released with a mouth full of white smoke.

"Then your mother's doing her job."

"She's definitely gonna do that," Nakeita assured.

Big Johnny walked over to give Ms. Matty Mae Strong a hand with carrying the cake and pie, so Bell took the advantage of their absence. He squinted his eyes at Nakeita.

"Did I see you earlier?"

"Not to my knowledge."

"You had on some white shorts and you had a head rag on your head," he reminded her.

Bell recalled seeing Nakeita as she took out the trash. He was walking down the street on the opposite side of her. Nakeita was always somewhere trying to keep her presence from going unnoticed.

"You probably seen me, but I didn't see you."

Bell pushed his plate to the side because food no longer interested him. If he needed to, he could finish the meal later. He saw Nakeita as top priority.

"This makes twice I seen you in the same day. You know, I don't believe in coincidence." He sucked on his teeth as his lips were in motion to continue speaking. However, Ms. Matty Mae Strong beat him to the draw.

"Don't listen to him, he's no good. If he looks at you too long, you'll get pregnant. If he breathes on you, you'll get pregnant," she warned. "Boy, you can go on somewhere else and leave my grandbaby alone. You can ring your bell somewhere else. Before I start ringing off them damn buckshots at your ass." Bell smiled, trying to play things off.

"Ms. Matty Mae Strong, the food was delicious. Now I'm ready for the dessert. You got some dessert for me?"

She sat Nakeita's cake and pie on the table, "Yeah, I got some dessert for ya. I got a fat and juicy slice of shit-outta-luck pie for you."
Bell threw both palms into the air as if silently asking for mercy.

"Ms. Matty Mae Strong, what have I done to you to deserve all of that? I ain't done nothing, all I've done was come down here and enjoy myself a meal like I've always done. Now am I wrong? And if so, then please acknowledge me of my wrong doing, so I can immediately apologize and redeem myself."

Ms. Matty Mae Strong went to pointing that favorite finger of hers and shaking it at Bell as she publicized his business.

"You messed up by try'na sweet talk my fifteen-year-old granddaughter, when you know you're the age of Michael Jordan's jersey, twenty-three and you're still living in the projects under your Mama's roof. You got two children, a one-year-old son and a three-year-old daughter, and between the both of your kids, you ain't seen nor toted a can of milk or bag of Pampers their way. Son, you think I don't know you. I remember when Mary and Sonny Boy had you."
"Grandma went on one, didn't she Unk?" Nakeita shot Big Johnny a question.
"Didn't she?" he replied. "Better him than me," Big Johnny smiled. He really wanted to spit Bell's words back in his face, he thought. *Bell, she got you then! That was cold, that was cold Bell, real cold.* But he didn't indulge in childish games, because the Bible taught him, when you are a child you function like a child, and when you become an adult, you put all childish things aside.

"Ms. Mattie Mae Strong, you need anotha swig before I pull out?" Big Johnny asked, thinking she could use another stiff drink of liquor to calm her down.
"No," Ms. Mattie Mae Strong spluttered with her right palm held out, "I need you to pay me my five dollars for my plate of food."
"I'mma give you six, one as a tip," he retorted.

"Did I ask you for a tip, Mister?"

"Nope, but do you have a problem with a gentleman try'na show his appreciation?" Big Johnny questioned, holding out his tip.

"Thank you very much, Sir," she politely said, gently snatching the money from Big Johnny's open palm. "I ain't the needy or the greedy."

"You know what?"

"What?"

"I done figured you out," Big Johnny counted, giving Ms. Matty Mae Strong a frown. "Yeah. You finally exposed your hand. Thank you for that."

"What is there to expose?" Ms. Matty Mae Strong queried. "I have nothing to hide."

Big Johnny smiled, "You're bipolar," he laughed out loud. "One minute you're talking with sense, and then the next minute you're talking like you don't have a lick of sense. It's either you're intelligent or you're not intelligent. You can't be both. It's not possible."

"Mr. BJ. . . Have you ever heard the saying, 'A wise man can play the fool, but the fool can't play the wise man'?"

"Ms. Matty Mae Strong. . . Have you ever heard the saying, 'Be careful not to cast your pearls before swine'?"

Nakeita rolled with laughter while Bell stood there sweating her, and she wasn't planning on giving him the time of day.

***

By the time Darrel reached cigar length of his decade and a half sentence, he knew he had nothing coming. It would be unnecessary to go before the parole board, knowing he had not met their criteria. The court papers he signed fifteen years ago clearly promised and guaranteed him parole if he would maintain a clean conduct. Darrel set out to win back his freedom, but the reward was not accomplished. He tried hard to control his destination; he thought positive and acted positive, but that wasn't enough to stop him from catching two DR's, which were discipline reports.

On Darrel's first day in the penitentiary, his victim waited until he went into the bathroom to try his hands. Darrel stood over the urinal, relieving himself when a brother doubles his size and weight rushed into the bathroom with a thick, broken broomstick.

"You're fresh meat and I choose you. You'll be my property! I'll be your war daddy," the guy predicted. Uncontrollable rage filled Darrel's body, he'd just been disrespected and verbally assaulted. This event surely couldn't go unnoticed and required serious immediate attention. When situations like this take place, two things can occur. One, you man the fuck up or bitch the fuck up. The alternative was surely in his corner and the other individual's corner as well. Two, he could fight for his crown or be face down with his butt in the air; and before the sun rose, the opponent was sure to have been converted over to a female.

Upon speaking his foolishness, the guy swung a stick as if it was a Louisville Slugger. Suddenly, the weapon connected with Darrel's rib cage. *He ain't got but one swing*, Darrel consciousness alarmed him. So, Darrel sprung into action. Assuring that he had the last hit, the powerful punch Darrel returned knocked blood and mucous from the guy's nostrils. Yet, the blows didn't stop there. Darrel worked the guy's body and face over as if he were imagining him to be a punching bag. After Darrel first drunk punched the predator, he could've easily used the guy's broomstick, because when it fell, he had open access to it. But Darrel taking into account the bad experience, feared using a weapon and even possibly catching another body.

Darrel being forced to fight, he got forty-five days in the hole. He was also placed on a six-month phone and visitation restriction, and lost thirty days of good time. As a result of his actions, now he wouldn't be able to see Ebony and Nakeita on the first of the month as planned, nor would he be able to hear his daughter's voice. Darrel's being restricted from family contact fueled him even more.

Darrel's next write-up came into play behind him forgetting to scan the callout sheet, which each and every prisoner was required to do on a daily basis. It's was the inmate's responsibility to handle this, and if they missed a callout for any reason, there were consequences to pay. Callout sheets notified inmates of appointments they had with medical, dental or job changes. This list also instructed inmates on issues regarding their daily scheduled destinations, including time and location. Darrel had missed his dental appointment, and that's how he ended up getting his second report.

He did take responsibility for his actions and he also admitted that he didn't look at the list and ask to be exempt from the write up on the strength that he had been D/R free for the last ten years. The people declined, stating that because his background was too positive, they believed he was out to beat the system.

To keep himself occupied, Darrel enrolled in college classes, computer class, and he was even a tutor. Since he'd first become incarcerated, Darrel felt the need to spend his time assisting other guys with the completion of their G.E.D. Nakeita's birth gave Darrel the motivation to be all that he could be, so he also went overboard with the Real-Estate and Business Management courses.

After having his parole hearing, Darrel dismissed the old contract and focused on the new one at hand. He received a five year set-back, and realized that the parole board would revisit his file at the beginning of his two-decade mark. He hoped and prayed that the Lord would not allow any obstacles to come between him reuniting with his wife and daughter. Frustrated with the outcome, Darrel felt the need to be in the company of his two best friends, paper and pen, so he got some out of his foot locker and began to get in the wind...

Dear Nakeita,

Sweetheart, you want to hear something funny? Smile, Lil' Lady. My Celly brushed his teeth only twice in two months, and both times were in the same month? That's no exaggeration!

Chapter 3

Thanks to their favorite uncle, Quasha, Keyandra and Keke finally got together. He'd been trying to get them together for some time now to ensure that they could and would assist one another in a demonstration of what a beautiful family structure looked like.

Nakeita entered the library with her backpack in her arms. While approaching her seat, she hugged it close to her body. It was almost as if the material were a small child. She dropped down in a chair next to the oldest niece.

"Y'all, I sincerely apologize for being late, now no more delays, let's get the show on the road," Nakeita exhaled. Throwing her backpack on the table, she took out all her books, stacking them on the table in a neat stack.

"Quasha, since you are the oldest, we expect you to lead the pack," Nakeita expressed.

"I'll try," Quasha shyly replied.

Keyandra placed her elbow on the table, making a kickstand for her head; she was ready to lead the group in her favorite subject, social studies. She loved that subject and a little bit of her excitement spilled over on the rest of the group. Surprisingly, they became more interested in the subject as well.

"Keke, what did you make in social studies?" Keyandra began her interrogation.

"I got a B."

"It's better than that C," Quasha chimed in, assuring her cousin.

"So what did you make?" Keyandra cut her off.

"I got a B too, cuz," Quasha reported. "But you can bet your bottom dollar that next time we get our report cards, I'mma have an A, if not an

A-plus."

"That's right big cuz, step your game up," Keke encouraged.

"You better believe it," Quasha added.

"Big cuz, you ain't gonna be getting the A by yourself," Keke promised. Keyandra looked over in Nakeita's direction, "we ain't even gonna waste our time and energy asking you what you got, cause girl, you stay on the A-B Honor Roll."

"It ain't easy," Nakeita warned. "Those good grades come from studying and re-studying."

"I get tired of studying something," Quasha admitted. "Girl, I study so much that when I'm try'na sleep, my mind won't let me rest. I'll get up out of my bed, get my books and read until I get sleepy. I got it so bad, I can wake up at one or two o'clock in the morning and start reading or writing like it's a normal thing to do."

"You're addicted to the right thing. And girl, I promise you that it'll pay off in the long run," Keyandra explained.

Nakeita gave her the notion that something was on her mind, so she zoomed in on her, "So Nakeita, what about you girl? Do you get tired of studying?"

"That would be like saying I'm tired of wearing Gucci, because everybody knows Ebony's gonna buy her only daughter anything and everything as long as the good grades remain," Nakeita teased, because her mother had earlier threatened to stop buying her the expensive clothing. Flashing back, Nakeita remembered coming home from school without her backpack, which caused her mother to do a double-take.

Ebony felt an unusual event in progress as a result of the picture not looking right. She was used to seeing her daughter with that backpack daily.

"Where are your books?" Ebony wanted to know.

"In my school locker."

"In your school locker?" Ebony repeated.

"I left 'em at school today. I don't need to be bringing 'em home with me every day anymore," Nakeita said. "Bring 'em home every day for what?"

"What are books for?"

"Ma, I make good grades." Ebony squinted her eyes at her daughter's comment.

"Look here, Ms. Comfortable, I'ma tell your smart ass one damn thing. If one of your A's drops, I'm going to slack the fuck up on spending my hard earned money on your ass. Child, I'm telling you now, if one damn grade slips, you'll be wearing cheap clothes, and knock off shit made from Hong Kong. I promise you that! If I'm lying, I'm flying! I can't even afford to put them high ass clothes on my ass, cause I'm spending all my money on your ass. Umm... and now you goon' tell me that you got to relax? And then you so damn confident with yourself that you're too good to study? Heifer please."

Nakeita snapped out of her daydream, feeling the need to share her thoughts with her friend.

"Keyandra, girl, didn't I tell y'all about the time my Momma almost had a heart attack."

"For real! When - Girl is she alright?"

"Relax, Chick. Not seriously, I'm talking about the one time I came home without my school books? I'm talking 'bout the woman actually went AWOL when she didn't see me with that backpack," Nakeita sighed, pulling her backpack closer.

"Oh, I believe you told me about that," Keyandra replied.

Nakeita smiled because she finally overcame the embarrassment. "I'm tellin' y'all, my mama blew stuff way out of proportion. Something that frivolous became such a big deal to her."

"Then it couldn't be that frivolous, because it mattered to her," Keke smiled.

"See, what we fail to realize is that sometime we're going to see things as being frivolous," Keyandra explained, feeling the necessity to elaborate on the touchy subject. "Things that are not so important to us, are to our mothers. Each of them would be able to identify with the seriousness of these issues. They can relate because they're speaking from experience or from someone else's experience. We can accept it the way our mothers give it to us or we can accept it the way that we want to accept it, but the main factor is that they don't mean any harm. Your mother was only speaking out of concern. Truth be told, if we listen to our mothers and value their guidance more, it would save us from a lot of headaches and pains. We probably could avoid more than just being brokenhearted, because most often older, wiser people know best." Keyandra paused to catch a breather, then she continued as if her breath was fire, "I'll go against my mother for no man."

You know how you can hear a person, but not really hear them. Well that is how it was for Nakeita. Maybe Keyandra's words went in one ear and out the other, because she had all her focus locked on the father and daughter when they entered the building. Nakeita yearned for her father.

Darrel always promised to do better, but his situation didn't permit. She strongly believed that Darrel hadn't learned from his mistakes. Empty from the void, she was convinced that he repeatedly lied to her about not going to the hole, and it looked like he wasn't going to keep his promise about making her senior graduation. She knew when he told her, he'd make it, he wouldn't. Nakieta needed Darrel to be a father to her. She didn't just want a daddy either, because in her mind, any male could become a daddy. Yet, it took a real man to be a father. What separated the two to her was the fact that a father was going to be there for his child. No matter what, he was going to be a functional parent, who guided, molded, encouraged, financially supported, and most of all took on the responsibility of fatherhood.

She snapped back to her senses by inserting a derogatory comment in her conversation with her friends.

"Y'all, I went to the Wal-Mart the other day and they had a poster on the entrance door of all the local deadbeat dads," Nakeita laughed, making her statement out of hurt. "And that's what they get since they ain't handling their business. All fathers should be takin' care of their kids like that guy over there," she pointed at the man she'd earlier observed.

"Some of them sorry niggas would even lie to a newborn baby," Keke unfolded her arms.

"You ain't lying," Keyandra confirmed.

"I know these deadbeat daddy's gon' start acting right one day," Nakeita frowned, stopping the wheel before it really got out of hand. She didn't want to spoil her friend's day, just because her father's absence had corrupted hers. Secretly, in all reality, they all shared the father-figure fantasy. Yet, Nakeita's two powerful remarks put to rest Keyandra's query as to why she wasn't in high spirits or full of energy as usual.

"Girl, you alright?" she whispered to Nakeita.

"Why complain when it can't help anything?"

"I was always told if you can change something, then change it. And if you can't change it, then leave it alone." Keke shared.

"Take it to the Lord in prayer." Quasha guided. "Once you put it in the Lord's hands, you can leave it alone."

Keyandra squeezed Nakeita's hand, "I'm always here for you. Girl, you can call on me anytime, day or night about anything."

***

Cigarette smoke shadowboxed with clean air, while the rest of the smoke wrestled with germs in the midst. Silk took one last drag of the Newport, before flicking it out the window crack.

"My body needs the nicotine, but I hate the aftertaste," he admitted, stabbing the butt into the astray. "That's crazy," he laughed, watching smoke now belly dance out of his side window. He rolled down the passenger window to set his vehicle smoke-free. Silk was always extremely cautious not to leave behind any type of evidence for his jealous wife to find. Had she known he was smoking, that issue alone was sure to lead to a good cursing out about cancer. Two quick sprays of cherry air freshener in the front seat followed by a drop of Betty's favorite conditioner roughly handle over his hands. Silk slipped from behind the wheel.

"Shit, it's chilly out here," he shivered, as rain lightly sprinkled inside the car along with the cold wind. He took a wet cloth, dabbed it on his ashtray, then cursed. After regaining his focus, he immediately threw two Altoid breath mints into his mouth.

"I'm in full control of my mind and body, but at times I allow this craving to get the best of me," Silk began talking with his body. "I stop smoking for five years, now I have the urge to smoke again. Sad! I can't stand not being willfully powerful enough to defeat this small craving. Am I not able to yield to temptation?" he questioned, remembering what his grandfather once told him, '*Son, sometimes even the strongest of us will sound like a man with a paper ass and when that time comes, you can do either two things: record yourself and play back that foolishness, or you can talk to your damn self. But son, don't be a bigger damn fool to answer yourself.'* As Silk reflected, he smiled, utilizing the wise words of wisdom given to him.

Swerving back into traffic, Silk sung along with the OJ's. *For The Love of Money.* "Money, money, money. Some people gotta have it; some people really need it.   …do thangs, do thangs, do thangs - bad thangs with it."

Two blocks from home, the last traffic light caught him. Sitting underneath the light with a great deal of patience, he watched the soft rain sprinkle over the street lights. Suddenly, he noticed how it hammered its way to the ground. While soaking in his surroundings, the walking victim popped up on his radar due to being the only female out walking the cold, wet streets. The neighborhood was dark, not many porch lights were on, and not even the sound of a barking dog occurred, because everything and everyone sought shelter. 7:30PM, darkness held the sky hostage.

This little young girl shouldn't be walking through this neighborhood alone, he thought. As Silk slowly rode the gas peddle, he continued studying the teenager. The thought crossed his mind to ask if she need a lift, but his grandfather's past cautions dissolved the idea.

Crazy man! Do you know how that would sound? You stopping to see if you could give her a lift. You think the young girl's going to say yes Sir and just hop in and ride with your overgrown ass? She going to decline, give you a polite no thank you and start walking faster. So why spook her, you stranger? Silk smiled at his crazy thoughts, but continued riding slow behind her. Suddenly, his headlights gave him away, and as predicted, the young lady started walking like she was trying to win a walkathon. Her swagger gave her away. Silk stopped the car and got out. He tried to keep his distance in order to avoid frightening her any further.

"Nakeita? Nakeita, is that you?" he shouted. The girl turned in his direction, as Silk's voice echoed once again. "Nakeita, ain't that you?" She started walking towards him.

"Yes, yes, it's me Uncle Silk," she shouted back, recognizing the voice and his black Lexus. Silk took off his black blazer before Nakeita reached him.

"Girl, what are you doing out here in this cold weather?" he asked, covering her head.

"I'm coming from the library. I should've left three hours ago when my friends did, but I wanted to stay and study a little longer. I wasn't in no hurry to rush home to a lonely house, but now I wish I would have been," Nakeita explained.

"Girl, it's cold and wet. This is pneumonia weather. Where's your hat and why you don't have on a heavier coat? This thin jacket isn't going to keep you warm," he fussed, walking her over to the passenger side to open the door for her. Nakeita slipped into the seat, and Silk ran around the car to jump back behind the wheel. Immediately he turned on the heater for Nakieta. "Girl… " he shook his head in disgust. "Promise me this won't happen again. I don't need you walking through nobody's neighborhood this late at night. You hungry?"

"Not really."

"Well, I sure can use a bite, so what you have a taste for?"

"I'm a beggar and a beggar can't be a chooser."

Silk smiled, while continuing to travel through traffic. When Silk was ready to eat, Nakeita knew better than to voice her opinion. Immediately, she was reminded of the last time her Uncle was trying to take her to eat. She was so busy getting him to stop at McDonald's that she missed out on getting a twenty-five-dollar feast from Red Lobster fest.

"I have a craving for some shrimp pasta. How does an Italian restaurant sound? What you think?"

"It sounds good to me."

They stopped at Zio's and after they finished eating and while ready to exit the building, Silk placed a healthy tip on the table and gave Nakeita two twenty-dollar bills. He advised her that a young lady should always keep at least fifty dollars in her purse at all times. As well as not allow the evil of the money to trap her, because the mean carried a lot of weight, and some women made the mistake of even selling their precious body for a few bucks.

"You done seen one of them cartoon monsters on TV with three eyes before, haven't you?" he questioned, reaching the aquarium at the restaurant's front door.

"I think so, why you ask?" Nakeita questioned, watching a large crab crawl around in the tank with a very confused look on her face. She'd never heard Silk drop his intelligence level to mention something about kid's entertainment before.

"Nakeita, come here," he said, with his arms open wide. She walked into his embrace, "I don't know what it is. Maybe I just need a hug today," he said, using reverse psychology. He kissed her forehead, "Now that's the third eye most monsters have, but we humans also have what we call that third eye. And young lady, when that third eye of yours is open, you won't be able to be led astray."

Silk continued to provide fatherly guidance to his God-daughter. Nakeita hugged him tightly. *Man, why he can't be my father*, she thought. Silk looked down in Nakeita's watery eyes and spoke as if he could read her mind.

"Look Lil' Lady, I'm your father and your uncle," he smiled. "Is that cool with you?"

"Y-E-S," Nakeita said.

"What time does your mother get off?" Nakeita looked down at her watch.

"In about twenty minutes."

"Well let's go pick her up. By the time we get there, she should be getting ready to walk out of Wal-Mart's front door."

When they reached the parking lot, Ebony was beating her feet out the door—she saw Nakeita waving and made her way over to the car. Easing into the back seat, she instantly started talking.

Ebony smiled. "Man, I earned my check today. The line to my register stayed long, customers raided the store for my whole eight-hour shift. Silk, how nice of you to come and pick me up. You sure know how to save a working woman a few dollars. I can save that twelve-dollar cab fee and spend it on a Captain D's meal tonight."

"Mama, we just finished eating."

"Y'all two been hanging out?"

"Actually, I just picked Nakeita up. She was walking home from the library," Silk expressed, looking into his rearview mirror.

Ebony dug around in her purse unable to find what she was looking for.

"Walking homein this pneumonia weather?"

"I was studying. I lost track of time."

"Young lady, you need to start listening to the daily weather reports and keep some gloves, a scarf, and a skull cap in your book bag at all times," Silk advised.

"Umm huh," Ebony agreed.

"It'll be done soon as I get home," Nakeita assured.

"So Silk, how was work today?" Ebony questioned.

"Sista-in-law, you know me. I work smarter, not harder," Silk grinned. He was a 39-year-old professor, who was making a six figure annual salary doing something he enjoyed. "You know everyone has a purpose in life, so I guess teaching was my call."

"How many knuckleheads you have in your class?" Ebony questioned.

"At least two," Nakeita predicted.

"Actually one," Silk smiled. "But sometimes Nakeita, there are two."

"See, Mama, I told ya."

"You know a funny thing that amazes me about my college students?"

"What?" Nakeita queried with enthusiasm in her voice because she loved to hear stories about the people on campus. Once Silk began, you were sure to learn something. Now rather you used it to follow in that individual's footsteps or to avoid falling victim to the individual's bad experience, Nakeita always got comfortable and mentally took notes.

"One of my female students..."

"Umm, mmm." Ebony intervened, moaning.

Silk continued, "She's a very, very intelligent young lady. Has a good head on her shoulders, but she invests too much time in this guy and he's taking her on a roller coaster ride of a lifetime. She has all this book sense, but it seems to me like she doesn't have any common sense. At least that's what she has led me to believe. She's still sticking her hand in the fire to see if it's hot."

Chapter 4

Ebony smiled even on the days she didn't feel up to it. Actually, polite words spilled from her lips without her consciously giving it a bit of thought. This professional conduct was a part of her makeup and character. Once she entered Wal-Mart, her train of thought kicked in, allowing her to perform activities out of habit. Whether she was up to the task or not, she'd grown accustomed to this pattern.

However, today she was only there physically - not mentally, because her mind rested on Nakeita. She was concerned with her baby girl's safety, and she knew no one had her daughter's best interest at heart more than her. A father's obligation was to teach their sons how to be men; while a mother's obligation was to mold their daughters into becoming women of standard. And most know that in a woman's world there are courses and stages that have to be taken in alphabetical order.

When Ebony taught Nakeita her ABC's, if her baby girl skipped a letter, she immediately took Nakeita back to square one. Taking time to give the proper guidance and coaching was important. She wanted to ensure that Nakeita got the full understanding of life, so Ebony didn't count on any schools to do her job or play her role. She knew it was not the school's job to nurture her child, so neglecting her duties or her responsibilities was never an option.

Ebony's fingers danced across the cash register and when her thumb hammered down on the total button, her lips relayed the price total, time slipped away; she'd been standing on her feet for half of her eight hours, but to her it didn't seem like it. Ebony felt like she'd just walked behind the register. She continuously watched the clock and time was not moving fast enough for her. As a customer approached, she exhaled, putting on her best salesperson smile and voice.

"Hello? How are you doing today?"

"I'm doing just fine young lady. Thank you for asking. So how are you?" the elderly lady inquired.

"Tired, and the day ain't moving fast enough for me."

The elderly lady's blue eyes smiled, and blue, green and red veins invaded the back of her wrinkled hand as she passed over her food stamp card.

"The day ain't moving fast enough for you?" she smiled. "Young lady, that's what they say 'bout my driving. Have you ever heard of a person receiving a ticket for driving too slow? I guess I'm the first person in America." She paused, raising her right hand. "I received a ticket yesterday for driving too damn slow. I'm the first elderly lady to make history." She gave Ebony a friendly look. "Do you think I'll be the first person and the last person to collect that kinda ticket?"

Ebony gazed at the woman's smile, and mirrored it, "I surely hope not for your sake."

The elderly woman failed to tell the whole story, because there are two sides to every story. The first time she had received a warning, which the officer respectfully gave her after learning that she had a valid license and full coverage insurance.

"He had the nerve to tell me, Ms, you're too old to be on the road. You're seventy-eight. Please do yourself and everyone else a favor by playing the passenger seat," she laughed. "Next he'll recommend me a rockin' chair and graduate me to the old folk's home."

But, no more than two days after that encounter, they had bumped heads again, which the lady didn't tell Ebony about. The elderly women quickly thought about the conversation she had with the officer.

"Ms... you remember me?"

"No," she played senile, using her age to her advantage.

"Ms. We just had a talk a couple of days ago, I warned you about driving. I personally have nothing against you being on the road, but if you're going to drive on these streets and travel back and forth across my highways, you're going to have to drive according to the speed limits. You can't continue driving 35 miles per hour in a 65 mile per hour zone. You are holding up traffic, you're gonna cause someone to get hurt. Now we don't want you to get hurt, do we?"

Quickly dismissing the officer's warning, she added him to her pay it no mind sheet, along with her daughter, son, and husband. Now here a few days later, the elderly lady appeared to be driving like she was in a parade. Vehicles behind her rode down on their horns as she should've rode her gas pedal. They lost respect for her; no one hid their contorted faces and voiced their nasty opinions.

'Take her old ass to jail"

"She needs to be behind a walker."

"She'll look good behind a push mower."

The crazy suggestions and comments did not damage her, she continued smiling and waving at the passing vehicles as if her parade was still in full effect. She played the sideline until her daughter and son arrived to collect her and her last-year brand-new white Cadillac.

"I ain't driving today," she admitted to Ebony, manifesting the office invisible leash was still around her neck, "cause I ain't trying to go to jail. I'm too old for that."

"Yes ma'am, you're too old for jail."

"Behind them bars made Momma get some get right," her daughter confirmed. "Before that Momma didn't have a do-right bone in her body."

"I like to drive."

"Drive it, Ms. Daisy!" A noisy bystander said.

"Shut your mouth. I taught you how to drive," the elderly lady said to her daughter while finally abandoning Ebony's register.

"Yeah, you did that and Momma, I appreciate it."

"No, you don't, you ungrateful thing... just like the rest of them. You side with your father against me. All y'all some unappreciative people."

"I'm all you got and you're all I got," the daughter paused. "Remember ma... I'm your only daughter."

Ebony's heart skipped a beat at the thought of Nakeita increased. She collected the time again, but only two minutes had escaped.

"It's going to be a long day," she predicted.

Customers raced through her line as if they were being fast-forwarded, for a good two hours. She lost track of time until this wanna-be player tried his hand.

"Wha's poppin' Shawty?"

"I'm not your Shawty, your Shawty supposed to be your kids."
"Damn baby-cake, don't be so mean!"
"Mean is my middle name."
"And Mr. Green is mines," he lied. Thumbing through his bank roll, the guy had a hundred-dollar bill on top, three twenty-dollar bills and fifty dollars worth of ones.
"Sir, money don't impress me," Ebony muttered, giving him the evil look.
"This shit here pays bills and buys meals."
"I'm a working woman," she offered and thought, *this lame with this pathetic ass game.*
He winked at Ebony, "Sweet thang, why get paid for standin' on your feet when you can get paid the easy way... by wallowin' between some sheets?" He smiled, showing off his five thousand dollars' worth of diamond dental work.
Is that what your mother do? Is that what your sista do? So that's you family occupation? Ebony thought, rolling her eyes, *"I'm not going to blame this bastard, I'mma hold myself responsible for this one because I put myself in the line of fire. Giving this low-life the opportunity for me to smell his shitty ass breath.*
"Baby girl, it's cool. Everybody have to tap dance every now and then. But, baby, you sit on a gold mine. You're definitely a walking treasure," he offered. "Baby, I knew you tried the taste of lemon ice tea, now try Pimpin T."

Ebony massaged her temples, burying her assaulting thoughts as she regained her professionalism because her ghetto side begged and cried to give this nutcase a suggestion.
"Sir, is this it?" she asked, touching the top of his beer.
"I'm not interested in nothing else in this store but you. So do you come with it? What's your price tag? Everyone can be bought," he said, handing her two singles because the register displayed one dollar and eighty-nine cents. "You can keep the change, Shawty."
Ebony politely dropped the change into his sack, "No thank-you sir, you're better off with it, it might save you one day from having to tap dance."
He gave Ebony a mean mug, "You're not my type anyway."
"The feeling is mutual."

"I used to like 'em from age 8 to 80 blind, cripple or crazy."

"Uh, huh. I can imagine."

"Now I don't want nothing over seventeen," he licks across his diamond grill, "I like 'em young, juicy... like plums."

He picked up his beer, "Ma, this the new millennium and the planet is full of young girls going wild..."

Big Johnny was next in line. He didn't like the way the guy was conversing with Ebony, so he intruded.

"Bur, why you going there?"

"Excuse me!" The customer gave Big Johnny a deranged look.

"Why are you disrespecting this nice young lady?"

"Man, get the fuck out of here, Ol' Captain Save-A-Ho ass nigga," he growled and brushed past Big Johnny, on hot pursuit behind a group of teenaged females. The oldest appeared to be about fifteen and a half years old. The guy hollered like a lonely wolf at them.

Ebony shook her head. After him, she was ready to call it a day and only needed four or five more precious minutes to complete her total eight-hour shift. That last customer almost made ending the day on a peaceful note impossible. Suddenly, she felt sick, light-headed and had the urge to vomit on the counter. She flicked off her light and raced off to the manager's station, so she could report her health problems. She also wanted him to know she needed to go home, because only her home-sweet-home would be her cure. Nothing under Wal-Mart's roof would do her any justice.

Ebony already didn't think she would work the length of time she did, but something in her helped her keep her sanity. She grabbed her things and rushed out of Wal-Mart.

"Nakeita, baby. Hold on honey. Momma's coming," she mumbled.

***

Nakeita sat on her bed, bored to death. She knew there was a healthy eight hours in-between the time her mother would be home from work. Tired of being sick and tired, she bounced to her feet.

"I'll spend the day trying on all my clothes. Anything I have that's too small or fits a little tight, I'll get rid of it, cause I don't wanna hear that woman's mouth," Nakeita insisted. "Oooh... it's about income check time too. I know Ma gonna hook me up. Ebony will have two big checks, I know she ain't gonna have no problems with setting it out for her only child, for her only daughter."

Nakeita attacked her closet like she was on a serious mission. She wanted to have the clothes covering her bed by the time Ebony arrived,

"I might as well do the shoes, too, cause I damn sho ain't try'na wear no tight shoes to mess up my pretty feet," she smiled. "Shoot, some guys like sistas with small, cute feet," she laughed, wiggling her toes. "They call him a foot man," she said.

She tried on some pants that stopped at her calf muscles, and a matching button-up blouse. Nakeita turned a couple of times, posing in the mirror at different angles to see what she looked like in the outfit.

"Ooo naw, these pants are a little too tight. Ebony would have a fit if she caught me in this," she talked to herself as she faced the mirror, realizing after a second glance that the bottom of the blouse rested at the top of her stomach. "Oh! Umm hum, you gotta go too... I got way too much flesh exposed."

After going through several outfits, Nakeita gave five outfits the boot back to back. She was serious about pleasing her mother and living up to Ebony's expectations. She knew she had more to gain than she had to lose. Nakeita reminded herself, *I'll get rid of about ten outfits and I'll have Ma to get me about twenty new ones*. Her greed sunk in. As Nakeita continued rumbling around in her closet, she came across a pair of black jeans, and held them up to her waist line.

"I remember when you used to be my favorite pair of jeans." She slipped into them, but they hugged her body like a glove. "Too tight. I can't even fasten the button, so your ass gotta go too," she said, throwing them on the bed. "While I'm bullshitting, it's clearly obvious that I have way more tight clothes than I thought," she fussed. Her cell started ringing. "I'm coming, I'm coming," she ran to get the phone.

"Hello?"

"Nakeita, what's up?"

"Hey Keyandra, girl? What's with you?" Nakeita asked, shoving her clothes to the side to make room on the bed to sit down. "I gotta write an essay."

Nakeita made a disgusting face, "Yuck."

"Girl, you know how I hate writing them things," Keyandra began. "It wouldn't be so bad if we could write about what we wanted to write about, but we have to write about the subject they give us, and it's hard for me to get in a comfort zone on someone else's topic."

"Keyandra, you know nobody likes writing them essays."

"Quasha don't like them, Keke don't like them."

"Girl, don't feel bad, cause I don't know nobody who does either," Nakeita said laughing. "Oh Keyandra, girl, I take that back. My mother! Girl, she can write the mess outta some essays. One day I came home from school complaining about how I didn't like writing them. So Ebony called herself try'na give me a lecture. I told her let me see you write one since they so easy."

"Your mother wrote an essay?"

"Did she!" Nakeita barked. "The woman wrote three."

"What did she write about?"

"She played the good student and I played teacher."

"That's not tellin' me what she wrote about," Keyandra sassed.

Nakeita looked at her raided closet as if it could produce the answer needed, "Mmm, mmm," she hummed, "I forgot."

"Some schoolteacher you are. So what's on your agenda for today?"

Nakeita's eyes roamed. As she surveyed her bedroom, she smirked, because it looked like a storm zipped through it.

"I'm in the middle of doing some spring-cleaning," she exhaled, "But before that I was bored to death and was just sitting around looking stupid."

"Where's your mother?"

"Why?"

Keyandra smiled, "Cause I need her to give me some assistance with this essay." Ebony would be a good person to ask for assistance, because she wouldn't move forward until you had it down to a science. She would explain until you understood.

"Keyandra, Ebony's at work."

Every time Quasha, Keke and Keyandra do their studies at Nakeita's house, Ebony would sit with the girls. She claimed she was kinda rusty in some areas, but Ebony was still on top of her game. Once they introduced the subject, she took off. She enjoyed Nakeita's friend's company, and encouraged them to come over more often, but the girls took turns doing their homework over one another's house.

Keyandra's mother Cynthia loved the girl's company as well, she also claimed they helped polish her up in certain fields, but Cynthia's mind worked like a true computer. Her brain dug up accurate knowledge, and she always wanted to be a schoolteacher. Now her precious daughter and girlfriends gave her the opportunity to act out that role.

So when Keyandra's oldest sister, Punky, who had a Master's Degree in Education, visited all the way from the ATL, they would sure enough be blessed, because Punky would step up their game and share with them the knowledge they needed to acquire before they reached the twelfth grade. She explained the importance of their education, and she would also get on them about taking their studies for granted, as if she was each of their sisters. They listened to Punky because they valued her advice. She was their role model and had influenced them all to want to finish school, go to college, and also get a few master's degrees under their belts.

She made everything sound easy and reachable, so each of them wanted to follow in Punky's footsteps. *Punky did it, so can I,* they all thought. Every single one of them loved Keke's mother, because Carrister was a young intelligent mother, and she lived by example. She worked and continued to go to college to further her education. She had two Bachelor's Degrees, one in Computer Science and another one in Accounting, plus she owned her own business.

She was the mother that rewarded everyone on report card day. All A's got the kids one hundred dollars. All A's and one B would get them ninety dollars, and anything below that remained a mystery, because none of them ever made anything lower.

"Where is your mother?" Nakeita queried.

"My Momma's at work, too. If she wasn't, trust me, I'd be in there working her brain."

"When's Punky coming back down here?" Nakeita further queried, because Punky promised to bring some college books that she still possessed. Punky had challenged them that if they could pass various tests, she'd take them all out to eat and to catch the latest movie.

"The weekend," Keyandra replied with excitement.

"Friday or Saturday?"

"The weekend child, the weekend," Keyandra laughed.

"Well, sista, we'll chat later. I gotta have this here mess cleaned up before my mother comes home cause I really don't need to hear the woman's mouth."

"Nah, you just try'na act right cause it's income tax time," Keyandra corrected.

"And you too," Nakeita laughed.

"Call me later, Nakeita, girl."

"Alright."

Nakeita spent the next full three minutes singing along with Keisha Cole, *"I used to think I wasn't fine enough, I used to think I wasn't wild enough*, she sang, moving around her bed. Occasionally, she'd pose in the mirror, and rake her fingers through her hair. The music added some pep to her step, and she raced through the remaining clothes. Now with that part out of the way, she began rearranging things, storing her winter clothes in one section, spring clothes in another location and giving her fall and summer clothes an area of their own as well.

As she continued to clean, Lyfe Jennings voice started filling in the silence, "S-E-X," Nakeita began to get light on her feet, because this song always put her father on her mind. When Darrel was millions and millions of miles away, she dropped down in a chair and got deep off into a meditation as Lyfe's song did its thing on her.

"Daddy gonna go crazy when he finds out his baby having S-E-X," Nakeita found it hard to find air for her lungs. The female voice didn't make matters any better; her lyrics damaged some of Nakeita's nerves,

"Lyfe, they'll understand it better coming from a woman's point of view, He'll tell you anything to get into your panties."

She stayed glued to the seat until they were finished torturing her. Then without hesitation, Nakeita stood and turned the radio off. She moved on to attack her next task. She pulled her shoe boxes from the closet shelf, and then Nakeita sat Indian-style on her bed. Hugging one box, she had multiple reflections of her father teaching her numbers over the phone, as well as her alphabet, and how to spell her name.

Though her lessons were given over the phone, her father's phone calls always made her feel loved, a sense of connection, and most of all, she felt like his child. She loved herself some Darrel. His voice always uplifted her, his fatherly advice and encouragement was desperately needed. By him not physically being home, Nakeita often longed for him, but his frequent calls made her pain bearable because she knew he was there mentally. She followed his instructions and tried to live up to his expectations. She would do everything under the sun to keep her daddy happy, or to make him proud of her. As she reminisced, she could hear his voice so clearly.

"Baby girl, don't be giving your mother a rough time."
"Yes, daddy."
"Nakeita, Daddy knows that you don't like doing your homework right now, but trust me, there will come a time when you'll learn to enjoy doing your homework. You'll fall completely in love with doing it," Darrel said, trying to speak things into existence.
"I know I will too, Daddy," she agreed, accepting her father's word of wisdom as law of the land.
"When you going to start?"
"Tomorrow," five-year-old Nakeita would then promise to write. *"Tomorrow, Daddy. I'll start early in the morning. As a matter a fact Daddy, as soon as I get up."*
"You gonna be a good girl for Daddy?"
"Yes."
"Yes, what?" Darrel questioned, checking to see if Nakeita began to fully use the manners he'd been going over with her.
"Yes Sir. Daddy, I'm a good little girl, ain't I?"
"Absolutely. Now Sweetheart, you're going to be starting Head Start soon. Very soon, so I need you to make all good grades for Daddy, you hear me?"
"Yes, Sir."
"Nakeita, you think you can make Daddy all A's?"
"Yes," she said, with confidence.
"Are you sure?"
"Yes, Sir."
"How do you know you can, if you've never been to school?"
"Cause I just know."

"Can you make them all the way through your schooling?"

"Yes," Nakeita stated and corrected him, *"Daddy, I'mma try and I'mma try hard, cause I wanna be able to give all them A's to you all the time and guess what? Daddy guess what?"*

"Oh no, tell me?"

"Me and my Momma be playing school," Nakeita said almost out of breath. *"Daddy, we play school every day. Every time my Momma comes home from her job, she wanna do numbers, ABC's and she spelling. She has me spell my name and pronounce my name over and over, all day. Daddy, me already in school right here with Momma. And every time you call, you wanna do the same thing that Momma be doing. Daddy, is that all grown people know to do? Even my Auntie Betty be talking that talk, but Uncle Silk gives me a break. He said he's gonna buy me candy and ice cream before he starts that same grown people talk."*

"Nakeita, I don't care how big you get or how old you become, Lil Lady, you'll always be Daddy's Little Girl. I love you Lil Lady," the phone line beeped, notifying them that Darrel's fifteen-minute phone call was about to end. *"Baby girl, you're well-loved and well-missed."*

Tears crept down Nakeita's face.

"You're well-loved and well-missed too, Daddy," she whispered as the tears raced past her cheeks. She used her hands as windshield wipers, because her water-filled eyes began to blur her vision. "Daddy, I wish I could hear your voice now," she cried. After a few sniffles, she got herself together and did the next best thing, which always seemed to remove her burden or hardship. Smiling, Nakeita removed the shoe box lid, she looked down at all of Darrel's missives. There was no particular letter she needed to revisit, because they all were laced with fatherly guidance, warm words, and his love. Now she could really escape for a while and go into a world only her and her father shared. The papers somewhat served as fatherly shoulders whenever she needed to get her cry on. For some reason, they gave her a sense of comfort, and helped her feel her father's presence. To her, it was almost as if they were engaged in a face-to-face conversation.

***

Big Johnny threw on his right signal and coasted to the side of the curve.

"Home sweet home," he announced, knocking the vehicle's gear in neutral.

"Thanks, BJ, I really do appreciate the lift," Ebony stated.

"I'm just glad that I was able to assist you," Big Johnny sincerely replied. "I'm sorry I didn't arrive sooner to run that creep away."

"He didn't know any better, because if he did, he would've done better."

"There you go making excuses for grown folks again," he gave Ebony a look. "E. . . when you going to stop that?"

"Maybe when I die," she joked, trying to spread some sense of humor, because she noticed Big Johnny was on the edge of getting angry.

"E, you know I look at you like the little sista I never had, and people don't allow anyone to disrespect family. When someone hurts my people's feelings then it's no different than them tampering with mine. What I really needed to do was break that guy's face into two pieces."

"Violence doesn't solve any problems."

"Sis, I agree. But it sho would make the people get some get right," Big Johnny spoke from experience. He'd been on both ends of the short stick.

As a young boy, his father had to knock some sense into his hard head. That was before he came around into his full potential, and started acting like he had some sense, instead of carrying on like a hothead all the time. He acted as if he wore his emotions on the bottom of his sleeve, but time cured that behavior. Also by Big Johnny giving a couple of guys two across the lips, there had been no more problems at his club, and the guys still come around. However, they know to leave their foolishness at home. So when under Big Johnny's roof, they bring their best of personalities.

"Well, Big bruh, I better get going, my job isn't over yet," Ebony notified him. "I gotta get in here and cook my baby her meal for today."

"How's Nakeita coming along?" Big Johnny asked, out of concern. "I mean, how's she getting on without her father? How's she dealing with his incarceration?" he asked, making his sentence less complicated to answer.

"I'm a female," Ebony paused, trying to choose the right words. "And by me being her mother, I can feel my child's pain, because sometimes there are days when I'm affected by Darrel's incarceration myself. But, we both are strong and blessed to have him to miss. He could be dead."

"With that sista, I'll seal my case." Big Johnny said, not wanting to emotionally upset Ebony. Ebony slid out of the passenger's seat.

"Drive safely," she suggested, shutting the door.

Big Johnny considered telling her, "*I've been driving safe since that maniac cut my damn break line,*" but ruled against the idea. He knew if he went there, he would reopen another terrible wound.

"E, I keep both hands and both eyes on the road, cause I know I'm driving for other drivers as well. People got their driver's licenses from Wal-Mart. Do they sell'em at Wal-Mart?"

"No BJ. For your information, Walmart don't sell licenses," Ebony said, laughing.

"You oughta know. You work there, not me," Big Johnny laughed. "Well, if they didn't get their license at Wal-Mart, then they hadta come outta a bubblegum machine."

Ebony threw her right hand on her hip, "You would've been better off saying the people got their licenses from in the bubblegum wrapper called, Chew Man Chew."

Big Johnny scratched his scalp, "Now come to think of it, that's where this old lady I knew got hers from, cause she drives so super damn slow."

"BJ, cut it out," Ebony laughed.

"E, tell Nakeita I said hello."

"I sure will."

"Have a nice day."

"I sure will," Ebony gave Big Johnny a wave good-bye. "And you have an even better one," she replied, watching the truck work its way back into traffic. Slowly, Ebony turned on her heels. With keys in hand, she headed straight up her four porch steps, ready to give her baby girl the lecture of her life.

As the door closed behind her, she yelled, "Hi honey, I'm home." Ebony started to sort through the things in her purse. Suddenly, she pulled out a DVD, automatically assuming once Nakeita sees it, she'll know her mother had been to the Redbox to get movies.

"Nakeita! I'm home. Baby, where are you?" Ebony's voice echoed throughout the house.

"In the shower," Nakeita hollered back.

Prior to her mother arriving home, Nakeita decided to take a hot shower to relax her mind. She was so emotionally drained from all of her crying. Once inside the shower, she put her face directly under the shower to help relieve the tension and built-up frustration she felt. The water pressure massaged her body and made her fully relax. She knew afterwards she would be able to sleep like a baby.

"Well when you finish, come to the living room. I have something special for you." With time to burn, she did something she liked to occasionally do when she felt it was really necessary. She went into the kitchen and poured herself a drink. Ebony had been working on this half-pint bottle for the past six months and still hadn't knocked a dent in it. She smiled as she realized that the bottle was still three-quarters full. She did not want to behave like a drunk, so she would only pour enough gin in her glass to cover the bottom. Then to give the drink a better flavor, she'd add in some Cherry 7-Up. It would take her a half an hour to drain the glass, but today she did it in four swallows. She wiped her lips free from the residue and went back into the living room to patiently wait on her daughter.

Nakeita went through her normal hygiene and cosmetic routine, and then she rushed to brush her teeth. Normally she'd brush her teeth three times and her tongue at least twice. Once she finished, she walked in on Ebony wearing a white robe with a white cotton towel wrapped around her wet hair.

"Hi, Momma. How was your day today?"

"Beautiful," Ebony lied. "Sweetheart, come over here and have a seat."

Nakeita walked around the couch and sat on the loveseat, "I see you have us a movie. You need me to make us some popcorn?" she queried, knowing they would always have butter popcorn, sodas and king-sized candy bars whenever Ebony brought home movies.

"That wouldn't be a great idea."

"So what movie did you get?"

Ebony knew she had to answer her question with caution. "Nakeita, we as the human sometimes do things without considering the consequences first. Our actions may sometimes not be the logical thing to do, but we do it anyway," she stated, picking up the remote to push play.

Ebony was trying to avoid all of the intense questions her daughter might present, and she also noticed the expression on Naketia's face, so she was trying to prevent any suspicions her daughter was having. Within seconds, the screen came to life.

"Get educated, there are millions of males and females walking around in today's society with the virus known as AIDS. Some know they are HIV positive, but they are afraid to seek medical attention. What they don't know is the virus can be treated, especially when caught at an early stage."

The narrator on the DVD explained. This was not the typical kind of movie Ebony and her daughter usually watched, this was one that individually explained each and every type of Sexually Transmitted Disease that was out there to help make Nakeita aware of this sensitive subject. She was able to see pictures of infected sexual organs dealing with every form of STD's. She even learned about diseases that she didn't know existed. As Nakeita looked over at her mother, Ebony was intensely focused on the movie and sucking up all the information like a sponge. When it ended, Ebony looked at Nakeita with a serious expression and informed her that the DVD was hers to keep.

She wanted Nakeita to review it again at her leisure, and become comfortable with asking her questions. Ebony knew people would often lay important questions to rest, because they felt like they were asking dumb questions, especially kids when in front of a class full of their peers. Now Nakeita wouldn't have any reason to feel embarrassed about asking her mother questions. Ebony had her daughter's best interests at heart. She was her teacher, protector and wanted to make sure that she provided great guidance. And since Ebony opened up the platform for questions, Nakeita took a deep breath and began to let them fly. She literally interrogated Ebony, but she didn't mind. She needed her daughter to know about the importance of using caution about her decision to become sexually active, because there would be no room for excuses or statements like she didn't know, if she ever contracted one.

She hoped with the information from the DVD, her baby would practice safe behaviors instead of being sorry later. No matter what, Naketia was fully aware of the birds and the bees, and so the rest was up to her.

Chapter 5

Bell, Life and Kenny took the bench by the wishing well, knowing just about everyone visiting the mall would want to sacrifice a penny, dime or nickel in hopes of their dream coming true.

"That's right, Pops, you gotta keep hope alive," Bell said, watching an elderly man on a cane, close his eyes to thumb a quarter into the wishing well. After Pops threw the coin over his shoulder, he questioned himself.

"Is it supposed to be the right shoulder or the left?"

"It all depends on what you're wishing for Dad," Kenny said.

"If you're wishing for something stronger than vinegar, then it should've been your left shoulder. Now if you were wishing for a young girl fourteen, fifteen or sixteen to give your social security check to, then you should've flipped that guarantee over your right shoulder like I always do," Bell said with laughter.

The old timer did not find any word Bell spit funny. But, Bell pointed out that he used a quarter when he meant to use a nickel.

"Then you should replace my quarter."

Bell stood, "I wouldn't give a cripple crab a cracked crutch to help cross his crippled ass across the mothafuckin' crossing street."

"Now that was cute," the old man laughed. "Boy, you know you used a lot of C's, Boy don't you, Boy."

"Boy, don't you know, Boy, you used a lot of B's. Boy, don't you, Boy," Bell fired back.

"Old man, get the fuck outta here try'na use my shit back on me. I invented this shit here. Kick rocks, old man, before I kick you in the ass."

"Your feet are made for walkin'," the old man growled, "And son, it ain't that much kicking in a game of soccer."

Bell held his right arm parallel with his shoulder, kicking his finger tips, "When I played school football, I used to be the kicker. I know I can kick your old dried up ass over a field goal." Kenny and Life laughed.

"Heh, heh, heh," the old timer fake-laughed. "Larry, Curly, and Mo," he looked at Bell. "Big mouth, you must be Mo cause you doing all the talking." He began shaking his dog finger. Kenny and Life tried to dodge the finger because they were suspicious. "Y'all boys very, very disrespectful. Y'all don't respect your elders. Y'all fucking monkeys don't respect not one living soul, but mark my words, neither one of you bastards will live to reach my age. Won't live to get old." Before Bell was able to grow some nuts and act out his threat, Pops eased on down the road.

When Bell and his boys went to the mall, they spent their time chasing teenager females and making fun of people. They kicked the homeless guys around when they saw them sleeping peacefully in their cardboard boxes. They always took the beggar's money, so now when the beggars see a group of youngsters in their area; they always stop begging out of fear of being robbed. As two grown females walked toward their direction, Kenny nodded.

"Big Playa, there you go."

Bell knew Kenny was talking to him because that's how he addressed him. Sometimes he used a bigger handle, giving Bell the title of, *Boss Playa*. Bell leaned forward.

"Hi, ladies."

"Hello," they both replied in a chorus voice, which allowed Bell to know he had both of the ladies' attention. Suddenly, Bell dropped the bomb.

"Where y'all teenage daughters at? Cause I know y'all got some. Shit, at least I know y'all got one a piece." They had to give Bell a second glance. He threw them his best smile, and as they frowned, they continued walking, acting as if they had not heard the terrible words that came out of his mouth.

"Got damn, Kenny Penny, is you going to holla? If so, when?" Bell asked.

Kenny blushed. Bell and Life knew just as well as Kenny did that his chance of catching a female was slim to none. Kenny had bad skin and when his skin wasn't kept moist, he would shed like a rattlesnake. He also had an odor that refused to abandon his body. It was almost as it they were married, or joined together until death do them part. Even if he bathed, the odor would immediately pour out of his skin seconds before putting on his underwear. The longest the odor had ever separated from his body was for about ten minutes, and that was only because this female sprayed him down with mace until the can was empty. He never smelled mace before, so Kenny thought it was Lysol. Until he learned it was body spray for women.

"Kenny baby, I know you can pull us something," Bell recapped. "Somebody's daughter."

Kenny was a damn fool in many, many areas, but this wasn't one of them, so Bell's encouragement tickled him. It wasn't any military secret that Kenny didn't start knowing females existed until crack came to town. Other than that, he still would be a 32-year-old ugly virgin.

"Boss Playa, you know I ain't got no problem with try'na shoot my shot, but here you and I both know damn well that I'm handicapped. You Mr. Charm, me and L just tagging around waiting on you to catch some, so we can have a party cause we know B that you don't love them hos," Kenny leaned forward. "Tell him, L," he added, looking for Life to support him.

"You said all the right things then, Baby," Life agreed.

"Now Homie, y'all can wait until we get back to the hood and it all will be good," Kenny advised.

"A nigga don't want no wore out ass crackhead," Bell interjected. "A nigga after these first offenders."

"Try'na give Shawty some and some she can remember," Life agreed with Bell.

"Shit I'm just try'na get my dick wet," Kenny admitted, speaking nothing but the damn truth so help him God. As he did, a snow bunny walked by. "Hey cutie," Kenny put forth his Mack, feeling like he had a better chance at the opposite race. He was hoping everything would not be the rejection, which he had grown accustomed to. Even when the fellas joked with him about his ugliness, he accepted it as a compliment. His feelings could not be damaged, because Kenny lost his feelings when he was twelve years old.

"Man, when I was growing up I got called ugly a million and one times a day. No lie. Shit, now I start laughing when somebody calls me ugly," Kenny admitted, "Bru, not one single day went by that I didn't hear 'ugly' or 'Kenny you ugly.' Hell, they didn't have to call my name or tap me on the shoulder, cause I knew it was me they were talking to. Hell, I might have been ugly, but I wasn't deaf, too."

Since Kenny made himself the center of attention, they joined his bandwagon.

"Will all the ugly people please be quiet," Bell said, laughing.

"Bru, I'mma tell ya when I met our boy Kenny," Life chuckled so hard, he had to beat himself in the chest to avoid choking to death on his own saliva. "Me and my grandmother was coming down the street and Kenny and his Momma was coming up the street. My grandmother stopped Kenny's Momma and said, *'Ooooh Ms. Lady, that's a pretty baby you got.'* And back then B, Kenny wore them thick-ass glasses. The young nigga's lenses were thicker than the bottom of a drinking bottle and my grandmother had the damn nerve to ask what was wrong with Kenny's glasses," Life slapped his knees with laughter.

"Damn, Kenny Penny. You was ugly as hell and blind as hell at a young age," Bell shrugged. Kenny nodded.

"Boy, yeah boy. I used to be an ugly duckling, now I done turned into the most ugly duckling."

"I have seen some females grow outta that shit. They ugly while they young and by the time they get around twelve or better they become a fuckin' butterfly," Bell licked his lips.

"I'm in my thirties and I ain't got pretty yet," Kenny barked, "Not even a lil pretty."

"Shit, I can tell," Life chuckled.

"Boy, I hope to God that before I die, I get a little pretty," Kenny said.

"Playa, you need to be throwing shit in that wishing well," Bell advised. "Get you twenty dollars' worth of pennies and throw all them bitches off in there. My nigga one of your wishes gotta be granted."

"Homie, that shit you just said don't sound logical, not at all," Kenny continued, "I'm spending my dub on me; two ten-dollar dime rocks. So I can get my nuts outta the sand. She'll get one dime and I'll smoke the other one my damn self. Shit, according to how I feel at the time. I might just fuck around and pocket my dime rock and help her smoke hers."

***

Nakeita paced back and forth, while waiting on the bus. Today the sun was smiling, and there wasn't one cloud in the sky. A cool breeze would visit every now and then, but yet the weather was still beautiful. Since the bus was taking longer than usual, and the climate was so nice, Nakeita pondered over pocketing her bus fair and walking to the mall. As she picked up her things, a candy apple red Caddy cruised by. The driver was bobbing his head to his loud music, and started bumping his horn.

"Hey lil Momma, you workin'? How much it cost to be the boss?"

Nakeita immediately frowned and dropped down on the bench. She didn't need somebody's son to receive the wrong impression about her, because her body wasn't for rent. She didn't have a "for sale" sign in her two hands, nor did Ebony and Darrel make her work for hire.

A cute six-year-old girl rode her big-wheel down the sidewalk, and as she stopped behind the bench, Nakeita quickly twisted her body around to see the little girl's face.

"Hello?" Nakeita greeted the shy little girl. The girl waved and smiled, showing her four front missing teeth. "What's your name?" Nakeita asked.

"Tia."

"You have a pretty name."

"Thank you," Tia slurred. "Everybody tells me that."

"You live around here?"

"I live rat down there," Tia pointed to a nearby set of projects.

"What happened to your teeth?"

"I fell," Tia swallowed. "I fell on my big-wheel cause I was going too fast."

"Then you need to stop going fast. So don't go fast anymore, okay?"

"Okay," Tia smiled. "but you know the fairy tooth man gave me four quarters," she smiled.

Nakeita thought her smile was so adorable that she picked through her spare change and handed Tia four quarters as well.

"Thank-you," Tia said. "So you the fairy tooth girl. And you came over here to give me some money too."

Nakeita nodded, smiling.

"But I don't have any teeth to give."

"That's perfectly okay."

"You sure?"

"I'm positive," Nakeita smiled. "I'm absolutely positive."

"What's your name?"

"Na-kei-ta," Nakeita pronounced, thinking Tia would have a problem saying her name like most kids had in the past.

"Na-kei-ta."

Nakeita nodded and stood up, because the bus was getting closer. "Has your mother informed you about talking to strangers?"

"Yes, ma'am," Tia replied, noticing Nakeita put her sweet voice aside and now spoke with a sternness to her tone.

"Then why did you start talking to me and accept my money?"

"Cause," Tia cried out. "Cause you was a girl. You gonna tell my mommy on me? Please don't tell her, her gonna whip me cause her told me bout riding my big-wheel down here, and her gonna think I been begging again when she sees all this money."

"I'm not going to tell your mother this time, but promise me you'll keep your tail up there close by your house." Tia nodded. "And promise me that you won't accept nothing else from nobody, no money... no nothing. And that includes no more talking to strangers. You're too damn young to be pedaling around here try'na make friends. Now get your tail home."

"Yes ma'am," Tia whined, peddling full speed ahead. She was trying to distance herself from Nakeita's presence before she went back on her word and told Tia's mother.

Nakeita burst out into laughter. She knew she didn't know Tia's mother from Mother Nature. She stepped onto the bus, fed the meter the required fee and swung her sweaty body into a seat. The half stack Ebony had given her was burning a hole in her pocketbook, and Nakeita planned on spending every penny of the five hundred dollars as soon as she made it to the mall.

Funny, because Ebony knew her daughter like the back of hand. She knew Nakeita would spend all of her money and just couldn't wait to cry out that she needed more money. Her first intention was to give Nakeita the whole stack at once, but she had to catch herself, because she was sure that Nakeita would come back home whining about not having enough to get accessories or a matching purse or pair of shoes. Ebony wasn't going to entertain the conversation—she'd already planned to just politely hand over the other half and Nakeita would think she was ahead of the game.

Nakeita went into Macy's and balled out of control. She bought all of the latest hip-hop fashions. As she finished shopping, she was exhausted, but she had to snatch Ebony up a pair of Nike's before exiting the doors. Nakeita staggered into the Ladies Footwear. As she made her way to an unoccupied chair, she exhaled while placing her bags right next to her.

"Miss, may I help you?" the store's top assistant asked.

"Not really," Nakeita smiled at the female. "But if you're willing to assist me that would be nice." The assistant smiled. "Would you bring me a pair of size seven Nikes, please."

"Not a problem," she smiled.

"Ms... Ms?"

"Yes," she stopped to face Nakeita once again. Nakeita held up two fingers.

"Could you please make that two pair? The other one a size eight. I hope that eight runs small," she said.

"I hope so too."

Bell watched Nakeita go into the store. He wanted to lose Kenny and Life fast because he did not need the extra luggage.

"I'm going to the bathroom, boy a nigga gotta shit badder than a mothafucka," he lied.

"You better hurry before shit runs down your pants leg," Kenny teased.

"You'll need Huggies?" Life joked.

"Yeah playa, you gonan need a Pamper?" Kenny laughed.

"For what? So I can bring y'all a shit sandwich back?" Bell fired back, laughing his way into the Footwear store that Nakeita was trying on her shoes. Bell made it to a spot right by Nakeita. "Say Baby Cakes. What's the B-I?" he greeted.

"I'm minding my own business just like you should be minding your own business," Nakeita rudely stated. "You know my grandmother here with me."

Bell watched her come into the store alone, but his eyes scrambled around anyway.

"Naw, you by yourself; I can see that you'll tell a lie in a heartbeat. You lie just because you have a mouth. So do you always volunteer to tell lies?"

"Mister, that's my polite way of saying I don't want to be bothered," Nakeita replied, putting the shoe back into the box. "Man are you stalking me?"

"Should I be?"

Nakeita looked around the store. The place had eighteen other females Bell could have harassed.

"Man, all these women in here and you come over to bug me. Why?"

"Nakeita, I can see it now that you're going to play hardball with a brother."

She gave Bell a sour look because he'd just used her name as if they were friends.

"Man, what do you want? Why are you bothering me?"

"Be easy," Bell encouraged. "I'm not out to bite you—you just caught my eye."

"Then your eye need to catch somebody else," Nakeita stood, propping her hand on her hip. "My grandmamma already gave me the 4-1-1 on you."

"Ms. Matty Mae Strong?" Bell laughed. "She senile and you know it and I know it too. Hell, we both know it." Nakeita laughed at his comment. "Sweetheart, the only thing good about Ms. Matty Mae Strong is her cooking," Bell confirmed laughing. "When it comes to cooking, she's the truth."

"Boy, ease up on my granny."

"No, what you need to be doing is telling Ms. Matty Mae Strong to ease up on the people," Bell paused. "Listen, I'm going to be truthful with you. Yes, I watched you come in here and yeah, I followed you, but only to ask you did you need some help with your bags. Or maybe I was going to ask you did you wanna grab a sandwich, or did you need a lift home, especially since we both live on the same side of town," Bell grinned, jiggling his step father's car keys.

"Yes, I could use a bite and a lift."

"On one condition," Bell said, holding up a finger.

"And what's the condition?"

"That you don't tell your granny, cause I don't need Ms. Matty Mae Strong all up in my video, and trying to get into the mix of things."

Nakeita crossed her arms across her chest and they both laughed. Bell told himself if he could get her to agree to allow him to take her home, then that would be the beginning of their relationship.

Chapter 6

Silk held the door open for Betty and Ebony, as they all proceeded to walk into the casino. In the casino, people were busy trying to win money, while on the other hand the casino's main agenda was to beat them out of their house and home. Some were going to be winners and some were going to be losers. Everybody couldn't be a winner, but they all could allow their money to entertain them. Once the people entered the building, no other world existed. Some people gambled for fun, while others gambled to satisfy their addiction.

"Ladies, are y'all ready to have some fun?" Silk asked, smiling. He looked forward to visiting this place; Silk called the casino his paradise.

"Umm, huh?" Betty mumbled.

"I don't know about y'all, but I'm here to win me some money..." Ebony replied.

"You can't win much by playing slot machines..." Silk pointed out.

"I can't lose much either," Ebony alerted. Palming her hundred-dollar bill, the casino was not getting a penny more, "I make my money by standing on my feet."

"I make mines by sitting behind a desk," Silk offered, "But when I come to this place, sista-in-law, we're in the same boat because I might stand at that table throwing them two dice for over eight hours."

"Do your thing, high roller... Good luck..." Ebony cheered, walking off on her mission to an unoccupied slot machine.

The gamblers were in a world of a world. Furthermore, they had everything that was needed under one roof; restaurants, banks, teller machines, a hotel, plenty of waitresses at their leisure, free drinks, free food, a shopping mall, and a club with live bands with different artist to entertain its guest.

"Oh God, what am I gonna play today?" Betty questioned herself out loud. She loved blackjack, and at one time became too addicted to shoot craps; in addition, the slot machines were not fast enough for her. She didn't have the patience of a farmer like Ebony. Ebony worked the machine from sunup to sundown. *'Ebony got more ass to sit on than me,'* Betty thought, laughing at her own cute little joke. The Roulette table was packed, and the dice table was crowded as always, it would be abnormal if it wasn't. However, the blackjack and poker table guaranteed to have a seat or two open, they both were back-lock, fast paced activities games, but most customers favored the dice and slot machines. Silk eased over to the dice table, the table pit boss came over to greet him.

"Hello, Mr. Davis," the table pit boss greeted Silk. "Nice of you to join us on this lovely afternoon."

"I'm glad to be here." Silk gave the guy a firm handshake.

By Silk being a connoisseur, he was always greeted with his last name and they always put a handle on his name. The hotel rooms, meals, and tickets to events were free to him and his guests. Silk always received the royal treatment; his signature alone was worth a couple million. He'd blow twenty to thirty thousand before the sun set, and then run through six figures before sun rise. Also, Silk had thirty calendar days before he had to pay one dime. Silk's grandfather's father was one hundred percent Indian, Chief Green Foot. His grandfather, Bread Crumb, had a serious addiction, and had settled his million-dollar deal trading off portions of his land. However, but the casino could stay in business a million centuries and still wouldn't be finished paying Silk off for the rest of the land his ancestors sold.

"How much chips you need, Chief?" a different pit boss asked.

"Davis will be just fine..." Silk replied feeling verbally assaulted.

"Yes sir! Sorry sir," the pit boss corrected, "Mr. Davis sir, would you be needing any chips tonight, sir?"

"My usual will be just fine, Al..." Silk replied.

Al placed twenty-five thousand dollars' worth of hundred-dollar chips in front of Silk. Silk collected two of the chips and dropped them on a silver tray.

"Thanks for the tip, sir."

"You're most welcome."

Two Hours Later...

Everyone agreed it was time for some brain food; something else to go in their stomachs besides alcohol. Silk cut into his well-done thin-cut steak.

"Everyone's winners, right?" Silk asked, while he continued cutting.

"I'm up a few thousand," Betty blushed, as she took small bites of a breadstick.

"Good girl."

, "I'm not up yet," Ebony shifted in her seat, "But I'ma get 'em before the night is over," she promised.

"Keep up the good spirit, Ebony; with your positive attitude you're bound to win..." Silk took a bite of his steak. "You'll tear 'em off before the night is over, I have faith in you."

So how 'bout you, baby?" Betty queried, toying with a breadstick.

"I'm up a few stacks..." Silk unfolded, driving another piece of meat into his mouth, "Ladies, the steak is delicious."

"Go ahead honey, take mines." Betty pushed her untouched steak over towards him.

"She can't eat, she has the jungle fever," Ebony claimed. Betty smiled and winked at her.

"Well, sweetheart, make sure the casino feeds your purse," Silk advised, stabbing his fork into her steak.

"You better believe it, darlin', " Betty stated.

Ebony smiled while playing with her salad. She added more dressing for what reason only God knew. She wasn't going to put another bite into her mouth; she was ready to get back to the machines. *"What've I been doing wrong?"* she silently questioned herself. *"Was I pushing the coins in too hard or was I dropping them too soft? Do I need to wait a second after I drop the first coin before I add another coin?"* She smiled down into the salad once again.

Al walked over to the table, stopping a foot away from Silk.

"Mr. Davis, sir, I've been looking all over the place for you, sir. I said, I'll find you and your family here..."

"What's the problem?"

"I thought maybe you and the young ladies..." Al paused, as he went into his double breast pocket, but then realized he was in the wrong pocket. After correcting his mistake and retrieving the contents from the accurate pocket, he continued. "Now here we go," Al mumbled, placing four tickets on the table by Silk's plate. "Sir, here's some tickets for tonight's show. I thought you might like to enjoy some nice entertainment."

"How nice of you, Al," Betty thanked.

"Why four, when there are only three of us?" Silk spread the tickets

"I wasn't sure how many guests you had, sir," Al responded, thinking there was a guy for Ebony as well. "It's better to have too many and not one short," he added.

"Smart fella," Silk congratulated, "That was very thoughtful of you, Al."

"Who's doing tonight's show?" Ebony asked, laying her fork down because there was no sense in continuing to hold the damn thing especially since she was not going to use it.

"We have Mr. John Legend in the house," Al looked down at his fingers and touched each one in order to countdown the artists. "Mr. Kenny Lattimore... Ms. Anita Baker... Ms. Melody Fiona... And, Ms. Sade..."

"Sade don't play," Ebony whispered.

Betty reached across the table taking Ebony's hand squeezing it.

"Girl, you're a soldier of love too..." Ebony and Silk both knew the reason why Betty made the true statement, because Ebony stayed strong and faithful by Darrel's side.

"Y'all please excuse me and enjoy yourselves," Al spoke. "Mr. Davis, sir, is there anything specific you need me to attend to, sir?"

"No Al, not at all," Silk said, "And thanks once again for the tickets."

"You're quite welcome, sir..." Al replied, and started back on his mission to give a couple more high rollers the same tickets for that evening's show.

Silk reached across the table, to palm Betty and Ebony's hands together, giving them the strength that was needed.

"Now Ladies, are we going back to finish getting into the casino's deep pockets, or is we going to sit around here praying at the table all night?"

"We're here for the money, right?" Betty offered, hypothetically speaking.

"I know I am!" Ebony shrugged.

"That cheddar makes ya feel better…" Silk teased.

"I know that's right, honey!" Betty agreed.

"Silk, we gonna stay and catch the show too, right?" Ebony asked.

"If you want to…" Silk answered.

"I would love to." Ebony locked her hands together in prayer form.

"Sista-in-law," Silk winked, "The show it is."

"Thank you brotha-in-law," Ebony threw back her best salesman smile, "Now let's go beat the casino outta house and home."

"Tear 'em a new asshole, huh?" Silk joked. "Ladies, please excuse my French, but it just had to be said in that form and fashion… In any other language it wouldn't have sounded so tempting."

"Okay now y'all," Betty began. "Let's do just that."

After they decided not to try and win all the casino's money in one night, they put the tickets to good use and drank two bottles of champagne while being entertained. As a result, no one could wait to crawl into their own bed.

Ebony sat in the backseat as Silk slumped down in the passenger seat allowing Betty to chauffer them to the house. Silk talked her fortune into existence; she was eight hundred dollars richer, and the thought of her earnings wouldn't let her mind rest. Ebony mentally split her winnings into three groups, *Two-fifty for Darrel, three hundred for Nakeita to shop with, and two fifty goes towards my bills*, she thought, always putting the two loves of her life before herself.

"Ebony?"

"Yes, Silk?"

"How you feel about coming back next week?" Silk asked, and then yawned.

"If I'm not working… Then it would be a lovely idea."

"It sounds like a beautiful plan if you ask me..." Betty said, speeding through the yellow light. The streets were too lonely to be sitting at a red light.

"Ain't nobody asking you!" Ebony barked, well heartedly.

"Then excuse me," Betty replied with a smile.

"Ms. Betty, how would you feel about going to the casino next weekend?" Ebony asked sweetly and in a joking voice.

"Mmm," Betty murmured, "I would love to, and thank-you for asking."

"It would be a pleasure to have you to join us..." Ebony teased.

"No, dear, the pleasure will be mine," Betty replied. "All mines."

"Ya'll too crazy and silly," Silk laughed.

"Ebony, girl, you outta try the craps," Betty suggested.

"Shoot dice?" Ebony frowned. "That's not for women"

"Child, you might win big... I did the first time I ever played the game--" Betty revealed.

"That's beginner's luck."

"Huh," Ebony grunted. "I'll have to think about that one because I don't know a thing about dice... I'm so green, I wouldn't know when I win or lose," Ebony admitted.

"Don't worry, say no more... You know Silk and I are not going to let the table cheat you; plus, the person running the table going to keep everything honest. He'll announce out loud whether you won or lost," Betty explained. "He's not out to cheat you, but to beat you."

"We'll see what next week brings because next week is not promised to any of us." Ebony said.

"Well, if the Lord still has us in our right frame of mind," Betty coughed, "And still breathing, me and you can shoot dice next weekend and I'll blow on your dice like Silk blew on mines."

"Sista-in-law," Silk began, "Remember you have to talk to the dice."

"Talk to the dice?" Ebony looked puzzled.

"Yeah!" Betty said.

"What am I supposed to say?"

"You can start off with; *my baby needs some new shoes...*" Silk laughed.

"Silk, you gotta be puttin' me on... Come on now, you can't

possibly be serious," Ebony pursued. "Silk, are you serious?"

"Very," Silk wailed, "Very serious."

"Ebony, girl, I know it might sound crazy, but watch, you'll see everyone who shoots the dice are going to talk to the dice while they shaking them or while they rolling them," Betty noted.

"Alright now…" Ebony replied.

"Girl, you probably have a good dice hand and don't even know it yet," Betty insisted, turning into their driveway.

"We'll know next weekend," Silk stated, getting out the car and opening Ebony's door for her.

"So did you have a good time?"

"You bet."

"That's good… So the casino can look forward to seeing you again next week?"

"Silk Davis, if it's the Lord's will."

"Ebony, good night, girl…" Betty said.

"Good night to ya'll, too, sleep tight and don't let the bed bugs bite…" Ebony responded, a little louder than she needed to. She went into the house and marched straight to her daughter's room. Nakeita was sound asleep with a big smile on her face. Ebony pulled the covers up to her shoulders and kissed her on the forehead.

"Baby, Momma won tonight… Now I got you some more money so you can go shopping again... Now Momma's baby can get that purse and open face sandals to go with her outfit." Ebony tiptoed back out the bedroom, not wanting to disturb Nakeita's sleep because from the sound of her light snoring, she could tell Nakeita had a rough day. *'Tomorrow I might go to the mall with Nakeita."* Ebony thought, heading to the bathroom to run her some bath water.

***

Five hours earlier, Nakeita had gone to the trailer court. She loved to hang out at Toni's run down trailer. The outside of the trailer showed it should be in somebody's junk yard rather than in somebody's trailer park. Three other females lived there as well; they sold their bodies and worked at strip clubs. With everything in common, they all were in the same boat: high school dropouts, weed-heads, and alcohol and X-pill abusers. They laid on their backs more for the sack than they did for the paper greenbacks and they had the nerve to call themselves, PPB:

The Pussy Power Bitches.

Toni had been forced to go to prison for a crime she didn't commit. She had claimed her boyfriend's drugs like a damn fool when the police raided. After completing the one year girls group home, the guy introduced her to drugs and by her not being able to financially support her addiction, she began doing the things she thought a cave woman would be able to do with only a ninth-grade education.

Tasha got turned out at the age of sixteen. Two guys dropped pills into her drink and after they finished having their way with her body, they notified twenty-six more of their gang-banging homies, giving them the opportunity to join the party. As a result, Tasha had a daughter and didn't have a clue the first of who is her baby's father.

Wonder jumped off the porch early as well and started smoking cigarettes that had been dipped in golden-looking pee-water. Not long at all, the PCP had her on a desperate and suicide mission to feed her craving. These young ladies showed her from experience the easy and faster way to get paid. Wonder got turned out by Toni; Toni got her drunk and high on weed and started charging guys fifty bucks for Wonder's goodies. After that, she continued allowing Toni to hook her up with dates and they used the money for getting high. Wonder looked up to Toni and trusted her judgment. To her Toni was out for her best interest.

Toni used the butt of her pink lighter to crush seven X-pills. She applied pressure down on the one-dollar bill, once the solid rock form converted to powder form, she laced two blunts and five cigarettes. The trailer living room smoke produced a cloudy fog as if it came out of a fifty-seven Chevy with a blown head-gasket. Nakeita fought away with the air by fanning her face.

"You fool, if you hit the blunt or the cigarette you won't have no contact high," Toni misguided.

"You sure?" Nakeita cautioned, but accepted the blunt from Wonder anyway. Wonder gave Toni a wicked smile. Nakeita choked on the first drag.

"Swallow the smoke," Toni instructed.

"Shut your mouth when you do, so all the smoke will come out your nose," Wonder coached, as she stared through her baby-doll brown eyes. Her forehead became sweaty every time she began smoking blunts or cigarettes.

"Why you decline the cigarette," Tasha questioned, "But tried the blunt instead?" Nakeita hunched her shoulders, but knowing she only smoked because she grew tired of hearing Toni nag about she's a party pooper. She wanted to fit in; she did not want them to think she was trying to be different or better than her friends by not smoking.

"How you feel, Nakeita?" Wonder asked.

"I'm alright."

Nakeita first came in contact with the girls when she accepted Bell's offer to give her a ride home from the mall. When they arrived, Toni, Tasha, and Wonder had the living room coffee table decorated with a week supply of alcohol and X-pills. Bell, Life, and Kenny helped themselves to the treats immediately. Since they always looked at the Pussy Power Bitches as gold-diggers and free-loaders, Nakeita turned down all of their handouts; she wouldn't so much as have a beer. She made the girls feel uncomfortable; Toni even complained that Nakeita blew her high by always watching everybody and everything. Tasha made the deranged comment that maybe Nakeita could be an undercover cop trying to bust them, but Wonder finally spoke up in their private three-woman meeting and said, *"The girl is young and if you really paid attention, you would've noticed Nakeita more likely ain't never been around drugs before, nor interacted with bitches like us before in her damn life."*

Nakeita's second visit supported Wonder's statement. Toni and Tasha learned that Wonder had been one hundred percent accurate. She had judged Nakeita correctly, and yes, once again Nakeita declined their handouts, *'Thank-you, but no thank-you,'* she had said, staying true to what the school and her mother trained her to do, and that was to say "no" to drugs. However, Toni also had been able to see deeply within Nakeita, she felt the curious energy coming out of Nakeita's pores as Nakeita began to ask questions about how each individual controlled substance affected them at the end of the day and in the morning. They took turns glorifying the pills and weed, they bragged so much that Nakeita almost felt the need to experience the pill. She asked the million-dollar question, "What you think a half a pill would do for a person who never took the pill before?"

Toni explained the situation so beautifully and encouragingly that Nakeita wanted to say, '*let me try it,*' but she just couldn't fix her mouth to say the words. Tasha broke a pill in half, "Here girl, go ahead and try it. I promise you'll like it."

Nakeita's mind was telling her *no*, but her body was telling her *yes*. She battled hard with the temptation and finally batted down the idea.

Now here she was again in the Pussy Power Bitches' trailer, smoking weed and faced with the same decisions as before.

"You like it?" Toni pursued.

"Not really, but it's cool..." Nakeita stated, with her eyes growing large without her noticing. Tasha smoked on the blunt and monitored it.

"This some good shit, Nakeita, girl--"

"T, give her the blunt, let Nakeita get another drag!" Wonder commanded.

Tasha made the offer and Nakeita wasn't shy with the accepting. She handled and controlled the smoke much better this time.

"You like this shit, don't you girl?" Toni's asked, as her eyes sparkled.

"Not enough to buy none!" Nakeita said, speaking the truth.

"You will sooner or later..." Wonder predicted.

Toni took the blunt from Nakeita's fingers without asking. She smoked the blunt like a professional.

"She true to it, not new to it..." Wonder revealed.

Toni held hostage a mouthful of smoke, then leaned into Nakeita's face and exhaled.

"Breathe the smoke in through your nose, Nakeita girl," Tasha insisted, knowing that would give Nakeita a rush that could not be explained. "God, I love them shotguns!" Tasha cried out.

"Huh, huh, huh..." Toni grunted.

Seeking to give her the same treatment, Tasha captured the smoke in each nostril one by one and then some in her mouth. She held her breath long as she could before releasing what little smoke she had left.

"You rollin'?" Tasha questioned Nakeita.

"Yeah, I feel good..." Nakeita blushed. "I'm high."

"You rollin'? You rollin'?" Tasha repeated her question to Wonder.

"Bitch, I might be," Wonder spit forth the answer Nakeita was supposed to breathe on. So now Wonder took the matter before hand and replied the question to Nakeita again. "You rollin'? You rollin'?"

"Bitch, I might be," Nakeita barked, "Bitch, I might be."

"Gucci!" Toni yelled out the artist's name. Not one of the three young ladies had stumbled upon the age of twenty-one, but their fake ID's registered them as adults and put them over the grown folk's mark.

"Here Nakeita?" Tasha offered the blunt.

"I better decline," Nakeita pushed her hand away. "I can't handle anymore..." she admitted, trying to focus back on reality. *Ebony will kill me if she thinks I've been smoking that mess,*" she reasoned with herself.

"Nakeita go ahead and get you one more hit," Toni encouraged.

"One hit is one too many and a million hits is not enough..." Nakeita growled. "Once you take the first pull you'll never be able to get that same high again because your brain is paralyzed. Our brain is already paralyzed now, all we doing is wasting the stuff!" Nakeita warned.

"Ain't this your first time smoking?" Tasha asked.

"Yeah."

"Then what makes you say that?" Wonder fished.

"I saw it on a tape..." Nakeita paused. "They show you that in the tenth grade." Their high stopped them from being embarrassed. They never made it past the ninth grade, nor thought about stepping another foot into a school house.

"Damn that tape!" Tasha roared.

"That tape fake," Wonder laughed.

Nakeita came to her senses; she didn't want to hurt her friend's feelings so she spoke up.

"You're right--" she agreed.

"I know damn well I am!" Wonder barked.

"They always showing fake-ass tapes in school," Tasha waved as if knocking something out the air. "That's why I quit that shit. I'll be damned if I continue let them pull the wool over my eyes."

"That school shit is just in the damn way..." Wonder claimed. "Nakeita girl, you might as well go and quit too... Come live with us and then you'll be one of us."

"Girl, get with us Pussy Power Bitches, this shit here is what's up." Toni climbed to her feet. "We got these damn niggas noses' wide open, girl. They love Momma Kitty cat," she said, patting her womanhood.

"Ebony would kill me!" Nakeita spoke out of fear.

"My momma can't tell me shit!" Toni fired off. Her mother had kicked her out the house because she was on the verge of taking her mother's man. He became addicted to Toni's young sweetness and gave her more attention than necessary.

"Mines can't either!" Tasha stated. Her mother had a serious drug problem. She started off on crack, and as a result, didn't have a favorite drug of choice anymore. She just had a need to stay high so she wouldn't have to cope with reality. She auctioned off Tasha's treasure when she was five years old. Guys were smoking crack in her kitchen and Tasha staggered in with sleep in her eyes. Once the first guy stated he'll pay two ten-dollar pieces of crack to have sex with Tasha, the auction went into effect and the bidding ended with one hundred dollars' worth of crack. Six years later, Tasha was smoking crack.

The girls started having their little pep rally dancing around the house shouting, "PPB". They would sound off and clap twice, Nakeita, shouted and clapped right along with them. Next, she cupped her hands over her face and exhaled. "Yuck," she grunted, smelling her breath. Nakeita's mouth stunk, giving her a scent she never smelled before in her entire life. She raced home to bathe and brush her teeth; if Ebony saw her large eyes and large pupils, there would be trouble she did not need or want.

Chapter 7

The next day couldn't get there fast enough for Nakeita. The whole school day seemed endless for Nakeita; she was impatient about getting to Toni's trailer, afraid she might miss out on something. Finally, working her way to the trailer park, she sat back grinning from ear to ear. The blunt had her flying high in the sky with the airplanes and helicopters.

"Damn, I love weed," Tasha admitted.

"Bitch, you're a straight up and down sack chaser..." Wonder revealed, clapping her hands.

"And you too!" Tasha publicized, not liking for her secret to be uncovered.

'Bitch ass Wonder got me fucked up! She ain't hit on shit, the dirty and low-down bitch let Kenny's ugly ass fuck her eight-year-old daughter. The nigga tricking with her and her fucking child. Wonder

needs her ass kicked! The bitch lucky I ain't gonna put her dog ass out there on Front Street... That shit not my business, but for real I need to throw the ho-ass back up underneath the damn bus just like she just tried to do me!' Tasha thought. *'Let me stop thinking about this bitch, she's a waste of time and energy. I'll be a goddamn fool to sit here and let this broke down ass bitch fuck around and blow my damn high...'*

Toni danced her way into the living room wearing a belly cut tank top and red boy shorts, her pinned up hair and her firm breasts bouncing along with her. Her small feet and small frame fit her 5'6 height to a tee. She looked every single day of her eighteen years; her beautiful body matched her beautiful face.

"Jig... Jig... Jig..." Toni sang, while juggling the twenty triple stack ecstasy pills.

Tasha was cute in the face, slim in the waist, stood 5'0, and weighed a hundred and forty pounds even. The fake one-carat earrings made her look extra cute, and she had a nice butt and a handful of tits. Her short-cut hair style made her eye candy material. She joined Toni's cheering section. "Jig...Jig... Jig," she danced and sang.

Wonder had a petite body; the Creator was in a good mood when he made her. She had the prettiest set of white teeth; her 5'5 frame forced her to religiously throw up her fake ID to shield her seventeen-year-old mark. Wonder was a real redbone with reddish hair, turning her cap to the back she leaped in the circle as well, "Jig... Jig... Jig," her voice echoed, as she snapped her fingers repeatedly.

Toni worked her way over to Nakeita, grabbing her by the hand and pulling her to her feet. Nakeita stepped out her open toed sandals to get barefoot with the crew. She could dance her ass off, showing that now they were in her field, in her line of fire. Nakeita danced, making her ass cheeks flip like a butterfly. Tasha juggled over to the stereo and put on their theme song, and Sean Paul's, voice had them dancing and carrying on as if they were in his video. Tasha dropped down and started dancing low to the floor, proving to the room that Sean Paul's dancers did not have a damn thing on her. Wonder fell in line also imitating the dancer's style of dancing. She started off with a Reggae dance and then converted into a duck-walk sexy dance; the guys in the club would go bananas when she did this while looking back over her shoulders.

Toni called herself the best dancer, so Nakeita set out to prove her wrong. They battled against one another, and they both were determined not to be outshone. Enjoying the competition, Nakeita closed out the show with a video performance as if she was, Ciara. She dropped to the floor with her waistband pants pulled down to her knees. No longer was her yellow thong incognito; both of Nakeita butt cheeks took turns bouncing off the floor as if they were a baby's basketball.

"That bitch can use them ass muscles," Toni shouted. "Damn Nakeita, girl, you done some shit that I can't do. You gotta show a bitch how to do that shit."

"It's easy," Nakeita said, almost out of breath. "It's like riding a bicycle."

"Ride a bicycle my ass!" Toni shrugged.

"Girl, I ain't into that gay shit, but your ass looked pretty than a mothafucka…" Wonder threw one of her arms around Nakeita's shoulder. "Girl, you got a fat beautiful ass!"

"Girl, you bust Toni's ass with that one," Tasha gave Nakeita high five. "She'll know better from this day on 'bout fucking with you."

"Yeah, she did that," Toni argued, "But I bust your ass and I'll continue busting your no dancing ass."

"Bitch, you been stripping longer than me, too! Ho, what you want an A-plus for that?" Tasha barked, immediately defeating herself.

"Naw bitch, I don't need a fuckin A-plus," Toni grinned. "I just need you to stay in your fucking lane, lil' girl, that's all.'"

"T and T…" Wonder laughed.

Nakeita put back on her sandals and began to head for the bathroom to wash her face, but Toni's voice gave her no choice but to abandon the thought.

"T, girl, this power pellet here might help you to knock me off…" Toni gave Tasha two double-stack ecstasy pills.

"These butt-naked ladies the shit," Tasha admitted, but knowing what worked for her body might not affect the next person system the same.

"Bitch, speak for your damn self," Wonder advised. "Two won't do me no damn good. What's good for the goose ain't always good for the gander."

"What's good for the goose ain't always good for the gander," Nakeita repeated.

"Girl, that saying so damn old..." Wonder added.

"True, but brand new to a sucka," Toni agreed, and they all laughed.

"Toni, girl, you ain't trying to call me a sucka on the sly is you?" Nakeita returned.

"Shit, you just punished me in dancing. Hell, I ought to!" Toni replied, handing Nakeita two pills as well. Nakeita looked down at the pills; her judgment got the best of her.

"Two pills might be too much for me, what y'all think?"

"This child told y'all witches she was brand new to this." Wonder walked over to Nakeita and scooped one of the pills.

Tasha waited until she finished washing down the pills with a hundred percent juice before she decided to speak her piece.

"Bitch, you got veins like a hog, five minutes from now you'll be ready for three more."

"I'll eat your ass..." Wonder replied.

"Catfish, I ain't eatable," Tasha laughed. "At least not by another bitch, anyway."

"For a sack of pills you will!" Wonder responded.

"Here we go again with this bullshit," Toni growled. "Can't we all just get along?" She spun around in her tracks and pulled out her sack giving out pills again with a wicked smile as she hollered, "Trick-or-treat." Toni gave Nakeita two pills again and encouraged her to take them both. Nakeita wanted to protest, but Toni assisted her with getting the wheel in motion by handing her the bottle of juice as well. Nakeita threw the pills in her mouth and washed them down to her stomach and then wondered how the three pills would affect her. She braced herself for whatever wild experience stood before her.

"Nakeita?"

"Huh?" Nakeita smiled in Tasha's direction since she called her.

"Girl, them pills gonna take you to another world..." Tasha counseled. "It'll have you on another planet," she tipped her juicy, "but remember, you gotta keep plenty of fluids in your body."

"Ok..." Nakeita nodded. Wonder walked over to Nakeita and looked down at her.

"You rollin' girl?"

"Bitch, I might be!" Nakeita smiled, remembering the appropriate way to answer the question in the correct form.

Toni went into the back room so she could be in privacy when she phoned her customers, *her clients*, to notify them that the cathouse is open for business. The menu: young flesh barely legal mommas ready for whatever.

***

Kenny and Life walked out the grocery store carrying two cases of beer they'd chipped in on. Bell opened the back door to his stepfather's Suburban; Kenny threw in his two twelve-packs and Life did the same.

"How long we got the truck, Boss Playa?" Kenny asked.

"We can ride this bitch all night long, but I got to take his shit back before 5A.M." Bell answered.

"Dude work in the fountain?" Life asked.

"Yeah…" Bell replied.

"I don't see how a mothafucka can work around all that damn iron…" Kenny said, slipping into the backseat. He busted open a twelve-pack suitcase, snatched out a beer and opened it. "I can't do no work like dude--"

"Nigga, you allergic to work man…" Life said, twisting his upper body towards the backseat. "Damn, ole ugly ass nigga, you done pop you one already and ain't try to pass us shit up here."

"Bru, all I was doing was waiting on y'all two pretty muthafucka's to ask for this shit…" Kenny went into the half of case freeing two beers at once with his large hand. "You know I was gonna slang this shit up there in a heartbeat."

Life made the collection and said, "Thank you, beautiful," as a joke. He opened Bell's beer and waited until he finished turning the curve before giving it to him. Next, Bell took a couple long swallows. Each swallow could be heard.

"That nigga drank like a horse…" Kenny claimed.

Bell brought the can down. "Boy, the mothafucka was good and cold just like I like my beer to be," Bell stated. "And ugly, for your information, I was thirsty than a mothafucka."

"Boy, I gotta get me one." Life noticed the black Benz on his passenger side. Kenny saw the car as well.

"Nigga, get you a job in the fountain and then you can my nigga."

"The fountain not for me, a nigga gotta work hard there, boy…" Life said, taking a swallow of beer. "A nigga gotta bring butter from the duck so I can't work there because I'm not no mothafuckin' duck and I have no butter to give."

Bell thought about asking his mother's boyfriend to help him get a job, but by the way his two partners talked about the hard labor, now he decided not to. Truly he's afraid of hard work, he had worked at McDonald's for two weeks. Bell enjoyed flipping burgers until Kenny and Life began teasing him, so he walked off the job.

"While y'all two niggas bullshit, I was thinking 'bout going to work for Hardies…" Kenny lied, throwing a hint into the air.

"Shit, flip two burgers and steal me five of 'em.".

"So that's what the fuck I should've been doing, huh?" Bell grinned and then turned on his right signal light. "Huh, Kenny Penny?" Bell asked, after making a right turn at the light.

"Man, you know he's just talking shit. We miss those free ass burgers and fries you was hooking us up with, my nigga. Now we gotta pay for that shit, boy a nigga used to look forward to them sacks…" Life sighed.

"My nigga, you ain't lying," Kenny agreed. "Every time I got in a mothafuckin car, the first thing I said was let's shoot by Bell's j-o-b so we can get a healthy ass sack for free. Playa, playa, playa, I fell in love with McDonald's ass…"

"You too?" Life spitted.

"Man, no bullshit," Bell began, trying to justify. "I got that job chasing the honeys not the moneys. While y'all niggas bullshit, ain't nun but young babies working there and if a nigga got a half ass decent conversation 'bout himself, he gonna come up and fuck good. Man, I'm talkin' 'bout them lil' girls gonna be throwing so much pussy at a nigga, a nigga gotta have hands like a fucking octopus."

"Mickey D's in the morning, here I come…" Kenny joked.

"What time we gonna bust that bitch wide open?" Life asked Kenny, playing along with the joke.

"We gonna be sittin in the fuckin parking lot waiting on that bitch to open up," Kenny teased.

"Ole dumb ass nigga, the mothafucka never close, it stays open

24/7!" Bell growled.

"Nigga, you ought to know, your burger-flipping ass worked there and not me." Kenny laughed.

"While you bullshitting, I'm thinking 'bout going back," Bell said, truthfully.

"Boy, if you do, I'm going wit'cha," Life shrugged.

"What y'all think I'm gonna say, count me in, that makes me three?" Kenny smashed his beer can using both of his hands and smiled. "It's not gonna happen; I ain't flipping no fucking body's burgers. I don't flip my own burgers, so what the fuck I look like flipping burgers for somebody else. I'ma continue coppin' these pills for five dollars and slanging these bitches for ten dollars…" He spread both arms wide and hollered, "I gotta stay the pill man, baby. Everybody in the club be hollering, 'where the pill man at?'"

"Nigga, everybody be hollering, 'where the ugly man at!'" Bell taunted.

"That's cool, too…" Kenny said, calmly.

Bell spotted several females hanging out in front of some projects, so he parked beside the road. Life called them over; two girls came. Life gave them a beer, and he and Bell had a good conversation going until Kenny decided to butt in. Once one female saw Kenny, she made a *yuck* sound; the sight of him frightened her. *Kenny looks like a rapist* she thought. As she backed away from Life, she called out to her girlfriend, "Come on girl, let's get the fuck away from this truck, they got somebody in their backseat that looks like he belongs in a fucking zoo." She didn't bite her tongue or cared how Life, Bell, nor Kenny took her words.

The language crushed Kenny's world, and verbally assaulted him deeply. He was embarrassed, and upset, and his face became uglier as he called them everything but the child of God.

"You once-a-month bleeding bitch!" Kenny screamed.

"Ya momma a bitch," she fired back, twisting her neck while waving through the air and the other hand rested on her hip. "And the bitch bleed once a month, too!"

Her words knocked all the fight out of Kenny, and he calmed the fuck down. He could do nothing but laugh. Then the other female gave him something else to laugh about, "Ole ugly ass nigga, you look like the type of nigga who love to eat a bitch pussy when her period on."

"Damn, Kenny Penny, sounds like Shawty and baby girl know you--" Bell laughed.

"They don't know shit 'bout me!" Kenny grunted.

"Are you sure?" Bell interrogated. "Because it seemed like it to me…"

"They know you ugly as hell!" Life joined in.

"Man, we need to go somewhere and chill because I'm tired of riding around," Kenny suggested. "Let's go over to the car wash and hang out."

"What, you gonna wash the truck?" Bell asked, getting back into traffic.

"Hell fuckin' naw," Kenny frowned. "The only damn thing I wash is my ass."

"And you ain't doing a great job with that…" Life joked.

"Man, fuck you," Kenny laughed, "With your beautiful self."

"Man, ride around drinking with y'all niggas ain't gonna cut it." Life threw his three beer cans out the window. "My old man told me, 'son, you can't be drinking and get tipsy with a bunch of hard legs. You gotta do that with the women because then you can get something out the deal. Riding around with a group of niggas, all y'all dicks gonna be rock hard.'"

"Shit, my nigga, say no more, we'll go down to Toni crib where we all can get some play," Bell reported, "And where our nigga Kenny's presence is always needed."

"Kenny a fuckin' celebrity at Toni house…" Life added.

"You fuckin' better believe it!" Kenny put forth.

"Ole ugly ass nigga, them hoes ain't thinking about you," Bell stated. "Them young hoes chasing that pill sack my nigga."

"Don't hate me, playa, hate the game…" Kenny chuckled. "Don't get mad because I'm beautiful."

"My grandma used to say you were pretty…" Life reminded. They all shared the laugh.

Not long after, Bell coasted the vehicle on Toni's trailer park grounds. Toni raced to the door looking forward to seeing her 45-year-old and up customers. She sent them pictures of Tasha, Wonder, and

Nakeita on her camera phone. One gentleman promised to pay a half a stack, *$500*, to have a cat nap with Nakeita. Other bids came in as well, another elderly guy offered to pay a stack, *$1,000*, if Nakeita was able to make time for him on his day off.

"These niggas done threw a fuckin' monkey wrench into my plan!" Toni cried under her breath as she watched them exiting the truck. *'There goes today's hustlas straight out the window because these busters not like my older guys, wham-bam and thank-you ma'am. These niggas make a bitch earn the money,'* she thought. *'They'll wanna fuck from sun up to sun down.'*

"T, what's up with you?" Bell greeted, as she held open the screen door for them.

"Ma, what up?" Life said, sweetly as he followed Bell into the trailer.

"There goes my girl," Kenny hugged her. Toni returned the hug, but hers was fake. "How's my favorite people?" Kenny greeted everyone. Tasha and Wonder walking into his arms, he kissed them both on the cheek. "You know Daddy got some good shit for y'all."

"What you got, Daddy?" Wonder asked, in a child's voice, playing her role.

'This bitch here deserves a fuckin' Oscar,' Tasha thought. Next she started laying game on Kenny thicker than honey and he was eating every word up as she stroked his ego. Kenny was the center of attention and he loved every minute, with his tomcat smile.

"Daddy?" Wonder began as she rubbed his face.

"Yes, love?"

"You got a girl medication?"

"Ain't no question."

Tasha rubbed Kenny's back and then licked his neck making his eyes roll in the back of his head. Tasha always had something new for him. She scratched his head, licked behind Kenny's ear forcing him to purr. Life and Toni fell into one another's embrace; Bell rested his bones next to Nakeita.

"Damn Shawty, I didn't know you smoked weed..." Bell said, smelling the scent of Nakeita's breath.

"There's a lot of things about me that you don't know--"

"Like what?"

"Like I said a lot of things…"

"Damn girl," Bell looked into her eyes, "You look so damn sexy high."

"I look sexy regardless…" Nakeita said, folding her arms across her breasts. Watching the other girls with Kenny and Life made her want to get busy; she couldn't stop moving her legs. Bell leaned into her neck and started attacking the spots he thought would do the trick. Nakeita welcomed him by rubbing his head.

"Damn, you smell good," he whispered.

"I know," she purred.

Bell ran his palm through her hair finally accomplishing one of his fantasies. As he massaged Nakeita's scalp she moaned and groaned. Bell worked his lips up to hers; Nakeita opened her eyes as Bell tried to brush her lips with his.

"Boy, before I bust the slob with anybody son, he gotta get tested first because I know I'm clean."

"Yeah, them ya words," Bell breathed, his hot beer breath on her. "Anybody daughter I mess with gotta get tested, too." He continued kissing and massaging her, and Nakeita melted into his arms. Bell was driving her young body crazy because she never came in contact with male hands or tongue. The experience was breathtaking. Bell climbed to his feet and pulled her up into his arms.

"What are you doing?" Nakeita asked.

"We going into the bedroom."

"I don't want to go into no bedroom…" Nakeita protested, but didn't put up a struggle. "What we going back there for? We ain't gonna do nothing."

Bell took her into Wonder's bedroom. Kicking the door shut, he led Nakeita to the bed and gently laid her down. He immediately went to work on her breasts, trapping one nipple between his fingertips and the other nipple between his lips. Nakeita's breathing became heavy, her chest rose and dropped. She massaged Bell's head and encouraged him to suck harder. He obeyed like a good little boy. When his hand snuck down in her jeans and panties, Nakeita spread her legs. Bell's skillful fingers made all the right connections. Her womanhood was warm, wet, and tight.

"You're a virgin ain't you?"

"Umm," she moaned between her heavy breathing. "What makes you ask that?"

"Are you?"

"Yes," she mumbled. "Like I said, there's a lot of things you don't know."

"The good thing about it, I'm willing to learn," he answered, getting more excited.

"You going to take time out to learn, baby?" Nakeita's purred.

Bell kissed down her belly and ran his tongue from Nakeita's navel button down into her ocean. He sucked her clit as if they were a match made in heaven.

"Oh God!" Nakeita exhaled as Bell French kissed between her legs.

Bell spent a good forty minutes with his tongue buried between Nakeita's legs taking his sweet time because there was no sense in rushing. He needed for his tongue and Nakeita's vagina to become better acquainted. He enjoyed giving head more than she enjoyed receiving it.

"*Please don't stop...*" Nakeita murmured, "*Please don't stop...*" Nakeita was coming for the twelfth time; her lips trembled as if she was cold. "Yes baby, suck my pussy... I love it! I love it..."

Bell swallowed all the bodily fluids that her body could spit out. He wished he had more tongue to shove, ram, and throw up in her. Nakeita cried tears of joy.

Bell stood up kicking off his pants and underwear, he finished helping Nakeita out of hers. As she looked at his erect penis, her heart started beating fast, and she asked herself could she take the whole seven inches. She wanted the meat; she needed some dick in her life. She felt his tongue, now she needed to feel his manhood so she would no longer be a vegetarian; she was ready to get her cherry busted.

"Where your rubber?" she asked.

"What rubber?"

"Boy, you need a condom."

"I don't have one…"

"Bell, if you don't have no condom then you can't get this pussy…" Nakeita said, sounding like it hurt her heart to say those heart-breaking words.

"Shit!" Bell cussed.

"I'm sorry, Bell," she shed a few tears. "I'm so sorry." Nakeita wanted to have sex with Bell at this very moment worse than he wanted to have it with her.

"Shit, I'm sorry too," Bell exhaled. To breathe those words sliced his heart into a million and one pieces.

"Don't worry, they'll be another chance, I promise," she assured him.

"Well, if a nigga gotta wait, then a nigga gotta wait," he began getting dressed.

"I'll make it up to you," Nakeita wiped tears of joy out of her eye.

"Did I make you feel good?"

"Yes," she nodded. "You're the best," Nakeita paused, smiling.

Chapter 8

Sunday Morning

Nakeita slept like a baby until 4:39 A.M. When her eyes opened and seized the room's darkness. As she slipped from the sheets, she realized she needed to pay her water bill, so she rushed to go use the bathroom. While there, she studied herself in the mirror, searching for the glory Bell left her with. Then she hopped back into bed with Bell on her mind; how could she possibly lose the thought of him. *I wanted to give him some, but how could I when he didn't have a condom? I'm not having sex without a condom; it's not a trust issue, it's a health issue. If I was to have sex without that condom, it would have been like me having sex with everyone he has had unprotected sex with,"* she reasoned with herself.

Nakeita's right hand traveled down into her panties and dove into her wetness, allowing her fingers to bring her pleasure as if it was Bell's tongue.

"Oh Bell," focusing one hundred percent, "I need you," she moaned. "Oh baby, eat this pussy. This all your pussy, baby…" Nakeita whispered, as she slowly penetrated herself, using two fingers to slide in and out of her hot vagina. Each time, Nakeita made sure her fingers dragged across her erect clit. She was in no rush to cum, but instead took her precious time with getting to know her body.

Eyes rolling behind her eyelids, she closed her eyes while barely arching her back to meet her fingers for a better penetration. Nakeita's fingers took a journey between her legs, leaving no stones uncovered.

"Oh, God this feels so good," she cried out. The more she discovered her *g-spot,* the more she moaned and rotated her hips. Not being satisfied with four climaxes, Nakeita sought for further justice by exploring and giving her clit a thorough investigation, a serious evaluation. Her pussy was in store for a full invasion. Nakeita's mind and body was on a need to know basis, and she felt embarrassed with Bell knowing her body better than she did. Nakeita captured her clit between two fingers and while holding the erect infant penis hostage stroked back and forth until becoming four more climaxes free. She smiled because now she knew her body like the back of her hand. She could coach, guide, and give instruction to her happiness. Nakeita was the captain of the ship; she needed to know the motion of the ocean. "Damn, that was good," she breathed. "I came so many times I lost count… I think I played with my pussy better than Bell ate it," she lied to herself. As she rubbed her sticky fingers together, curiosity got the best of her, she felt the need to lick her middle finger.

"Mmmm, my pussy juices taste like syrup…" She sucked the two fingers clean before climbing out of bed. *'Ain't nothing like getting a couple nuts off and a good hot ass shower to start the day,'* Nakeita thought, as she made her way back to the bathroom.

***

"Keke, girl, what's on your agenda today?" Keke yawned at Keyandra's question.

Keke wasn't out of the bed good, and here was her first cousin asking her what she was going to do today. *I should've let the answering machine pick up and took my shower like I planned to,'* she thought.

"What time is it?" Keke asked, because she was too lazy to get the time off her nightstand clock.

"9:20."

"9:20?" Keke repeated. "Girl, today is Sunday."

"Okay, and?" Keyandra said. "What Sunday got to do with anything?"

"Rest day."

"So what time are you planning on getting up?"

"I'm up now," Keke spoke without thinking. She was procrastinating about calling her Daddy and giving him a piece of her mind, something she thought Keyandra should be doing instead of breathing down her throat that early in the morning.

"So what's on your day's agenda?" Keyandra repeated her very first question.

"Girl, I don't know yet. My feet ain't touched the floor yet and you calling me early in the morning," Keke replied, swinging her feet to the floor.

"Okay, then get your sorry tail outta bed and tell me what we're gonna do or where we gonna go, because we going somewhere," Keyandra offered.

When they didn't go to church on Sunday, they would hang out and go visit their 84-year-old great-grandmother.

"You ain't even giving my blood the chance to circulate yet... Can the blood rush to my brain first?" Keke questioned while climbing to her feet. "We gotta go by Big Momma's house first before we do anything," she finished stretching. She knew if they didn't pay their grandmother a visit first, then it wouldn't get done. That was Keke's head agenda, top priority.

"I agree and then what we gonna do after we leave Big Momma's house?"

"Keyandra, you talk to Auntie Lisa lately?"

"Yes… Last night."

Keke's brain wasn't functioning properly, she ran out of things to say. She just popped off a few quick questions trying to give her brain the chance to kick in, but it never occurred. As a result, Keyandra took matters into her own hands.

"Let's go over Nakeita's house after we leave Big Momma's house."

"I have no problems with that."

"Keke, I'll be over your house at twelve o'clock, so go on and get ready… Keke, be ready when I get there because I ain't trying to sit around and be waiting on you to get ready," Keyandra advised.

"How many times you had to wait on me?" Keke challenged.

"How many times haven' I had to is the key question?" Keyandra smiled.

"I'm going be ready when you get here," Keke promised. "What time you say you coming?"

"Twelve o'clock," Keyandra dragged out.

Keke gave the nightstand clock some attention for the very first time.

"Make it twelve-thirty?"

"Do I need to change that thirty into forty, or forty into forty-five?" Keyandra asked, joking.

"That would be nice, but I'll be ready."

"Now that I gotta see."

"Keyandra girl, now let me get off of this phone because now you're cutting into my time," Keke chuckled. Her brain was coming around to its full potential.

"Yeah, we better do just that because we got people to see and places to go…" Keyandra paused. "Twelve-thirty?"

"Twelve-thirty," Keke noted, hanging up the phone, ready to shower and get herself together so she wouldn't have Keyandra waiting, not this time, but the next.

***

One good thing about Ebony, she always cooked for an army, never knowing when there would be company. *There should always be too much food, instead of not enough food,'* Ebony would always say. She and Nakeita enjoyed the left-overs better. It gave the food more time for the flavors to mix; besides there was some days she was not able to prepare daily meals. So while she put in her twelve-hour shift, her daughter could still come home from school to a home-cooked meal. Also, it worked to her advantage as well, as she could walk through the door and always count on a delicious meal waiting on her.

Ebony opened two packs of hickory-smoked sausage. She produced six light-bread length pieces per pack and threw them into the frying pan. "Now, add more flavor to my cut up garlic, chopped onions and bell peppers. And one more thing, I know you make your own grease, but I'll add a couple spoons of butter." She placed the lid and peeked in on her cabbage after giving them a good stir. She reapplied the lid and pulled open the stove to see how her baked beans were coming along. "Y'all doing just beautifully, and let's keep it that way," she instructed, smelling the bacon's juicy flavor in her beans. She reached into the oven taking a small slice of bacon off the top of the beans. Ebony couldn't cook without nibbling; any real cook knows that.

"Nup, we ain't ready for you yet," Ebony gave the four bags of Uncle Ben's rice her undivided attention. "If I throw y'all in a boiling pot of hot water, ya'll little babies will be finished in no time," she snapped her fingers. "So y'all asses will fall in the tail end of the line."

She added a large cup of water to the cabbage; not because water was needed, but she wanted to be on the safe side and the water couldn't hurt anything. After lowering the fire, Ebony was ready to check on that daughter of hers, but three knocks at the front door captured her attention.

Knock... Knock... Knock...
"Yes, I'm coming… I'm on my way," she said sweetly as the visitor could hear her voice.
Knock... Knock...
"You should've called first," Keke counseled, "Before we left Big Mommas."
"You right," Keyandra agreed.
Ebony smiled while looking through the doors peephole and knowing who was on the other side of the door, she heard and recognized their voices.

"Hello and good morning to you, Keke and Keyandra. How are you both doing on this blissful morning?"

"We okay, Ms. Ebony, we don't see anything to complain about," Keyandra said, speaking for them both.

"Is Nakeita home?"

"Yes," Ebony said, welcoming them into the house. "I haven't seen her or heard one word out that child's mouth yet, but I know she's still around here somewhere. I was getting ready to holla for her." Ebony closed the door. "Have y'all eaten yet? Are y'all hungry?"

"No," Keke said.

"Was that a 'no' to my first question or was that a 'no' for the second?"

"I'm sorry," Keke smiled, "No ma'am, we not hungry. We just finished eating at our Big Momma's house… Ms. Ebony, she won't let us walk out her front door without us putting something in our stomachs."

"The same here," Ebony said, with authority. "Now y'all go upstairs and wake Nakeita up and wash y'all hands while y'all up there… I'll give y'all a good twenty minutes to chitchat before I start setting up the table."

They watched Ebony's head back to the kitchen before exercising their voice.

"I'm full already," Keyandra brought forth.

"Me too," Keke agreed, thinking about how Big Momma had loaded their plate with bacon, fried fatback, pancakes, scrambled eggs with cheese, and a bowl of grits. They didn't have room for the orange juice, which Big Momma stressed the vitamin C was needed, but put her mouth to rest by them drinking a glass of milk. *"At least y'all drunk the milk to feed the bones,"* Big Momma laughed.

"Keke, Ms. Ebony cooks good," Keyandra reminded.

"I know," Keke replied. As they both wolfed at the lovely scent, it did the caliente dance around their faces.

"I'mma eat," Keyandra stated.

"Me too," Keke noted, letting her first cousin know they'd be gaining them two pounds together.

"Let's go wake up Ms. Sleeping beauty," Keyandra said, as she lead the way up the stairs.

"She's not no sleeping beauty?"

"Why she can't be?" Keyandra asked, knowing keke was going to say something funny cause it never fails.

"Because the sleeping beauty would be me."

"I knew you was going to say that,"

"Wake up monster," Keke's voice rang out, "we coming for you, monster, Na-kei-ta, Na-kei-ta, monster, Na-kei-ta."

When they reached the top of the stairs, Nakeita's bedroom door was open, and she sat on the bed getting ready to polish her toe nails.

"Look who's up mighty early," she smiled. "How you manage to make that happen?"

"Trust me it wasn't an easy task," Keyandra exhaled.

"Girl, I go to school five days a week and deal with y'all sometimes six days a week," Keke clarified. "So if y'all two ain't got sense enough to know that Sunday is a rest day, then I'm sorry. I'm young and still growing, so I do need my beauty rest, thank-you."

"You're most welcome," Nakeita said, being sarcastic, while shaking a bottle of cotton candy blue nail polish, "So ladies, what's up? What y'all two up to?"

"I was just trying to get out the house," Keyandra threw herself into a white soft chair. "You know, move around and get some air."

"The early bird gets the worm," Nakeita said, as she began applying polish.

"That's what they say," Keke added, looking into the mirror and seeing more of her father's features than her mother's. Keyandra leaned forward and looked at Nakeita's nails.

"You know your nails gonna turn yellow in the long run, don't you?"

"True that," Keke confirmed.

"Now why is that?" Nakeita stopped applying the polish and gave them her full attention.

"Because you're not applying the clear nail polish first," Keyandra began to explain. "You suppose to always lace your toenails and finger-nails with a coat of clear polish first, and then put down your colorful polish. Now that's how you protect your nails and will keep them from becoming yellow." Keke nodded, because that's the same instruction Keyandra shared with her, and she not only mentally took notes, she applied the method and did her nails in that order, form, and fashion.

"Okay," Nakeita approved, immediately correcting her mistake, using the wet cloth to remove the fresh polish. Not all the polish came off, "Now I'll use a little bit of this…" Nakeita mumbled, adding polish remover to the cloth after freeing the nail clear of polish, she worked in the direction of her advisor.

"Now is that better?" she inquired.

"Honey, them your nails, not mines," Keyandra pointed out.

"Nakeita," Keke stemmed, "Stop trying to be a problem child with that thick skull of yours… Try doing the right thing for once in your life, everything in life don't cause for trials and tribulation."

"Look who's talking," Nakeita laughed. "The sleepy head."

"She's alive...she's alive," Keyandra teased, getting in a good laugh as well while covering her mouth because she's the shy type.

"Nakeita girl, you picked the wrong time in the world to wanna play with your toes," Keke offered, looking at the bedroom door.

"And why is that?" Nakeita asked.

"Because your mother is about finished cooking," Keke replied.

"Your mother said she'd be setting the table in twenty minutes," Keyandra unfolded.

Nakeita examined all five toenails, her right foot was finished.

"That food ain't going nowhere, it can wait," she said out her mouth, but her stomach objected by growling. Nakeita had been waiting to hear Ebony's voice hollering about breakfast being ready all morning. She was just killing time fooling around with her toenails; she opened her bedroom door thirty minutes' prior waiting for the call, hoping it would come seconds later, and not wanting minutes to come into the equation.

"Girl, go wash your hands," Keke teased, "Because you been playing with your funky toes."

"My toes ain't funky," Nakeita said, heading to her bathroom.

"I applaud you," Keke clapped being silly. "You're supposed to stick to your story."

"I smell feet," Keyandra covered her nose using her right hand and laughed. "Somebody toes stink! It's stinking up the whole room."

"I see how y'all on a sista case early in the morning?" Nakeita called out the bathroom drying her hands.

"What you talking about girl?" Keyandra asked, mirroring a fake serious frown.

"I heard y'all this morning," Nakeita said.

"You heard us what?" Keke asked.

"Holla bout I'm a monster in baby-doll clothes," Nakeita put on her best little girl's voice. She tried to say it in a serious tone, but could not hold her composure, so she burst out with laughter.

"Mmm," Keyandra frowned. "Girl, I'm scared of you."

"See ya and don't wanna be ya," Keke said to Nakeita ready to visit the kitchen.

"Come on here, Lil' Nicki Minaj," Keyandra joked.

"Okay…" Nakeita began in her Nicki' Minaj voice. "After breakfast, do you think we can go out and have a few drinks. You know, so I can put salt all around that rim, rim, rims." She enjoyed impersonating her favorite artist.

"Only if you promise to let us meet Usher Raymond," Keke sighed as she laughed with crying tears.

"I promise," Nakeita spitted, feeling the need to say the last words.

Chapter 9

"Are you sure this gonna work?" Nakeita second-guessed, as Bell threw the truck in neutral. She had heard so much about Big Johnny's club, she was dying to hang out in there for a few hours.

"Yeah, it's gonna work. If I thought it wouldn't, no way in hell I would've came way up here; this damn truck drinks gas like water. Nakeita, it ain't like they be posted up by the door collecting fees. They ain't even checking ID's," Bell informed. "Just do like I told you."

"Alright."

"Just keep your head down and follow me," he advised, while watching Nakeita tuck much of her hair under the black cap he gave her.

She climbed out the vehicle and walked around to his side forcing a smile from Bell. Nakeita looked sexy in the blue jeans and button up long sleeve blue shirt he loaned her, even though the cloths sagged. Nakeita looked boy cute.

"Them clothes fit you, Ma."

"You think so?"

"Yeah." Bell's pants weren't that much too big on her, but she still used a belt because she wanted to dress like a male as much as possible.

"You ready, Shawty?" Bell asked, as they grew near the front entrance.

"I guess so," Nakeita replied, taking a deep breath.

Bell swung the door open and walked into the club. His eyes were trained and commanded to locate Big Johnny's whereabouts. Big Johnny sat at the bar doing what he did best, running off at the mouth, and entertaining the customers with lies and two percent of the truth. Bell's eyes immediately did a full interior scan of the room searching for a nice seat out of the way. "Bingo," he said under his breath once locating an empty booth in the back. He couldn't have hoped for a better place. Putting his feet to work, Nakeita fell into his foot tracks. He slipped into the booth, and Nakeita was getting ready to sit directly beside him, but she caught herself and slid into the seat across from him. Bell nodded his approval.

"That's right, Shawty, two niggas can't sit together without drawing attention… Since when you start seeing shit like that?"

Nakeita wasn't paying him any attention, but was soaking up her surroundings. Everyone seemed to be her mother and father's age.

"This a real old-school club," she said.

A female waitress stopped beside Bell.

"What can I get for you guys?"

Nakeita blushed, but kept her head down towards the table. A few strands of her hair gave her away. The waitress knew she was a female, but couldn't care less because she too used to sneak into the same club while she was under the age of twenty-one.

"Two beers… Two beers," Bell ordered, trying to take the waitress focus off Nakeita.

"Beer cool with you, Ms.?" The waitress smiled at Nakeita. "Or would you prefer a peach wine cooler?"

"The wine cooler would be great," Nakeita replied, pulling the cap down on her head more.

"I thought so," the waitress agreed, walking off to fulfill their order.

"You think she gonna tell on me?" Nakeita questioned.

Bell's eyes watched the waitress's every move. She went straight to the bar, nowhere near Big Johnny or his two brothers.

"Naw," Bell responded, "If she was, she wouldn't of mention shit about the order. She would've asked us to leave."

"That's what's up," Nakeita whispered as she danced in her seat to the song of, Drake and Briana, *Oh na-na, what's my name? Baby, you're a challenge, let's explore your talent.*

"You come here a lot?" Nakeita asked after the song went off.

"Yeah," Bell nodded. "It's a cool lil' spot," he answered, not once taking his eyes off the waitress. She returned with the same smile she had before she left them.

"One beer for you," she said, placing the glass of beer in front of Bell. "Young lady, here's one wine cooler for you," she said to, Nakeita. "Now don't have too many of them because they'll sneak up on you."

Bell gave her a five-dollar tip knowing it would hurt his pocket, but she deserved the money because she kept her mouth shut. She recognized Bell as a regular customer; she wouldn't know Nakeita from a can of paint. But her guess was as good as gold that Nakeita wasn't old enough to be in anybody's club. She wasn't a betting person; wouldn't bet water was wet, but tonight she would've laid odds twenty to one that Nakeita wasn't female law grown, which was age eighteen, and for certain not male grown, age twenty-one. Nakeita was adult grown only in her mind.

"Good and cold..." Nakeita sipped from the bottle.

"That's how it's supposed to be, ain't it?" Bell questioned, focusing only on her.

"Tasha, Wonder and Toni like this place, too."

"Them dizzy bitches be up here catching these old ass tricks…" Bell smiled into Nakeita's eyes. *'They beat these old farts outta their wallets,'* he thought, while continuing to smile.

Nakeita had the wine cooler bottle close to her lips, getting ready to take a swallow. Bell's eyes puzzled her.

"What? What are you smiling about?"

"Damn Shawty," Bell licked his lips, "You have some pretty lips… You have a smile to make a nigga wanna die for. Damn Shawty, I can see it now, you gonna fuck around and make a real nigga fall in love with your young ass."

"Huh," Nakeita mumbled, taking a sip, "Boy, stop."

"I'm serious," Bell said. "You ready to get serious or what?"

""B", I'm still in school… I ain't finished school yet, I have two more years to go…" Nakeita explained.

Ebony's words did the moonwalk across her brain. *'Nakeita, you don't have time for nobody's son! Them boys can wait… Ain't nothing more important than getting your education. You don't need to be running up behind nobody son, your top priority is your education… Them lil' boys don't give a damn about you or your education… All he'll be interested in is getting between your legs. Now days, you have more guys dropping out of school, at least 75 percent of them, if not more. When a boy do pop up in your face, ask him did he finish school, and soon as his ass tell that big white mule lie, tell him to show you his diploma. I'm willing to bet you he can't show you a piece of paper showing he got him a damn G.E.D.'*

"Bell," she began.

"Yeah, what's on your mind, Shawty?"

"I forgot what I was gonna say," Nakeita lied, wanting to ask him did he have his high school diploma or a G.E.D.

"Damn Shawty, I was always told if a person forgot what they were gonna say, then it must of meant it wasn't important."

"They lied to you, baby," Nakeita said, jamming along with, Willow Smith, *I whip my head back and forth*, she sang and waved into the air. She would give anything to be able to skeet across the dance floor. Nakeita wanted to dance badly, but her cover would be blown.

"Bad idea, Shawty," Bell objected, "I know ya lil' ass want to hit the disco floor..."

The waitress stopped by on her journey to the bar. Bell notified her that they were ready for round two. And after the third round he planned on throwing in the towel by exiting the building, but instead saw Big Johnny and his two brothers storming in his direction and looking like three silver backs, they caused him to panic.

"Got damn," he whispered.

***

A super healthy young lady traveled over to Big Johnny, she was a big boned 26-year-old with a head full of good hair.

"What can Big J do for you tonight, sweetheart?" he asked, ready to go into his wallet and give his secret lover a few dollars.

"I wanna dance," she said with her lips poked out.

"Oh no, sweetheart, them days been long gone for me," Big Johnny declined. "The only dancing I do is in the bed."

"You so nasty," she playfully slapped him on the arm.

"That's how me and you got here," Big Johnny laughed, pulling her closer so he could smell her cheap cologne which smelled mighty damn good to him. "Girl, you smell edible... "He laughed. "Are you edible, sweetheart?"

"You tell me?"

"See, that's why I like you because you have a good sense of humor," he said, rocking his finger at her.

"Johnny."

"Yes, sweetheart?"

"Johnny, I ain't dumb," she clarified. "You like me because I got a

113

p-u-s-s-y."

"Cause you got a what?"

"A p-u-s-s-y."

Big Johnny looked into the female's mouth as she pronounced the word once again.

"Sweetheart, I love how you say that word because you definitely have a mobster between your thighs," he laughed. "You got an octopus down there because you sure know how to squeeze on ol' Big Johnny and make him feel good."

"I used my p-u-s-s-y muscle to milk you dry--"

"And leave me feeling like I done died and went to heaven."

"Is the Mask Dro there? Is Al Green up there, too?" she asked, being sarcastic because she made all seven of her children off of their songs.

"I don't know about that heaven," Big Johnny pointed to her kitty cat. "I'm talkin' bout that heaven right there." She slapped Big Johnny's hand down.

"Are you stopping by my house tonight? Because tomorrow I got a few bills need to be paid."

"Why would I not be over there?" His voice grew deeper. "I need to get to know you mentally, physically and immediately."

"Uuuhh. You sound so damn sexy just like, Barry White..." She kissed him on the lips and lied through her teeth again. "You're a damn good lover... lover boy." When Willo's song sprayed the club, *I whip my hair back and forth*, she sang, *I whip my hair back and forth*, making her tongue dance in his face. Big Johnny's eyes roamed the club because he wanted to see how many people vibed with the song. As his eyes danced around the club, Bell's company caught his attention. Big Johnny recognized the prey since birth. He rounded up his two brothers, Big Jimmy and Big Jack, and they beat their feet behind their big brother without asking the question first.

Bell braced himself, not knowing what was in store for him or Nakeita. By the look on the brother's face, he knew it wasn't going to be a pretty sight.

"Bell, you got some nerve to bring my god-daughter here in my place of business... You know she's a minor... You know this! I outta break your body in two pieces with my bare hands," Big Johnny growled, sweat skipping down his nose and his nostrils wider than a double-barrel shotgun.

"Unk, it's my fault, I--" Big Johnny pointed at Nakeita, cutting off her sentence.

"You sit your ass tight, I'mma take you home personally." He frowned towards Bell. "Ya'll throw this piece of shit out." They snatched Bell out the seat, his two hundred and twenty-four pounds feeling like paper to a giant; the two brothers could bench press over four hundred pounds apiece. While they carried him by his armpits, Bell kicked like a three-year-old, spoiled rotten, little bad-ass, hard-headed child. Big Johnny kicked the door open and they sent Bell's body sailing through the air.

"Punk, act like a cat and land on ya feet," Big Jack woofed.

Bell's head connected with the concrete first, and then his shoulders and the rest of his body tumbled down. The collision scared the hell out of his oxygen, and Bell's oxygen fled from his body as if the brothers were coming to finish the job. Bell was in so much pain he was forced to lie still and shed a few tears.

* * *

The fresh 2 AM air watered Nakeita's eyes as the wind blew in her face. She stared out of the passenger window, allowing the street and car lights to play tricks with her pupils.

"If you want to, you can roll up the window and I'll cut on the AC," Big Johnny said, changing gears.

"Naw, I'm cool… I need some fresh air."

Big Johnny went from the third gear to the fourth gear making the truck haul ass down the back streets.

"What do you see in the boy, Bell?" Big Johnny fished.

"He's cool."

"Cool, my damn ass," Big Johnny snapped. "That fuckin' little punk!"

"He cool, you just gotta get to know him."

"I know enough about the little rascal. He's a piece of shit just like his father."

Nakeita gave Big Johnny a deranged look as if he had said something wrong, *'If you not gonna say nothing nice about a person then you don't suppose to say nothing at all,'* she thought, but would not

115

dare fix her mouth to say it.

"That boy mean you no good, Keita," Big Johnny stated, taking his eye off the road for a split second to look at her. Nakeita sat in the passenger seat with both palms buried between her legs. "You cold?" She gave off the impression.

"No," she nodded.

"You know, I used to be a young boy myself so I know how some boys can think, and most of these young freaks mean you no earthly good," Big Johnny explained, rolling up his window so that it would be less air Nakeita would have to worry about. "Some guys will try to take advantage of you, especially when you're young. They'll try to pull the wool over your eyes when they think you're green."

"True enough I'm young, but I ain't dumb," Nakeita shrugged, wiping the falling tears from her eyes. She was tired of everyone giving her lectures and trying to run her life. They had lived their lives, now she wished that they would back the fuck up and let her live hers.

"You know--"

"I know what?" she interrupted.

"Last week, Atlanta, Georgia was the AIDS capital, the week after that it was South Carolina. The week after that, it was North Carolina, then it was, Washington D.C...." Big Johnny paused, and then broke the gear down from fifth gear, so he could turn the corner. Going in to first gear, his conversation continued. "Every week it's a different state, a different city, and then a different little bitty hick town. Before long the whole world gonna be full of disease. The people feel like he/she gave it to me, now I'mma pass the shit on, too. Nakeita, no one wanna go get tested, they too afraid they'll be positive. They not looking at the bigger picture, which is curing themselves. People rather walk around infected than to seek professional help, and the sad and bad part about it is most of the medication will be free. What is America coming to these days?"

"I don't know," Nakeita mumbled. "Honestly to God I don't know, I wish I did, I'll tell you," she said, and meant every word. This drug addicted woman's daughter had lived only four precious years before she returned back to the Creator because she inherited the package at birth. They had lived in the same duplex as Nakeita, and the tragedy touched every family in the building. The female didn't start smoking until she was into her sixth month of pregnancy. She had caught her husband cheating, so she turned to drugs as a solution. Not long after the child's death, the mother committed suicide.

"Keita," Big Johnny continued, getting back to the real subject. "Guys today not like guys who came up in my time frame. Some of them are unappreciative. They don't know how to treat a woman; they feel as though they have to beat her to show they love her. They don't know how to respect themselves, so how in the world is it possible that he'll know how to respect you? I know you probably tired of hearing me wailing, but I'm talking only outta concern. I'm concerned about you and your health."

"I know," Nakeita said.

"Well, do you know you're not Bell's cup of tea?" he frowned. "The scumbag is just not good enough for you! He has too much extra luggage with him. Too much unnecessary propaganda comes with the territory. He ain't gonna do nothing but use you, misuse you, and then abuse you."

"How you know?"

"I told you," Big Johnny looked at her briefly, "Like father, like son."

"You can't judge a book by its cover, Unk!"

"I'm just calling it as I see it," Big Johnny gripped the wheel tighter. "One thing about me young lady, I'm gonna call a ball a ball and I'm gonna call a strike a strike when I see it."

"Obviously, you have something against Bell…" Nakeita turned to face Big Johnny. "What do you have against him?"

"Not a thing."

"You and him beefing over a woman?"

"Heck no," Big Johnny barked. "I deal with strictly women, not minors."

"It's something."

"Nakeita, you right… You're 100% right about that."

"So what is it, Unk? Will you please tell me?"

"Look into the mirror," Big Johnny instructed. "I have a problem with the no-good slime-ball because I know sooner or later he's going to break your heart. I'm trying to save you the trouble and prepare you for the pain because it's coming. Just as sure as there is a God in Heaven."

"You think so?"

"I know so," Big Johnny smiled. "You should know I'm right. Ask Ms. Matty Mae Strong why she don't like him?"

"She don't like nobody."

"She likes you," Big Johnny's words struck a nerve. Next, Big Johnny made a deal with Nakeita: he promised not to tell Ebony about the club situation if she agreed not to see Bell again. She agreed. Nakeita snuck into the house and went straight into her bedroom, showered, brushed her teeth, and then hopped into bed. However, at 4 A.M., a pecking noise coming from the window, *Peck…Peck… Peck…* awakened her.

She dragged her worn-out body to the window; there stood Bell in motion to throw another rock. She raised the window.

"Fool, you better stop throwing them damn rocks before you break out one of my Momma's windows."

"Then you better come down here and let me in," Bell said, dropping the other rocks and dusting off his hands. Nakeita let him in and they tiptoed back to her bedroom. She examined his bruised forehead, and then cleaned the infected area with turpentine. His shoulder was damaged as well, and after attending to his wounds, she used a whole roll of gauze to keep blood off her sheets.

Bell ate four ecstasy pills hoping his pain would fade away. He grunted while pulling Nakeita's gown over her head. Nakeita's nipples stood at attention as tears slipped from Bell's eyes. She brushed his tears away with her thumbs, for some strange reason it turned her on seeing this grown-ass man cry. Their kissing started out gently, and then escalated into an animal lust. Bell sucked at her breasts.

"You have a condom?" she asked, gently biting and sucking his thumb. He reached into his pocket pulling out a box. "Thank-you Lord," she whispered.

"Mmm, you smell good… You taste good," Bell cried out in a low voice.

"Baby, you have to take your time with me," she warned.

"I know," Bell spitted between tongue kissing her breasts. "I ain't forgot you're a virgin."

"Come, baby come…" She forced out. "Take me. Make me a woman."

Nakeita climbed into her bed and watched Bell strip naked. His erect curved penis looked more beautiful than the last time.

"Put it on." Bell handed her a condom.

She nodded and slipped it on his shaft and stroked him a couple times as she got the feel of a male tool for the very first time.

"You ready?" he asked, while crawling in the bed over her like a lion.

"Yes, I been ready," she admitted, removing her thongs.

"You sure you want this?" He asked, knowing he was going to talk her into it even if she would've said she wasn't.

"Yes," she nodded, biting down on her bottom lip as he worked his penis between her virgin lips. Nakeita opened her legs wider, she rotated her hips the same way she did when masturbating. "Ohhh," she breathed, feeling Bell push past her cherry. He took his sweet time, long stroking her, giving Nakeita's pussy a good feel of his dick.

"I need for you to get used to the dick before I dick you down."

She nodded and scratched at his back. Sharp pains took control of her body for a brief moment, then everything after that was good as gold.

"Give it to me, baby," she begged.

"What you say?" Bell asked, knowing he heard her the first time.

"I've been wanting to do this for a long time..." She confessed. "Oh, it feels good... Oh Bell, I'm coming... I'm coming again for the second time already."

Bell put one of her legs over his shoulder, making her flinch. He delivered short fast jabs, stabbing her with his penis, and, she continued humping back. As he threw the other leg over his other shoulder, she wanted to protest but endured the pain.

"You gonna have my pussy sore..." she moaned. "Oh God, I hope I won't be walking bow-legged."

Bell's four bare-naked lady pills kicked in. Plenty of blood rushed to his penis every time he pushed forward giving him a falsehood of cumming, but bursting off wasn't happening and time soon. Nakeita's fresh young womb had a promising future of straight punishment. Her body would be well beaten up and tortured good before Bell considered spilling out his first semen. Nakeita wailed as though she was a wounded animal, while Bell carried on like a wild animal. As the pain increased, her mood decreased.

'What have I got myself into?' She questioned herself lying motionless. Nakeita held Bell tightly and cried into his neck as she raked his back skin and flesh caked in her nails, but Bell felt not a thing. The feeling of ejaculating engulfed the tip of his penis.

"Baby?" she said, drumming him on the back.

"Huh?"

"I'mma take you to a hospital tomorrow so they can take a look at your bruises."

"Ummm, huh," he mumbled and continued to hump as if there was no tomorrow.

Chapter 10

The classroom noise rose above average, and the teacher pounded down on her desk bell, *Ring... Ring...Ring*!" The students lowered their voices once again for the fifth time.

"Ladies and gentlemen, we are finally here..." she stated, waving a stack of papers in the air so everyone could get a good look at them.

"We ain't ready yet," one of the students shouted. The teacher did not entertain the young man's train of thought.

"We studied for this test two weeks..." She reminded, holding up two of her fingers, "For two whole weeks, so there's no reason why everyone of you shouldn't pass with flying colors."

"Teacher...Teacher... We'll pass with the same color that's on our American flag," a female hollered. The teacher overlooked her sarcastic outburst as well. Nevertheless, she learned that she had a female classroom clown as well. *'They say there is somebody for everybody,'* she thought, as she focused on the students more closely.

"Please save all of your comments, and if I catch this classroom clown who's continually interrupting me, I'll have you suspended so you can fail this test and will have to repeat the tenth grade. Now, do I make myself clear?"

"Yes ma'am," a deep male voice railed through the air.

"This is a very, very important test," she held up a booklet showing both sides of the classroom. "This C.A.T. test will go straight to, Washington. This test came straight from Washington D.C., and this test will determine whether or not you promote to the eleventh grade or if you will remain here another year with me. This test is not important to me, but important to you and you alone." She looked at some of their faces to see if she got her point across as she continued hammering home with her subject, "If I catch you cheating, then guess what, I'll personally flunk you myself..." She patted her chest. "There will be no cheating, ladies and gentlemen, not in my classroom... I don't play that... Ask around the school, everyone will tell you there's nothing more that I hate in the world than a cheater. I believe everyone should get outta life what they earned. If you deserve an 'F', you'll get an 'F'! If you deserve a 'D', you'll get a 'D'! If you deserve a 'C', you'll get a 'C'! If you deserve a 'B', you'll get a 'B'!" She paused, catching her breath. "Now, if you earned an 'A', you'll receive an 'A'. Each and every one of you is capable of making an 'A'. Each and every one of you is capable of passing this test with a 'B'! There shouldn't be any reason for anyone to make anything less than a 'B', there shouldn't be any justification. We went over these questions and answers for ten days. The answers to every one of these questions should still be fresh on your brains. All of you here are intelligent students... I know at one time or another, someone will feel the need to act like a no-brain by making a frivolous input, but I do know that those two individuals have plenty book sense and not a lick of common sense."

The class laughed.

"Teacher, now you got jokes," a female alerted. "I feel that, that's what's up." The teacher spent the next fifteen minutes passing out the tests along with a couple sheets of notebook paper so they could use it for scratch paper. Every time she placed the material on a female student's desk, she would ask, "Are you gonna be the next, Sherry Pacely?" And every time she placed the material on a male's desk, she would ask, "Are you going to be the next Obama?" Once she got to the short stack brother's desk, she looked down into his curly hair because he held his head down. "How are you today?" she asked. He looked up at her smiling showing off his buck baby teeth.

"Hello," he returned the greeting.

"Young man, are you going to be the next, Obama? Our next president?" She question.

"Yeah... Yes ma'am, that can be arranged. What you think I'm not capable of making that happen? Teacher, you just talked something serious into existence," he smiled, "once I get in the, White House, I'mma paint that thing black, too."

"Snack..." The class laughed and started calling out the brother's name. "Snack... Big Snack... You're a giant, big boy."

"But for right now you can start off by calling me, Mr. President," Snack said. The teacher failed to hide her smile.

'I set myself up for that one,' she thought, because she had knowledge of Snack being the classroom mascot. "Okay now Mr. President, calm down and let's get this test completed. You get me an 'A', okay?"

"Of course now, teacher... Why wouldn't I?" Snack replied.

She traveled to the center of the room and recounted her students because there were seven extra tests in her hand, when there should've only been two.

'I warned everyone beforehand about this test, they know this is an important test and Washington D.C. needs to have their IQ scores and they didn't have the common courtesy to call in sick or to report their reason of absence. What is wrong with my young people,' she thought. While searching for her roll book, *'After they finish testing, I'll call those five students' houses to see why they were absent. I need to see who'll have a legitimate excuse, and whose excuse isn't legitimate enough,'* she mentally noted.

***

"Man, 'B' said they throw him outta the club like he was nothing but a cigarette butt," Kenny laughed.

"Oh catch me, I'm falling," he threw his left foot behind his right knee falling to the ground and immediately bouncing back to his feet. He did a smooth spin, and his foolishness to rest with two dance steps.

"Boy, I see you still, Disco Dynamite…" Life said.

"Still the one and only," Kenny stated, brushing dirt from his knee.

"Say Bell, were up there fucking with them boys who look like sumo wrestlers, huh?" Life asked.

"Life, man, all them boys name begin with a fuckin 'J'," Kenny grinned. "They all strong as a fuckin' ox. Playa, them nigga's thighs is bigger than our fucking waistlines."

"Lover's Lane is an old folks club," Life reminded. "I wouldn't get caught dead up in there."

"Man, this nigga need to hurry the fuck up," Kenny said, "they should've went and got a room."

"He didn't wanna waste any paper on a room," Life supplied. "And why should he when all he's after is a quickie?"

Bell and Nakeita used the truck as their love nest. At first she protested, but after a couple more ear nibbles and a few more times of his tongue being shoved down her throat, she gave in and submitted to every one of Bell's suggestions. The backseat where their oral sex lesson took place, Nakeita wasn't the receiver this time around, she was the one doing the giving.

"Girl, you gotta start givin' what you wanna receive," Bell whispered into her ear while she stroked his hard on.

Nakeita fell head over heels for Bell the night he gave her some head. His talented tongue gave her more orgasms than she could keep track of; they came flying back to back. Truthfully, Bell's tongue owned her body. Nakeita set out to make him fall in love with her as well, so she took heed to his instructions and followed Bell's coaching.

"Ma, don't use your teeth."

"What you mean?" Nakeita stopped sucking and started stroking, not knowing she was cheating Bell out of his full blessing. "I don't have false teeth. I can't take my teeth out."

"You're using your teeth…" he said, calmly. "You're scratching the side of my dick up."

"Oh, what am I supposed to do then?"

"Go slower until you get the hang of it."

Nakeita's jaw was hurting. It wouldn't be much longer and she would have the lockjaws, she predicted. However, deep in her heart, she wanted for her lover to get his rocks off.

"Come on baby, we almost there," Bell encouraged. "It won't be long before I release some of this pressure. Ma, my dick head bout to explode…" He needed her to hurry the fuck up before Kenny or Life fucked around and got stupid by coming over to the truck.

"Man, what the fuck that nigga in there doing, making love?" Kenny questioned, pointing to the truck. "Shit, it don't take a nigga that damn long to fuck."

"I agree, that nigga should've bust a nut by now," Life said, noticing they had been waiting for over thirty minutes for Bell to handle his business.

"Shit, I could've got off two times, in all that time," Kenny blew.

"I could've got me about three or four nuts," Life snapped his fingers. "Bomb, bomb, bomb."

"I'mma bust that nigga's bubble…" Kenny pulled out his cell.

"Give him a few more minutes," Life pleaded.

"Naw, fuck that," Kenny replied… "A few more minutes my damn ass."

"Pretty boy," Life smiled, "Don't cock-block because that's not the game. The game is cop and lock, so let playa finish getting off his rocks and knock Shawty's socks off."

"Fuck that!" Kenny said, dialing Bell's cell number.

Bell was almost ready to cum, Nakeita's head game was getting better and better with each suck, but then the phone rang.

'Who the fuck can this be,' he thought. "Hello?" No one said a word. "Hello?" he said again. Nakeita had stopped sucking; she wanted to see who was calling as well. "Go ahead, baby, you doing a good job. I was almost there."

She started back bobbing for apples.

Kenny pushed the end button the second time Bell's voice rang out. He palmed the phone real well, 'Hello? Hello?' He repeated Bell's words. "Nigga, ya ass should be through by now, that's what the fuck up."

"Boy, you wild," Life laughed.

"I'll show you wild," Kenny pushed redial on his cell. Bell palmed his cell, afraid this would happen.

"Yo?" He answered on the very first ring, but he got no answer. "Man, who the fuck playing on this fucking phone? I'mma grown-ass man and I ain't got time for no fuckin' kindergarten-ass games..." He got a dial tone. "Girl, you ain't gotta fucking stop every time you hear a fucking bell go the fuck off," he barked at Nakeita.

"Man, you should've heard that nigga mouth." Kenny laughed. "He's madder than a mothafucka.".

"Give him a break," Life bargained "I got two hos we can call; I got one for you. She won't know you ugly through the phone, but once y'all meet in person, you're on your own."

"Fuck that, I'm not giving Bell no break, now he'll see how we feel... Ain't no fun if the homie can't get none."

"Pretty boy, you sick with it."

"Ain't no question."

"Pretty boy, let me find out that you're a fucking hater on the DL."

"A hater my ass..." Kenny howled, acting like AT&T, reaching out to touch someone. "Pick up Southern Bell," he altered Bell's name.

Bell grew angrier as he allowed his phone to ring a few times, *Ring... Ring... Ring.*

"Yeah?" He accepted the call, but no answer. "I don't know who the fuck this is that keeps calling me, but I'll advise you to go play with your fuckin' momma and leave me the fuck alone!" He disconnected the line.

"Who was that?" Nakeita asked.

"How the fuck would I know?"

"I know who the fuck it was," Nakeita exclaimed, using her sleeve to wipe her mouth.

"Who the fuck was it? How the fuck you supposed to know when I don't even fucking know?"

"That was one of your bitches," Nakeita shouted as she threw herself on the back seat.

"You ain't heard no bitches voice!" Bell growled. "How the fuck you heard something when I didn't hear nothing, girl, you ain't heard jack shit."

"Then who the fuck was it then, Bell?"

"How the fuck I supposed to know?" Bell fixed his clothes. "Nobody knows everybody who calls they phone. Shit, people do dial the wrong number."

"Three fucking times."

"Nakeita, I don't know what to tell you. What am I supposed to say when I don't know who the fuck playing games on my damn phone?" he asked mockingly. Nakeita reached for his cell, but he jerked the phone back.

"What the fuck you doing, girl?"

"Let me see your phone?" She asked, hand still held out.

"What the fuck you want my phone for?" he frowned.

"Let me see your phone… I'll tell you who been calling you all three times," she said with her right hand still flipped out.

"Shit, I can do that my damn self…" Bell looked down at his caller ID. "Shit, girl, a nigga forgot all about that caller ID shit. Damn, I must be dumber than a box of rocks."

"Try two of them," Nakeita watched his facial expression.

"I'ma kill that fuckin nigga," Bell snarled.

"Which one of your bitches was that?" She persisted, still mad. She could strangle Bell's ass to death right about now. She went through a lot to spend the day with him and here he was taking her for granted already. *'Early in the game,'* she thought.

"I told you that wasn't no bitch…" Bell tried to hold the phone in her face so she could see the phone number. "That was the ugly duckling."

"Umm huh…" She mumbled, knocking the phone from her view. "You didn't wanna let me see your phone the first time, so now all of a sudden you wanna try to let me see it after you done erased the bitch number."

"Ol' crazy ass lady, I just sat right here and told you that was Kenny ugly ass?"

"You think I'm stupid, don't you?" Nakeita got into Bell's face. "That's probably why you don't fuck with nothing but young girls," she screamed, but didn't mean to mention the second sentence, so continued her delivery. "Kenny, calling while we up in this mothafuckin' truck, huh? So why in the fuck would he be phoning us three times and not saying a damn thing as you fucking claim?"

"Bitch, I don't fuckin know," Bell shuddered. "Ain't I sitting up in this bitch with you? Huh? Huh? You ask some of the dumbest shit in America!"

"Oh, I'm dumb, huh?"

"You fuckin' right you dumb. You gotta be dumber than a mothafucka to keep asking me why in the fuck the nigga keep calling me."

"Let me get the fuck up outta here…" Nakeita reached for the door latch, Bell grabbed her pulling her back into the seat. "Boy, get your fuckin' hands off me!"

"Girl, sit the fuck down!"

"Man, are you fuckin' crazy?" She gave Bell a crazy look. "You not my fuckin Daddy! My father's name is Darrel Donnell, and that shit don't sound shit like B-E-L-L." All the little girl came out of Nakeita.

"Nakeita, listen… A nigga ain't trying to play games with you, I fucks with you," he pleaded. "A nigga beginning to catch feelings for your young ass…"

"Nigga please," Nakeita threw an open palm into his face. "I may be young, but not dumb."

"Lil' ho! Who the fuck you think--" Bell was about to blow, but caught himself and started laughing. "A bitch better off laughing instead of crying."

"Yeah nigga, speak for your mothafuckin' self."

"Girl, you got a fuckin' slick-ass tongue."

"Mothafucka, I might be, but I ain't dumb," she said, feeling hurt. Her feelings raced off in a million directions. She felt played and that he handled her like a fucking yo-yo. She really wanted to cry, but refused to do it in Bell's presence.

Bell looked at her and was at a loss for words. The shit he wanted to say, he couldn't because it truly did sound stupid as a mothafucka even though it was the truth. So he just let the sentence play ping-pong on his brain. *'Why in the fuck Kenny's ugly ass playing and fuckin' around.'* A cell phone began ringing, Bell sat back into the seat with his eyes closed.

"You ain't gonna answer your phone? What, you scared it's one of your lil' boyfriends?" Bell asked

"That's your damn phone again… The bitch calling you back again."

"I cut mines off," he opened his eyes and looked into her sad eyes "So if the stank bitch did decide to call back, she knows that I'm not trying to fuck with her no more. Now she knows I done fired her for you." Nakeita opened her book bag; her cell wailed worse than a hollering baby.

"Hello?"

"Nakeita, where are you?"

"In the store buying me a soda," she lied.

"Come home now."

"I'm on my way," she heard the line go dead. The anger in her mother's voice couldn't go unnoticed. Nakeita knew something was wrong, but wouldn't know exactly what the problem was until she got home.

"Which one of your lil' boyfriends was that?" Bell pressed. "I see you told him you're on your way."

"That was Ebony…" She said, trying to focus on the problem that laid ahead.

"Who the fuck is Ebony?"

"That was my mother on the phone," Nakeita dropped her phone back into the backpack. "I gotta hurry up and get home."

"Come on, I'll take you," Bell opened the door, stepping out the truck.

"I can walk, " she stepped out as well.

"What, you don't want me to see where your lil' boyfriend lives?"

"Yeah," Nakeita threw the bag across her shoulder and went to stepping knowing it wouldn't be wise to keep Ebony waiting. The longer it took her to get home, the angrier Ebony would become due to her absence.

Kenny and Life watched as the two leapt from the vehicle, Kenny waved at them and flooded the Soulja Boy song, *Pretty boy swag, pretty girl swag*. He laughed taking giant steps.

"Boy, you're a silly nigga," Life assured.

Nakeita raced off in the opposite direction with the word, *"worry"* written all over her pretty face.

"Damn playa, me and my nigga thought for a minute y'all wasn't coming up for air. Like y'all said 'fuck oxygen' and died up in that mothafucka…" Kenny said.

"Boy, we thought y'all overdosed on that four letter word called love. Some shit a real ho catcher like myself wouldn't know shit about, but welcome back to society…"

"You don't know shit 'bout catching hos either," Bell sputtered, "Life, tell that nigga he don't get no points for catching hoes who's not content, them ho's you fucking with chasing that high. Give me your sack and let me see you come up off your mouthpiece."

"Nigga, a come up is a come up! A fuck is a fuck," Kenny stated. "From 8 to 80 blind, cripple or crazy." Kenny was dead ass serious about each and every one. He wasn't playing no games.

"Man, fuck that shit y'all niggas talking. Let's go bust that strip club wide open," Life suggested, cocking his cap over to the right side, trying to look real pimpish.

"My man," Kenny cheered, "you just spit some playa ass shit."

"And nigga, you always spit some ugly ass shit!" Bell reported. "And I'ma get your ass back for all that playing on my fuckin' phone bullshit. Nigga, karma is a mothafucka; the nigga had me chasing a nut like I was a fuckin' ho."

"Playa, when it comes to getting a nut, me and a ho be in a rat race," Life joked. "Because I'm try to get mines off before she get hers."

Once everyone was seated, Life made the strong suggestion they swing by Ms. Matty Mae Strong's house and get their grub on. Kenny was cool with the idea, but not Bell; he objected.

"Bad idea… Super bad idea. Man, that old ass woman won't rest until she make a nigga the biggest fool since Chicken Little."

***

Ebony stared out the window with both arms behind her back. She was madder than a disturbed honeybee's nest. With clocking off work early, she demanded some immediate answers. Watching Nakeita climb the stairs fueled her even more. Soon as Nakeita entered, she got deep off in her shit.

"How was school today?"

"The same as every day…" Nakeita huffed and puffed. "There wasn't anything special 'bout today." Nakeita kept her distance; she was afraid Ebony would smell the weed, alcohol, and penis residue on her breath.

"Are you sure there was nothing special 'bout school today?" Ebony re-questioned, giving Nakeita the chance to come clean and redeem herself.

"Why you ask that, Ma?"

"Your teacher called me on my fuckin job. You skipped school today. You missed a major test," Ebony's eyes narrowed. "So I wanna know where the fuck have you been?"

"Oh my God," Nakeita slapped her forehead, "We went to McDonald's for lunch and I missed Ms. E's class."

Ebony went for the lie since Nakeita came halfway clean. She really didn't know if Nakeita skipped the whole day or just one class because she didn't check. However, she did call Cynthia, Yolanda and Carrista to see if the same teacher called them as well. Keyandra, Quasha and Keke were good as gold; they didn't have a problem in the world concerning their school issue. But still, Ebony wanted to have all her facts in order.

"Lil' girl, don't you know education is a key factor," she stated, leaving the skipping school issue alone because Nakeita was prepared to carry her lies the full length of a football field.

"Yes," Nakeita shrugged. "How can I forget when you always breathing it down my throat." Ebony didn't like what she just heard.

130

"Girl, get your ungrateful ass outta my fuckin' sight before I stomp a damn mud hole in your ass. And the next time you fuckin' skip school, I'ma put my foot so far up your damn ass the doctor gonna have to do surgery to remove my foot… Do you understand?"

"Yes ma'am." Nakeita started heading for her bedroom.

"No! You're going the wrong way!" Ebony pointed towards the front door. "Take your unappreciative ass back to that school house because that teacher is waiting on you! She staying late for you and if you don't pass that test then I got a trick for your overgrown ass."

"I need to use the bathroom first before I go," Nakeita trembled from her lips.

"You hurry the fuck up and use my bathroom," Ebony said, with strong authority. "Then you hurry the fuck up and get outta my house… And when you get back, you go straight into your room for the next eight days. Now take your ass straight to school and bring your damn ass straight back home. You on room punishment and that do mean no talking on that damn phone. If I catch you on that phone, I won't pay your bill for two months. I'll let the shit get turned off!"

Nakeita lowered her eyes and started making her way across the living room floor so she could go use the bathroom and brush her teeth. She lied earlier about having to go pay her water bill, but now she actually had to pee for real because Ebony put the fear of God in her.

"How long you gonna be?"

"Huh?" Nakeita asked, not fully understanding the question.

"How long you gonna be in my bathroom?" Ebony re-asked, looking at her watch.

"Long enough to pee and brush my teeth," she said dryly, refusing to make eye contact.

"I'll give your ass a full ten minutes…" Ebony looked at her watch again. "Nine minutes and fifty-nine seconds you better be outta my fuckin' house." Nakeita gave Ebony a sad look, but Ebony still didn't light up.

"Ain't no sense in looking at me, you need to be trying to get in my bathroom and outta my fuckin' house because your ass is definitely on the clock," she said in an icy tone.

***

The club began to fill early; the senior citizens huffed and puffed into the building. Once they stepped foot into the place they individually clapped their hands because to them that was their imagination finish line. As three guys wheeled in, two of the men hopped in with the assistance of crutches. Four used iron walkers; thirteen with canes. The doorman asked his boss, the bartender, "What all this be about?"

"How the fuck would I know…" his boss humped up both shoulders. "I don't have no senior citizen's night and I damn for sure not going to discriminate against them. Shit, they money spend, too," he laughed. "And you better not give not one of their asses a senior citizen's discount unless you want to get fired…" He paused, looking around the club. There were more senior citizens than there were young guys. He threw the doorman a wicked smile. "Shit, charge them old farts double." The old timers texted and phoned one another stating this was the place to be, and the event needed to be seen. Once seated, they gave one another two thumbs up.

"Playa, this shit look like a fucking old folks home," Bell claimed.

"Smell like one, too," Kenny laughed.

Life soaked up his surroundings. There weren't many unavailable seats.

"Man, this joint got paid tonight… Boy, a nigga might need to fuck around and rob this shit. We'll get good paper. I know there's 'bout four stacks ($4,000) strong."

"A nigga needs to hurry the fuck up and get us some fucking seats while y'all bullshit," Kenny addressed. He walked away from Bell and Life in order to claim them a table before there were no more seats. Playing the wall wasn't a part of his agenda; the wall could stand without his company once the club got packed. Unfortunately, some guys would have to run parallel with the wall.

Half-naked females mingled with the crowd chasing table dances. They wanted to collect enough money to help pay school issues, day care fees, house bills, car notes, etc.... Girls of every size, shape and color, they were out to please a guy's fantasy, which were so small to these female giants. They were live tigers roaming this jungle without a leash, but for a small fee leashes could be applied. The ladies submitted to the mighty dollar. They worshipped the US currency more than anything else.

"Everybody in the club holla… 'Where the pill man at?'" Kenny yelled.

"Slow ya roll. Be easy, baby…" Bell coached.

"Slow down my ass, I gotta get paid and get laid," Kenny scolded.

"That's right you do, my nigga," Life encouraged.

"That's gonna be done without question," Kenny replied.

"Hell yeah," Some of the senior citizens whistled and shouted as the lights began to dim, "Let's get the fucking show on the road."

"Pop, when your ass nod the fuck out, I'ma beat them hos to your pockets," Life joked while watching one of his elders with an iron four leg walker.

"Ole timer, that nigga dead ass serious," Kenny grinned.

"Serious as a heart attack," Bell breathed.

"What, y'all niggas thought this shit a game?" Life smiled. "I gotta get it before them thirsty ass hos get it."

The black curtain parted as though it was the Red Sea. Toni, Tasha, and Wonder stood there looking as lovely as can be, true eye candy. Their hairstyle gave them an innocent naive school-girl look as they twirled the blow pops in their mouths. Dress code consisted of a black see-through bras showing off nipples as an appetizer. Short green cheerleader skirts exposed the bottom of their butt cheeks and black thongs. The six-inch heels added height to the girl's small frames.

"Now that's what I call ass all outdoors," a senior citizen whistled. "Happy Birthday and Merry X-Mas to me."

"Baby, show a playa what's for sale?" One of the seniors yelled.

"Let me see what I gotta bid on?" another senior citizen shouted, who was enjoying the view.

The DJ finally got the music playing. The girls did the Naomi Campbell walk around the stage once Keri Hilson song, "Do the Pretty Girl Rock" laced their ears. They went to work dancing, singing, and altering the lyrics by using their names. Toni lead the group, *"My name is Toni, I'm so very, fly oh my it's a little bit scary, boys wanna marry, looking at my derrière, and you can stare, but if you touch it, I'ma bury,"* she squatted so the audience could have a presidential view between her legs at her shaved completely bald-headed kitty cat.

"Baby, is them thongs edible?" Fat Mack hollered licking his lips. The girls claimed his initials, F.M., stood for Free Money, because he had a misquote peter and raccoon tongue. He could lick for days; Fat Mack licked the tip of five of his fingers. "Finger licking good… All of you, I just wanna eat all the meat off of y'all lil' bones. Dolls, you're all barely legal, my type."

Toni blew him a kiss, rising to her feet. She waved over to Tasha.

"Tasha can repeat it for you."

Tasha moved swiftly around Toni so she could please and tease the crowd. She had to sell herself as well, and no one could do a better job than she. This song and dance could and would benefit her good. She repeated Toni's paragraph with adding her name and deleting Toni's name. As soon as she finished, Wonder replaced her, *"I'm pretty as a picture, sweeter than a swisher, mad because I'm prettier than the girl wit'cha. Don't hate me because I'm beautiful; don't hate me because I'm beautiful."*

Toni and Tasha strutted up beside Wonder, leaning forward as well, bouncing on their toes and butt cheeks, behaving like jello, shaking and bouncing like crazy. *"Do the pretty girl rock, do the pretty girl rock,"* they sang together. They removed their skirts and threw them into the crowd. Wonder's skirt landed in Bell's chest instead of Kenny's. Bell flicked out his tongue and leaned back into the wood chair making a wolf noise, as if hollering at the moon.

Once the first senior citizen balled a five-dollar bill up and threw the money on stage, his comrades followed suit to show their appreciation.

"Them lil' hookers don't need that, I do," a hustler stated, while swinging a bag of pills in the air. "Ya know the demo brings all that money over here to Daddy." He balled up his cigarette pack forgetting there was one left; he threw it on stage catching the girl's attention, which he always did. They nodded, giving him the sign that his presence was surely needed.

"Who the fuck could this be?" Bell questioned himself as his cell vibrated. "Not right now Shawty," he mumbled, viewing Nakeita's number and planting his attention back to Wonder.

"Boy, them lil' hos showed their asses tonight, huh, man?" Life asked.

"Umm huh," Bell mumbled.

"Boy," Kenny laughed. "Y'all niggas done fell in the category with them senior citizens tonight. Y'all niggas are ass drunk because those hoes done let the monkey out the cage."

"Nigga, you out your damn cage," Bell assured.

"And you, too…" Kenny replied.

"I'm an animal," Bell stated.

"Naw homie, that's the whole fucking club," Life said, while the older guys waved large bills into the air. They were serious about outbidding the next senior citizen.

"You ain't got nothing there but bra money and thong money because I'ma put a stack down as a payment on the kitty cat," one senior citizen alerted another.

"Don't worry. My crazy check start back up next week."

"Man, fucking with these young girls nowadays, we'll have to fuck around and become drug dealers to take care of their high maintenance asses," stated another senior citizen.

"Tom, how much money you got?"

"Two hundred," Tom breathed. "Two hundred dollars…"

"Shit, that's not ass fare, you can take that back to the nursing home with you and use that to finish playing two dollar games of checkers."

"Johnson, everybody don't have money to throw away like you."

"Bro…" Johnson thumbed through his stack of ten one hundred dollar bills. "It ain't called tricking when you got it."

Chapter 11

Everyone got prepared for the walk. Today was a beautiful day; not too hot, but just right and not a cloud anywhere to be found in the light-blue sky. When this type of weather was present, the girls loved to take advantage of it. As everyone gathered in the school yard, Keke leaned on the outside stair rail to replace her two-inch heels with her pink and white Air Force Ones. Keyandra pulled her hair up in a ponytail to avoid having sweat drip down her neck. Quasha removed her thin sweater, which she'd used earlier to for the morning chill. As Nakeita waited on her slow poke friends, she stood around preparing herself for the long walk home.

"Y'all ready?" Quasha asked, watching all of her friends nod yes in unison.

The girls were not only best friends, but each of them enjoyed walking home from school. For them the long walk gave them more time to gossip, catch up on stuff happening around the school and with their individual friends. Most of all, they looked forward to the exercise.

"All ya'll slow pokes should've been ready," Nakeita said, "Soon as y'all hit the door, y'all should've got in gear, because you know this was our day to walk. Shoot, y'all know we been waiting on this day for weeks."

"I can't argue with that," Keyandra agreed. "Cause when you're right, you're right." Quasha nodded in approval.

Keke felt the need to interject her opinion, "Ya'll might can't argue with it, but I can," she said, joking as she pulled her hair up into a pony tail.

"Look who's talking. Girl, you'll argue 'bout the sky not being blue," Keyandra fussed. "And at the end of the conversation your opponent has already surrendered, and let you win. And you'll still continue to argue."

"Why's that?" Keke queried.

"Cause Cuz can't nobody out-talk ya," Keyandra quickly stated. "Well, you oughta know. Cause on the for real, for real, you be with her more than I do," Nakeita teased Keyandra.

"Look who's try'na talk," Keke gave Nakeita a friendly shove.

Quasha brought her palms together. "Now since we'll soon be out for the break, what you guys have planned for the summer?"

Keke pointed at Quasha, "Now what do you have planned?" she wanted Quasha to share first, since she was always good about popping off questions.

"Well, to be honest I haven't given it much thought myself," Quasha admitted.

Keke laughed.

"So what you have planned?" Quasha redirected the question back to Keke.

"I'mma go work with my cousin Kieron," Keke said, offering a fake smile.

"Yes that's exactly what we both been talkin' bout," Keyandra confirmed, "So I guess that's what the two of us will be doing for our summer break."

"That sounds like a plan," Nakeita interjected, "Nothing like working for your people and with your people."

"Keyandra and Keke girl, y'all came up with a great idea," Quasha said, letting them know they couldn't come up with a better idea.

"Nothing like a functional family," Nakeita stated.

Now since they mention it, she might mess around and do the same, because she enjoyed Keiron's company as well. Even though he was first cousin as well, but she looked at him more like her little brother.

"I don't know what I'mma do with myself," Nakeita mentioned. "I'm going to have so much free time on my hands; but I'm quiet sure I'll find something to get into."

"Mmm huh," Quasha mumbled. "Just make sure it's something positive."

"Oh, I'm not a negative person," Nakeita defensively said.

"And not one time did I say you were," Quasha replied. "Just be careful, girl. That's all I was trying to say, cause now days us young people have to be careful of the company we keep."

Quasha had heard rumors about Bell being no good, but she didn't want to come straight out and tell Nakeita. She didn't want her friend to get the wrong impression, or think she was hating, so that was the best way she could caution Nakeita without causing any damage or suspicion.

"She ain't negative," Keke laughed, "She just Ni-dy with a capital N."

"With a capital N, cuz?" Keyandra questioned, to flame up the joke.

Nakeita couldn't resist laughing, "I done heard it all, Ni-dy with a capital N," she laughed again. "Keke girl, is that what you do all day, sit around and find something slick to say?"

"Only when it comes to you," Keke replied. Keyandra gave Keke a grin look. It was one that said, Cuz be nice, falice.

"And why's that?" Nakeita pursued.

"I used the N cause you're a Nicki Minaj fan," Keke smiled.

"I forgot about that," Quasha murmured. "Nakeita girl, let me see if she really can spit better than Lil Kim." Quasha walked over to Nakeita and gently helped her out of the backpack. "Here, hold this trouble," she said to Keke.

"Trouble," Keke repeated the new name Quasha had just openly given her.

"Cuz trust me, you earned the title," Quasha replied, rummaging through the backpack.

"Let me find out you a Nicki fan, too," Keke fired off.

"Quasha girl, now that's what's up," Nakeita cheered.

"How could you possibly not be one too?" Quasha began. "Cause she's the hottest female artist out there, and she's on everybody's shit."

"Cause she is the shit now," Nakeita verified.

Keke smiled because she didn't need for them to get a misconception, she too gave credit where credit was due. She had the same CD in her CD player.

"That song she got with Keshia Cole is an animal," Keke stated.

"You should know it by heart," Keyandra assisted Nakeita with putting the backpack back on.

When they got ready to cross the street, a four door dark blue Cadillac slowed down. Three guys occupied the vehicle.

"Whas up ladies?" the driver greeted.

Keke looked into the car, "Man how you gonna tryta holla at us, when it's only three of y'all and four of us?" she fanned him off as though he was a fly. "You can't try no mess like that. So keep it pushin."

"Baby Girl, I can respect that," he replied, and got back into traffic.

Keke held her frown longer than necessary, as Nakeita pointed at her stone face.

"Girl you a fool with it."

Keke burst out laughing, "Nakeita girl, sometimes that what it takes. You better get with the program."

"Now you see why I keep her with me," Keyandra said.

"The bodyguard huh?" Quasha exclaimed, half listening to their conversation. She was more focused on the music, as she tried to learn some superfly lyrics she could apply to her conversation when needed.
As the friends continued to make their way home, they discussed various world events as their feet beat the pavement.

* * *

Bell mean-mugged his mother from behind the wheel, as she made small talk with their neighbor about senseless conversation over a putter, which was a damn dog she was not going to buy. To him it was a waste of time to hold even friendly conversation over a creature she didn't like.

"*Mom you need to bring your in the way ass on,* " he wanted to scream, but instead blew the horn twice. Irritated by his gesture, she waved him off.

"Boy, don't rush me."

"Man, this woman here will fuck up a wet dream," he mumbled to himself, beeping the horn again.

"B-b-b," the horn echoed.

"Alright neighbor, let me get on cause that boy of mine is gonna beep on that poor horn until it dies," she teased, walking to hop in the truck.

Once she got inside, Bell looked in the rearview and sped away from the curb.

"Boy, don't be drivin' my man truck like you some kinda bat outta hell. If you tear up this man's truck, you know you can't afford to buy him another one. If it wasn't for me, you wouldn't even have money to put gas in this here truck," she sighed, rolling up her window to turn on the air conditioner.

"Woman, we don't need no air," Bell fussed.

"Look ol' big head boy, speak for yourself. I know what I need and I need some air." She paused. "You say we? Since when you learn to speak French?"

Bell didn't say a word. He just turned on the air to put his mother's mouth to rest. But as usual, it didn't work.

"Son, whoever you're in a hurry to get to can wait. So don't you mess around and get me killed."

As Bell sped through a yellow light, a green fastback Mustang slammed on its brakes and swerved hard into the opposite direction to avoid crashing into him and his mother.

"Lord have mercy, I don't know why this man keep giving this child the keys to his truck. He knows good and damn well that this boy don't have a lick of license."

"I do have a license."

"Since when?" she asked. "The only license you think you got is the one to get all these here girls pregnant." She shook her head, "And sad thing, but just like your damn daddy, you're no earthly good. Bell you ain't about shit, and you know I'm telling the truth. You keep having babies, and these females gotta be dumb as hell, which is why you runnin around here thinking you're some kinda big playa. Son, you ain't hardly cool. Actually, you're more like a damn fool. And you're messing up these lil girl's lives. To be frank, I wouldn't put shit past you. You probably got them to drop outta school witcha, so y'all can have more time to lay up." Bell looked at his mother like she was crazy. "Don't look at me like that. Boy, you know better than I do that you need a job. These babies' mommas need to put your ass on child support and stop coming outta their panties for ya." Bell gritted his teeth, but remained silent.

"Boy, you making all these babies. Hell, what you tryta do, keep up with the Mexicans? Cause shit you can't do nothing for them. Do you spend any time with 'em?"

"Mom it's OK to be quiet."

"Boy, you claim you know everything. You think you got all the sense in the world, but yet your ass ain't got sense enough to leave these babies where they at. Shit, these girls following behind you like they can't do better. Hell, it's like the blind leading the blind. Where were you when God was handing out brains?" she paused, watching a flock of birds fly south. "I bet'cha if I was to put your damn brain in a bird, the damn bird wouldn't fly any faster. Bell, you don't know nothing and don't care about nothing. Boy, all you care about is screwing. I just pray to God that you don't catch nothing you can't get rid of."

Bell wasn't interested in his mother's lecture or conversation. He blocked her out, allowing her words to go in one ear and out the other. Highly irritated, it was clearly irrelevant to Bell what she thought. All he wanted to do was put all of his energy into quickly getting her to her destination. Bell tried hard not to be too disrespectful, so until he dropped her off, he held a conversation within his mind. To him, he knew himself far better than his mother.

Bell finished fighting through traffic to get to his next destination. When he arrived at the school ground it was nearly empty. As Bell circled the parking lot, a few guys wrestled on the front lawn. When he got a little closer to the youngsters, he questioned them.

"Say fellas, I was supposed to pick up my lil sista Nakeita. Have y'all seen her?"

"You lookin' for who?"

"Nakeita."

"Playa, you're super late," one guy managed to get out before his friend tripped him. As soon as he touched the grass, the boy felt a hard elbow drive into his chest. *Oh shit, that nigga set me up good*, the boy thought.

"Man, had you gotten here twenty minutes earlier, you would've caught her," the opponent stated.

"Shit," Bell cursed, punching the wheel. He knew the guy hadn't given him any kind of information he didn't already know. "Was she out here waiting, or did she take the bus?" Bell asked, remembering

Nakeita told him that she and her girlfriends would sometime walk home on sunny days, especially if it was not too hot.

"She took off towards the traffic lights," the smallest of the boys said.

"Nigga, you should've said that from the rip," Bell frowned, turning the vehicle towards the only set of traffic lights in sight.

Zipping through traffic like a madman, after they crossed the bridge, Bell reached the girls.

"Yo Nakeita," he yelled.

"Umm huh," Keyandra nodded, mumbling.

Keke rolled her eyes, "Nakeita girl, you need to drop that zero and find you a hero." Keke frowned, as she was known to be one who always spoke her mind.

As Nakeita traveled towards Bell's vehicle, Quasha slipped off her headphones. "Here, Nakeita, you can keep them till tomorrow."

"Okay! Thanks, Girl." I'll see y'all tomorrow." Nakeita said as she opened the car door. "Call me early. We can go job hunting together."

"We'll see," Keke shouted.

Before she could close the door, Bell fired off a question.

"So what did your lil friends have to say?"

"Say about what?" Nakeita questioned, clearly aware of what Bell had in mind, but she intentionally played dumb.

"What they have to say 'bout you leaving with me?"

"What could they say?" she asked as they headed to the motel.

Once he got her butterball naked, she was ready to give Bell instructions on how to please her.

"Kiss my fingers," she ordered, followed with request for him to kiss her toes and ankles. When Bell went on to honor her request, he overlooked the two cherries and his name tattooed on her ankle. The only thing that interested him was getting between her two thighs. But because Nakeita felt hurt and depressed, the mood for making love abandoned her mind and body. Sadly, her sorrow went unnoticed. Tears streamed down her face as Bell humped away on her body.

Chapter 12

<u>Three weeks later</u>

Nakeita woke up one morning feeling sick. She fixed herself a cup of coffee and two slices of toast. After forcing the breakfast down, twelve minutes later the meal forced its way back up. For some strange reason that day Nakeita wasn't able to keep anything on her stomach. Each and every meal caused her to be dizzy and continuously throw up.

Nakeita finally built up the nerve to phone her doctor's office. Once the on-call nurse returned her call, she informed Nakeita that she had symptoms of pregnancy. Immediately, Nakeita hopped into some jeans and a t-shirt. She quickly grabbed a brand new pair of white Nike tennis shoes and rushed to the nearby grocery store. In her frantic search, she could not find what she was looking for.

"Excuse me! But could you please tell me which aisle the pregnancy tests are on?"

"Aisle four," the female pointed, continuing to ring up a different customer's merchandise. Nakeita zipped away in search of a test. While in route, she crossed paths with a male salesman. "Excuse me Sir, would you please be so kind as to tell me where your restroom is?"

"Sure, walk straight and once you pass the butcher on your right, you'll run into two wooden swinging doors. Once you go through them, you'll see the lavatories."

"Thank you," she said, racing off.

"Don't mention it. I'm just glad I was able to help."

Nakeita speed-walked as if the bathroom could run away from her, "Why that mothafucka couldn't just say bathroom? *Why he had to use the term, lavatory, like I don't know it's just another word for bathroom?"* she argued with herself.

Once inside the bathroom stall, she dropped her pants and panties. "I can't sit on these people's nasty-ass toilet," she fussed, reading over the instructions because she'd never done a pregnancy test before. Praying the nurse's speculation was incorrect, Nakeita stood over the stool, allowing urine to stream from her bladder onto the strip.

After a few seconds, she eased the soiled strip to her eyes and freaked out.

"Oh no, God, oh no," she cried out, as the white applicator turned from clear to a light pink plus. Nakeita could not believe her eyes; her pregnancy test was positive. "Oh God, what am I gonna do now? Oh God, Ebony's gonna kill me," was all Nakeita could whimper. She couldn't tell her mother her news. Nakeita just didn't have the stomach to break her mother's heart. How was she going to tell Ebony about her pregnancy, especially after she'd recently been warned, lectured to and prayed with over a million and one times about sex. Her mother had constantly warned her that she was only a baby her damn self and to leave them babies where they belonged.

Her mother explained the delicate situation of teen pregnancy to her as if she was a newborn baby herself. Ebony had spoon-fed Nakeita day in and day out about how a child would hinder her future, and dampen her chances of furthering her education. She also explained to her how it would interfere with her desire to buy and wear name-brand clothes. Ebony said everything in the world that she could to Nakeita to try to keep her from having a baby. She even told her that she was a hundred percent against abortions because that was the number one killer amongst African Americans.

"What the fuck am I gonna do?" Nakeita questioned herself as she stumbled out of the stall, throwing the pregnancy test into the bathroom trash can.

Pissed, she spits at the trash as if it had done something wrong. While Nakeita washed her hands and her face, two female employees burst into the bathroom.

"Girl, I got this fine-ass man I'm tryta get pregnant by, so I can trap his black ass," one of the females said.

Nakeita looked at her in disgust and felt the urge to vomit.

"You better hope like hell he's family oriented and ready to raise a kid," the other female expressed, giving Nakeita a fake smile.

"Fuck that, if the mothafucka buck then child support will fuck his ass up."

"Child support keeps a third of the money and give you and your child the crumbs. So y'all both can't live off that."

"How you know?"

"From experience," she collected more thoughts "They encouraged us to have more kids and be a single mother, that's why they give us them Habitat houses. They want us to be low income, and keep our men from living with us. You know President Clinton was cutting our welfare check off after a certain period of time. So I had to get up offa my ass and start career chasing just to take care of my four sons. I'm glad he did because I couldn't have taken care of them nor myself without an education."

"I didn't think about all that."

"Girl, that's what gets the best of us all. Not thinking."

The positive female appeared to be in her mid-twenties, and spoke with a wise woman's tongue. Nakeita did not want to hear any more of their conversation, so she exited the bathroom with the quickness. Nakeita exited the grocery store totally clueless about what she should do, where she should go, or who she could tell. Scared, she just started walking until she came upon Toni's trailer. Nakeita knocked on the door several times, but her knock went unanswered. She tried the doorknob and fortunately it was unlocked. As she traveled through the house, she saw Tasha stretched out across the living room couch naked as a jaybird. Wonder laid across her two floor mattresses in her birthday suit. The whole trailer was junky, clothes, beer bottles and ashtrays that were piled up with cigarette butts.

"Jesus," Nakeita whispered, thinking, *do these people ever clean up around here?* She found Toni lying in her bedroom on two mattresses, which were on the floor. Toni was naked too, and the room carried the odor of hot stinky sex. Dirty ashtrays and beer bottles from the night before were scattered everywhere, along with her clothes. Nakeita grabbed Toni's big toe.

"T get up! I need to talk to you," she said, shaking the girl's feet.

"Later, later," Toni mumbled, turning over on her right side, trying to catch back up with the celebrity she was talking to in her dream. He was getting ready to propose to her with a quarter million-dollar ring. when disturbed. He was promising to take care of her for the rest of her life.

"Why y'all sleep this time of the day?" Nakeita asked, dropping down on the mattress.

"We partied all last night," Toni answered, clasping her hands together to lie on the back of her hand.

"A party," Nakeita frowned.

"Mmm huh," Toni mumbled, "Girl, we had the whole club here last night. There were so many niggas in here, we danced all night long, we just went to bed bout five-thirty."

So that explained where all the cigarette butts and beer bottles came from, as well as why all their clothes were scattered all over the place. It seemed like people stripped piece by piece and dropped their bras, thongs, and skirts wherever they stood.

"Toni, we need to talk."

"Talk, Nakeita. I'm listening."

"Toni, I have a serious dilemma and I don't know what to do," Nakeita stated, covering her face with both palms.

Toni rolled over because she heard the sadness in Nakeita's voice. She raised to her feet and slipped into a nightgown.

"So what's the problem?" she asked in a motherly fashion.

"I'm pregnant, and I don't know what to do. I can't have the baby, because I'm too young to be having anybody's child. I'm scared. I don't know what to do. My momma's gonna kill me if she finds out," she became teary eyed, looking at Toni. "My situation doesn't look good. What would you do if you were in my shoes?"

Toni sat down beside Nakeita, "First of all, you got pregnant by giving up some free pussy and that couldn't have been me. Girl, you have some abortion money?"

"No."

"You mean to tell me the nigga didn't give you any abortion money?" Toni questioned, in a serious tone of voice.

"I didn't ask him for any money," Nakeita hung her head in shame. "He doesn't even know I'm pregnant. I didn't tell him yet. Actually, I just found out this morning, and you're the first person I told."

"You're supposed to know when your period is due, so you don't be having sex without protection two weeks before it's due," Toni pointed out, before she considered who she was talking to. This was Nakeita, not Tasha or Wonder. "Nakeita girl, your solution is within your problem."

"I don't understand."

Toni went over to her mirror and started brushing her hair, she wanted to be able to see Nakeita's face from a good angle as she explained her comment. She was more than positive that Nakeita would leap at the idea, because she had no choice.

"Nakeita?"

"Yes, T."

"What I meant by your solution being in the problem, you can use one of these Johns to get you out of this situation."

Nakeita rose to her feet, really not liking the conversation, and she still was confused. She knew Toni was trying to say something but was beating around the bush.

"Toni, I'm sorry, but I'm slow. What is a John?" Ebony taught her if she didn't understand what a person was saying, always admit that she didn't understand. She knew that by not doing so, she'd end up doing something wrong and becoming the laughing stock of the block, and that was the last thing in the world Nakeita wanted.

"A John is a trick," Toni said politely.

"Oh," Nakeita whispered. Now getting a better understanding, Toni advised her to use their occupation as a way out of her dilemma.

"You think I should start stripping and selling my body?"

"It'll beat giving it up for free any day," Toni explained. "It'll pay for that abortion and put money in your pocket at the same time. Girl, your mother wouldn't find out 'bout you being pregnant either."

"Now that would be a very hard pill to swallow."

Toni smiled, because Nakeita did not shoot down her idea.

"Come on here, hard pill to swallow, and help me get this mansion cleaned up."

Once the house was clean and the girls had bathed and gotten back into their Barbie Doll gear, they sat around the living room doing the girly-girl talk. As they recaptured the events from the night before, their story seemed too unreal to be true.

"Girl, I manipulated this trick outta a whole stack," Tasha publicized. "I'd just left the doctor's office and he gave me a fresh bottle of sleeping pills."

"Them shits came in handy, huh girl?" Toni questioned, already knowing what Wonder was about to say.

"Tricks are definitely a treat and that's for damn sho," Wonder laughed as Nakeita was the only one fascinated by their stories. "So Tasha, what happened?" she asked, resting her hands between her legs.

"I asked the John did he like X pills and he said yeah," Tasha smiled, "So I gave him two pills and by the time he got naked, the pills kicked it."

"That warm water did the trick, huh Bitch?" Toni asked. She always encouraged them to drink warm water while taking pills, because it caused the effect to take hold sooner. Warm water seemed to rush the medicine straight to the bloodstream.

"He ain't get no honey, but I got all the money," Tasha said proudly. She gave her two counterparts a hundred and fifty dollars apiece, because they were having a rough time and business wasn't going as well for them. Besides, things didn't look too good for the home team and by her being a team player, she allowed nothing to kill her girlfriends' spirit.

"Tasha you came through for a poor bitch. Bringing the pills and the bud was a good look on your part," Toni said, showing gratitude. "Cause girl, you know a bitch can't function too damn good without that medication."

"Who can function without them ex-pills?" Tasha challenged.

Nakeita wanted to raise her right hand and holla "Me," but she knew that wouldn't be a great idea. Reluctantly, she sat there taking in all the story lines that they could possibly throw her way. She had nowhere to go and nothing to do for another six hours. As she listened, she sometimes wondered if her friends were making up stories, because they never seemed to run out of tales, and they seemed to always have some of the most amazing shit to talk about. So amazing, that they made her wonder where she was while all of the magnificent events were taking place. As they talked, Toni studied Nakeita.

"Before long, she'll eventually let the monkey outta the cage and start slanging pussy like she's got a Pussy License, which will allow her to sell that shit over the counter, especially if I got something to do with it."

Toni concluded that because she witnessed the excitement in Nakeita's eyes. Though she tried hard to resist, she was always impressed with their livelihood. Nakeita always asked questions about what they did the night before, clearly aware of the fact that they worked at the strip club Monday thru Saturday, from 6PM until 2 in the morning. Nakeita had to admit, at least to herself that her friends' stories made her day, and sometimes left her panties wet. After hearing some of their sexcapades, she'd have wet dreams and kinky daydreams. On a few occasions, there were times when her girlfriends going wild wouldn't escape her thoughts.

Toni knew Tasha and Wonder like she knew the back of her hand. She could read them as if they were a book, but as for Nakeita, well, she couldn't judge her by her cover, but she was damn sho trying to.

Ms. Goody Two-shoes curious as a mothafucka and being too damn curious is what got the cat. I know this young ho try'na come out the closet. If it can be done Tasha is the one who will probably do it, cause Nakeita seems to always be most fascinated with what Tasha has to say, Toni quietly analyzed the situation. *Nakeita acts like she came from a home with two parents though,* Toni prejected, second guessing herself.

Nakeita kept a huge smile on her face.

"Tasha, you was a mothafucka, girl," Nakeita praised.

"Naw that pussy eatin' nigga was the mothafucka," Tasha corrected, laughing. "Girl, you just don't know what you've been missin'. You better let somebody's son suck all that built-up honey out of your bee-hive, and get on our team and let's get this money."

"She young and full of cum," Toni teased. But out of respect, she left off the dumb part, because she did not want to offend Nakeita.

Wonder's eyes went to sparkling, as her body language began to unfold a hidden secret.

"That bitch can't sit still. She done went to foaming at the mouth, knowing perfectly damn well her mouth can't hold nothing, so ho spill your guts and drop the 411," Toni encouraged.

"Bitch, drop it like it's hot," Tasha cheered Wonder. "You know good and damn well ain't no secrets and shit around here. Bitch, you know we don't play that. Ain't no dick nor dollars gonna come between us."

"You forgot to say ain't no nigga gonna come between us," Wonder added.

"Bitch, just tell us 'bout how you got your funky little rocks off, and who the fucking nigga was," Toni insisted.

Wonder fumbled around on the couch, faking like she was trying to get more comfortable. She'd been holding this secret now for some time. The guy made her promise not to talk about the details of their sex scene, although she did not give him her word, she did hold out for a little while. Besides, she figured he should have known that all females and their crews had conversation about how they got dicked down; and her and her girls were also very well known for going back on their word.

"Bitch, what nigga did what?" Toni challenged.

"Ho, let's hear it," Tasha breathed.

"I'm listenin'." Nakeita smiled.

Wonder looked at both of her girlfriends, but she wasn't ready to look Nakeita in the eyes just yet.

"Y'all remember that night at the club when we turned that mothafucka out?" Wonder began.

"Umm huh, how could we forget," Tasha said. "Them niggas went crazy, Nakeita girl, you shoulda been there. The niggas started out betting one another 'bout who was gonna leave the club with us. Honey child, I'll tell you the truth. The price of pussy went sky high that fucka night, Girl. If I'm lying, I'm flying."

"O, K heifer, keep it coming," Toni demanded, trying to get the conversation popping and in full effect. Before Tasha took back the conversation to share the whole event all over again, which she would normally do, Wonder took a deep breath and let the cat out the bag.

"This nigga ate my pussy so damn good, I had one argin after another. I ain't even going to lie to y'all that was the first time in my life I ever came like that. Girl, the nigga tongue fucked me so damn good."

Wonder told only half of the story. Yes, her vagina was well worshipped, but she also worshipped his penis as well, and gave his dick the royal treatment. She gave him such a blow job that she took him to another planet. So of course he wanted to return the favor. Not to mention that Wonder brought him so much pleasure that he went from saying *damn you give a nigga some good-ass head,* to saying, *goddamn, Girl, I love you.*

"Girl, you sure you had an argin?" Tasha asked, laughing, "Cause I ain't never had one of them my damn self."

"Tasha, I had so damn many of them back to back," Wonder snapped her fingers. "I lost count," she burst into laughter, closing her eyes. Suddenly, she shivered. It was as if she could feel the wide tongue French kissing her lil man rocking her boat once again. "I believe my spare tongue grew two inches, my shit swollen and wouldn't come back down to its normal size," she exaggerated.

"Bitch, you might know what an orgasm is, but you damn sho can fuck the word up," Toni said, wishing she'd had that tongue instead of Wonder. "Wonder, the word's not 'argin', it's 'orgasm."

"So who was this lucky guy?" Tasha asked excited. "Cause once you give him up, I'ma need him to take care of my kitty cat, too."

"And you too," Toni blurted.

Wonder looked over at Nakeita, "Shit, believe it or not, y'all already know who the damn nigga is."

"Shit, we can't because nobody had that special kiss between the legs but you," Tasha said. "So girl who the fuck is this nigga with the fucking magic tongue."

Toni became moist between the legs, "Damn girl, you got a bitch horny and jealous," she admitted, waiting on Wonder to spill the beans.

"Girl who is this mystery lover, lover man?" Tasha questioned.

"Bell," Wonder finally answered.

Nakeita's oxygen abandoned her body. She found it hard to breathe and felt the urge to throw up, when she discovered that Bell had obviously cheated on her with this slut. Bell crushed her world twice in one day.

Toni bounced out her seat and slipped down beside Nakeita to bring her back to reality.

"Girl, you can't allow no nigga to come between you and anotha bitch, cause you know all males are dogs. A man will fuck a mother and daughter, so it ain't shit for him to fuck two best friends. Do you think a nigga would get mad at anotha nigga for fucking his girl? Shit, if anything they gonna talk about how he beat the pussy up."

Everything Toni told Nakeita was true, but Nakeita wasn't trying to hear shit she said. She was in love with Bell. He was her life, her first love, her world. Bell stayed on her mind 24/7, and she couldn't possibly do anything without him being on her mind. She actually loved him more than she loved herself.

"I need to use the bathroom," Nakeita announced, excusing herself. Once the door was closed, she stood over the stool and stuck two fingers down her throat, forcing herself to throw up. Afterwards, she washed her face in cold water, and took a long look in the mirror. "*This creep is fucking up my life! Why am I allowing this man to do this to me?*" she questioned, looking at her reflection in sheer shame. Finally, guilt swept down on her like a hawk. She wanted to breakdown and cry. *But for what,* she questioned herself, "*Cause it's not gonna help, it's not gonna change the fact that this mothafucka got me pregnant and cheated on me,*" She fussed, before pulling out her cell. As anger and embarrassment consumed her, she began dialing Bell's number, hoping he could convince her that Wonder was just making up another story about her man.

* * *

Kenny adjusted his frames, the glasses Life called birth control. Life stated he wouldn't get any pussy with them because the lenses were, thicker than the bottom of a Coca-Cola bottle. Today they decided to take Kenny up on his offer. They joined him in his place of business, in a super cheap run-down motel where Kenny sold crack, pills and partied until he could not party anymore.

Kenny gave the four girls fifty dollars' worth of crack so they could entertain him and his crew. This female's addiction fully controlled them. There wasn't anything they wouldn't do for the cooked up cocaine. They had no morals, and privacy and respect meant nothing to them. As a matter a fact, was not in their vocabulary. They knew their role and played it well. Kenny was the superstar, and they were the rock stars. Due to their habits, they kept him on celebrity status, but the game was to be played on him. Women sought attention, but no one loved attention more than Kenny.

"Kenny, you want me to suck your toes tonight?" one of the crack heads asked.
"Naw, not tonight Baby."
"Kenny, you want me to suck ya dick and lick your ass?" another junky asked, trying her hand, cause she wanted to smoke for free as well. Not to mention that one of her get-high buddies highlighted how Kenny was a freak for getting his ass licked.
"Maybe some other time, Baby."

Jazz took the top mattress off the bed and threw it on the floor, "Yo K, man, don't give them crackhead ass hos no mo crack until they perform," he stated, standing in nothing but his boxers.
Kenny had all the girls immediately strip completely naked, as soon as they entered the room. He enjoyed showing Bell's little brother the power that crack and pills gave him.
"You hos heard the young boss," Life said, giving off some direction. "Y'all take that other mattress off the bed and throw it on the floor, too."
Two girls promptly jumped to his order. Once the mattress hit the floor the girls found them a comfortable spot to sit.
"Yeah, now that's what I'm talking 'bout," Bell said, staring between one female legs. Her vagina lips were thick and juicy. "Man, Baby Girl, shit looks like a hot dog sitting between a hot dog bun," he stated because she had a large clitoris, and it gave him a hard-on. Bell licked his lips and used the back of his forearm to wipe his lips, trying to prevent his mouth from foaming.
"That's the way you like her, ain't it?" Kenny queried.
"And you too," Jazz said.

As she flicked her tongue, the girl laid back on her elbows, spreading both legs to display all of her goodies. This was the same female that offered to give Kenny the great ass-licking.

Bell handed Jazz a condom, "Here lil bru, use this shit."

"Man fuck that rub shit, I gotta feel this hot, juicy, gushy stuff," Jazz replied. "Lace up, young playa," Life coached.

"Yeah, young buck, it's too much shit out here for a nigga to be going raw dawg. You feel me?" Kenny counseled.

"Fuck that, a nigga gotta die of somethin'," Jazz said, showing his impatience by climbing on top of the girl. She wrapped her long legs and arms around him. Bell escorted the girl of his choice to the bathroom, because what he had planned to do, no one needed to know. He always licked before he stuck it. *"Once her body comes to life, she'll fuck me senseless,"* he reasoned with himself.

Bell dropped on both knees and peeled back the girl's pussy lips as her foot rested on the commode. She heard about Bell's skillful tongue and was dying to get a piece of the action. He knew oral sex was what seriously got chicks head's sprung to the extent of following a man's demands, even if unlawful, or ready to battle with other females about him.

"Ring, ring, ring, ring," Bell's phone rang out.

"Baby, don't answer it," she instructed.

"Bitch, I do what the fuck I wanna do," Bell snapped. Had she remained silent, he wasn't going to answer the phone. However, he'd changed his mind.

"Yeah," Bell answered aggressively.

"Stay away from me! I never want to see you again! You cheated on me with that garbage," Nakeita whispered in pained and emotional distress.

"What the fuck you talkin' bout?"

"Bell ate my pussy so good that's the first time in my life I ever had an argin," Nakeita said, trying her best to imitate Wonder's voice. Tears showered her face, "The dumb-ass bitch so stupid, she can't even pronounce the word orgasm correctly."

Bell knew Wonder had finally behaved like a nasty-ass cat, and unburied her week old shit. Nakeita gave Bell the chance to explain, the chance to say Wonder lied and she was going to give him the benefit of the doubt, but Bell had other things to do with his tongue instead of wrestle.

Without one explanation, he looked at his phone, and gave Nakeita the dial tone. At the moment, trying to explain was not a necessity to Bell. He knew females were possessive and Nakeita was always whining and nagging, so he did himself a favor before she got started. Since she was just like every other female, Bell decided he was going to cut Nakeita off and leave her young ass alone.

Nakeita sat on the toilet crying. She tried to cry quietly and cautiously, because she did not want the girls in the living room to think she was a little girl. After that, Bell's conduct gave her a misconception that every male with a swinging dick was no good and not to be trusted and you gotta use them before they misuse and abuse you.

Nakeita girl, you too damn smart! You can't allow this man to have you fucked up in the head, she reasoned with herself, giving herself a couple of pounds to the head in an effort to knock some sense into herself.

Chapter 13

Ms. Matty Mae Strong placed a saucer in front of the girls and gave them each a fresh slice of pastries she'd made from scratch. Nakeita chose the sweet potato, Keke wanted pumpkin, Quasha and Keyandra settled for the cheese cake. To help wash the sweets down, three pitchers filled with ice water, ice tea, and freshly squeezed lemonade rested on the table.

The weather was beautiful. Ms. Matty Mae Strong's picnic tables sat under four large trees, which shielded off the sun pretty well. The girls enjoyed the baby picnic as well as the company of Ms. Matty Mae Strong. Because she was always joking around, they thought she was a comedian, a talented cook and very wise.

"I hope I'm multi-talented like you," Keke praised.

"Child, anything's possible," Ms. Matty Mae Strong gave off a note of wisdom. Once Ms. Matty Mae Strong went back into the house, they took advantage of her absence and went about discussing the reason they'd gathered for this meeting.

Nakeita gave Ms. Matty Mae Strong's back door her full attention as she told her crew her burden, her headaches and her heart breaking story. Sure not to hold back anything, she released everything she had to say.

"Bell got me pregnant and I don't know what I'mma do," she unfolded, covering her face.

Quasha pulled her hands down, "Don't worry, we'll help you. That's what friends are for. We'll come up with something before we leave," she promised.

"I knew that boy was no good," Keke confirmed.

"Everything gonna be alright, Nakeita," Keyandra assured, she reached across the table and squeezed Nakeita's hand. "The Lord won't put on you more than you can bear."

Nakeita nodded and felt like Keyandra was a lying ass, because she didn't have the slightest idea of how she was going to get out of this situation. She looked terrible and felt like she looked.

"Bell ain't shit. How he gone eat the coochie of a girl I know?" Nakeita publicized, wanting to curse, but managing to maintain herself. She didn't want to compromise her character, so she didn't go ghetto, no ghetto bones existed in her healthy body.

"Yuck," Keke huffed and puffed. "Now I bet'cha you won't be kissing him no mo."

Keyandra gave Keke a shove to the shoulder, "Girl, you silly."

"How's that?" Keke frowned. "For saying she won't be busting slob with Bell anymore?" Keyandra decided it was best not to respond to Keke's comment, because if she did, they would be on a new topic. It was obvious that Keke wasn't going to allow the conversation to die, and she was going to escalate the foolishness to the point of no return.

Keyandra looked at each one of her first cousins, "Anyone have any suggestions? The floor is open." She wanted to see where their minds were.

"Nakeita, I know you still ain't messing with that nasty boy," Keke said.

Nakeita nodded, "Not no mo. I told him to stay away from me and I never want to see him again," she reported, freeing her face of tears.

Quasha took a couple of swallows of her lemonade before she spit a few questions.

"So what did he have to say when you told him you was pregnant with his child?"

"The baby ain't mines," Keke quickly stated three times. "The baby ain't mines, the baby ain't mines."

Keyandra reached over and pinched Keke on the arm and wolved "Shhh."

"What he say?" Quasha re-interrogated.

Nakeita couldn't look anyone in the face. She dropped her eyes to the saucer, allowing tears to splash on her untouched pie.

"I didn't tell him," she whispered, wondering if she should regret the fact that she didn't.

"You did not tell him?" Keyandra blurted out in shock.

"Why not?" Keke further pressed.

"Nakeita, why didn't you tell that man?" Quasha asked.

"On-no," Nakeita hunched both shoulders. "I guess cause I was too busy telling him that I knew 'bout his fornication."

"What's more important?" Keyandra fussed. "Talking 'bout him cheating on you, or talking 'bout this innocent child in your stomach that you're not ready for? Nor able to take care of?"

"You're right," Nakeita whispered.

Ms. Matty Mae Strong started making her way to the table. She noticed everyone got quiet as she passed around napkins. After asking the girls if they need anything else, and each declined, she slipped into a seat.

"Woooo! I been on my feet since 4 this morning."

"Ms. Matty Mae Strong, what were you doing?" Keke fished.

"Cooking, child, cook-ing," Ms. Matty Mae Strong replied. She liked Keke because Keke always had something sarcastic to say and that reminded her of herself when she was in her prime. Like Keke, she would have been unsettled if she couldn't get in the last word.

"Keke, I used to have pretty hair like you back in the day," Ms. Matty Mae Strong pointed out, trying to find more ways to connect herself to Keke.

"Her hair used to be longer, that is until her crazy self cut it," Keyandra reported, raking through Keke's short hair.

"So! It was my hair," Keke smiled. "And while you talking, I'm thinking about cutting it again."

"No baby, let it grow," Ms. Matty Mae Strong encouraged. Once she was finished with the small talk, she wanted to be a part of the delicate conversation the girls were having and felt the need to speak on the more serious issues. "Now why every time I walk up, y'all stop talking?" she addressed the group. No one responded, so Ms. Matty Mae Strong continued. "I know y'all having y'all's girly girl talk, but I was once y'all's age before. None of you have no reason to hide anything from me, cause I'm only here to help. I can see it written all over y'all faces. Y'all are stressed out with some kinda dilemma, and if I was a bettin' woman, I'd say it has something to do with one of them pissy tail boys. Am I right?" she paused, looking at each girl to study their individual faces.

Everyone carried a stone face, but Keke had to be the only one with a mischievous smile on her face.

"I'mma tell y'all this before I get the hell on," Ms. Matty Mae Strong continued. Nakeita made the big mistake of glancing into Ms. Matty Mae Strong's eyes for a brief second, and that was one second too long, "I get up with the roosters and it's hard to fool me," she stated and had to catch herself before she slipped back into a joking manner. She could tell that this was no time for jokes, so her serious tone took over. "If y'all young girls are not cautious and careful, y'all will make the tender mistake of lettin' a man lead you into a brick wall. It'll be like he's physically ripping your heart out of your chest and throwing it as hard as he can into a brick wall. He'll kick that same heart around like it's nothing to him but a soccer ball," she paused, looking at Nakeita, hoping she'd lock eyes with her just once more. "Nakeita, you hear me?"

"Yes, Grandma."

"I'mma tell y'all young ladies, please don't allow nobody son to drag you through the mud, cause I'mma tell you the truth, you don't mean nothing to him, and he'll dog you out if he's able to. He's capable of taking any girls love for granted. And most of all, don't allow him to stop you from getting your educations." Ms. Matty Mae Strong had to catch her breath. "For a young single mother, life is hard, but it's extra hard if she's uneducated. And for God's sake, please don't let him have you fooling around with him tryta sell and traffic them damn drugs."

With that said, she excused herself from the table and hoped the girls could and would now discuss some of the serious issues she tapped into. Ms. Matty Mae Strong often reminded herself that her knowledge could not help every girl in the world, but it didn't stop her from trying once the situation manifest.

Today she wanted to open up a door for Nakeita and her girlfriends. It was her hope that they would bring their problems to her, so they could talk them over. Ms. Matty Mae Strong wanted them to feel comfortable opening up to her. She didn't want to see anybody's precious daughter destroyed, or hindered from the future because of someone else's son.

One of Ms. Matty Mae Strong's daughters brought home a slick talking, light-skinned, pretty cat-eyes guy. Her daughter talked about nothing other than the beautiful babies they could have. Ms. Matty Mae Strong done some investigating and was very, very displeased with the information she obtained about him. The so-called perfect gentleman was a well-known trouble maker and a drug dealer. Ms. Matty Mae Strong caught the guy without her daughter present, and she put her double barrel shotgun to his temple and promised to pull the trigger if he didn't get completely out of her daughter's life. The brother sweated bullets. After her threat, he was so scared there was nothing Ms. Matty Mae Strong's daughter could offer him that would even allow him to meet her in a motel. Surprisingly, that was a secret he and Ms. Matty Mae Strong would take to the graveyard with them. Her daughter cried to her and asked why the guy didn't want to see her anymore. Ms. Matty Mae Strong showed no sympathy. She'd just always say, *"Cause you still wear them damn bloomers,"* she laughed. *"Don't no man want no big ass woman, wearing big ass draws."*

"Then I don't want him either," her daughter responded.

Ms. Matty Mae Strong didn't waste her time trying to use reverse psychology, she'd find something off the wall to say and a person would fall victim to her comment every time, it never failed.

Now as for Nakeita's situation, Keyandra made the suggestion they all chip in and use some of their allowance to help pay for the abortion and Nakeita promised to repay them, but Quasha told her there was no need for her to do such a thing.

"Girl, we're friends. We ain't got no problem making the small sacrifice to see you better your life." Quasha stated.

Keyandra designated herself for the bus ride to the clinic with Nakeita, and Quasha promised to stop by to check on her.

"Shoot Nakeita, you're gonna have to do some of my homework for this," Keke said, joking.

Keyandra smiled because she knew Keke would not rest until she said something that did not fit their game plan.

"Nakeita, you hear me?" Keke smiled.

***

Silk parked in one of Big Johnny's brother's parking spots.

"Well here we are people. If you ain't ready, then you better get ready."

Ebony smiled.

"Who are you talking to?" Betty questioned. "Cause me and my sista stay ready."

Silk exited the vehicle and opened Ebony's back door. Once she stepped out, he closed and locked up his vehicle. Then he and Betty walked side by side to the door.

"It's been a long time," Ebony said, trying to overlook the tragedy. She thought honest to God that she wouldn't be able to step foot on Big Johnny's property again never in life.

Silk held the club door open, Betty paused, giving Ebony the opportunity to walk between the doors first, and then she would follow. Once inside, the club was packed and Mr. Cain was on the dance floor doing the funky chicken, which helped Ebony forget all about her past parking lot experience. As she laughed with her friends, she cried tears of joy.

"Look at your Uncle Bubbu," Betty whisper to her as Silk lead them to a table closer to the dance floor.

"Cut up, Unk," he shouted, wanting to hit a step or two himself to show Mr. Cain that he could jam too.

Once they were seated a slim waiter raced to their table to collect their order. Silk decided they'd drink champagne and orderd the finest bottles that Big Johnny's place could produce.

As soon as they walked through the door, Big Johnny spotted them. He was good about keeping a steady eye on the people who entered through his front doors. Finally, he was able to break away from a begging female after he promised to give her a few dollars before the club closed.

"How's my family?" he asked, giving Ebony a kiss on the cheek, then he worked his way around the table to give Betty a kiss on the cheek and a firm handshake for Silk.

"So what we need to decorate the table with tonight?" Big Johnny asked.

"BJ, we on champagne tonight," Silk replied.

"Champagne, huh," Big Johnny mumbled.

"That's right," Betty exercised her voice.

"Try that NUVO," Big Johnny recommended. "That's some good stuff and I'm more than sure the ladies will like it."

"We'll do just that," Silk assured him.

"The first bottle's on me," Big Johnny offered. "That way you'll see how it tastes for free and not for a fee."

"BJ, you're a gentleman and a scholar," Silk stated.

"I know that's no lie, cause females are always telling me the same two words," Big Johnny smiled, shooting Ebony a wink.

The waiter returned with the bottle of Dom-P. Big Johnny instructed her to take the champagne back and bring the good people a bottle of NUVO. He kept them company until the waiter returned.

"You'll like it; it's smooth," Big Johnny informed Silk, as he did the waiter's job and placed glasses on their table. Once he gave the tray back to her, he informed her that that bottle was on the house.

"You the boss baby and bosses make the rules." she replied, walking off to go handle the needs of her other customers.

The Delfonics sang *Lying to Myself* while Mr. Cain entertained their eyes with the bounce rock skate dance. He had energy for days; the two glasses of cheap wine were his energy booster. A horse would stop running before Mr Cain would get tired of dancing. When he started doing the Chuck Berry dance, people started clapping and cheering him on. Mr. Cain moon-walked behind the stage curtains and reappeared with a black cape draped over his shoulders and started performing the James Brown dance.

"No, he didn't," Betty cried out, covering her mouth to laugh.

"Oh, he's good," Ebony smiled, pointing at Mr. Cain.

Mr. Cain was dead-ass serious; he didn't crack one smile. The man truly thought he had the Godfather of Soul's shoes on both of his feet, but he definitely had the spirit because he didn't miss a step after doing the splits twice. He decided it was time to start singing.

"Sittin' here in this chair, waitin' on you to see things my way," he sang along with Rose Royce. A female walked over to Mr. Cain and started dancing around him. Mr. Cain continued to put his voice in the wind. "Girl, I'm spending my time, spending my time. Girl, you make me feel so insecure, knowing I'm not your kind, you're so fine. I just wanna get next to you."

The sister spun into Mr. Cain's arms to slow dance with him. He pulled her in close to him and she leaned backwards, touching the stage. He eased her back up, and as soon as they were once again face to face, she kissed him on the lips, and then spun out of his embrace.

"You're my dream come true, I just wanna get next to you, I promise I wouldn't make you blue," Mr. Cain sang, before quickly starting a new Rose Royce song. "Good things come to those who wait, but we can't wait too late. Just the two of us, we can make it if we try, we can build a castle in the sky."

The lady blew Mr. Cain kisses as she hip-hop danced. The crowd thought Mr. Cain's show was over, but they were wrong. He was miles and miles away from throwing in the towel. As the Commodores song rushed off his tongue, his mid-section gyrated.

"She's a brick-house, she's mighty, mighty… lettin' it all hang out. The clothes she wears, her sexy ways, makes an old man wish for younger days. She the one, the only one, built like an Amazon. I want a brick-house."

After his performance, Mr. Cain bowed in three different directions before abandoning the stage. The crowd gave him a standing ovation. It was almost as if he was truly a celebrity, a real artist or sho-nuff superstar. With all the attention he got in the club, Big Johnny gave Mr. Cain his own personal table. That way he would have privacy when he finally worked his way back to his seat. As usual, the table was loaded with drinks and tips, because people grew accustomed to contributing to Mr. Cain's cause. The small sum of gifts excited him and made Mr. Cain feel the need to perform day in and day out. Big Johhny's patrons loved Mr. Cain as much as he loved alcohol. He brought forth happiness and the people had no problem rewarding him. Once the first person stepped forth and left blessing on Mr. Cain's table, others followed to also show their appreciation. They created more fans for Mr. Cain, which caused him to put more big bills into Big Johnny's already deep pockets.

People around the community always advised family members, friends and co-workers to pay Big Johnny's club a visit to witness the super live, disco dynamite Mr. Cain, a.k.a. The Electric Man, as he called himself in person.

"It takes a bad mothafucka to do the James Brown," Silk said, enjoying the show.

"He's multi-talented," Ebony shared, "He can dance and he can sing."

"You're right about that," Betty agreed, looking into her glass at the light pink liquor. "You like the drink?" she questioned Ebony.

"It's alright," Ebony answered.

"See that's what's wrong with your uncle," Silk grinned, "He's full of that drink. Ya Unk Bubbu sucks up all that alcohol, then he'll tear the stage up until his fuels start runna low."

"Baby, when does his fuel start runnin' low?" Betty asked.

"When his brain goes to playing tricks on him, or how bout when they holla last call for alcohol," Silk said.

The liquor had him in a good mood. He wanted to compete with Mr. Cain, but that would not have been a good idea, so he left that rodeo for Mr. Cain, AKA Uncle Bubbu.

"Ebony, what you think about your Uncle Bubbu?" Silk asked.

She smiled, feeling light-headed because she was not a drinker. "My uncle definitely taking home the trophy tonight," she stated, claiming Mr. Cain for the very first time as a family member.

"We need him dancing with the stars," Betty said.

"Mmm huh," Ebony mumbled, taking another sip of her drink, "Now that would be a good sight to see."

"Things can be talked into existence, you know," Silk enlightened.

"We didn't say they couldn't, professor," Betty replied.

Big Johnny came back to the table and whispered into Ebony's ear, "When you get a moment, I'd like to speak with you alone. Preferably before you exit the building."

"BJ, we can talk now."

"Suit yourself," Big Johnny said.

Ebony turned her attention to Betty and Silk, "Y'all two love birds, please excuse me for a minute," she said, getting up from the table. As she extended her body to make it straight, she staggered a little.

"You had one too many ain't you girl?" Betty questioned Ebony.

"You might be right," Ebony exhaled, slowly walking away.

As Big Johnny lead Ebony to his office, two of his secret lovers saw them and got jealous. One vowed to make sure she gave Big Johnny a good cussing out once they were alone.

Big Johnny motioned for Ebony to take a seat, and then he begin to tell her about the night Bell brought Nakeita to his club. He also apologized to her for not updating her on the situation immediately. He informed her of the conversation him and Nakeita had, and she agreed not to see Bell again. Ebony respected the fact that Big Johnny was trying to build a family bond with her daughter, and thanked him for personally making sure Nakeita got home safely.

"And hopefully Nakeita will soon feel comfortable enough to talk to me again, once she learns that I kept her secret," Big Johnny said, winking at Ebony.

"Don't worry; Nakeita's secret will still be you alls secret. You can rest assured that I'll safeguard it," Ebony said.

When Ebony returned to the table, Betty had gone to the restroom. At that moment, Ebony took the time to enlightened Silk on her and Big Johnny's conversation. As she talked the song, *Wildflower* blared out all across the club.

"That's New Birth's song right?" she paused to ask Silk.

"Yeah, but you know the OJ's later remade it, right." Silk paused to listen to the words... "You know she's just like a Wildflower, just growing wild," he added.

Ebony appeared distracted, and then finally spoke.

"Silk, you need to tell my baby don't be no fool for no man. I've had this conversation with her several times, but maybe she'll respect it more coming from you, because you're a man."

"That's not a problem," Silk assured her. "I'll make time to talk to her immediately."

"The sooner the better."

"I agree," Silk stated. "I'll make it my business to be in Nakeita presence sometime tomorrow."

"Thank you, Silk."

"There's no reason to thank me," Silk patted his chest. "That's my job. Did you forget who I am?" he asked, smiling.

"Who are you?" Ebony asked, wanting to hear what he concealed behind that smile.

"I'm her Godfather."

Chapter 14

Ebony spent her first day off in misery. She laid in fetal position with her knees resting in her chest. Tear residue stained her beautiful face as thoughts of Darrel flooded her mind. She couldn't eat, sleep, nor speak. The thought of Darrel had her unaware of if she was coming or going, and even though the bed had her right thigh sore, she refused to reposition her body. Weeping like a baby, Ebony stared at the walls, and mentally licked her wounds. The antique, wooden stereo system played Stacy Lattisaw's song repeatedly. The music did not stop until Ebony lifted the needle off the record. For two and a half hours, all she heard was, "*I found love on a two way street and lost it on a lonely highway.*" As she listened to the lyrics of that song, her eyes repeatedly teared up on the verse, "*his lips would gently say, honey I love you.*" Ebony was broken, and under a lot of stress. She hadn't felt that bad in some time. However, she was so emotionally crushed that her self-esteem was even low.

Darrel was her life, her spirit, her motivation. She learned to live up to his expectations. He had a beautiful sense of humanity, and even in prison, he'd always provided her with encouraging words to keep her strong. When things didn't look so promising, he never stopped thinking and speaking positive. That's why without him, she felt empty, helpless, and sometimes like life wasn't really worth living. It felt like he was millions and millions of miles away, but she still continued to survive off of his energy and strength.

To her they were separated physically, but not mentally, Ebony brought him into her room and into her world as often as needed. Her mind always played tricks on her, and she was always thinking of him, and talking to him.

"I wonder what Darrel would do in this situation? I wonder what he would have to say about this or that? I wonder. I wonder. I wonder." Ebony's mind would ponder. The crazy part was that she wouldn't allow herself to think outside the box, or outside her space. She couldn't envision any further than her two eyes could see. She seriously and actually tried to picture herself in the kitchen, while wallowing in her misery. Sadly, she couldn't escape her space. It was unfortunate, but her vision of Darrel held her captive. She was literally a hostage in her bedroom, mentally and physically as a result of Ebony allowing herself to be locked down with Darrel.

Coming to her senses and back in tune with reality, she threw the covers off of her body and sat up in the bed. As she brushed the last few large tears away, she fussed at herself.

"Ebony, get your ass up outta this bed and cook your daughter something to eat. Hell, I need to eat something my damn self. Look at me, lying around here looking all pitiful ain't gonna help shit. This is not something Darrel would do."

Ebony stripped herself naked and went to wash all the misery from her body with a good, hot shower. With her positive thinking, she talked things into existence. And once she stepped out of the shower, she was fully burden free and a hundred percent back to her normal self. Yet, that didn't stop her from singing her theme song. Yeah, Aaron Hall was her boy and she love his song, *I miss you.*

"I'm talking to you baby, I miss you. We use to talk and laugh all night, what happened to them days? Holding you in my arms made me so happy. I miss you from the bottom of my heart. Please come and rescue me from all this pain and misery," Ebony sang with everything inside of her.

Once back in the bedroom, Ebony grabbed her favorite picture of Darrel and kissed his lips. She hugged the photo to her chest and slow danced with it around the bedroom as she continued singing. "I miss how you use to hold me. I'll do anything to have you back in my life again. I miss you in the winter, summer, spring, and in the fall, when we were together…. I love how you use to kiss, how you use to hold me. Now, all I do is cry."

Ebony got herself together. She looked beautiful, and she felt like she looked. After realizing it was 2:30 in the evening, before she headed to the kitchen, she decided to look in on Nakeita to make sure she didn't spread that Darrel sickness on her.

***

One hour earlier, Nakeita's cell phone rang.

"Ring, ring."

"What's the itness," she answered.

"How you feeling girl?" Keyandra asked.

Nakeita was now into the fifth day of her abortion. Her body wasn't all the way back to normal, but she was a whole lot better since she no longer had to worry about carrying Bell's seed.

"Thanks to y'all, I'm now trouble free," Nakeita said with sincerity.

"What kinda symptoms you had?"

Nakeita smacked her lips, "A whole lot of sleepiness. I stayed nauseous, but I didn't have that much pain. Keyandra, everything came out good. So that lets me know that the doctor knew what he was doing. He gave me his card and told me to give him a call if I have any problems. But I ain't had a problem yet. Thank God."

"Girl, you better not do that mess again."

"Who you tellin'?" Nakeita sassed. "Girl, you ain't gotta worry about that 'cause that mess had me scared to death. I can't afford to do that again. That was my first and last time. Trust me, I done learned my lesson."

"People suppose to capitalize from a bad decision and not repeat there faults. But Nakeita, some people will turn right back around and do the same thing again."

"Well, you ain't gotta worry 'bout me. I can promise you that."

"Alright," Keyandra said, and changed the conversation. She wanted to know what Nakeita had in mind since they were out of school for the break. She was curious as to if she was going to find her a job for the 90 days or use the free time as a vacation.

Keyandra shared with Nakeita each place of business she planned to fill out an application and hoped her friend would do the same, but Nakeita didn't say yay or nay to the suggestion.

"It would be good if we both got a job at the same restaurant," said Keyandra. "And on the same shift too, that would be real cool. Nakeita, girl that's what's up."

"I hear you talking," Nakeita responded, rubbing her stomach thanking God that there wasn't a breathing soul utilizing her body as living quarters.

"So girl, what's on your agenda for today? You should be tired of lying around the house. You wanna go to the library and hang out?"

"We can, Keyandra. It don't make me none."

"I'll call Keke and Quasha to see if they wanna come."

"Hold that thought, my other line is beeping," Nakeita said, putting Keyandra on hold as she clicked over to the next line. "Nakeita speaking."

"How you feeling, girl?"

"Keke, we were just talking 'bout you and Quasha. Keyandra wanna meet up at the Library. She's on the other line. Hold on and I'll merge you into our call," Nakeita said, thinking to herself, *Damn, if you talk about the Devil, then the Devil will show up. But that girl can't be the Devil, because she helps me out when I really, really need someone. And honest to God, that says a lot to me on her behalf. And I owe her a lot for that.*"

"Girl, you talked Keke up", she reported to Keyandra, adding her in.

"What's up, Cuz?" Keyandra addressed KeKe.

"You and sometimes me," Keke replied in a rude tone.

Keyandra instantly picked up on her cousin's attitude and knew Keke had a lot on her mind. Keke always shot straightforward, she didn't hold any punches, bite her tongue, choose her words, or beat around the bush. That was not something that was going to happen.

"So Keke, girl, what's up?" Nakeita asked.

"That's what I called you to find out," Keke replied.

"Keke." Keyandra spoke. Keke knew Keyandra was giving her a signal to be cool and not to instigate any negativity, but Keke ignored her warning. That mess went in one ear and out the other. "Keke." Keyandra repeated, hoping Keke would respond and give her full attention.

"Keyandra, would you please, for God's sake, stop calling my name!" Keke immediately roared on Nakeita. "Nakeita, girl, I know you still ain't messing around with that no good boy."

"I ain't talk to him since I told him I knew he cheated on me. And for your information, I told him it was over between us and I never wanted to see him ever again in my damn life!" Nakeita snarled.

"Girl, you let that no good boy put that D in your life and now he done messed your whole damn life up. You gonna sit back and let that messy man mess up your life, destroy your future! He's no good for you. He don't deserve you! You can do better than that. There's plenty more fish in the sea. What you think God only made one man? Girl, be patient. You have your whole life ahead of you. Trust me; one day God will send you a good man and you'll know he's the right one. So don't let that Bell boy mess things up for you."

"Bell kept coming up to me," Nakeita tried to justify. "I ain't run behind that boy not one time. So I don't know where you're coming up with all this mess from," she tried to explain with an attitude.

"Nakeita, just because the man continued coming to you doesn't mean you suppose to give in," Keyandra advised in a calm tone, not taking anyone's side, but hoping to get both of them to remove the hostility from their voices. "If anything, you shoulda took that as a warning to make it your business to stay away from him. But that's the past, only the future is what counts. We have to safeguard ourselves, because some boys will try'ta handle us as if we were only a damn dish rag, but he can't do no more to you than you're willing to allow him to do."

"I agree," said Nakeita.

"That boy Bell don't mean nobody no good," Keke grumbled. "All he wants is girl's stuff."

Keke's statement made Nakeita hype. She became tired of hearing the girl carry on like she knew Bell better than her.

"I know Bell ain't no good. I know he don't mean me no good. I also know he has two children and ain't doing nothing for them! I know he still staying in the projects with his mama, and he dropped out of school in the eighth grade. So trust me Keke, you ain't telling me nothing I don't already know."

"Since you know all that then tell me why you went ahead and messed with him anyway," challenged Keke. "I mean common sense would've told anybody to tell that duck to find him another duck to pluck."

"Keke," Keyandra chanted, enjoying how her cousin put Nakeita on point.

"Bell has no significance in my life. That boy ain't nothing special to me!" Nakeita screamed. "I hate his fucking guts! I'll never let him put his hands on me again."

Keyandra could foresee the situation getting out of hand, so she calmed Nakeita down with some encouraging words and advised her not to allow any man to have her making bad decisions and doing things that she would later regret in life. She made it clear that neither she nor Keke were out to tell a grown person what they could or could not do. She explained that they were only speaking out of concern and for no other reason. She admitted that they held her best interest at heart and wished her only the best, because that's what friends do.

Keyandra informed her that she and her cousins were still going to meet at the library and it would be nice if she joined them. Nakeita said she would think about it. Before their conversation ended, Keyandra made sure Nakeita wasn't upset with Keke, not that Keke was the least bit worried. But Keyandra just wanted to be sure that everything was peace, love, and respect.

Nakeita sat in bed. She was still confused. She wondered why Bell hadn't called her or tried to argue with her concerning his cheating. The questions ate her alive.

At 2:00 PM, Nakeita decided to go downstairs and get something cold to drink. Before she could make it down the twelve stairs, there was an impatient, urgent, and disturbing knock at the front door.

I wonder who this could be knocking on my mother's door like they're crazy, she thought, rushing to the door. When she peeped through the peephole and saw that it was Bell, her heart began hammering away. Bell pounded a couple of times then put his ear to the door, trying to listen for a voice or some moving around, but to no avail. He continued pounding on the door. Nakeita didn't know what to do, whether she should answer or not. She didn't have to worry about her mother hearing the banging, because she had the music on, and she knew from experience that Ebony was in her own world. The only thing that would run her out of that room was if the house was on fire. Nakeita had her back to the door.

"Bell, what do you want?" she asked, with tears racing down her face. "Please go away, please."

"Nakeita, I need to talk to you. Please let me in. I need to talk to you. I have been sitting out here for a while."

"No. Get away from my door."

"Let me talk to you for two minutes," Bell begged.

Nakeita cracked the door, giving Bell a good view of her wet face. She wore boy shorts with a tank top, and her hair was in a double ponytail.

"God, you're beautiful," Bell poured on the charm. "Nakeita, let me come in for a few minutes. That's all it'll take. I promise. It don't look good with me trying to talk through a cracked door. Listen, all I need for you to do is hear me out before you cuss me out."

"No," she nodded. "That's not a great idea. A great idea would be for you to turn back around and go back down the street where you came from. And I'm pretty sure it'll lead you to one of them girls' doorstep. Bell, please do us a favor and get outta my life and stay outta my life."

As Bell stared into her eyes, his jaw vibrated. He was more mad with himself than he was with her.

"That's what you want me to do, huh? Say it!"

"Yes."

Bell laughed. "I tell you what," he wiped the smile off his face. "If that's what you really want, then I'll do that. But you gotta let me in and tell me them same words to my face. Fuck this through-the-door shit."

Nakeita pushed the door close and unlatched the chain and reopened the door. Bell was surprised; he didn't think in a million years that she would go for the idea, but it didn't stop him from trying his hand. He had nothing to lose and everything to gain. He stepped in and Nakeita's voice echoed.

"I'm through with you, and I want you outta my life. Now, please leave."

Bell close in distance reached for Nakeita and wrapped his arms around her.

"Nakeita, don't do this to me. I love you. I need you. I can't live without you, and I'm not about to spend another lonely night of my life without you!" He palmed both sides of her face. "Look into my eyes and tell me you don't love me, and I'll walk right back out that damn door."

Nakeita cried uncontrollably. Bell shoved his tongue down her throat. She sucked on his tongue as if it was a pacifier. They had a good, strong and lustful animal rumble-in-the jungle sex scene that required no foreplay. Nakeita encouraged her lover to rip off her shirt and bra. Their bodies collided together like two rams bumping heads with all their might. Bell held a palm full of Nakeita's hair while penetrating her doggy style.

He rode Nakeita as if he was riding a real live horse. Her eyes rolled back into her head. They missed one another's body and were trying to make up for lost time.

After a hard and long thirty-five minutes of gorilla lovemaking, Bell was ready to do the pillow talk thing. He made Nakeita a pack of promises, knowing good and darn well that he intended to break each one of them, willingly and unwillingly. To Bell, making promises was as easy as breathing. In his childish mindset, promises were made to be broken.

Nakeita was so excited about being back in Bell's arms and good grace again that she forgot that once the music stopped playing in her mother's room that her mother would be back on the prowl again. The love birds circling in her head distracted her even while Bell continued to make watered down promises. Suddenly, there was a knock at Nakeita's door.

"Nakeita! Girl, you up?"

"Shhh," Nakeita hushed Bell, instructing him to be quiet.

She no longer saw her mother's shadow under the door. Nakeita sensed the trouble coming. She shoved Bell away from her.

"Get your clothes and go out the window," she demanded.

"What?"

"My momma is coming," she warned him, jumping out of the bed and throwing on a gown. "Boy hurry the fuck up, 'cause Ebony's gonna come in here."

Bell jumped into his jeans and had only one shoe on when Ebony burst into the bedroom.

"Nakeita, why the fuck you got this man in my fucking house?" Before Nakeita could respond, Ebony slapped her. Ebony overlooked the fact that while she raced back to her bedroom, she'd prayed to the Lord for strength and the will power not to kill anyone. Bell gave Ebony an evil look.

"Man, don't be looking at me like that. The best damn thing you can do is get the fuck up outta my motherfuckin house. And I do mean quick, fast, and in a hurry. You need to carry the rest of your shit. You can put that shit on outside of my house."

"Lady fuck around with me if you want to, I'll have your ass dialing 911," Bell growled.

Ebony held the pistol in plain view. "I don't dial 911, I dial .357," she snarled.

Bell wanted no parts of that iron. He refused to challenge Ebony further. She was armed and he wasn't. He chased sex, not death-wishes. Before the emotional mother had second thoughts, Bell followed Ebony's instructions and collected his shirt, hat, and other shoe and headed for the door. Once he was gone, Ebony started a shouting match between her and Nakeita.

"Didn't I tell you that boy don't mean you no good? You don't need him as your friend!"

"Momma, you can't tell me how to pick and choose my friends!"

Ebony couldn't believe her ears.

"Since I can't pick and choose your friends for you then get the fuck outta my house, because you're obviously grown, and grown folks take care of their damn self!"

"But momma..."

"But momma my ass. Get the fuck outta my house, Nakeita. Please pack your shit and leave." Ebony scolded.

Their mother and daughter relationship went straight out the window. Now Ebony talked to Nakeita as if she was the average Joe Blow on the street. She refused to continue to put up with a hard-headed child. Her mother did not put up with the nonsense, so why should she put up with her daughter's nonsense?

After Ebony showed Nakeita the front door, she relapsed and experienced another one of those Darrel attacks. She crawled back between her sheets and allowed her music to play on repeat until the next morning. It was the same song. *"I'm Forever a Rolling Genie, rolling around until I drop. But what am I to do when my mind is in a whirlpool. Giving me a little hope, but one small thing to do to please you? You got me going in circles. I'm sprung out over you. I need you ba-by. I said I'm sprung out over you. I need you ba-by."*

The song was guaranteed to rock Ebony to sleep and promised to greet her when she decided to wake up. Tomorrow would be another long and boring day for her to fight through without Darrel.

Chapter 15

Keke phoned Keyandra whining about having to wash her mother's car. Keke wasn't trying to be a part of washing anyone's vehicle, so she played on the computer, something she often did in order to waste time and allow the day to slip away. The guys she had been conversing with on-line were her father's age, however, she didn't know. One of the men introduced himself as a seventeen-year-old after learning that Keke was still in high school. He used everything to his advantage, since he was double her age and had been in the world twice as long as her. Without having to ask specific questions; just by her conversation he was able to identify with her youth. It has always been a no-no to ask a females age. So he simply used his intelligence and a few words, 'I can't wait until I finish school.' And then his victims along with, Keke, would respond by saying, 'me either.' Using his imagination, along with the assistance and guidance of his son who was truly the age he claimed to be, he played the high school event to a tee.

"My birthday is in December, that's why I had to start school late," He began the conversation in an area which he knew Keke would fall for the bait.

"I know you hate that."

"They wanted to skip me to the ninth grade when I was in the eighth grade, but my mother wouldn't go for it. She said it was best if I didn't skip because I might miss out on something. And she didn't even ask me what I thought about the situation…"

"That's crazy!" Popped up on Keke's screen.

If Keke would've paid attention to his spelling instead of the conversation, she would have noticed his typing skills were pure garbage, and so was his grammar. For instance, there were often run on sentences, and the statement he just made did not add up to his so called intelligence.

'This boy can't type, I type better than him and sometimes he don't use periods, commas, and he never indents. He keeps some run on paragraphs, but girls have always been smarter than boys. I'm the one they should have been trying to skip not you, you fool. I bet you got all bad grades and are just sitting there behind the computer trying to fool me. You're probably an ugly boy anyway," Keke joked with herself, but she kept typing.

"I wish they would have tried to skip me."

"Now I'll be nineteen when I graduate."

"Not me. I'll be eighteen like I'm supposed to be."

'Thank you for the free info, all I have to do is keep the conversation rolling and this young girl is going to tell me any and everything I need to know. Yeah, Tenderoni, exercise your freedom of speech.' He thought, and then typed, "I know you'll be glad too when school is over with?"

"You're right."

"You going to college?"

"Most likely, yes, because my mother wants me to go… She suggests I choose a good career so I won't have to depend on anyone to take care of me."

The evil predator's fingers began to cramp up. Keke had him going back and forth longer than he expected. Normally, they'd be on-line no longer than thirty minutes, which he had trained his fingers for. Now, they were going into another twenty-five minutes!

'Shit, I never thought I'd allow one of these little pissy-tailed heifers have me sit behind this laptop for no damn hour. We ain't even talked about jack shit. Come on little girl, open up the door for some freaky shit because I'm tired of babysitting you with this frivolous shit.' He said to himself while typing, "Do you drink beer and smoke cigarettes?"

"No, never have and never will."

He gulped down the rest of his beer and stabbed out the cigarette butt. *'She ain't got any of my habits, huh?'* He talked out loud and replied, "You smoked some weed before, I know you have?"

"No, you're incorrect my friend."

"What's up then, you like them, X pills?"

"Heck no, no pills for me boy, I heard they'll put a hole in your brain. People say them pills have you wildin' out."

'Shit, that's what the fuck I'm try'na do. Today is Friday and I'm try'na make this shit our wild out Friday. I've been babysitting your ass for over two week now. It's time to break the ice." He thought, as he typed, "I'm still a virgin and my parents think I should stay that way until I get married."

"Boy, you have some good parents," Keke typed while smiling.

"You a virgin, too?"

"Now boy, you try'na get too damn personal." Keke typed back immediately, almost breaking a nail.

"Sweetheart, you can stay a virgin because all I want to do is kiss you between the legs," he typed, knowing if he could get her to give an inch; he'd be able to take the whole damn mile.

"This man got me messed up," Keke said, out loud. Next she typed, "Man, who you think you talking to? My name ain't Nakeita! You ain't gonna put your lips on me nowhere. The only kissing you'll be doing is try'na kiss my two hard fists, while I'm busy trying to knock your lips off. Have you tried kissing some punches? What they taste like? My big brother, Tray, will knock your tongue down your throat, crazy man. My Daddy will probably cut your tongue out and then cut your whole neck off your shoulders for asking me some mess like that. Now, don't get on my line again, and if you do, I'm going to put the law on you." She clicked the computer off. She couldn't believe the guy tried her like she was a lollipop. Keke knew the guy was dumb, but she didn't think he was dumb enough to let anything fall out of his mouth. When she mentioned Nakeita's name, if she would've given him the time and opportunity, he would have been bold enough to ask how he could get in contact with her. He was a pervert and couldn't care less who he preyed upon. The man was an animal and had served eighteen months in prison for having sex with his girlfriend's two-year-old daughter.

Keke couldn't believe this man just tried her with the okey-doke. She needed someone to talk to about this subject, concerning this issue. Since she was educated at a very young age to report if a grownup or anybody tried to touch her private parts, she fled from her bedroom with tears running down her face, yelling for her mother.

***

Nakeita sat on Toni's couch, revisiting her tragedies with, Bell and Ebony. Toni assured her it would be a pleasure to have her stay with them and that she could stay as long as she wanted. Nakeita was embarrassed to publicize her situation among, Tasha and Wonder, so, she pulled Toni over to the side and simply admitted she needed a place to lay her head. Toni did not ask for an explanation because she saw the hurt and damage in Nakeita's eyes. She could relate to the trouble and was able to feel her pain. Nakeita felt betrayed and abandoned. The two people who she loved dearly had let her down and left her scarred for life.

'I don't need Bell or Ebony, I can take care of myself,' she thought. *'I don't need Ebony; I can make my own money and buy my own clothes. And like Toni said, men ain't no earthly good no way. You have to use them before they use you. They ain't nothing but male dogs anyways. They'll drive you crazy if you allow them, and like Toni said, they can't do no more to me then I allow them to do. I'll have them eating out of the palms of my hand. I'll have their asses fucked up in the head. I'll show them they need me and I don't need them. They'll jump when I say jump, and ask how high. Toni knows how to handle these older men. I remember her telling us about one who used to pay her good just to give him spankings. And then there's the other man who used to pay her two hundred dollars just to pee on him. Tasha says that some of the older guys give up their security checks just to suck her toes--'* Nakeita would've continued holding a conversation with herself if Wonder hadn't butted in.

"Nakeita girl, take a couple pulls of this blunt so you can relax."

Nakeita looked troubled and felt disturbed. She wanted to escape reality; she wanted to land on planet mars or get on cloud nine as the girls always joked about while getting high.

"Maybe it will make me feel better." Nakeita said, accepting the blunt. She inhaled and swallowed the smoke, taking heed from her first experience.

"That good weed gonna be like medication to your body..." Tasha predicted.

"I hope so," Nakeita replied, while releasing the smoke her lungs rejected.

"Girl, you'll be lightheaded in a minute and won't have a problem in the world," Wonder explained her condition. "I love smoking weed, it lifts me of all burdens."

"I just want to party..." Toni said, displaying the clean Ziploc bag with fifty ecstasy pills. She had just re-upped; she caught a steal of a deal by having sex with a big time pill man. Toni traded tricks for treats. "This the real medication," she said, dropping two pills in Nakeita's open palm.

"More powerful than pain killers," Wonder spitted.

"Uh shit, Nakeita, them pills are the best damn thing smoking on the fucking market." Toni said, as she crushed a couple of them bad boys and laced the weed with them. "That blunt had a bitch really out there and I was feeling good as a bitch," she unfolded.

The very first time Nakeita experienced the pills, her mood swing enhanced everything she came in contact with. The girls were in a happy stage and she immediately became in a happy mood. But Nakeita truly didn't embrace the pills full potential because she had to be home and didn't want Ebony to catch her out of character. Her body no longer persisted a must seed of her mother's fear, so now she could relax and allow the pill to reach every vein, muscle, and blood vessel. Nakeita was high and would remain on that plane for another eight hour flight. Once Nakeita put those two pills in her mouth, Toni continued feeding them to her as if they were Skittles candy. Tasha played bartender by keeping a bottle of water and juice in her hand, and the liquid further enhanced the pills.

When Wonder's time arrived for her to play the waiter, she also took time out to elaborate on her and Bells situation. She explained to Nakeita that no man walking on God's green Earth is any good. Since it was her story, Tasha and Toni sat back and let her tell the story the way she wanted to because they wanted to see how Nakeita would accept the story. From Wonder's point of view, or from her own understanding, Nakeita smiled. She digested every piece of misguidance thrown her way, in every form or fashion; she saw the girl's words as law. Law of the land to her; now they had a beautiful plan.

"Men ain't shit but ho's and tricks," Toni stated.

"I break'em and dump'em," Tasha blurted.

"You have to train, control, and mold his ass..." Wonder said. "And have his ass paying all the damn bills."

"Nakeita, you agree?" Toni asked.

Nakeita smiled and nodded, yes.

"Bitch, is you rollin'?" Toni leaned forward and screamed in Tasha's face.

"Bitch, I might be," Tasha replied, and attacked Wonder with the same question, "Bitch is you rollin?"

"Bitch, I might be," Wonder spitted with joy and addressed Nakeita with the question as well.

"Bitch I might be," Nakeita smiled and whispered. It would take some time for her to become accustomed the curse words. Cursing was not a part of her agenda. The way she was raised up, such language was not permissible, as well as not lady like. Darrel even went about mentioning that a person who could not communicate without using such derogatory words was a person who didn't have a vocabulary. For the majority of the time, her father's words of wisdom overruled every bad decision or misdeed Nakeita could and would think of.

Toni whispered in Tasha and Wonder's ears and instructed them to go slip into their lingerie and high heels. They escaped the room one by one and returned in their sex gear. Afterwards, Toni did the same and returned carrying red lingerie with matching six inch heels.

"Here, Nakeita, get more comfortable with us."

Nakeita looked confused at first, but went along with the program before the guests arrived. Toni personally handed Nakeita two more triple stacks of Butt-Naked Lady ecstasy pills, and before long the group of girls were chanting, "I just want to party."

The majority of the clients favored Nakeita. The older guys saw her as fresh meat. Nakeita's line grew and seemed as though it wouldn't end. Toni increased the price hoping the fellas would choose Tasha, Wonder, or herself as a cheaper piece of flesh. But her mouth was overlooked; all eyes remained on Nakeita. After more than a dozen tricks had tampered with her young pure flesh, Toni went into the room to see how Nakeita was coming along. The pills had Nakeita completely out of her mind. She made no complaints and only boasted about how the men worshipped her precious body. Nakeita continued bragging while Toni gave her a bird bath, got her clean and free of semen for the next group of guys who waited impatiently for their one on one expensive private sessions.

Toni encouraged her no raw sex unless they were willing to pay extra. Ebony's voice echoed in Nakeita's head, '*no condom, no sex, you don't need no germs that your ass can't wash off.*' Since she was angry with her mother, she didn't care to take heed to Ebony's words of wisdom. Now she lived to break every rule in Ebony's book.

"You okay, girl?" Toni asked, showing some fake concern.

"Yes," Nakeita nodded and bit down on her lower lip.

"What you think about the gentlemen so far?"

"They love me."

"Huh?" Toni breathed hypothetically speaking.

"They all love me. My body makes them happy! My sweetness is their weakness." Nakeita's words made Toni regret she ever asked the question.

'*I think I have created a fucking monster,*' Toni thought and reassured herself that Nakeita wanted to do this. "Everyone has freaky events balled up inside of them, but don't have the nerve to release those demons." She turned around and second guessed herself, '*Is this innocent child really one of us? Is she seriously cut from our cloth?*' Sympathy and jealousy had Toni discombobulated.

* * *

Ebony exited the cab two blocks from her home. Claiming she needed the exercise, she truly thought the fresh air would bring her some justice. Her mind stayed cloudy with her and Nakeita's falling out.

'*I should've done this. I should've done that. What if I wouldn't have done that? How would she have responded*?" She held herself responsible for the incident. She claimed if she didn't work two jobs, she would be able to spend more time with Nakeita. "Then I wouldn't be able to support her more financially." Poor Ebony, her mind wouldn't allow her to rest.

She wanted to drop Darrel a few lines last night to explain the situation, but she couldn't stay focused. Everytime she began writing, she would wind up balling the paper up. On the fourth try, she laid her forehead on the paper and cried. Trying to release her frustration with the tears, she hoped and prayed that Darrel would call home and her prayers would be answered. Darrel explained the delicate issues; his voice relieved her of her guilty burden. He stated that Nakeita was the one at fault because she should've known better; and when people know better, they supposed to do better.

"Nakeita's up in age now, she knows wrong from right! She had no business having that man in the house. They lucky you were the one who caught them instead of me."

"Darrel baby, be cool."

"Honest to God, I don't know what I would have done."

"Darrel, don't you go get yourself all upset."

"Ebony, I don't know what I would've done. Only God knows… You know we all good about saying what we would've done if we walked in on certain situations, but once that time comes only God knows what would take place, because Ebony baby, I probably would have lost it. I don't know if I would've been as strong as you. To allow the guy to walk out of my front door the same way he walked in, and he's a grown ass man too." Darrel tried to speak with sense, but his tongue forgot about the intelligent aspect. "This motherfucker gotta be crazy for fucking around with my fifteen-year-old baby. This shit is considered statutory rape."

"Darrel baby, please stop the cursing, you know the profanity is not you."

"You right, E... You right, but I can't get over the fact of this guy actually going to damage my baby for life. There is no telling what he'll drive her into doing. Lil girls will take the wrong path behind a boy's unlawful action."

Ebony held her tongue; she needed to let Darrel get everything out of his system because she was afraid he might do something crazy out of anger. She wanted him to stay focused and on a positive level due to his environment. Knowing that a prisoner could cross her husband's path with the wrong intentions and Darrel could be placed in another situation that would cause him to take a life or lose his life in the same process. Ebony's agenda was for Darrel to keep a level head and to stay in control of his temper.

"Baby, you all right?"

"Yes, E, but how are you holding up?"

"I'm okay."

"That's my girl," he paused collecting his intelligent train of thought. "You know a female is mentally stronger than a male."

"Darrel, stop it... Cut it out, baby."

"No, seriously, this is no joke."

"And how's that possible?"

Darrel went into the spill about how a woman can handle more pain and deal with more emotional activities. God wanted it that way because if he didn't then they would have been different.

"You dealt with more things than me."

"Repeat your sentence again?"

"You dealt—"

"You said the key word." Darrel cut her off. "I was dealt, and by me being dealt that hand, I was forced to do what I had to do, and I have no regrets. If I was faced with that situation again, I wouldn't change a thing because I'm a man and a man protects what he loves… It hurts me that I'm not out there to protect and take care of you and my daughter. You just don't know how bad it hurts not to be able to do my fatherly job." He bowed and stretched his head because he really didn't mean to make that last statement. He was truly in pain. This conversation made him feel helpless, less than a man. He wanted to destroy something to exercise and challenge his physical strength.

"Darrel, I love you and I rely in the Lord, God will make a way for us."

"And Ebony sweetheart, I love you and my baby girl more than I love life itself. Now, all I want to do is come home so I can take care of you and Nakeita. Nothing hurts me more than not being able to protect the two people that I love. Sometimes I feel less than a man. I know Nakeita needs me in her life."

Chapter 16

Toni took it upon herself to go shopping for her and the girls. She bought Nakeita a few pieces of clothing, something Ebony surely would disapprove of. Meanwhile, Tasha and Wonder made it their business to teach and train Nakeita to live up to Toni's expectations. By Nakeita being a natural intelligent human being, it didn't take a whole lot of babysitting; she didn't need instructions but once. She comprehended very well. There wasn't any reason to pacify Nakeita with the likes and dislikes, she pretty clearly had the do and don't memory padded, which she learned from her mother. Sassing around the house, they continue to mold and counsel Nakeita with their elementary water down game. It was still brand-new to a sucker for the very first time. They mentally spoon fed Nakeita with propaganda conversation. Wonder took off first.

"I screwed the grandfather, his son, and his son's son."

"Ain't shit wrong with that… You just beat them to the punch… A man will fuck a mother and her mother, and her damned daughter and wouldn't lose one bit of sleep behind it. Hell, he might wake up the next day and try to do that shit all over again," Tasha instigated. "The granddaddy was fifty two, his son was thirty five, and the grandson was seventeen. I had them all sprung the fuck out," Wonder said.

"Girl, you ain't done shit wrong, get your papers," Tasha encouraged.

"They chased love and lust, huh?" Nakeita pried. Wonder giggled like a teenaged school girl.

"Bitch, you ain't told me about that one… When this happen?" Tasha questioned.

"When I was about fourteen," Wonder smiled, "Actually, they the ones that broke me in. The thirty-five- year-old one was well hung." She leaned forward choking and coughing with laughter. "That's when I learned a pussy will stretch a mile before it tears an inch." Nakeita enjoyed the story telling, but that did not stop her from thinking Wonder had a filthy mouth. She thought Wonder should've kept that secret to herself and carried it to the graveyard with her. There were some thing's that are meant not to be shared. Every female should have secrets that they keep in the darkness. Some are too painful to spill, but they need unloading so that they can relieve themselves of the burden and grow from their misfortunes.

Wonder snapped her fingers twice giggling some more because now it was the perfect time to let her peers know what had her brain rattling off and on. "I have been giving it a great deal of thought about becoming a Porn Star."

"A what?" Tasha asked, covering her mouth.

"I'm trying to get some real Benjamin's!" Wonder replied. "Fuck all this lil girl money. Shit, Tasha, if you really think about it, we already softcore porn stars. We might as well suck and fuck on a tape and get paid for it because the shit we are doing now is the same shit, but this time we'll get to watch ourselves on TV. And we can become famous, straight outta our anus."

"You don went too far!" Tasha seriously replied.

Tasha felt as though she heard it all. Internalizing the situation, she thought that all her girlfriends morals had done exited their bodies and now Wonder wanted to worship a dollar bill faithfully.

"Wonder, do you have a fucking moral bone in your body?" Tasha asked, after she walked into Wonder's face. "That would be a giant step, one too big for me. I mean, I can't see myself crossing that type of line. Wherever you stumble up on that crazy idea from, you need to hurry the fuck up and throw that shit back and I do mean fast as a mothafucka! What is it, the pills? The weed?"

"Tasha, we already crawling lower than four legged cockroaches, so what the hell…"

"Wonder, you're crazy."

"No, I'm not… I'm just trying to get to the papers," Wonder paused with both palms on her hips. "Oh, I gotta be crazy to want better for myself. I want to live in a big beautiful house, and drive fast cars and wear fur coats?"

"Nakeita, you heard this poor child?" Tasha replied.

"Yeah, and that shit going in one ear and immediately back out the other one," Nakeita replied. She was content with the thousand dollars Toni gave her out of the three thousands she earned last night from her unconsciousness.

"Wonder, you have a donut for a brain," Tasha said, before taking a long hard swallow of her vitamin water.

"Look who's talking!" Wonder spit with emotions. "You out of all people… I thought you would be on my side. But now I see you're going against the grain." Tasha threw off a crazy expression.

"Wonder, everything is not for everybody. We would be outta our lead, that's not for us."

"We, Tasha?" Wonder blurted. "Now you want to begin speaking in French. "

"What, I need to tell you in tongue like a preacher? "Tasha teased

"One minute, Wonder talking good now, she's speaking like an insane creature. 'She's moving too fast for me. No way, I'm not crazy enough to do porn stuff. I don't know how I was able to do all of that stuff last night.' Nakeita thought while looking back and forth from each speaker's mouth.

Wonder looked at Nakeita as if she were silently asking her to voice her opinion. Nakeita threw both palms into the air.

"You know I can't make a comment because you know I'm slow and I'm not afraid to admit that you are talking over my head. How y'all say it? I'm young, dumb and full of cum," she said, trying to bring some sense of humor into play.

"You can use that young and dumb part, but you can't get away with the still full of cum part since last night." Wonder said, being sarcastic.

"Let's just say I'm ten pounds lighter, Baby!" Nakeita replied.

"I can live with that, and Nakeita girl, you're fair for a square. As long as you stay around me you might fuck around and learn something," Wonder smiled.

"And what is that because you know I'm eager to learn, and eager to please, and them Benjamin's is most definitely what a bitch needs." Nakeita spoke coming out of her little girl shell.

"T, you heard that?" Wonder like what she just heard.

"Every single word of it…" Tasha nodded.

"Nakeita's been upgraded!" Wonder cheered.

"I can see, I can see, said the blind man." Tasha joked.

"Uhh, my game is on one thousand," Nakeita spitted.

"Overnight celebrity," Tasha said, shooting Nakeita a wink.

Wonder snapped her fingers a couple times because she was able to identify a little bit of Toni's spills out of Nakeita the same way Toni's ways of life rubbed off on her and Tasha.

"Young Nakeita, I ain't mad at'cha," Wonder stated.

"Who is the illest? Who is the shit?" Nakeita blurted, clapping as if she was just singing a song. Wonder turned on her heels and raced to the front door because she heard a vehicle approaching. Tasha hunched up both shoulders giving Nakeita a puzzle's look. Nakeita nodded towards Wonder as they both laughed out loud.

"I know ya'll two angels back there talking about me!" Wonder spoke out of curiosity. She nodded sadly once her eyes fell upon Gary's black Lexus parked with Toni occupying the front seat. "Damn girl, why it couldn't be me. The shiny Knight and Armor has landed in your fucking lap and you don't have sense enough to know it." Wonder thought that Gary was a dream come true and a blessing in disguise. He was definitely looking out for Toni's best interest, but she was too damn blind to see it. He wanted to treat her better than the other sisters that he was humping. Gary was a middle-class Caucasian, who married an extremely wealthy widow. She was friends of the family. Gary used his wife's wealth to take care of Toni's wants and needs. He offered to put her in a condo, bought her vehicles of her choice, and opened her up a Beauty Shop. Toni claimed she was not going to be his number two women and allowed Gary to handle her like she was just a piece of meat, which was her favorite excuse. Now with truth being told, Gary treated Toni as if she was his number one lady. There was nothing he could give his wife because she had everything. There wasn't any excitement in their life. Sex was twice a year, if that, and it was a waste of time and energy. Toni had good sex and she actually gave him that sex drive that he needed to satisfy a woman.

They enjoyed each other's company and loved to be in each other's present. Gary confessed, he was in love with her, and Toni secretly was in love with him. However, she fought the feeling and refused to admit it Gary more than often stroked her hair and admitted she was a fun person to be around. Toni joked that they were a match made in Heaven. She wanted to be with Gary, but she wasn't ready and willing to give up her bullshit life style.

Gary went out of his way to treat her special; especially in public he treated her as if she was his wife. They stayed hugged up, holding hands, kissing and feeding each other. He took her to opera concerts, plays and on cruises. He took her to parks and proposed, but she declined. Gary had no problem with giving up his worldly wealth to be with her. He was more than serious about spending the rest of his days on earth with her.

Wonder continued to stare as she sucked her teeth. '*Gary, man, can't you see that bitch afraid of a commitment? Scared of change… Man, that Ho playing games. Now I see you're dumb ass can't see through the muddy waters, ole crazy ass man. "T" gonna continue to put that pussy on you like a hu-lo-hoot and string your ass out for another two years. Man, you can't turn a Ho into a house wife. It is not gonna happen, it's not gonna work. My girl "T" is a young old Ho, and it's impossible to teach her new tricks. She's not gonna allow it. Man, you better try to find you another bitch neck to put that leash around. Toni always holla about she after of that cake, but her actions speaks for their fucking self. She only after the mothafuckin crumbs because she supposed to be milking your ass dry,*' Wonder's consciousness started talking to her; she placed her right hand on her hip.

"*Bitch, milk that dick and that pocket at the same time and stop fucking his ass so much physically and start fucking him mentally… Girl, spoon feed that mothafucka, he's already eating out the palm of your hand.*"

"Nakeita, I wonder what that bitch sees out that front door?" Tasha asked, as she crossed her legs.

"Mmmmh, huh," Nakeita mumbled.

"It must be something mighty interesting," Tasha said.

"To put ya two-Ho's lil pea brain to rest, I'm looking at the two love birds," Wonder replied.

"Mickey and Minney," Tasha joked, using the alias names they had given, Toni and Gary.

"Yeah, but that bitch Toni ain't trying to get that paper, that Ho stuck on the crumbs." Wonder said, as she walked away from the door. "Naw, the bitch don't wanna work smart, she wanna work hard".

"Now Toni doesn't want to work the brain, she wants to work the body," Tasha said. Wonder clapped, praising the answer. "Her mouth says one thing and her ass does something totally different."

Nakeita sat back and grinned, she loved when Toni was not around because Wonder and Tasha were able to speak freely. Nakeita had control of these absent moments because once Toni's name fell into the equation, every stone was going to be unturned. The *411* gets dropped like it's hot.

"If Toni plays her cards right, she can be living in a mansion," Nakeita said.

"A mansion my ass," Wonder huffed. "That bitch wanna stay in this position. You can't kick the Ho out of this funky-ass trail. She loves the ghetto. She's afraid to try another lifestyle; she's scared she'll miss something."

"The ghetto?" Tasha chided and moaned. "Bone, bone, bone…Talking bout the ghetto…"

"A change gonna come the girl way one day," Nakeita stated.

"When?" Wonder asked, with an attitude. "When hell freezes?"

"Naw, before then," Nakeita replied.

"When, Nakeita? When winter comes in July? When all the people in hell get a drink of ice water?" Wonder interjected.

"I aint even gonna lie," Tasha said, raising her right hand. "I know I have done some dummy shit in life before."

"Try plenty," Wonder interfered.

"But, I ain't dumb enough to let a mothafucka like Gary get away. If the man wants to buy me a house, I'ma let him. Shit, with the truth being told, I need somebody son, husband or grandfather to teach me the bigger and better things," Tasha stated.

"Tupac said it best when he said, 'why keep explaining the game when no one listens and still stuck in the same position," Nakeita yawned out while covering her mouth. Her aching body let it be known that it was time for sleep, but she refused to obey the body, afraid she might miss out on something.

"You know, Run DMC, made a song about Toni ass," Tasha said, giggling like a seventh grader, "dumb, dumb, dumb, dumb," she chided, "the girl is dumb!"

Shortly after, Toni walked in the house with an arm full of bags.

"What y'all no good ass ho's in here talking about?" she asked with a good sense of humor.

"You," Wonder stated.

"Shit, ho, if it all came from you then it was a compliment," Toni replied, and started filling their minds on some more of Gary's offerings. which she accepted the gifts, she only wanted the money Gary donated her way. Toni did not want him to think or feel like he owned her, so that was her biggest reason for accepting the small gifts. He was asset and not her liability.

"Y'all ho's listen up… There isn't a damn thing broken in my relationship with Gary, so there isn't a bitch ass thing that needs fixing," Toni announced.

"Excuse me, bitch," Wonder said.

"Yeah, ho... I knew a hit Dog would holla," Toni responded.

Tasha began making the noise of a lonely puppy, and they all had to laugh.

***

"Bru, we went by them ho's trailer, they had a yard full of Bentley and Beama's…" Jazz lied while laying his right hand on Bell's shoulder.

"Cut it out," Bell replied, as he choked with laughter.

Life phoned him immediately at his baby's mother's apartment once they pulled up to Toni to tell Bell that the girls had more company then the law would allow. The yard was loaded with senior citizens old model and beat up vehicles, and majority of the cars carried a senior citizen sticker.

"Yeah, Playboy, we couldn't lay and play there last night," Life reminded.

"Them old senior muthafucka's are the true Ballers, huh?" Kenny asked, joking.

"Toni said them old farts spend that bread and give them some head," Bell revealed, spitting Toni's words verbatim, not trying to add or take away anything from her sentence. "Them Senior Citizen can't get all the honey, they just wanna give away some of that first and fifteen of the month money." Bell replied. "And get a quickie as the Easter Bunny."

"Well, tonight is our night… I know that," Kenny said. Life held his fist close to his mouth as he laughed. "Damn, man, did y'all niggas see how ugly Kenny looked when he said that? Damn, Kenny, my nigga, you are one ugly mothafucka… Yeah, you one ugly ass, Brotha…"

"Shit, I couldn't get my lil' dick wet last night either, so I guess that makes me one ugly and mad mothafucka, too… "Jazz said, as he gave Kenny a wink. Kenny was his true partner; they had a lot in common. Jazz always stuck-up for Kenny whenever they begun to crack their jokes.

"So what you pretty ass niggas… What you gonna do? You gon' sit here and talk shit and swallow spit? Or is we gonna go over to them, ho's, raggedy-ass trailer?" Kenny asked and took a super long drink from his liquor bottle. He looked even uglier as the hot and nasty liquor washed down his throat.

"Shit," Jazz exhaled, "Now that's what the fuck I'm talking about playa, playa, playa…" He walked over to Kenny and gave him some dap, "my nigga, now what that Adidas shit stand for again?"

"All day I dream about sex…" Kenny huffed and puffed out.

Bell was ready to get to the trail as well because he had a bone to pick with Wonder. She had no right telling Nakeita about their business. And he was craving for another taste of her sugar walls also. With Wonder, he did not have to worry about pubic hairs getting caught in his throat because her vagina was shaved bald and smoother than a newborn baby's ass.

"Man, that bitch, Wonder," Bell began, "Can't hold water. She put a Nigga ass dead on blast!"

"That's why you don't suppose to eat out, you suppose to eat at home," Life said, laughing, putting Bell's business out in the open so that now Jazz and Kenny were aware of Life's reason for laughing. As a result, they joined in, and Bell couldn't help but to release his anger with a smile as well.

"No matter what, Boy, she still gonna continue being your, boo," Life said, as he held his longneck beer bottle in Bell direction.

"She gonna always be our boo, my nigga, check yourself before you fuck around and wreck yourself. I love her and my young nigga J loves the ground her dirty draws wearing ass walks on!" Life said, giving Jazz some dap.

"Tonight, Pimpin', we gonna run a train on her ass. You start off with the head and I'll start off with the tail, and after we both bust, we'll holla switch!" Jazz suggested, giving Kenny another pound.

"Why can't I start off with the tail and you start off with the head?" Kenny asked, with a smile. Honestly, he couldn't careless which hole he sunk his ship in. He was just ready to be about it, instead of continuing talking about it.

"You ain't said shit but a word," Jazz told him and addressed Bell since he had the keys to their step-father's truck.

"Bru, Bru, let's get the wheel in motion, so we can go play in the ocean."

"Yeah, all talk with no action ain't bout shit," Kenny breathed.

"Preach ugh Preach," Life shot the joke at, Kenny.

"For once in a life time, Life, I'll have to say amen to that," Jazz said.

Bell raced upstairs to his bedroom and went under his mattress collecting the last four condoms. He gave his brother two and kept the other two for himself. Jazz threw both of his into the kitchen trashcan. He realized that the only way he could use these rubbers was if he were in a water balloon fight. He chuckled to himself at his own private joke.

***

Ebony walked to the mailbox massaging the right side of her head. She had a terrible headache for the last couple of days and the headache didn't seem to be going away. She went to bed with it and woke up with it.

Once she arrived at the thirty-six inch steel mailbox, Ebony exhaled as she leaned up against it for support. Her eyes scanned the box until she found her house number. While shifting through the mail, Ebony over-looked her bills since she had to make payments as always. Three pieces of mail for her daughter caused her to stagger, making her headache begin to kick in more like a pregnant woman's baby. Ebony wasted no time at all opening up the first letter addressed to Nakeita.

"Oh, my God," she cried out. As she read on, the sheet stated that they wanted to give Nakeita a free Scholarship and that they were impressed with her grades and three point two GPA. Another missive was an invitation. They invited Nakeita to come to their college for the summer to get a feel of how it would be in college and around college students. They were also very interested in recruiting her as well. The last missive was from the school giving Nakeita a certificate for perfect attendance and for making all 'A's' and 'B's' on her report card for the whole semester. Tears raced down Ebony face, she loved her daughter and wondered for the millionth time where she went wrong and why was Nakeita wilding out? She gave her everything and anything she wanted. Ebony could only blame herself for keeping that leash around Nakeita neck too tight. No tight cloths, be home by no later than 9:30PM, and no grade less than a 'B' average on her report card. By making the decision for her that she was definitely going to college, she had her daughter's life planned out because Ebony wanted her baby to be successful and independent. Most of all, she truly was afraid that if she did not handle Nakeita with proper guidance and knowledge, she would be easily mislead down the wrong path and her future would easily slip through her fingertips.

"Oh, God, what am I gonna do?"

"Lord, I beg you Lord please don't allow my Baby to be led astray".

"Lord, Lord, Lord… have mercy on my child, she knows not what she do, protect her, Lord…" Ebony laid her head on the mailbox as if it was the shoulder of the Lord. She continued to shed tears and pour out her heart. "Oh, Lord, help me Lord, strengthen me."

Chapter 17

Tasha tried her damndest to teach Nakeita how to dance sexy. She was going to give her the fundamentals of basic stripper dances. Nakeita thought the moves Tasha taught her were nothing more than a joke. Nakeita loved to dance, but becoming a professional stripper was far from her agenda. Her mother had raised her with morals, so she didn't have the nerve to stand before men half naked, let alone completely naked. In trying to find the guts to get with the explicit moves she was being taught, she gave Tasha a disgusted look.

"Girl I'm sorry, but stripping ain't for me."

"So you done had me up there all that time wasting my energy," Tasha exhaled, dropping down in her seat.

"Aint nobody told your crazy ass to show them nothing," Wonder said, grinning.

Tasha gave Wonder a sour look, "Shut up."

"T, I can give you a few lessons," Nakeita paused, giving Tasha the opportunity to decline, but it did not happen.

"Yeah, she can use some lessons, some new moves to improve her stripper swag. Nakeita girl, some damn body needs to teach her ass something and girl nasty as you dance, shit that'll probably have mo Nigga's making them dollar bills rain on her ass. Cause sometimes Tasha be dancing stiff as a mothafucka," Wonder said.

"Tasha, you gonna let me upgrade ya?" Nakeita joked.

"Look who's talking," Tasha gave Wonder an ugly smirk. "Ain't you got some damn nerves? Bitch, I'll out dance your no dancing ass any damn day!"

"Don't out dance me, get mo paper than me," Wonder challenged. "Yeah, Bitch that's what the fuck you do, cause I'm truly a walking ATM Machine. And I don't always have to shake my money maker."

"Bitch, sometimes I can't stand yo' ass," Tasha rolled her eyes.

Wonder threw Tasha a wicked smile. "Ho that's ok. Your ass will get over it."

"Huh," Tasha mumbled, sucking her teeth.

"Huh, my ass," Wonder replied, digging between her breast to expose a sack of X-pills. "I got something to make you love me, Bitch" she sassed, swinging the sack over head as if trying to hypnotize Tasha.

Nakeita sat quietly, smiling from ear to ear. As her eyes darted back and forth between Wonder and Tasha, she couldn't wait to hear the next reply, as both of their faces mirrored a smile.

"Oh, Bitch, now all of a fuckin' sudden you can't stand me, huh"? Wonder asked, waling over at Tasha as she continued swirling the pill sack. "Say you love me, and I'll give you a couple."

"Bitch, you gonna break me off regardless," Tasha scolded, rolling her neck.

Wonder mimicked her neck rotation.

"I ain't gotta do jack shit, but two damn things and that's stay black and die."

Tasha snatched the sack out of Wonder's hand and buried the sack in the front of her panties.

Wonder dived on her, and Nakeita cried with laughter as the girls wrestled.

"H-e-e-elp! Somebody help me, this bitch is trying to rape me," Tasha managed to laugh out. "Somebody please help me. Rape! Rape!"

"Bitch, you can holla all that rape shit you want to. Ho, I'm gone get back what's mine," Wonder said, trying to rip Tasha's small ass shorts off her waist.

"H-e-e-elp! Rape! Rape!" Tasha playfully screamed.

"Bitch, you can scream until your damn ass gets blue in the face, but I ain't stopping until I get my damn sack," Wonder shouted.

Tasha jumped off the couch and tried to run, but soon as she climbed to her feet, the pill sack fell from between her legs onto the floor. Wonder dived on the floor to retrieve her sack.

"Bitch, you ain't shit and you ain't got shit," Wonder huffed and puffed, barely able to get her words out.

"Damn! I almost had that bitch's shit," Tasha snapped her fingers, sounding disappointed.

"Almost is not good enough, "Wonder replied.

"I know," Tasha said, walking over to Wonder. She sat down on the couch beside her and smiled, while Wonder secured the sack on the opposite side of her.

"I ain't gonna try to snatch it no mo," Tasha promised.

"Just make sure," Wonder laughed. "Cause I ain't gonna put this bitch close to your funky ass no mo. Girl, you done funked up my bag wit' yo stanky pussy. When the last time you washed your funky ass?"

"Ain't that a damn lie? I ain't funk up shit. I wash my ass every day and some damn time two or three times a day," Tasha corrected.

"Nakeita, that bitch is lying. Tasha doesn't have one bone nowhere in her damn body that tells the truth," claimed Wonder.

"Not even in her toe?" Nakeita questioned, playing along.

"Not even in her damn toe," Wonder said, laughing.

"I just wanna party," Tasha chanted the magic words, springing off the sofa. As she started dancing and snapping her fingers, she continued chatting, "I just wanna party."

Wonder was first to fall in line, she and Tasha pulled Nakeita out of her seat, so she could join them in their anthem. Moments later Wonder was loading Nakeita and Tasha's waiting palms with their medication. The magic pill they considered to be an energy booster as it often made them care free.

As soon as daylight came to a close, Wonder led Nakeita down the dangerous road, which was well known as the strip prostitutes made their money. Females from every nationality were posted on the block, trying to sell their bodies for a little of nothing. There were even a bunch of transvestites strutting up and down the stroll, or posted up on light poles in search of a trick. Years earlier when Wonder's mother fell on hard times, she used to bring her to this spot. Her mother came here sure she would escape their financial hardship.

"Them lil junky bitches worse than crackheads," fussed one redhead prostitute. She was accustomed to seeing Wonder, Tasha and Toni on the strip, but this was her very first time lying eyes on Nakeita. Her pimp informed her that she didn't have to worry bout them young ass bitches sucking up all the papers or catching the majority of the tricks, because as soon as they made a couple hundred dollars, they would be gone. And if the pill man tackled the block, they were gonna leave even quicker cause they were going to trick off with him for a fix.

"I know two young bitches out here looking for a pill man," the prostitute shouted. "Anybody know where the pill man is? Anybody seen the pill man?"

"The sooner the better," the prostitute's wife-in-law said with a lot of fear in her voice. She was afraid they might not be able to meet their Pimp's daily fee before it was time for them to pay up.

"We'll have Daddy's five hundred dollars a piece by midnight, cause if we don't make it by slinging ass, then we'll rob one of these damn John's or those two young ass bitches," the red head prostitute stated, hoping to calm her down. Wonder locked eyes with the prostitutes and got chills.

"That redhead bitch gives me the fucking creeps every time I come down here," Wonder confessed.

Nakeita looked in the two prostitute's direction. The slim pretty one had a shoulder length black weave and a huge mole on the side of her nose.

"You looking for a date, Sweety?" she said, smiling as a male crossed her path? When she blew him a kiss, Nakeita noticed that she had a gap between her two front top teeth. The prostitute held open her fake, ankle length solid white fur coat, showing off her large fake breast and her flat stomach, the result of a tummy tuck. Her Momma cat was hairless. Nakeita's eyes soaked up this part of the jungle and prayed to God that she did not get caught up in this spider web. Nakeita's heart was pounding with each and every step she took, this scene scared her to death. The pills she'd earlier taken like candy were wearing off fast. *I ain't never seen nothing like this before ,* Nakeita swallowed hard.

"This is like some shit I've seen on TV. And it didn't look this bad. This looks so spooky, don't it Wonder?"

Wonder wasn't trying to hear nothing Nakeita was saying. She wasn't talking about the Benjamin's, so she wasn't listening, cause in Wonder's eyes all she saw was dollar signs, and she knew from first hand experiences that this place was the spot to get it and get it quick.

Wonder scanned the area. Her eyes lit up like a Christmas tree once she located her target. The fifteen year-old boy, Ace wanted to be known as the pill man. She would always have the youngster tricking off his whole sack just to get get a taste of her twat.

"The games I run on these guys are so old, but brand ass new to a sucka!" She mumbled, picking up her pace. Nakeita had to jog here and there just to keep up with Wonder's fast walking, her long legs definitely putting her in the wind.

"First come, first served," Wonder mumbled, knowing she had to beat the other pill head females to the youngster. He was good about tricking off everything with the first female to open her legs to him. If there wasn't no such thing called X-pills, he would still be a virgin. He enjoyed this sex strip more then anyone else.

"The freaks surely come out at night," Ace whispered, watching Wonder and Nakeita close in the distance. "Got damn, who's that other chick? Oh, just as sho as grits are grocery, I definitely gotta get me a piece of her."

Wonder walked into Ace's embrace.

"Ace, baby, you looking good today….umm umm, and you sho' smell good as hell."

After their embrace, he put a lot of focus on Nakeita.

"Boo, who's our friend? You know how this shit works, your friend's - our friend."

Wonder smiled, looking over at nervous Nakeita.

"Oh, Ace, this is my friend Nakeita. Nakeits, this is a very good friend of ours. His name is Big Ace."

Nakeita manage to deliver a fake smile, as Ace tipped his hat in her direction.

"Wonder, y'all going back to the hotel with me so we can have some fun?" Ace question, rubbing both of his palms together. "Party, party, party."

"We wouldn't miss it for nothing in the world," Wonder replied. "Less snatch up some weed and beer while we out and about."

"That sound like a great plan to me," Ace said, putting more attention on Nakeita. "Say Shawty what's up? You can't talk? What, the cat got your tongue?"

Wonder stepped closer to Ace. He took her hand, making her finger tips lightly drag down the side of his face.

"Ace, my girl is a little uncomfortable. This is her first time in this area. I had a hard time convincing her to come down her with me so I could try to find you," Wonder told half lie and half truth.

"So you can find me, huh?" Ace blushed. "Wonder, girl, you full of surprises."

"Let's just say I know how to keep the party going," Wonder smirked.

"Now that's my kinda girl," Ace said, stroking one of her shoulders. "Y'all ready to blow this spot, cause ain't shit out here for us?"

Nakeita hesitantly nodded yes to his question.

"Lead the way, Big Daddy, and we'll follow," Wonder said in a sexy seductive voice. As she became Ace right arm piece, he looked back at Nakeita.

"Baby girl, you know we waiting on you, darling. So, sweetheart feel free to join in at any given time." Nakeita stepped up, becoming Ace's left arm piece. "Now that's what I'm talking about," Ace paused, smiling. "A dime on each arm."

"Only for you Big Daddy," Wonder giggled like a little school girl.

"Ma, you ain't gotta be afraid of me," he addressed Nakeita. "I don't bite, but if you do fuck around and bite me, I will bite'cha back."

Wonder laughed along with Ace because there was no question about it, she was definitely his yes man, and she made it quite clear that she had no problems kissing his ass behind closed doors or in public. As she talked with Ace towards their desitination, before they could reach the corner a blue and white police car blocked their path. Ace slipped from between Wonder and Nakeita, clearly aware of the fact that the cops weren't interested in him. From being on the strip so much, the law enforcement primarily had the females on their radar.

"Fresh meat," one said, understanding that everyone was accustomed to the law of the land. Yet, John and Brandy were after sex favors. It wasn't business on this night for them.

Brandy jumped out of the passenger's seat with his black night stick.

"You two get against the car. You know the routine, palms on the hood and spread'em fucking wide."

Nakeita looked in all directions. Her eyes full of fear, reflecting a look of, "please help me."

As Ace spread both palms, he hunched both shoulders. "I'm sorry ladies, but there's nothing I can do. I don't have a pussy," he laughed, continuing to travel down the street.

John walked around to Nakeita side playfully smacking his night stick in his palm.

"Don't fucking stare at me. Stare at the fucking hood."

"Y'all come down here and work my fucking streets, without my permission," Brandy spit.

The two dirty cops knew every female who worked these streets part time or full time. They made it their business to get to know them.

"You fucking trespassing. That's what the fuck you are doing. Y'all two are in big trouble for coming on my property. These are my grounds," John shouted, his nose inches away from Nakeita. She wanted to break down and cry.

"I-I-I- aint doing nothing," her trembling lips released, as four tear drops splashed on the hood.

"You didn't do nothing," John screamed in her face with his drill Sgt. Voice. Nakeita couldn't believe her eyes. While they were in the hands of these angry and intimidating cops, no one stopped to see whether they were alright.

"Don't I know you?" Brandy exercised his voice with Wonder.

She shook her head left and right, mumbling a dry, "No."

Brandy cupped her chin. "I'm pretty sure I've seen your lil hot ass prancing up and down my streets before. And every damn time before I can get my paws on your ass, you seem to vanish. But I got news for your young ass today, this is one fucking time you can't close your fucking pretty eyes and disappear."

"You got my money?" John screamed on Nakeita.

She was so afraid it was possible for her to have a heart attack or nervous breakdown at any second. He began frisking her. He started with her breast while his erect prick ground against her butt. She felt totally disrespected and humiliated. Her whole body shook with fear and it turned the dirty cop on even more. The exact same thing took place with Wonder. She knew their wasn't a damn thing she could do about it, so she played along with Brandy's game by spreading her legs even wider and grinding her butt cheeks up against his manhood, which he was no stranger to. On a regular basis, that's what all the ho's, hookers and prostitute would do if they were in Wonder or Nakeita's shoes.

"I'm sure we can work this little misunderstanding out young lady, don't you agree?" He whispered to Wonder.

"Urnmm, Hmmm," she replied, with pain in her voice. "It would be my pleasure to resolve this quickly."

"Oh God, I got a live one," Brandy said, louder than he meant to.

This Cracker thinks he's taking my black ass to jail, he got another thought coming. I'mma let him skeet then I'll be as free as a damn bird, Wonder thought. She saw the sad expression on Nakeita's face and felt sorry for her. She knew she had to be strong for the both of them.

"You think your friend likes me too?" Wonder said, catching John's attention.

"He probably can't handle what he's already got," Brandy assured with a chuckle.

John didn't like the sound of that.

"You want me to haul your ass to jail?" he screamed at Nakeita. She did not know how to begin to answer the question, so he repeated his question and also grab a hand full of her hair, jerking her head back into his chest.

"Hooker do I need to take you to jail tonight?"

"No please no," she cried out.

"I think I do," John said, changing his voice to a more friendly tone.

"I don't wanna go to jail," Nakeita whispered.

John had to strain to hear her words. The sound of loud heels could be heard, the clicking sound grew closer. Once the shoes stopped connecting with the concrete, there was a smooth and friendly voice.

"Say, J and B what kinda problem do we have here, gentlemen?"

The cops knew the voice belong to Pimp Black, so they were not in any rush to face him. The pimp immediately noticed Wonder and Nakeita the moment they stepped on the scene. *"There goes those pissy tail heifers, they don't want no real bread, they just want the crumbs off the bread,*" he joked with himself as he first laid eyes on them. "*Shit, they don't want the crumbs, cause they giving it up for a couple pills.*"

Black knew Wonder's M.O., but he had to study Nakeita a little more. Her figure, her face, he knew her from somewhere.

"*Man I ran across lil Momma some damn where,*" he racked his brain, trying to remember. "*Fine as she is, under no circumstances could I allow her young ass to escape this pimpin. She could be my prize, and the lead of my stable any time. She could lighten the load on my wagon.*"

After ten full minutes of thinking, he finally remembered. Some time ago, he saw Silk walk into a restaurant hugged up with Nakeita. He remembered congratulating Silk for having a show stopper. Silk became angry, voicing harshly, "*This is my goddaughter and if I ever hear of some pervert disrespecting her, I'll break his body in two with my bare hands,*" Silk growled, with his eyes mirroring death. Pimp Black caught chills, revisiting the moment in Silks present. This situation wasn't his call of duty, but for some strange reason, he felt this was his obligation.

"Black, mind your business,"John said.

"Fellas this is my business," Pimp Black smiled. "Come on you guys, we've known each other for too long and always done good business together. You know I don't get in nobody's business." John abandoned Nakeita and faced Pimp Black. He carried a serious grudge against him, due to the fact that Black had twelve white girls hoing out of a house and no matter how bad he wanted to shut Black's operation down, there wasn't a damn thing he could do about it.

"You too damn smart for your on damn good, ain't you boy," John said, with a venomous expression.

"What's the trouble?" Black asked, smiling.

"You the damn problem," John replied.

"Who, me?" Black asked, with a more serious expression.

"Fuck yeah, you! That's who."

"J-Man if I'm the problem, then don't take the problem out on my girls. We both men; let's discuss this like the gentlemen we are. That way we both can get back to our order of business and or families, which ever matters once this conversation ends."

Black used reverse psychology on John. John had four daughters. His

23-year-old and the 20 year-old always gave Black a second glance. Black was pretty popular in the city, and John would've murder Black many, many year ago if he thought he could've gotten away without any repercussions.

The tension in the air began to grow thick. Several small crowds begin to form behind Black. The young thugs, drug dealers and gang bangers stood with their chest poked out, hands behind their backs, or tucked under their sweater.

"Yo, O.G., is everything alright?" One of the gang bangers asked concerned.

"I don't know, I'm afraid that answer will have to come from Johnny Boy," Black said with cockiness in his voice.

Brandy did not want for his partner in crime to make this situation any uglier than it needed to be. Besides, they were outnumbered. There were groups of young brothers on every corner with weapons, and both cops knew from experience that youngsters now days were packing guns that held forty round clips. They also carried extra clips that forced a gun fight to last for days. Brandy exhaled, shaking off his gut thought, knowing it was time to think with his big head and not with his lil one. While holding both palms face level, he began speaking in a peaceful language.

"Now Black, you have been in show business for too long. You know from time to time my partner and I like to sample the merchandise."

"It ain't what you do, but how you do it," spoke Black".

"You know what, you are absolutely right," Brandy replied."

A drug dealer cleaned his throat. "Big Homie, we have a problem! Do we need to air this mothafucka out?"

"You already know these bitches can get it," a thug said. "That tin foil badge this bitch got pinned on his fucking chest doesn't give him the authority to fuck over people. This mothafucka can play dumb and get some. You know I enjoy wetting a bitch up. Shit, that's how I get my fucking hard on."

Black locked eyes with John, but John wasn't any fool. He knew if he breathed wrong, these guys were going to fill him with lead.

"You know how this shit works, you pay the cost to be the boss," stated John,

"You know I ain't got no problem with that," Black smiled. "I love to pay my taxes. I pay well, too! I'm like a slot machine!" he said, removing ten one hundred dollar bills from his bank roll. Brandy stepped forward to collect five big ones for him and the other five were for his partner.

"Yo! Black you know me and my partner take all of this as business and it's not nothing personal, right?"

"Business is business," Black agreed.

"Me and my partner are not here to get violent. Man, we're strictly about the Benjamin's," Brandy felt a need to say. He dealt with so many street guys; he finally started sounding like them.

"Yeah that's cool, B, but you can't speak for Johnny B too," Black said.

John gritted the hell out of his back teeth, because Black had altered his name.

"Na, we aint got no beef."

"Spit it like you mean it, Baby," Black popped slick.

Brandy patted John on the shoulder.

"B, you know for yourself me and my partner here are two of the good guys. Yeah the last of the dying breed."

"Last of the dying breed, huh?" Black corrected.

"You can bet your ass on it," Brandy replied.

"Say O.G, what's the word?" The gang banger inquired.

Black did not have to reply, because Brady spoke up before the young ones decided to become trigger happy.

"Everything here is all dandy. Everyone can go on back to doing whatever rocks their boat."

"So if everything is all lovely, then why do you still possess my property? Release the hostages," Black demanded.

Brandy turned to Wonder, waving her on in front of Black that her and Nakeita were free to go. She walked over and stood by Black, while Nakeita had an emotional breakdown. When Black lifted her from the hood of the cruiser, she cried as he carried her away.

Wonder couldn't help but ask Black why he went through so much trouble for them? For the first time in his life he did not have an answer.

"Man them two pieces of shit cops always trying to be the judge and the jury, "one of the thugs publicized.

"The best thing God gave the people is choices. My ho's choose to do things by choice, and I hate to see people doing things by force and most of all, I hate to see people being taken advantage of," Black expressed.

"Sir, thank you for saving me," Nakeita moaned.

"Don't thank me, thank your Godfather Silk. I felt like I owed him this much," Black grinned. "And I felt like I could at least do this for him."

Nakeita's heart was beating a hundred miles per hour at the mention of Silk's name. She held her chest as if Black did not know any better. From her actions, he would've thought she was about to have a heart attack in his arms.

"Nakeita, who is Silk?" Wonder asked looking concerned.

"He's my Godfather," Nakeita said, tearing. "Misters, please don't tell Silk," Nakeita pleaded.

"I don't get in grown folks business. I'm not ready to go to my own funeral," Black said, grinning at his own joke.

"Black, I owe you big time," Wonder admitted. "How can I repay you?"

"By staying the fuck off of my territory," he stopped walking. "If I ever catch one of you in my neck of the woods again, I'm gonna handle you like you my property. I'ma kick your panties in your ass. Do you understand me?"

"Yes," Wonder whispered.

"Yeah, you better understand, just don't fuck around and over stand. Because if you fuck around and do, that's where the fucking problem will come in at."

***

Ms. Matty Mae Strong was wondering what Nakeita was up to now days. She looked forward to her and her friend visit. She enjoyed their company. The last time they were over her house, she wondered what the conversation she tried to pry into was all about. She hoped to God that she didn't run them away from her, and for their young sakes, they needed to start running to her more often, so they could suck up the wisdom and knowledge she had to offer. She wanted to phone Ebony to ask a few questions about her grandbaby, but she did not want to further upset Ebony. She learned Nakeita got kicked out of the house from Betty and wished Nakeita would've come to her for help. She thought about what she would have told her.

Nakeita Baby, I told you that damn Bell boy was no earthly good just like his damn daddy, but naw you wouldn't listen to me. Child, you thought I was just an old senile woman, but I been in the world longer then you. Some things in life you won't have to go through, if you listen to me. Child, all you have to do is sit your tail down and listen to the people who love you. Ebony aint gonna tell you nothing wrong. Your mother gonna always be there for you. You never let one of these pissy tail boys come between you and your mother. Soon as one of them no good boys break your heart, you gonna run right back to your mother and she gonna always have her door and arms open for you. Baby Big Momma gonna pray for you. I wish you do the right thing and take your tail back home to Ebony cause she worrying sick about you.

Chapter 18

Silk walked in the front door and placed his coat and hat on the hat rack.

"Hi Honey, I'm home."

"Silk, I'm in the kitchen," Betty replied.

Silk entered the kitchen, untying his tie. He kissed Betty on the lips.

"Hello Beautiful, did you miss me, cause I sure missed you?"

"Yes, I missed you. So how was work today?"

He removed a glass from the dish rack and filled it with warm water from the faucet.

"Work today was just beautiful," Silk said, dropping down in a chair across from her. "So Sweetheart, what have you been up to today? Besides missing me?" He said, taking a sip from his glass. Silk loved nothing more than to look into his wife's beautiful eyes.

"Bout an hour ago, I just got off the phone with Ms. Matty Mae Strong"

He recognized the sad disappointment in Betty eyes.

"So what did Momma Matty Mae Strong have to say?" He took another couple of sips from his glass. "I hope everything is alright. Actually, I have been meaning to drop by her place."

"We talked about Nakeita," Betty said, leaning back in her seat as if the largest burden had been hibernating in her for a few decades.

"One of you spoke with her?"

"No."

"Where she's staying?"

"Silk, we still don't know."

"Lord have mercy on her precious soul, "Silk dropped his eyes to the table. "I hope she's not somewhere with that same guy who came between her and Ebony."

"She probably is. He's probably her first love. You know how these girls get when they think they in love."

"If so Betty, then that makes things even worse," Silk paused, lifting Betty's chin to look into her eyes. "So Sweetheart, did you allow your first love to force you to break a few of your mother's rules?"

"I guess so," Betty smiled. "Only a few, but he couldn't get me to do no insane shit like run away from home."

"Did you sneak him into your bedroom?"

Betty began to smile, because she was fully aware of where her husband was going with his selection of questions.

"I'm sure just about every girl has let a boy into their house."

"In their house, or in their bedroom?"

"Silk, what is your point?"

He leaned back in his seat crossing his leg.

"We all have made mistakes. Some of us have made more than others, but my point is this. No one is excluded from making mistakes and I'm sure that sooner or later Nakeita will come to her senses and capitalize from the error or errors that she has made. I love her dearly and would give the world to have here. Betty, I've see the hurt in your eyes every day. I hear the pain in Ebony's voice each and every time I speak with her. I know this thing with Nakeita is eating Ebony, Momma Matty Mae Strong and you alive," Silk took Betty's hand into his. "My Love, when you hurt - I hurt. I feel your pain, and I'll be glad when Nakeita brings her tail home, because she's causing stress in our home and relationship. Now all Ebony wanna do is stay cooped up in her apartment. This thing is extremely too hard for her. It seems like it's too much for her to bare. I only wish there was something I could say to ease her pain."

Betty tightened Silk's grip. She was aware of him spending late hours in the streets, searching high and low for Nakeita. He hoped he could run her down and talk some sense into her. He wanted to get her to think more seriously about her behavior before it was too late. He would say a prayer for her every night before going to bed, and say another one for her and for himself in the morning, immediately after opening his eyes. Now he closed his eyes and said another small prayer.

"Lord please protect this young and decent child. Please open her eyes and bring her into the light. I am one of your sinners, asking for forgiveness. If there's anyone who needs to be punished, please allow it to be me. Dear Lord please, I beg you not to allow her to come face to face with any challenges that she can't bear. Amen!"

When he opened his eyes, Betty was standing at the sink. Silk went over and hugged her from behind. She laid back into his embrace and cried as if she were a newborn baby. She cried for Ebony, for Darrel and most all for Nakeita. She loved Nakeita to death and now she felt helpless because there was nothing she could do to help and protect Nakeita.

"S-s-sh-sh," Silk tried to calm down Betty. He knew her heart was heavy, very, very, heavy. "Baby, I'll find her. I'll find her. I promise you that I'll find Nakeita and bring her home. I will not give up on her."

"Please do Silk, please do. You know we are all she has and by her going through life without that father figure it's extremely hard on her," Betty sneered. "She looks up to you."

"I know Sweetheart, I know," Silk said, stroking her hair.

"Silk?"

"Yes, Sweetheart?"

"Nakeita loves you like a father. I think for us, when a daughter cries, all we ever want and desire is to be in the comfort of our father's arms."

"Yeah, Yeah, and a daughter's cry will break a real father down to his knees, if he's unable to help his child through her problems. And because I've been there for her since birth, I really love her as if she's my biological daughter."

***

Toni staggered into the living room, wiping sleep from her eyes. She slept late this morning because she had a long night. She made the tender mistake of feeding her lover two ecstasy pills, so they had some of the roughest sex for five hours and fifty nine minutes straight. He tried to pound on her body all night long, but she lied about needing to get a soda out of the hotel soda machine, and instead of getting a soda, she hitch hiked her tail straight home. The only reason she coached him into taking the pill in the first place was because his sex performance was hitting on zero. He was equipped with the tool, but did not know how to use it.

He did not have a clue as to how to satisfy his sex partner.

"That nigga had all that damn meat and didn't know how to use it. I turned that zero into a hero," she yelled, as she stretched.

"Ha girl, I thought your ass was gonna be knocked out for at least half of the day," Tasha said, when she heard Toni dragging her feet and yelling.

"You thought wrong."

"Shit that aint nothing new."

"My house was too damn quiet, and that's what woke me up."

"Tell another lie? Your ass was scared you might miss out on something."

"And that too," Toni admitted, stretching out on the couch.

"Put some clothes on," Tasha frowned, "Ain't nobody trying to look at your naked ass. Toni was wearing some red thongs and a matching tank top that stopped inches from her belly button.

"Ho, you forgot, this my fucking house?" Toni rubbed her stomach from where the guy was going so deep after he took the powder pellet that he left her gut sore and feeling like it would fall out at any given moment.

"So where them two knuckle heads?"

"They out there somewhere hunting."

"That's good."

"I got em' good and loaded with the pills, so Nakeita can handle the mood swing," Tasha laughed. "I got rid of all those butterflies she had in her damn stomach. Wonder took her to the fast track."

"I hope she was ready for the ho stroll," Toni yelled, "Y'all sluts might have took the little girl too fast."

"She had to come off that leash. Shit, it was now or never."

Toni continued rubbing her stomach. She did not have any objections to Tasha's suggestion. "So what else is new?"

"Child please!" Tasha smacked her lips. "You know as well as I do, same old day, just different shit."

"My stomach hurts," Toni cried, rubbing her stomach again. "I don't feel too good."

"You might be pregnant, girl."

"Try I'm far from that."

Tasha sprang from the couch. "Don't worry. I got something to fix that small problem of yours," she said, getting six ecstasy pills. "Girl, you know as well as I do that these little babys are the body mechanics." With that, Tasha begin making airplane noises and telling Toni to open her mouth up wide, so she could land the airplane inside. After placing four pills on Toni's tongue she said, "Now shut your damn mouth before a damn fly flies in there."

"What I'mma wash'em down with my spit?"

Tasha jumped to her rescue by giving her a full glass of cold water. Once Toni's bloodstream became one hundred percent polluted, she couldn't sit still nor keep her mouth closed. She stated the less clothes she had on, the sexier she felt. Toni became extremely feminine.

"Girl, sit your ass down. You're acting like a bitch in heat."

"Maybe I am," Toni said. Before she took the pills, her thoughts were on sex and the love making session from the night before. So now her body enhanced the thought.

"Shake that money maker; shake that money maker," Wonder sang, trying to get Toni in one of her shit talking moods, but to no avail. "I aint seen Bell and them lately."

Toni rubbed up and down her body. "I need to be his lollipop," she laughed. "Those lil boys can't handle me. I'm too much woman for them. I have to turn my sexy game down when I'm dealing with them."

"You go girl."

"I'm the best thing that ever came into those little boy's life. That damn Bell can't seem to get enough of me."

"And you too."

Toni done a cute spin. "I feel so sorry for Nakeita because she's a little girl. Bell using her as a substitution, so he can be victorious, but like I said when he came in contact with real woman of our caliber, we'll have his ass eating out the palm of our hands. I trained Bell. I turned him into a professional; that's my work. I taught him everything he knows. Yeah, I created that Pac-Man."

"We gonna see. I'mma hold you to that."

"I expect you to."

"If Bell pulls up right now, bitch you will eat them words." Tasha said, grinning. She covered her mouth because Toni had her crying with her slick comments.

"The only thing Bell will be eating is my cookies." Suddenly, they hear the sound of a vehicle. "Girl, I'll be damn if I don't talk about the devil and the damn devil shows up. Bell, Life, Kenny and Bell lil brotha Jazz is out there."

"The more the merrier, I'm a meat lover," Toni started, performing like a tiger.

***

Bell looked in Jazz direction, "You wanna drive?"

"Fuck yeah," Jazz's said, knowing damn well he didn't have a lick'em license. Life jumped in the back seat. As he closed the door, the first joke escaped his lips.

"Yo J, you know K-mart got a special going."

Jazz frowned. "Man, I don' fuck with no K-mart like that. So what kind of special they have for me?" he asked, shifting the ignition into first gear.

"A set of license," Life laughed.

"Don't worry Playa, I got me some outta the bubble gum machine, "Jazz replied, eyeing Life in the rearview mirror with a cocky smile.

"Shit Life! Man, in that fucking case, you need to get you a set," Kenny said.

"And you need to get you a couple of them Halloween masks K-mart got on sale," Life responded.

"Boy, K-mart be full of them barely legal too," Bell reported, wanting to change their conversation. To him, it was too early for the bullshit. 24/7 his mind stayed in the gutter, and focused on getting laid.

"Damn Baby this gas hand's on E," Jazz revealed.

"Hit the gas station," Bell ordered. "Y'all nigga's know what time it is? It's time to ante the fuck up."

Normally Bell would foot the bill himself. His stepfather didn't mind him driving the truck. He just wanted to see the tank on full whenever he returned the vehicle. At first Bell protested his stepfather's request, until his mother stepped in and pointed out the fact that he kept her man's truck more than he did. And she also suggested that Bell chip in on the monthly payments of the truck as well. Bell left that suggestion in the air, he didn't say no and he definitely wasn't going to agree.

"Five dollars a piece, soldiers," Bell announced. "..and we got a full tank.

Life went into his front pocket and came out with only three dollars, "I'm two short. I don't have but three dollars to my name."

"Damn homie, I wonder why?" Kenny said, grinning. "A broke nigga only makes jokes funny."

"I'm fucked up cause I've been doing a whole lot of balling and not enough hustling and to be honest wit'cha, I'm ready to pull a lick," Life explained, because that's how he always came across a few dollars other than Kenny getting him to sling a hundred pills.

"I'll put the other two up for you, my Nigga," Bell said.

"You need to foot the whole bill, since I always supply the pills," Kenny fussed.

"Ugly ass Nigga, I aint like you. I got responsibilities. I got mouths to feed, "Bell reminded his friend.

"What mouths?" Kenny bucked his eyes. "What damn responsibility?"

"My kids, my son and daughter." Bell scolded.

"So those are the mouths that you feeding?" Kenny asked, forcing Bell to accept this challenge against his will. Everyone knew that Bell was not properly taking care of his children.

He was not handling his part of his responsibility, because if he was as he claimed, his baby's mother wouldn't be fronting him off in front of Kenny, Life and Jazz, or religiously complaining to his mother. So if Bell was handling his business, then they wouldn't know his business. When it came down to spending time with his kids, or taking care of them financially, Bell would say one thing and do another.

"Bell, the only mouth you come close to feeding is some vagina lips," Kenny laughed. "And the only way you feed them is by giving them

C.P.R."

"Oooh! Dawg that was low," Life laughed. "Boy, we've been riding ya ugly ass for too damn long. You were due for a score."

"Two points for Kenny. That's my Dawg," Jazz cheered.

"Boy, you need to try to learn my technique," Bell teased. "Cause with your ugly ass, you will have honeys jumpin' over one another to get to you, and you can save some money. You wouldn't have to feed'em all those pills, just to get them to over look your ugliness and lay down with'cha. I bet when a girl wake up with you, and comes to her senses, she probably has to do a double take. And then she ends up questioning herself, *how in the hell did I lay down with that baby Godzilla?*"

"You the famous tongue man and I'm the popular pill man," Kenny said in good spirit. "So what more can I say?"

"I'd rather be the pill man any day, "Jazz proudly commented.

"Shit me too," Life agreed. "Cause then I can have racks on racks," he said, fumbling with the three germ infested dollar bills.

Jazz whipped into the service station, he was getting ready to park beside the pump in front of the store until he saw a middle age sista in some tight jeans. She was twelve years-older than him, which was the way he liked them.

"I see you Cougar."

"Cougar?" Bell laughed. "My baby brotha wants the Momma and I want the daughter."

"I'll take an older woman over a younger woman any day," Jazz stated.

"Speak for your damn self, Young Playa," Life said.

"Yo J., don't get me to lying," Kenny replied. "Cause when they young, you can mold'em, train'em and when you lead'em to that brick wall, you can say you sorry and you didn't mean to do it. You can straight dog their young asses out. Shit, ask your big brother? Take Bell for an example. He keeps'em stacked like a Georgia peach. And treat'em like the dirt that he walks on. And they still love his dirty draws. Worship the ground he walks on, and at the end of each relationship they all will say Bell aint no earthly good. Nakeita say Bel--."

Bell cut Kenny off in mid sentence.

"Fuck Nakeita," He scolded. "That lil Bitch! Who the fuck is she? Who the fuck do she supposed to be." Veins showed in his neck as he spoke.

Kenny winked at Life, "She's the one who dumped your ass."

Bell twisted around in his seat, so he could face Kenny.

"You know what? I just figured the shit out. Okay ugly ass nigga, you want to be me. Don't ya?"

"You right," Kenny grinned. "Only when you get your lil head buried in between some legs." They all laughed.

"Nigga, you're not only one ugly mothafucka, but a funny mothafucka too," Bell cracked up with laughter along with his crew. To them they were so cool that they never took the jokes personally, and Kenny always got the short end of the stick.

As they talked, Life looked ahead for someone to become his victim.

"Damn, look, look," he bumped Kenny's leg twice.

"Look at what?" Kenny asked, looking around lost.

"Look behind the register," Life suggested.

The 58-year-old Asian male tended to his customer without breaking one of them a smile. He adjusted his super thick lenses to see better.

"Chew Man Fu," Kenny said, giving the stranger a first, middle and last name.

"If that's his real name, then what is his alias?" Life asked.

"Sucky, sucky one dollar," Kenny laughed.

"Oh, you bet your ass he's good," Bell said.

"Again," Jazz added to their scam.

"Jazz, you know the demo," Bell looked over at him. "Y'all let's go in the store. Man don't buy nothing but a beer."

"A beer," Life questioned.

"Yeah, the one that cost one dollar," Bell advised.

Kenny and Life walked into the store and followed Bell's every move. Once they arrived at the register, the Asian guy addressed Bell "One beer and gas on pump number nine?"

"No gas nothing," Bell replied, producing one finger. "Only one beer."

The Asian smiled. "No, no, I see you truck, yOU get gas too."

"What truck, me and my dawgs walked up here," Bell lied.

The Asian looked to where the truck once was parked. His smile faded. He pushed the glasses further to his eyes and took another look; frustrated, her exhaled.

"You try to play joke on me? Me know you truck. You pumped twenty dollars of gas. You owe me twenty dollars and ninety-nine cents for this one can of beer."

"You right I owe you ninety-nine cent for this here one beer."

The Asian wanted to reach under the counter to collect his pistol, and blow Bell's brains out. He did not like them calling him a liar to his face, actually he did not appreciate them trying to convince him that he was wrong. They were trying to play him as if he was illiterate.

"You play this joke on me before. You took gas, you move your truck while I wasn't watching."

"Listen old man, I'm no' fuckin magician. I can't make nothing disappear. I'm broke as a motherfucka, so I can't afford to buy a remote control to make a truck move or park itself. I'm a poor motherfucka. All I can afford is a one dollar beer."

The Asia refused to allow Bell to further verbally assault him, so he dismissed him. Once Bell got by the door, he became rude.

"Man, I don't appreciate you trying to beat me outta my twenty dollars. Next time I come back I want to speak to the manager."

"I am the manager and I'd appreciate it if you don't come back here, ever again. People like you are not wanted here. You thief, you took my gas two times! I never forget a customer. Don't come back here neither of you."

"And fuck you too, sucky, sucky, one dollar," Kenny said.

"Pop, be easy before I put this iron in your life," Life warned, wanting to rob the store and take more than just the twenty dollars worth of gas.

"You cheat me," the Asia shouted.

"Old man, I cheat on women," Bell said, laughing on his way out the door.

They laughed all the way back to the truck and joked about the Asian as they rode off. Once they pulled into Toni's lot. Life notice someone peeking from the living room curtains. He lifted his fist in their direction, while also aiming his hand as if it were a pistol.

"Fu, Fu, Fu," he uttered, trying to make the sound of a firing weapon.

"Damn Dawg! You sound like you still got Fu Man Chew on your mind," Bell teased.

"Shit, I do," Life replied. "I need to go back and rob his ass."

"Right now we tryna get some of that shit some people call sunshine, but I call it heaven," Bell said, leading the way up Toni's four step trailer.

"Shit I'm tryna go to heaven," Kenny joked.

"I amen to that," Jazz nodded.

"I just wanna party," Bell replied.

As they entered, Toni and Tasha sat on the couch with their legs crossed, smiling.

"How's my favorite two girls?" Kenny questioned, playing like he was the perfect gentleman.

"Lonely," Tasha purred.

"And horny," Toni confirmed.

"Where's everybody?" Life asked.

Toni strutted over to him to answer his question. Using her best sexy walk and voice, she replied.

"We're the only two here. And beside we're more than a handful. My sexy game is on one thousand, and I'll have to tone it down for you lil boys."

"That sounds like a threesome too me, "Kenny interjected.

"Two to one," Jazz rubbed his hands together. "Then we can holla switch".

"I keep telling y'all why settle for one cow in the pasture when you can run through them all," Bell said, as he and Life made a sandwich with Toni's banging body.

"Kenny and Jazz darling, I can hear y'all body calling me, "Tasha sang, doing a bunch of sexy and enticing dances.

"Yes Ma, whine for me," Kenny said, becoming hypnotized by the motion of her swaying hips.

"Yeah, whine for us," Jazz corrected, as he danced over to her. Tasha hypnotized him as well. There was no escaping her spell. Once he or she responded to each other, it was a guaranteed cop and lock.

Chapter 19

The closer they came to the trailer, the plainer the vehicle became. Wonder screamed out to Nakeita in fear. "Girl, that's Bell's truck."

Nakeita's worse nightmare was coming to reality. She was finally about to face her demon, and mentally questioned if she was ready.

"No! Oh my God, "Nakeita whined as her heart skipped a beat. Then it felt like it completely stopped beating all together. She hadn't seen Bell since she got kicked out. To her knowledge, they hadn't been in the same place at the same time. Now they were about to be under the same roof, and she was stressed out big time.

"Wonder, I can't do this. I'm not ready to see that boy yet." Nakeita said, admitting that she were still very hurt and discombobulated from the whole police issue. Now she was having to deal with this. "I can't take another bad surprise, "she whispered.

"You go through the back door and I'll go through the front. Go in your room and get some rest. Won't no one know you're in the house but me."

"Thanks Wonder, I like that idea," Nakeita mumbled, with tears streaming down her face.

When she slipped in the back door, Nakeita heard the loud moaning of a male and female. They were speaking real sexy to one another, and she immediately recognized Bell and Toni voices. Nakeita stopped in her tracks. As she grabbed her mouth in total disgust, tears ran even faster down her face. Wanting to confirm what she heard, she followed the voices. Nakeita held her breath as she turned the knob to Toni's bedroom door. Bell and Life were making out with Toni. Nakeita got sick to her stomach, and finally realized what was meant by the comment, *what's good for the goose, is no longer good for the gander.* This living arrangement was no longer for her. She was so hurt, she wanted to call Ebony and ask if she could come back home. However, Nakeita was afraid of being rejected by her mother. One night, Toni was high as a kite and so many guys had sex with her, they pounded and pumped away her intoxication. When Toni couldn't take the body banging punishment any longer, men came to Nakeita's room wanting sex favors. Some even asked to have rough sex with her.

"Man is you crazy, I ain't no fucking human walking and talking Burger King. This room aint called 'have it your way.' In fact, you can have your money back," she threw the fifty dollar bill at him. *"Now get the fuck up outta here."* Nakeita shook her head to shake off the flashback. When she came back to reality, she rushed to her bedroom, dove onto her bed and buried her face in her pillow. Nakeita was so traumatized that she blamed Darrel for everything that went wrong in her life.

"I hate you! Man you left me all alone," she threw her pillow across the bed. "You don't love me, cause if you really, really cared about me, you would be here with me. And I wouldn't have to live my life like this. Daddy, if you were here, I know you wouldn't let Momma put me out the house like this. I have nowhere to go, and I don't like these streets. Daddy please talk to Momma so I can come back home. Please!" she sobbed, rocking herself to sleep.

***

Kenny got up off of Tasha. Her love making was no longer exciting to him. *Danm, she was a waste of time and energy,* he thought. *Shit I'mma go join Bell and Life, cause Toni's damn super freaky ass always know how to turn a nigga on.*

"Say Dawg, what's up?" Jazz asked. He could tell from being around Kenny for so long that he'd lost interest.

"I'm going to see what Bell and Life working with," Kenny announced.

"With leftovers, "Tasha laughed.

"That's exactly what I felt like I just was getting," Kenny laughed, exiting the room. After using the bathroom, Kenny opened the first bedroom door he came across. Seeing Nakeita spread across the bed, he saw her sleeping and felt like he'd just stumbled up on a full supply of Viagra. He licked his lips and began counting his blessings. Kenny eased the door shut, careful not to startle her. He tip-toed back to the room where Jazz and Tasha were. When he arrived, they were now screwing one another's brains out.

"Yo Jazz! Man come here. I got something to tell you," Kenny said.

"Can't you see Jazz is busy," Tasha replied with an attitude.

Jazz wiped sweat from his face, "What time is it?"

"One o'clock in the morning. Now come out the room, so I can holla at'cha.' " Kenny said, almost in a low whisper.

"Make him wait bout ten minutes baby," Tasha begged.

"Naw that's my main man. I can't handle him like that, "Jazz replied, getting up off the bed and stepping into his boxers.

"What that young raggedy ass bitch say?" Kenny walked back into the room, closing in the distance between him and Tasha, but Jazz blocked his path.

"Jazz, man, that young girl wore out, she has no walls, and no corner for a nigga to bang."

"Ya' momma aint got no damn walls, or no corners for a nigga to bang, and she don't get wet no mo either," Tasha said, all out of hurt feelings.

"Bitch you better watch your mothafucka mouth, talking about my mothafucka Momma," Kenny pointed at Tasha. "Ho, on my Momma dead body, if you say something about my Momma again I'll break your fucka

221

neck." Kenny turned his full attention back to Jazz. "My nigga, come check this shit out."

"You have to forgive Kenny because sometimes my nigga will go the fuck off for no reason and really the shit don't even be necessary." Jazz said to Tasha, that was his way of apologizing on Kenny's behalf.

Tasha looked sad and disappointed; Kenny hurt her feelings. Never in a million years did she think he would fix his mouth to say such disrespectful words to her. He was so cold he forced her to feel as though she were a nobody.

"*That nigga is a fucking low life ass loser. Don't nobody want his ape looking ass.*" She said to herself, hoping to rebuild her low self-esteem. And honest to God, it did the trick.

"S-sh-sh," Kenny said, holding a finger inches away from his lips. He turned the doorknob and stepped into the dark room, motioning for Jazz to enter. Once Jazz stepped in, the reflection of the moonlight danced over Nakeita's body from head to toe. As she laid in the center of the bed on her back, she was still fully dressed, even still wearing her sneakers.

"She goes to bed dressed like a firefighter, don't she play?" Jazz sneered, feeling like he just had to get that joke off his chest.

"Sh-sh," Kenny whispered. "Man, I'm finna treat myself. Man, ya just don't know how long I've been waiting to get in her draws. You with it?"

"You damn right. It ain't no fun if the homies can't have none," Jazz said.

"Now, aint that the fucking truth," Kenny smiled, "that's what I've been tryna tell that damn brotha of yours."

"Fuck that nigga," Jazz said, closing in on Nakeita. Kenny refused to let Jazz beat him to the punchline. He sat down on the bed beside Nakeita. As the bed sank in, she opened her eyes. Once she locked eyes with a smiling Kenny, Nakeita's heart tried to jump out of her chest. The appetite of lust in his eyes couldn't be ignored. "Merry Christmas to me," Kenny said, smiling as he began to undress her.

"Boy, what you think you're doing,"Nakeita protested.

"I'm unwrapping my gift," Kenny replied.

As Jazz stood before her stroking himself, Nakeita tried to sit up, but Kenny punched her in the face, forcing her to lay there with her mouth closed and her legs open. Jazz jumped on the bed, giving her a few punches. He was letting her know they meant business, and he was not going to accept no for an answer.

"Lil Momma, we can do this here the easy way or the hard way. But either way, you're gonna lose and we gonna win," Kenny warned.

Nakeita just stayed there crying as they misused and abused her precious body. Now she experienced the tragedy her mother had once endured over a decade and a half ago. Nakeita moaned for help, hoping and wishing someone would come to her rescue. Forty-five minutes later, her prays were answered. While Jazz was about to move in on her for session three and Kenny session four, Tasha burst into the bedroom. Nakeita's squeals of pain led her to the door. As she took in what was happening to her friend, her eyes were filled with sorrow and a look of death.

"Y'all bastards get the fuck off that girl," she shouted. "Get the fuck off of her motherfucka," Tasha lost it and became a loose cannon. She dove on the bed and began throwing hard, wild and crazy punches every which way. She was swinging so viciously, that she ended up giving Kenny and Jazz a taste of their own medicine. Her first blow rested on Kenny's eye, and the next on his jaw. Jazz caught one to the mouth, giving him a taste of his own blood. The next punch knocked him off the bed. They couldn't stop nor block Tasha's deranged blows. She fought as if she was fighting for her own life. Jazz was finally able to creep up on Tasha and steal on her from her blind side. Other than that, it would've been impossible for them to duck and dodge Tasha's blows.

"Stinky ass bitch, I'll kill ya," Kenny growled, stomping her in the head. Jazz kicked her between the legs, which knocked all the fight out of her. All the commotion drew the attention of everyone else in the house. Wonder rushed into the room. She had a small container in her hand and after witnessing the commotion, she sprayed Kenny in the mouth and eyes with Mace.

"Oh-oh-oh-shit! Man, somebody get that damn bitch," Kenny screamed like a female.

Jazz tried to run, but she wasn't having that.

"Ut'un motherfucka! No you don't," Wonder cried out, racing over to make sure he didn't escape her wrath. "Naw! Bring your tough ass on over here and man the fuck up. Punk ass nigga, come get you some," she taunted. Jazz tried to use his hands as a shield, but to no avail. Wonder showered his face with almost the remaining fluids left in the can. The ten percent of feminine characteristics people claim are a part of every male came out of Jazz at that moment. He leaped around trying to avoid her and get as much air as possible.

"Ah-ahh-ah… Girl! Get the fuck away from around me with that smelly ass shit." Jazz fought to breathe. "I-I-I-, I can't catch my breath," he whined, bending over. Once Wonder ran out of spray, she begin beating Kenny in the head and face with the empty can. He was the first to stagger through the doorway, but she was not trying to let him off that easy.

"Ah, man, somebody get this crazy bitch. Bell, Life," he hollered at the top of his lungs. Bell and Life entered the room naked as a jail bird. They were about to swing on Wonder.

"Fuck that you ho ass niggas. If I was you, I wouldn't try that stupid shit."

When they tried to turn around, they ended up facing an also butt naked ass Toni, who had gotten Life's pistol, and was aiming it at them.

"Bitch, you aint gonna shoot," challenged Life.

"Which one of you bitches wanna die first?" Toni looked from Life to Bell.

"Nigga let's get the fuck outta this shitty ass dump," Bell said.

"Y'all asses leaving alright, but not like you came; go outta my front door, butt ass naked. I'll throw y'all shit out to y'all afterwards," Toni said. Life acted like he wanted to rush her. "Fuck! Nigga, I wish your coward ass would try me," she threatened.

"Bitch fuck you," Life spit.

"You already did. Now try me while I'm not in the mood! "Toni's eyes narrowed. "Nigga, play pussy and get fucked," Toni challenged, tightening up her grip on the pistol.

***

"Please help me, please help me," echoed through Silk's mind for the hundredth time. He continued slinging his head right to left, hoping to shake off Nakeita's crying voice. But she sounded as if she were lying right next to him. "Oh, God will someone help me," her voice rang out a second time, forcing Silk to wake up. As he opened his eyes, his wife's head was on his chest. While she slept peacefully, he cautiously removed Betty's arm from across his body and carefully emerged from the bed.

"1:20 in the morning," Silk yawned, after looking at his watch. He slid into his jeans and a black pull over T-shirt, and then jumped in the car and rode around in the dark and lonely streets. As he smoked one cigarette after another, he finally realized that the chain smoking did not calm his nerve as it normally would. Silk raced through two packs and felt the need for at least one more pack before his nicotine craving was finally satisfied.

"Nakeita, where are you?" he whispered, hoping a voice would reply with directions to her whereabouts. "Where are you Nakeita? Please tell me, where you are? I'm here. Uncle Silk wants to help you. I came to help you. Please where are you, so I can help you." The sadness of Silk's voice could be heard with each and every word that rolled off his tongue. Forty minutes later, he stumbled on two young females, staggering down the street in his direction.

Once their distance shortened, he focused more on the hugged up couple. When he recognized Nakeita, who was leaning on Wonder for support, Silk's heart stopped beating. Fear covered his face, and then slung the car over on the curb, frightening them both. Without delay, he hopped out of the car.

"Nakeita! Baby, is that you?" He asked, paranoid.

"Ohhh," Nakeita cried out, as tears fell from her eyes. She stopped in her tracks, because all of the punches she'd taken to the ribs caused more pain. And as she walked, she struggled to breathe.

"Baby! What happened to you? What have you gone and gotten yourself into?" He asked with tears and death in his eyes.

"They raped her," Wonder angrily stated. "And they beat her too."

"Uncle Silk it wasn't my fault," Nakeita tried to explain.

"Shhh, Baby Girl…Sshhh," Silk mumbled, taking Nakeita into his arms. "You're safe now. No one can hurt you anymore. No one will hurt you again."

"Please don't tell my mother. She'll think it's all my fault," Nakeita pleaded, before loosing consciousness.

Silk clutched her closer to his body. "Do you know how to drive?" He angrily asked Wonder.

"Yes," she replied, with trembling lips. "I mean, yes Sir."

"Get us to the hospital A.S.A.P."

"Okay."

Silk held Nakeita in his arms all the way there. Even though she was unconscious, he still felt the mask of tension in her body. As he thought back to the decade and a half ago when her mother was raped, anger consumed him. Now he was in the same mind set as Darrel. Silk wanted to take the life of whoever had caused Nakeita all this hurt. He knew from Ebony's experience, that Nakeita would now carry this same kind of burden until death do them part.

"Nakeita, you gonna be alright," Silk assured her, stroking her hair. As his tears splashed on her ripped clothes, he tried to keep her encouraged. "Hold on Ba-by, we almost at the hospital."

As Nakeita slipped further and further into a coma, she saw herself in a long white gown that rested right at the top of her bare feet. She felt like she was flying around in the sky and had been given wings. She could hear her uncle crying, she just could not respond…

"Uncle Silk, I will protect you. I'll be your Godly Angel," her mind silently screamed.

<h1 style="text-align: center">Chapter 20</h1>

As the tears washed down her face, Betty stepped into a skirt and slipped on one of Silks jackets, so her nightgown would be incognito. Now Ebony needed to be notified immediately caused Betty to hold her breath. As she dialed the number, pain and fear took completely over her body.

On the first ring Ebony eyes opened. There was no reason in the world for her phone to be ringing at 2 in the morning, unless something terrible had happened to her baby.

"NaKeita," she whispered with a dry mouth and watery eyes. The third ring caused her to begin praying, "Lord please doesn't let anything be wrong with my child."

Fear and pain spread through her body like cancer. Ebony finally found the strength to answer the phone.

"Hello." She managed to force out. After seconds of silence, Ebony said again, "Hello."

"Ebony!" Tension in Betty's voice could be heard.

"Oh God," Ebony cried out. "Betty what's wrong?" Ebony stated. "Please tell me this call has nothing to do with my ba-by. Please tell me that nothing happened to Nakeita?" Betty's crying and sniffling was a dead give-away. Plus her silence was used against her.

"Oh God no. No, not my baby," Ebony cried.

"Get dressed, we need to get to the hospital," Betty reported.

Ebony dropped the receiver and fell to the floor .She could hear Betty's voice, moans and cries while she talked.

"Ebony get yourself together, we have to go to the hospital. Nakeita needs us. Silk is already up there with her."

"Thank God," Ebony whimpered.

When Silk finished informing Betty of Nakeita's tragedy and her whereabouts, he recommended that she give Ebony the call instead of him, because he was trying to cope with his own emotions and demons.

"How is she, Doc?"

"It's too early to tell," the elder man replied.

"Let's just pray that she doesn't stay in that coma too long. Sometimes the patient will sink deeper in their darkness so they can't be hurt again. They have the tendency to feel safer, like they can hide from everyone."

Silk didn't like what had been said, so there was no reason to entertain the conversation with a response. However, he needed to be advised as to what was best for Nakeita.

"What can I do to help?" Silk questioned.

"Talking to the patient usually helps. They need to feel safe, loved and most of all protected," responded the Doctor. "Son, hold the Child's hand while you talk to her," he also encouraged. "She'll be able to feel your energy; because your strength is desperately needed for her sake."

The doctor left the room after he was called to the intensive care unit over the intercom. At that point, there was nothing else neither he nor his staff could do at the moment for Nakeita, but stay on standby. No medication could be provided to bring her out of her situation. If Nakeita came out of her coma then they'd be able to do a little more to comfort her. As Silk walked around the room looking at Nakeita's unconscious body, tears ran down his cheeks faster than he could wipe them.

"What creep would have the desire to rape a child?" he questioned himself, removing his jacket to drape it over the chair. Then he pulled up another one closer to Nakeita's bed. "Nakeita?" he whispered, first gripping, and then rubbing her warm hand. "Please come out of that coma. You're going to be alright, I promise you. Nobody's going to ever hurt you again. We love you. We need you out here with us." Silk continued to pour out his heart, while shedding tears. Once the staff saw this, they assumed he was Nakeita's biological father. They never would have guessed in a million years that he was only her Godfather.

During these moments, Silk made Nakeita a world of promises. He told her they'd spend more time together. He'd pick her up from school more. He'd buy her a couple of coats and hats, so she'd be well protected from the rain and cold. He also mentioned from that day forward, he wanted to screen every male before she even thought about giving out her seven digs.

He also told her, he thought it would be a great idea if she started spending her summers on college campus, so she'd be able to get a feel of college before hands. Silk expressed himself as the perfect father figure. Everything that rolled off his tongue were things a father needed to explain to his daughter. The present image of Nakeita tore Silk apart, but he continued to think as rational as possible for the both of them. Nakeita was his heart, his first responsibility, and he'd been overprotective of her since birth, loved her as his own flesh and blood, and was ready to kill or be killed for her. Silk's thoughts were interrupted as Ebony and Betty rushed into the small hospital room, which Silk knew would happen. They just came a little too soon, because it prevented him from getting the opportunity to get everything off his chest.

"Oh God, no! Not my baby," Ebony cried, entering the room. She hadn't seen her daughter in over a month, and now this painful sight caused Ebony to lose it. "Nakeita, get outta that bed!" she shouted. "I can't take my child being in no casket."

"She's not in no casket, E," Silk whispered.

Ebony took baby steps closer to Nakeita's bed. "Nakeita, where have you been? Momma missed you so much," Ebony said, rubbing Nakeita's hair. Tubes were in her nose, tubes were attached to both of her arms. Her face was badly bruised, black eyes, busted lips, and she was badly battered. Ebony felt every bit of her daughter's pain. "Girl, you were a good baby. Please tell me where did I go wrong?" Ebony sat down beside Nakeita calm and collected, but then all of a sudden, she lost control. She couldn't take the sight anymore. "Lord, please take me Lord! Don't take my baby from me. You're supposed to punish me for any of her wrong doing. Punish me, punish me," Ebony shouted and cried. "Don't take my baby."

Ebony would have snatched Nakeita out of bed had Silk not stopped her. As Soon as Ebony broke loose, the nurse fled the room. She could sense the shit before it could hit the fan. She had been a nurse for some time, and she thought Ebony needed to be sedated.

The doctor entered the room to calm Ebony. Two male nurses secured her, while the doctor informed her that she would require a shot to relax her. As the thick clear serum enter her body, within no time all the fight in Ebony's body came to a halt... Instantly, she felt light on her feet and fainted.

"Is she alright?" Silk asked, moving closer to the nurses.

"Sir, she'll be just fine," the doctor stated, stepping in Silk's path. "For her safety and most of all, our patient's, she needed to be calmed down. We don't want to lose Nakeita. Sir, only God knows her fate," The doctor sadly nodded. Silk looked over to Nakeita's motionless body. He did not like the look on her face one bit. Betty stood there shedding tears, and she didn't know what to do or what to say. She was tongue-tied and didn't know if she was going or coming. She thought sincerely about asking them to give her the same injection they had given Ebony.

"Ms, you alright?" the doctor asked Betty.

"Yes," Betty murmured, but truly wanted to say no.

Silk walked over to Betty to comfort her and she hugged him for dear life.

"Sweetheart, everything will be alright," he said, rubbing his wife's back. "We'll just have to sit back and let the Lord do his work."

Betty continued to cry as she watched the strangers carry her best friends unconscious body out of the room.

"She'll be over in the next room," one of the nurses said to help Betty and Silk's mind rest. The doctor held up a hand as if it was a stop sign.

"Please allow her to sleep for a couple of hours. We'll let the drugs wear off, but once she wakes up, there won't be any side effects. The drugs will be completely out of her system."

"You sure?" Betty asked?

"Yes," The Doctor smiled, "I'm more than positive."

Silk allowed the doctor to get within an arm's length from the door before he spoke.

"Doc will my family be alright?"

"Sir, I and my staff will do the best we possibly can," the doctor stated with a sincere expression. "We're here to save lives."

"Thanks for everything Doc!"

The doctor shot Silk a wink, "The man upstairs runs the real show. I say that to say, I always ask him for help and so should you. He's the real protector of our families, because at times our hands can be tied and there's nothing in the world we can do, but let things heal themselves." The doctors reason for saying that was because one day his eight-year-old daughter caught a cramp in her right thigh and there was nothing he could do about it, but he sat on the floor with his daughter to comfort her for hours and hours until the higher power decided enough was enough.

"But Sir, if it would help ease your pain, I'll have several nurses checking on your daughter every ten minutes. I love the kids as well. I have a few daughters and they are precious to me also. We will do our complete best for your family."

"Thank you, Doc, you're a good man," Silk said, turning his attention back to Betty.

Chapter 21

As Wonder went into Nakeita's room, Silk and Betty stood front and center, hugged up crying. Wonder's eyes were puffy from crying so much.

"Hi! Can I sit with her alone for a while, please?"

Betty whipped around to see who the voice belonged to. Thank God Wonder had changed clothes. She was dressed like a schoolgirl and could easily pass for one of Nakeita's classmates.

"She's Nakeita's friend," Silk whispered. "Sure, you can sit with her for a little while. If you need us, we'll be out front," Silk said, leading Betty out of the room to give Wonder privacy.

Once Wonder heard the door close, she eased closer to Nakeita's bed. She examined Nakeita's face, thinking how much she hated Jazz and Kenny's guts as well as Bell and Life too, since they were all running partners.

"Nakeita, I'm sorry. I'm so sorry." Wonder cried, as tears rushed over her thick lips. "Oh God- it's my fault. It's all my fault. This shouldn't have happened to you."

Wonder's mind began to play tricks. She started to envision herself in Nakeita's shoes. The burden began to immediately become more than she could bear. She promised herself she would throw in the towel. She was done; finished and retired with the streets, cause the streets didn't care about or love anyone.

"Nakeita, I'm sorry," she said an additional time. "Please come out of this coma. Nakeita, come on back. Your mother's here. Silk's and his wife are here. Girl, we wanna see you smile again."

As the door creaked opened, Wonder's head rested on Nakeita's forearm. The nurse waited for a second, because she thought Wonder was praying. Suddenly, their eyes met.

"Ms, sorry to disturb you, but you have to leave. This patient needs her rest. If she doesn't get her proper rest, she won't be able to build up the strength she needs to beat this."

Wonder climbed to her feet, put up two fingers, which represented the peace sign, kissed them, and then pressed them against Nakeita's forehead.

"Girl, get well. I look forward to seeing you soon." Without another word, she walked over toward the the nurse, and took another glance at her friend.

"Girl, I'm gonna pray for you."

Wonder never prayed for anyone, nor took time out to pray for herself. But she was planning on staying strong on her word. And just as sure as she had been about chasing that dirty almighty American dollar, praying was going to now play a major role in her life with that same intensity.

After hours in a coma, Nakeita was finally able to respond. She'd heard everyone speaking to her, and when the male nurse was in the room trying to grab her mother, she cried and reached out for Ebony. But, her arms weren't stretched forth long enough, nor could her voice be heard.

Nakeita saw herself in a scary house, which was two miles from her hiding spot. She could see a way out. The huge rooms were completely dark, but the open door presented light on the other side, which was her path for escape. She had to pass Bell, Life, Kenny, and Jazz, and in her mind, they were lying in the darkness waiting to hurt her again. Nakeita could hear them snickering, giggling, and whispering. They knew she was in the darkness with them, but could not pinpoint her whereabouts, and due to being frightened, cold and angry with herself, Nakeita just wanted to stay in her fetal position and cry herself to death. She was afraid to move a muscle; afraid that if she moved again they might find her. She put her back against the wall, and peeped out of one eye. For some reason when she used both eyes, her vision was blurred and she saw four sets of eyes in the darkness; a red, orange, yellow and white pair.

"Nakeita?"
"Here, kitty, kitty."
"Where are you?"

"Come out to play little girly-girl."

"You can run and you can hide, but I'll find you. And when you look around, I'll be standing right behind you." Bell said. Then his voice rung out with laughter and his crew's voices did the same.

Nakeita became consumed with fear. she closed her eyes tighter, and held her breath. The left side of her brain started to shut down. While the nurse was doing her rounds, she heard a beeping noise. It was one of the machines that were set up to monitor Nakeita's vitals. Upon seeing the light-green dot racing repeatedly across the screen, she alerted the nurse's station for additional assistance. The doctor and a few male nurses rushed to her aide. They hooked up a defibrillator to Nakeita chest, but to no avail. The doctor then increased the voltage twice, still to no avail. The doctor gave Nakeita all he had by trying to increase her adrenaline. Then the machine started to bounce around, making little mountains, then big mountains, super big mountains.

"Thank God!" said the doctor.

Chapter 22

The next day, flowers which were everywhere, brightening the atmosphere as everyone sat around in Nakeita's room talking. Betty had given her two French braids to the back, because she was tired of seeing her hair piled up underneath the surgical cap. They had each agreed to take turns staying with her and no one cheated. While each person did their shift, they spent the whole 48 hours talking to her to try to stimulate her. It was almost as if she was a child. Ebony told them they didn't have to stay, but they all insisted on sharing in the responsibility.

"Yes we do have to stay, because Nakeita is our baby also. Remember we were there when you brought her into the world."

Ebony didn't dare try to speak that foolishness to Ms.Matty Mae Strong. Once she learned that Nakeita was in the hospital, she flew up there and spent twelve days straight beside her grand-daughter's hospital bed. Neither doctor nor nurses could run her away. She prayed and guarded Nakeita's body as if she'd carried Nakeita for nine months herself. Ms.Matty Mae Strong also got to the point of having to regulate the visitor. She even insisted that Ebony stay away for 72 hours, so she could catch up on some much needed rest and meals.

As time passed, the hospital staff grew very fond of Ms. Matty Mae Strong. One nurse even went against hospital policy for her. Yes, she put her job on the line for a complete stranger. She didn't know Ms. Matty Mae Strong from a can of paint, but she rolled in another bed, so Ms. Matty Mae Strong could stretch out and get proper rest, while staying with Nakeita. The head administrator showed up without notice and walked into Nakeita room at 4:30AM, only to find Ms. Matty Mae

Strong in a deep sleep. He didn't intrude on her rest, but he did chew the nurses out and threatened fired them all since no one wanted to take the blame.

One day Ms. Matty Mae Strong gave the doctor and a couple of nurses a plate of her fried ribs. After eating, the doc asked her for her family's secret recipe. She told them that the secret ingredients were a pinch of patience, a dash of kindness, a spoonful of laughter, and a whole lot of love.

And within those 30 days of Nakeita's coma, Big Boss made sure Nakeita had the best of care that his people could provide. Ms. Matty Mae Strong also received the royal treatment.

***

Big Johnny smelled a set of red roses and a set of white roses.

"What's the difference in these flowers?"

"The color," Ms. Matty Mae Strong said.

"Oh, I can see that."

"Then why you ask the question?"

"Because I knew you were gonna be the person to birth the answer. Matty, you think you know the answer to everything, don't you? But you don't have the answer to everything Sugar."

"I have more answers than you," Ms. Matty Mae Strong sassed.

"I'm not knocking that," Big Johnny said with a smile. He loved Ms. Matty Mae Strong's good sense of humor. She knew how to cheer up a person when they were down and out. Silk and Betty smiled, they were waiting on this Esther and Fred Sanford moment to escalate, cause it never failed, and if they didn't know any better, they would've thought Ms. Matty Mae Strong and Big Johnny were the true example of oil and water. They kept a conversion going, kept you rolling in so much laughter that your stomach cramped up. They kept tears in Betty's eye, and Big Johnny treasured these moments. He and Ms. Matty Mae Strong would carry on in this fashion, even if they were alone. They enjoyed one another's company and lived for the moment.

Silk couldn't hold his laughter, he laughed out loud, wishing he had a recorder so he could record the comical encounters. Though they were all full of laughter, Ebony wasn't in the mood for fun and games. Her mind rambled with the conversation she had with Wonder. Wonder put the pieces to the puzzle together for her. She didn't bite her tongue either. She dropped the 411 on everyone involved, but she didn't say anything to incriminate herself or Nakeita. Wonder was no fool, she didn't throw salt on Nakeita's character. She left Ebony with the same respectful image she had of her precious daughter.

"BJ, the white roses cost more than the red roses," Silk announced to Big Johnny, giving him something else to play fight with Ms. Matty Mae Strong about. Silk didn't want the fire to cease. Yet, little did he know he had just thrown gasoline on the fire.

"Um-Ha,"Big Johnny exhaled. "Lady, you didn't know nothing bout that did you?" he smiled at Ms.Matty Mae Strong. "You didn't know the white roses were more expensive then the red roses - now did you?" He shook his head no and continued talking as if he had the microphone.

"You didn't know, because if you did, you would've said so."

"You didn't know ya'self," Ms. Matty Mae Strong fired back. "And you're a man. You're supposed to know that," she held up her big finger, (which nowadays youngsters call it the trigger finger). As she wiggled it at him, she continued. "I ain't no man. I don't run around buying people roses like you guys. Flowers mean life, they give off the symbolism of something that's alive, growing and reforming. Now, I bet'cha didn't know that. Did you Mr. Smart Guy?"

Big Johnny watched Silk nod in his direction insinuating Ms. Matty Mae Strong was stating facts and not just talking out the side of her neck.

"Yeah, yeah, yeah she knows a few things," Big Johnny laughed, "And I'm not disputing that." He hunched up his shoulders. "All I'm saying is that she doesn't know everything. That's the point I'm tryna get across."

"Point taken," Silk said.

"BJ, you mind if I use your truck for a while?" asked Ebony.

"Ebony, where you going?" questioned Betty.

"I need some air. I need to go out for a little while to clear my head. I think a long drive will do me well."

"If you want me to, I'll go with you."

"No, that's okay," Ebony gave Betty a pitiful look. "I just need some time to myself. Taking a ride will clear my thoughts."

Big Johnny handed over the keys.

"The truck is yours. Take all the time you need." He also handed her a fifty-dollar bill. "Bring back some more flowers, since I learned they represent life."

"Keep living, you'll learn something else new," Ms. Matty Mae Strong said. "Yes the 3 L's, Look, Listen and Learn. You know what's wrong with our people today?"

"No? Tell us," Betty said.

"We stopped listening! We think we already know everything and we believe we are too old to learn something new. We feel like we know it all, and don't want nobody to tell us nothing."

The room got quiet. Big Boss and two nurses walked in to tend to their patient. They also listened to Ms. Matty Mae Strong talk, and were able to kill two birds with one stone, as they sucked up some of her knowledge. They even altered Ms. Matty Mae Strong's name and gave her a handle, "Momma Ms. Matty Mae Strong."

***

While swirling through traffic, Ebony asked the Lord to be with her when she reached the trailer park. She handled Big Johnny's truck like a piece of cake. When Ebony finally reached her destination, two old school model cars set on the lawn. Before exiting the vehicle, she looked herself over in the mirror, making sure she didn't look as insane as she felt. The closer and closer she got to the door step, the louder the music grew. The booty shaking music caused her face to ball up, and when she looked through the screen door and saw Toni dancing half naked in front of six elderly guys who were old enough to be her father or grandfather, it caused the Holy Spirit to flee from Ebony's body. The devil took complete control over her God fearing body. Ebony banged with all her might on the screen door.

"Bang! Bang! Bang!" The knocking on the limber tin door rattled over the music. Toni strutted to the door.

"Yes," she said.

"I want to see the lady of the house!"

Toni gave Ebony a curious expression, thinking she was one of her client's angry wives.

"And who might you be?"

"My name is Ebony and I'm looking for the lady of the house," Ebony paused, trying to recall the bits and pieces of her and Wonder's conversation, because from Toni's expression, her name didn't ring a bell. Ebony, snapped her fingers, and spoke.

"Yeah, that's right; I need to speak with Toni."

Toni put her hand on her hip.

"I'm Toni; now what you need to talk to me about?" Ebony snatched the screen door open faster than a speed of lightning. As she used her other hand to retrieve a pistol from her purse, she begin to beat Toni in her face with the weapon while talking.

"You young bitch, you stand her before me in your damn T-shirt and panties, talking like you grown, and my fucking child laying up in the hospital on her death bed." With every swing Ebony knocked blood from Toni's mouth and nose. "Bitch, doctors don't even know if my child is gonna make it or not," Ebony screamed, continuing to hammer on Toni.

The guys present wanted no parts of Ebony wrath. They went coo-coo for the drugs and sex, but the violence they wanted no part of. They almost tripped over one another trying to get out of the trailer and back to the old folk's home where they belonged. Being around crime scenes and criminal activity wasn't a part of their agenda. They weren't trying to be on the news, talking before the cameras about who did what or about why and they witness the whole damn thing.

Had Wonder not come to the rescue, Ebony would've beat Toni senseless.

"Ms. Ebony! Stop! Stop! That's enough! Stop before you kill her," Wonder shouted. "You can't do anything for Nakeita if you're in jail."

The mention of her daughter's name brought forth some peace. Ebony looked down at Toni's bloody body. As Toni lay in a pool of blood crying like a child, Ebony remained heartless and still presented a demonic spirit.

"You ill bitch, my daughter got raped here and beat half to death and you got the audacity to shake ya half naked ass in front of them old farts. Lil' child, I blame you for the shit that happened to my baby." Ebony screamed, hawking up a mouth full of spit, and launched it right into Toni's face. "Bitch, I have no fucking sympathy. You lucky I didn't murder your fucking ass. You promoted that shit that happened to my child. And there's no telling who else's daughter you've led astray with your trifling ass. I outta blow ya fucking brains out right fucking now," Ebony stared at Toni without a bit of mercy. "Bitch, give me one reason why I shouldn't kill you right fucking now?"

Toni was in so much pain. She wanted to shout, *"Bitch go ahead and kill me now,"* but she didn't have the nerve to speak.

"Putting her outta her misery won't hurt anybody but you," Wonder said. "You'll only be doing her a favor and put yourself in more misery."

Ebony looked into Wonders eyes," You're right. You're one hundred percent right. But, this bitch need to suffer like my daughter is. Then just maybe this tramps sinful ways might be washed away." Ebony put her focus back on Toni. "And lil' hefer let me tell you something. You better be glad there's a God up above." Her eyes narrowed. "If my daughter pulls through this, and I ever hear of her setting foot in this shitty ass trailer again, I'mma come back down here and burn this bitch down to the ground. And guess what else? Your ass gonna be in it."

Ebony caused serious damage to Toni. As blood poured out of Toni's nose mouth and eyes, she could taste blood. She was in such bad shape that she only had about six to eight teeth left in her mouth. Her jaw bones were broken and there was no doubt that she'd be sucking her food through a straw for the next nine months or so.

Chapter 23

Darrel worked in the Law library, and he was always the last person to leave. His behavior had been exemplary, so the C.O's trusted him to keep the place nice and neat at all times. He wasn't like other prisoners; so in his work environment, there were no supervisors to breath down his neck. He worked on his on time and his own pace. If he felt like missing work, then he could do that without any consequences, because he was his own boss. At the end of this particular day, Darrel put chairs on top of the table, before doing a quick sweep of the room. The floor really didn't need sweeping; he just wanted to look busy, not to mention that it was part of his daily routine.

Officer Waters whistled his way into Darrel's area. They were both pretty familiar with one another, so they would conversate on a regular basis about worldly things that went on outside the prison. Darrel was not one to feel any pressure from talking to C.O's. He'd made it clear, from his initial day in prison that he was no snitch. When Darrel and Officer Waters became acquaintances, he told him to please try not to ask him any off the wall stuff concerning anybody in the prison, because he was there to do his time not police any of the other inmates or convicts in the facility.

During Since his incarceration, Darrel pretty much stayed to himself. Every once in a while he would walk the track with an old-timer, or go to the chow hall with one of his homies. But he was basically a loner, trying to do his time as comfortable and with as few problems as possible. He had already made up in his mind that he didn't need any friends, nor was he looking for any. When he began talking to guys, they would always assume he was their friend, and somehow would come up with the misconception that he was going to do deeds for them. However, he wasn't having that, because to have friends in prison cost. He knew they all stayed in the need or wanted for something, and with most, they all had some type of personal agenda or code of honor.

From his observation, he'd see how some would want to borrow commissary or ask too may unnecessary questions. So Darrel stuck to the "Law Of The Land," which was, don't borrow, loan, gamble, or do drugs. Don't drink, don't fool around with boys who wanted to be girls, and don't compromise your manhood.

"D! What up doe?" The officer inquired.

"Officer Waters. Hey, it's been a long, hard day," Darrel replied, continuing to try to beat the clock. There was little under ten minutes left before the day ended, and Darrel would be heading back to his housing area to shit, shave and bathe.

"Yeah, I have put in my eight hours for the day too. I'm so glad it's almost time for me to hit that gate," Officer Waters said, ready to go home to his beautiful wife and daughter. He could taste the ice cold beer right then slowly sliding down his throat and washing into his pot belly.

"D, what time did you go to sleep last night?"

"When the officer locked my cell door. Man, I can't rest well until my door is locked," Darrel said, giving the officer a look.

Darrel could take naps if he chose to. He could also go to bed before lockdown, because he was a good guy who didn't have any beef with anyone. Darrel didn't have one problem in prison, and he was well known and respected. When group wars broke out on the yard and in the units, Darrel was still able to walk around as if he didn't have a care in the world. And as long as a person minded their own business, then they had no problems with him.

"D, last night two guys got into a fight in your unit," Officer Waters said, laughing at the thought of saying something cute. "Playa, dude put that lock on Buddy's ass. I mean he worked him over good. By the time we reached the unit, the damage had already been done. That lock old boy used was something serious. Boy, that shit will put a zig-zag in a man's head for real. Bru, it's gonna take a cross-eyed doctor to sew his shit back up. That lock caused so much damage there was only so much that the Doctor could do to help ol' boy."

"That shit has nothing to do with me," Darrel said, mean mugging Officer Waters, as he gritted his teeth.

"Bru, you didn't see dude's shit split to the white meat?" Officer Waters asked, smiling. "Dude got seriously fucked up over the T.V. Playa I'm surprised you didn't warn people about that trick box. That TV got one muthafucka in a coma and the other guy bout to go back to court to get about fifteen mo years added to his sentence."

"Officer Waters, I mind my own business and keep my nose outta other people's affairs. I see no evil, hear no evil and definitely speak no evil," Darrel said, becoming more and more irritated with Officer Waters. He could tell he was trying to lead him into a conversation that he should have previously known he wouldn't discuss. He was already mad at the world. Little did Officer Waters know, he was talking to a ticking time bomb that was ready to go off at any moment.

"D-man, I bet'cha dude fucked around and changed the channel to that TV while them guys were watching the ticker, and they were probably tryna get them baseball and pre-season football scores. Playa, mark my word; before the year is out, there's gonna be plenty mo mothafuckas getting fucked up behind that TV."

Darrel picked up one of the wooden chairs and smashed it against the wall. Officer Waters stood there in shock with his mouth wide open. He actually thought Darrel didn't have a violent bone in his body. He thought Darrel was different from the rest of the dangerous inmates. Officer Waters was fully aware of Darrel's case; so he too said if he was in Darrel's shoes at that particular moment, and he found his wife raped and beaten, he too would've caught a murder case. The whole system came to the conclusion that Darrel caught his case by force and not by choice. They often joked that Darrel wouldn't harm a fly; the man wouldn't so much as kill a blood-sucking mosquito.

"D-man what's wrong?" Officer Waters asked, putting all the joking aside. He wanted to give Darrel the opportunity to explain where all his frustration and anger had surfaced from. Darrel dropped down into a chair to talk.

"Man, I'm fucked up in the head." Officer Waters remained silent for a slight moment.

He'd never seen Darrel so agitated, so he immediately sensed that Darrel had something serious going on in his life. *If I would have given my mouth the same chance I gave my ears, I would've smelled the shit before it hit the fan,* he thought, feeling guilty.

"D-man, do you want to talk about something? I mean is there something I can do?" Darrel balled up his fists, knuckles where bulging and his bones looked as if they were about to burst through his skin. Darrel's eyes were full of tears. "There isn't shit I can do, cause I'm stuck here in this fucking cage. Man, my daughter is lying up in the hospital in a coma and the Doctors don't know if she's gonna make it or not."

"Was she in a wreck?" Officer Waters asked concerned. "I mean has she been in a real bad accident?"

Darrel sadly shook his head no.

"She was raped by a couple of creeps and it hurts me to my fucking heart that I can't get my hands on them and rip out their fucking hearts out. It's a damn shame I can't do jack shit!"

"Man, I'm sorry," Officer Waters expressed his condolences.

Due to establishing a slight friendship with Darrel, he could actually feel some of his pain. Again, he realized that Darrel wasn't a bad person; he was just once again catching a bad break. Maybe the Lord was just punishing him for some strange reason.

First his wife, now his daughter. Lord! What did this man do to deserve all this? Execute Jacob's wife? Curse God? What! Officer Waters thought.

"D, I can't say I feel your pains because I haven't experienced anything of that nature. However, I can only imagine the feeling I'd have if it was my wife and daughter going through this. Man, I'm very sorry about what has happened, and the fact that you had to learn about your daughter under these circumstances." Waters paused to see if Darrel was paying attention. "I understand what you're going through," Officer Waters continued."I…"

"Mothafucka, you don't know what I'm going through and you don't know a fucking thing about me," Darrel lashed out at Officer Waters, cutting him off. As he fussed, spit flew from Darrel's mouth. "The only fucking thing you know about me is I'm black and I'm probably gonna die behind these fucking bars. I don't fear death," Darrel opened his arms as wide as possible. "I welcome it."

Officer Waters did not respond, he wanted to allow Darrel time to let out all of his frustration. When Darrel gave off the impression that he was finish with the conversation, he looked like he wanted to box.

"Darrel, hear me out, before you cuss me out," Officer Water said, watching Darrel's jaws vibrate. Darrel looked like trouble, and smelled like trouble. "Man, I know you're a good dude and I would like to help you as much as I can, so let me do you a favor. I'm going to put you in the hole for a couple days, or until you can get yourself together. Bru right now the S.H.U. would be the best place for you. Most intelligent and positive brothers such as you use the hole to their advantage. Sometimes it's best we think the problem out instead of fighting it. You too smart to mess up and do something stupid; something you'll regret later. D, right now you might mess around and hurt someone real bad or mess around and get yourself into a world of trouble. Man, you don't need that; you're not a trouble-maker. You're a wise brother whose tryna finish up the rest of your lil bid and make it safely back home to your family. At least that's what I've gotten from bits and pieces of our conversation, or maybe I've just been assuming things. But Bru, whatever the case, I know you're not yourself right now, so please let me put you in the hole and hopefully in a few days you'll feel a lot better and have a change of heart." Officer Water briefly paused. "Bru, I even had to get my life in order and find God to help me through some storms."

Darrel looked lost; it took all the strength he had to look Officer Water's in the face. The officer didn't feel endangered, he just want to avoid putting Darrel in his cell and in the line of fire, because one wrong word or the wrong movement could cost a person their ticket to freedom. And Darrel was definitely going to explode.

Officer Waters immediate notified the Psych Department about Darrel's behavior. After securing Darrel behind the glass, he also left the Chaplin an e-mail updating them of Darrel's status. To help ease his pain, they made extra sure that they gave Darrel a couple of phone calls, so he could speak with Ebony and other family members. He planned on giving Darrel a few calls himself because Darrel always told him how Ebony's voice healed his soul and gave him the strength and energy to make it through the madness of his environment. Darrel always spoke so highly of his wife and always bragged about how smart Nakeita was. In the past, Darrel had even shown Officer Waters copies of his daughter's report cards. So since Officer Water's had heard so much about them, he felt like he knew Ebony and Nakeita. Officer Waters knew how Darrel felt about the women in his life, and one thing for certain, he knew he had a few things in common with Darrel: their love for their wives, their daughter and how over protective they were over them.

<h1 style="text-align:center">Chapter 24</h1>

Thirty-seven days later.

Ebony sat by the door, talking to Darrel on the phone. As Nakeita's pupils tussled with the sunlight, she would've given anything and everything to hear her father's voice. Nakeita's eyes squinted as she saw six plastic bags hanging from a rack. The tubes running from her nostrils and both arms displayed the reason for the bags. Every time Nakeita breathed, she smelled nothing other than medication.

Oh, God! she thought. *What have I gotten myself into this time?*

Even though Nakeita had a headache, she still could see her attackers violating her body. Tears poured from her eyes, and Scooby dived into her ears. Some of the blows she endured revisited her mind. Nakeita didn't blink, or try to avoid the punches, but by the Lord's grace she found the will power to finally want to strike back. She was ready to stand toe to toe with Kenny and Jazz. She knew she couldn't defeat them both, but now fear didn't dwell in her anymore. She was willing to fight back instead of being used as a punching bag. Nakeita wanted to scream out all kinds of foul language.

"Come on mothafuckas, I ain't scared of yall, y'all might beat my ass, but I ain't runnin no mo. I'll fight you two mothafuckas! I'll fight! I won't run again!" Rage took completely over her mind, and Nakeita found herself unable to shed another tear. Wanting to abandon her bed so she

could storm the streets until she found Jazz and Kenny, she found the strength to fight. If possible, she wanted to kick her assailant's teeth down their throats. Nakeita promised if given a second chance, she wouldn't go down so easily.

Hearing Ebony's voice brought her back to reality.

"Darrel, I don't know what to do. I've been here with Nakeita and the doctors don't know if she's better or worse. They say there's nothing more they can do. They say she has to come outta the coma on her own." She paused to affectionately look at her daughter. "She has been in that coma for sixty-seven days now and the doctor say she pregnant! Darrel, I don't know what to do, them creeps raped my baby, now she has one of their babies living inside of her."

The pain in Ebony voice killed Darrel. It just tore him apart. He was so broken down; he couldn't retain for crying. There wasn't anything else for him to do, so out of frustration, he hammered himself in the head with a closed fist. Ebony felt Nekita's small belly. It did not feel like she was pregnant, nor like something was living in her.

"Yes, Darrel. I love you too and continue to pray for our baby, because that's all we can do. Yes, I heard your phone beep for the second time. Oh, God. Darrel, I wish you were here with us. I wish you could stay on the phone, but anyway. Honey, please calls me as soon as you can? Better yet, please make sure you call me back! Please Darrel! Please, Please. Baby we need you."

Once the line went dead Ebony punched the wall a few times and allowed her weak body to slip onto the floor.

"Oh God, why me? Why me, God? Why me? What have I ever done to you to deserve this? What have I done wrong? You took the only man, I ever loved. Now you're after my only child."

After shedding plenty of tears, Ebony pulled herself together, knowing she had to be strong for herself and Nakeita. Wiping away her tears, Ebony walked out of Nakeita's view. Had she been paying attention; she would've noticed that Nakeita's eyes were open. But Ebony's mind was focused on getting some aspirin out of her pocketbook. She'd been dealing with a three-day old migraine, and was ready to abandon it.

"Lord, I'ma eat these aspirins like candy," Ebony said, filling her palms with four pills instead of the two. "I hope these bad boys do the trick this time," Ebony whispered, leaning over Nakeita to kiss her forehead. "Baby you father asked me to give you a kiss for him. Darrel also asked me how you were doing. You need to come outta this deep sleep, so you can talk to your father for yourself."

Ebony brushed Nakeita hair with her fingertips, as she fought back her tears.

"Nakeita ba-by, come on outta that coma. Please baby! Please do it for momma. Sweetheart, you're worrying me and your father to death. I don't think I can take any more of this. I mean sittin' here helpless, watching you suffer is killing me. I know there's nothing else I can do, but Nakeita momma need you to wake up for me. Please!"

Ebony put her palms together to pray and afterwards she continued stroking Nakeita's hair. Unable to help herself, she gave her daughter's forehead another kiss. "Baby, I'mma run down to the cafeteria and grab a bottle of vitamin water. When I get back I wanna see you wide awake, and sittin' up in the bed. Okay?" Ebony squeezed Nakeita's hand, then she exited the room.

Nakeita counted to ten after she heard the door shut and readjusted her eyes to the sunlight. Her legs and arms felt as thou they weighed a hundred pounds individually. Finding strength from somewhere, Nakeita ripped the tape and tubes from her arms, and carefully removed the one from her nostrils. As she tried to move, her lower body felt numb, but Nakeita manage to get both feet over on the side of her bed, and then on the floor. Sore and afraid to take the first step, tears begin to form in her eyes, and then they crept down her face. Nakeita knew she had to move and move fast, because time wasn't on her side. Ebony could walk in at any moment, any given second, so panic and fear put her body to work. Nakeita held the bed as a walker while traveling to Ebony purse. She wasted no time opening the purse to take out the bottle of aspirin. She took baby steps towards the bathroom, and then filled the first cup in sight with water. As she slipped one hundred 325mg coated pills in her mouth, she gasped as each group washed down her throat. Seconds later Nakeita became lightheaded, the bathroom began to spin, and shortly after everything was a blur. As her body collapsed to the floor, once again her body became still as a doorknob.

When the Asian nurse on duty came in to check on Nakeita, she discovered Nakeita wasn't in her bed, and she noticed the bathroom door was closed. Concerned, she walked in the direction of the shut restroom door.

"Thank you, Lord, for answering my prayers and allowing this here poor child to wake up," The nurse smiled, knocking. "Ms.," she said. But there was no response. The nurse slowly turned the doorknob, praying that she didn't find anything upsetting. Once her brown eyes locked in on Nakeita's body, her heart begin to beat a hundred miles per minute. "Oh, no! Not again," she cried out and raced to the room door to scream for assistance.

***

Four hours later Nakeita had recovered from the fluids she was given to flush out her system. And now she and Ebony were having their mother-daughter talk. Neither one held back any punches or secrets. Nakeita broke down and told Ebony everything. She confessed as if she was speaking with a priest.

"Ma, I took the 'pills because I couldn't face you. I was afraid you were going to blame me for everything and say everything was my fault."

"It's as much my fault, as it is yours," Ebony said, looking Nakeita in her eyes. She knew she made some irrational decisions based on anger and explained to her daughter that she'd always love her, no matter what. Nakeita desperately wanted to have another abortion, but Ebony was a hundred percent against taking the precious life. She convinced Nakeita to see things from a better point of view. She expressed to her that the innocent child didn't asked to be conceived and should have the right to life.

"Remember when the Game said; what if his mother would have had an abortion?"

Ebony asked her daughter, only using that example because Nakeita related to rappers and their music. It was not to insinuate that the rapper and her grandchild had anything in common. Nakeita loved her mother and most of all valued and respected her opinion. She regretted not taking heed to everything that her and her mother fell out about.

"Ma, I'm sorry I stopped listening to you."

"It's okay, Baby," Ebony replied, trying to air out all the kinks in their relationship. "Sometimes crazy things happen to the best of us."

"It won't happen again, Ma," Nakeita mumbled, tearing. "It won't happen again, I promise."

"Okay Baby," Ebony nodded. "I believe you."

"I'm sorry Ma. I know I let you down."

"No! I'm the one who's sorry Nakeita. I let you down," Ebony hugged her daughter. "And it won't ever happen again."

Nakeita wanted to reassure Ebony that she had done nothing wrong. To her, Ebony was a perfect mother; the number one mother in the whole wide world. Nakeita wanted to be held accountable for her own actions. She knew she was to blame for her own wrong doings, and fully took responsibility for her actions. She felt guilty for remaining silent while Ebony blamed herself for her nonsense, but Nakeita wanted to move forward and distance her memories far away from the pass as possible.

To move the conversation, Ebony rubbed Nakeita's spreading belly.

"You and the child are going to be a'right, cause the Lord and I are going to take very good care of you both. Nakeita, you have to give this baby a lot of love, especially because of the way it was conceived. Sweetheart, every child needs to know they are loved. It's important."

"I will," Nakeita assured Ebony. "Ma, I love you."

"And I love you more."

"Ma?"

"Yes, Dear?"

"I'm scared."

"Scared of what?"

"I'm scared for my baby."

"There's nothing to be afraid of."

"What will I tell my child when he asked about his father?"

"We'll cross that bridge when we get there," Ebony smiled. "You still have faith in the Lord whole-heartedly, don't you?"

"Yes ma'am, "Nakeita smiled. "I'll always have my faith. I just won't lean on my own understanding again."

We'll just pray about the situation and once we do," Ebony looked into Nakeita eyes, "…Once you put things in the Lord hands, you leave them there. Meaning you don't worry about them anymore. Lil girl, you're too young to be worrying. I refuse to let you beat me getting gray hair."

"You're right Ma. I listen and obey. I know the Lord will make a way for me, because he made a way for us."

"Good girl and never ever forget, as long as there's a will, there's a way."

Chapter 25

Ebony wanted her and Nakeita to get back on the right track, and establish a balanced spiritual life. As a way to make that happen, they attended church on the first and third Sunday. They listen to media preachers on the radio, six days a week, which helped them keep the Lords Words prevalent in their minds. *"When the Lord is with you, no-one can be against you,"* so they thought.

At the morning service, Nakeita fell to her knees to plead to God. Tears streamed down her face.

"Oh God! Why do you take me through all of this? What have I done to you? Why do you think I deserve all of this; and what do I have to do to get my life right with you?"

Ms. Matty Mae Strong counseled Nakeita a million and one times about how the lord would open all kind of doors and send multiple blessings her way, once she got her life right. Ms. Matty Mae Strong patted Nakeita's knee and whispered, "Child, this preacher here can preach his tail off."

"That's our favorite preacher," Ebony whispered to Nakeita.

"Ain't that the truth," Nakeita mumbled in agreement.

The preacher always preached long, good services, but people in the congregation never became bored. It appeared as if they wanted to hear every word that came out of the wise brother's mouth. They had no problems with him holding them spiritually hostage, longer than the usually church hours. *They only had an attitude with short church services cheating them out* of God's Word. The church stayed focused on the preacher's lips, afraid they would miss out on something important. For most, the right word at the right moment was all a person needed to get back on the right track. As the pastor stood at the pulpit, his eyes scanned the congregation. He was serious as a heart attack about saving lost souls, and everyone knew that his primary goal was to bring people back to the Lord, where they belonged. And that was to be with God Almighty, in order to allow God to be the head of their lives.

Suddenly, the preacher and Nakeita briefly locked eyes, and for some strange reason she felt as though he was talking about her. You know sometimes the Holy Spirit will speak to you and force you to take the pastor's sermon personal. So Nakeita thought the Pastor was reading her soul and making her misfortune his topic. Nakeita's guilty conscious had her mind on one crazy roller coaster ride.

"See! At one point or another, sometimes we come into a divided intersection in our life. We don't know which way to go. To the right – or the left? We question if we should go forwards - or backwards. If we continue looking backwards, dwelling on our past, it can hinder our growth; hinder us from the future, and most of all - it can block our blessings. We may come to church often, but our heads and our life still remain full of questions and focused on the wrong things. But God says lean not to your on understanding, but instead acknowledge Him, and He will guide and direct your path. Sometimes we have to get like Jacob. Genesis 32 tell us about Jacob wrestling with the Lord and the Lord broke both of Jacob hips; but poor Jacob told the Lord, 'Lord, I'm not going to let you go, until I get a blessing. But y'all don't hear me."

Some members of the congregation clapped, others screamed, and some had to make a joyful noise.
"Preach! Brother preach!" One decon shouted.
"Lead the people to the Promise Land."
"Hallelujah - Thank ya Jesus. Thank ya Lord."
"Amen, Amen."
"Pastor Lead the people to the water and make'em drink."
"Let the church say Amen," said the Preacher. "People you're too blessed to be full of stress." The Pastor walked off the platform, and begin preaching with each step. "See, my Bi..Ble tells me to 'trust in God, because faith and prayer change things! God gives us tests to measure our strength. If the devil can't hold us down spiritually, then he can't tempt our flesh and blood. Lord some of your children were once lost, but now

they're found. We don't learn by education, but by revelation. We don't call God --- ha!" the pastor hooped. "- God calla us, --- ha! God don't need us, --- ha! But we sho' need God, --- ha!

I thank God for bringing us out of the darkness, --- ha! Cause you sho wouldn't have been able to see without Him--- ha! I wouldn't have been able either, --- ha! But I'm so glad for God! --- ha! Because he keeps me in my right mind when I'm not able to deal with life --- ha! So what you sayin' Preacher Man?" he said to himself, before responding… "I'm sayin' you and I need a higher power, --- ha! Let the Lord fix you, so he can use you," he moved to a calmer tone. Then without missing a beat, he changed up the pace. He stretched out his right palm to offer an invitation.

"Rejoice in the Lord and whatever you are going through, God will restore you. Come give your life to God today and surely peace will flow through your body like a river."

As people started to make their way to the altar, the choir rose to sing, *Jesus will fix it.*

"So much trouble in my life, I have to cry sometimes, but Jesus will fix it. I lie awake at night, but I know my Lord will fix it. I know you will, Lord, I know you will. I have to talk to someone who will listen, who knows what I'm talking about. Jesus will fix it, Jesus will fix it."

Nakeita found herself singing along, "Jesus will fix it. Jesus will fix it. Jesus will fix it," she sang, feeling a sense of peace. It was as though the weight of the world had been lifted off her shoulders.

"Thank you Lord. Thank you for cleaning my daughter's heart and restoring her soul. I'm always and forever in your debt Lord." Ebony lifted her hands in praise and then had a tender cry.

* * *

As Soon as church service was over Quadiri and his childhood friends hung out in the church parking lot. They reminisced about the old days and how it felt damn good to see one another healthy and still in their right frame of mind. Chuck, Capone, Small and Tutu heard so many prison stories from his homies who'd already done time, and felt their pains. As a result of mentally putting themselves in their homies footstep, they decided as teenagers that involvement in criminal activity was not going to hinder their agenda for life. They decided to grow up and stop worrying their mothers with life threatening encounters with the streets.

Small had an extremely bad attitude, and would fight at the drop of a hat. Determined to prove to the school and neighborhood that his mother and father weren't raising no punk, the skinny framed kid stayed on the A and B Honor Roll and could ball his tail off. He began dunking at age twelve and by the time he reached fourteen, he was dunking with both hands. Once his father explained that he couldn't get a trophy for his disruptive behavior, Small got his act together.

Chuck was on a whole different issue. He was the one in the crew that stayed in chill mold. He loved smoking weed, drinking alcohol, and he certainly loved the ladies. Yet, it was no secret that he was a young man who loved to paper chase. Chuck believed in treating himself to the finer things, instead of cheating himself, so once he crossed paths with Jennia, he elevated his game. He did away with the B\S and allowed his mature side to come full circle. He decided to become a man of standard, because Jennia was a queen, and he knew beside every queen there had to be a king.

Capone loved money and the fast lane, but soon as his wife delivered their twins, his criminal activity went straight out the window. He wanted no parts of living that double lifestyle, nor did he want to leave any type of negative footprints for his junior to follow. Chasing dirty money was not what he wanted for his kid's legacy, so he changed.

The whole time Chuck was explaining the game of cut it and push it with Quadiri, Quadiri's mind and eyes stayed focused on the double wood doors of the church. It was good to see his old friends, but it was even better to see the female who he used to secretly admire, and just so happened still remained the apple of his eye.

When Nakeita was a sophomore, Quadiri was a senior with a very high GPA. He'd skipped a grade. When in school, Quadiri would often break into Nakeita's locker to leave teddy bears, boxes of candy and roses. She noticed him on several occasion watching her, but they never spoke to one another. She later learned Quadiri was the one always leaving her the gifts, but it was too late, because Quadiri had graduated and was millions and millions of miles across the seas, living in more water than he and his 250 man crew could possible drink. Yet, that didn't stop Nakeita from investigating his character. She made it her business not to rest until she found out what type of person Quadiri was. And what she discovered is that she loved everything she heard about him, and hoped that one day she would come face to face with him to thank him for all the presents. Nakeita told Ebony about the mystery man, she too looked forward to meeting Quadiri, especially since her and his mother both were members of the same church.

Crowds and crowds of people begin to pour out of church. Quadiri's heart skipped several beats the moment he laid eyes on Nakeita. She was still beautiful. Quadiri couldn't forget her face in a million years. Out of sight, out of mind didn't seem to apply to either of them. Even after joining the Navy, and while living on the ocean in the submarine, Quadiri interest still seemed to be anchored on getting to know Nakeita. He knew he would one day have a chance to tell her his true feelings. As Nakeita and Ebony made their way through the parking lot, Quadiri finally built up the nerve to go over and introduce himself. They both immediately recognized each other.

"Please excuse me for the intrusion," he said, more so out of respect to Ebony, studying her facial expression and body language. "My name is Quadiri Adams and I—."

Ebony interrupted him.

"So you're the famous Mr. Quadiri?" she said, smiling and truly impressed with the studious look his Navy uniform gave him. "I'm Nakeita's mother, Ebony - and Mr. Quadiri, it's a pleasure to finally meet you."

Quadiri remained silently. He didn't know how to respond.

"Quadiri, is that you?" Nakeita asked, blushing. Quadiri nodded. "Oh, my God. I can't believe it's really you - Quadiri. ….Quadiri Adams."

"Live and in the flesh," Ebony anxiously interjected. "So Quadiri, what made you rush off and join the Navy?"

Quadiri had been asked that question over and over, so he wasn't caught off guard, nor did he have to give the question much thought.

"I wanted to make something out of myself. Common sense told me if I sat around here unproductive that I wouldn't amount to much. The world has enough losers, enough nobodies. And I wanted to be a better man than my father; a better son for my mother, so when I was ten years old, she made me promise that she wouldn't lose me to the streets. She also told me that it takes a man to raise a man, but she did her best, and I turned out pretty good."

Ebony smiled. She liked every word she'd just heard. Quadiri's first impression was most certainly his best impression and was sure to leave a stain on Ebony's mind that she could take to the grave yard.

"Now Ms. May I please have a few words with your lovely daughter?"

"She's all yours," Ebony said, giving Nakeita a wink.

While Quadiri and Nakeita talked, she unloaded all of the burdens, misfortune and painful trials and tribulations she had been through. Old wounds were reopened, and the pain felt almost unbearable as she explained how she was beaten and raped. Quadiri felt her pain, and wanted to comfort her. Without warning, he leaned in and hugged her while she spoke as if her situation was not one she needed to concern herself with. Quadiri heard her, but it was almost as if he didn't hear one word she'd spoken. It wasn't that he was ignoring her, he just refused to allow what she'd gone through prevent her from understanding just how blessed she was.

"Nakeita, I don't believe in coincidence. I firmly believe today was our destiny to meet once again. My mother always used to say, '*If you love someone and you set them free; if y'all reunite, it was meant to be.* I have always had feelings about you that I can't explain, but I know we'd be good for each other, "Quadiri empathetically said, hugging Nakeita tighter. "Mom also explained to me that I can't miss what I never had," he smiled.

"Now that comment there, I know she was wrong about."

Nakeita rested her head on Quadiri shoulder. After paying attention to his level of compassion, she felt safe and comfortable in his arms. Quadiri continued stroking her hair and back, while he inhaled her perfume, thinking of the beautiful plan the Lord may have in store for him and Nakeita.

Awww.... sometimes the Lord will take his children through the realms of pure hell in order to give them a taste of heaven, Ms. Matty Mae Strong thought, watching Quadiri and Nakeita.

<h1 style="text-align:center">Chapter 26</h1>

One year later

Ebony sat in her bedroom feeding Quadiri Jr a warm bottle of milk. As she rocked him to sleep, she counted her blessing. To her, he was the spitting image of her daughter. He had Nakeita's eyes, nose and mouth. Ebony's grandson was her pride and joy. While rocking him, she fumbled in the infant's curly hair. Suddenly, one of her favorite songs comes on the radio - Teddy Pendegraph.

"It doesn't hurt now. No more sleepless nights. No more headaches, no more fights, all that has changed. Now I got someone to help ease my pains." Ebony smiled, thinking, *Nakeita's, firstborn better learn to love oldschool, cause he gon' sho nuff grow up loving or hating this song. In the next few years, I can promise he's gonna hear that record at least a million more times.*

That song along with the time Ebony spent with Nakeita's son helped her mind and soul wash away lots of bad memories.

"Lil Boy, why weren't you a girl? I could've been doing your hair?" she laughed. "That's right Granny wanted a girl. Had that been the case, I could've put some cute little ribbons and bows in your hair."

Ebony removed him from her lap, giving him a kiss on the cheek and another one on the forehead.

"Momma's baby got some sweet sugar," she said in a baby voice before kissing him again on the opposite cheek. "I got me some more sugar. Three times." The infant stared at her with his big, beautiful and brown yes. "Yeah, umm hum," she winked, tickling his chin."You're Grandma's baby. I'mma have you speaking multiple languages and able to do things that even I can't do. You'll be ready to go to any corner of the world," Ebony paused to catch her breath. "You're gonna know Spanish because it's a must now days. Son, everywhere you go, the people are speaking that mess. I also want you to learn Arabic, Chinese, and sign language too. You think you can do that for Grandma?" Ebony slung promises left and right, as she assured her grandchild that he was going to be smart as his mother, if not smarter.

Ebony carefully laid the child across her shoulder, and then proceeded to burp him. She rubbed and patted him on his back. It was a good thing Ebony had a towel thrown across her shoulder, because he immediately spit up some milk on her. Nakeita was accustomed to putting towels across her shoulder, because Quadiri Jr had thrown up on her several times, causing her to smell like spoiled milk.

Running up and down the stairs during the late-night hours had taken a toll on young Nakeita's body. But she wasn't going to complain about that, because after all she'd been through, she'd learned to enjoy every moment in life for what it was worth. As Nakeita folded her son's clothes, she reflected over the affection her mother expressed for her son. Now she wouldn't admit it in a million years, but sometimes she got a little jealous of all the love and attention her mother gave her baby boy. Ebony was still a good, loving and caring mother, and her son was her top priority.

***

Quadiri and Nakeita sat around Ms. Matty Mae Strong's lake, chit chatting. Love was written all over their faces and could easily be seen in their eyes. He placed a thin throw sheet around Nakeita's upper body to shield her from the mosquito.

"I wonder how long this will last, "Nakeita said, easing into Quadiri arms. She was more or less hypothetically speaking, but Quadiri's interest in her question was sparked.

"How long will what last?"

"I mean, you doing all the right things,"Nakeita said. Like most women today, she'd heard so many stories of guys who started out their relationships as the perfect gentlemen, but somewhere along the line, they stop being the nice guy and transform into the Dr. Jekyll or Mr. Hyde.

Quadiri laughed.

"What so funny?" Nakeita asked with seriousness in her tone.

"You."

"How's that?" Nakeita looked puzzled.

"Nakeita," Quadiri whispered, hugging her from behind. "I know what you are thinking. I know what you're trying to say. And to put your pretty little mind to rest; Baby, you're not going to ever have to worry about me mistreating you. God gave you to me. God put us together, so God will have to be the one to take me away from you. No male or female can separate what God has put together, do you agree?"

Nakeita nodded.

"Yes!" She was glad her back was to Quadiri, so he wasn't able to see her tears of joy.

"Nakeita, I loved you before I knew you."

"And Quadiri Adams Sir, I'll love you for the rest of my life."

"That's good to hear."

"Quadiri, you might not believe me, but I love you more than I love myself."

"Is that good or bad?"

"I don't know; you tell me?" she responded.

"I can't answer the question, because I feel the same way you do. Nakeita, you can stop wasting your precious thoughts on negativity. My Love, I always think in a positive manner and your always gonna get positive results from me."

"Okay Baby," Nakeita smiled.

"Nakeita?"

"Yes," she immediately answered, anxious to hear what was about to escape from the love-of-her life's two lips.

"We'll grow old together," he chuckled. "Naw, better yet, we'll be runnin' back and forth to get one another's false teeth."

"Quadiri, you're crazy."

"No, I'm serious."

"I love the idea, please tell me more."

"No."

"No," Nakeita repeated laughing.

"Ma, I'm not going to let you hear it, I'm going to let you see it. I'm not going to talk about what I'm going to do, because talk is cheap.

You'll see for yourself that my heart is into you by my actions. I don't toy around with words like some people who only talk, cause they have a mouth. I'll spend my entire life proving to you that I love you, and if I ever jump off track, please don't hesitate to bring it to my attention."

"Now that I will do."

"You promise?" Quadiri asked, being humorous.

Nakeita took her fingers and made an X over her chest. "I cross my heart and, boy, I don't play when it comes to them crosses."

"Why you couldn't say you put that on your momma? Or on everything you love?" Quadiri asked joking.

"Oh, it's not too late. I still can."

Quadiri wrapped his arms tighter around her waist.

"Baby, you don't have too, because I believe you, and I'll always give you the benefit of doubt. That is until you show me something different."

"Now you don't have to worry bout that."

"Oh, yeah."Quadiri said.

"That's correct."

"But yet you can worry about me, huh?"

"Quadiri, I'm only human. I'm a woman and you know how a female can think?"

"I don't know, because I never been a female."

"Do you believe in reincarnation?" Nakeita asked, repositioning her body to face him.

"Yes, I believe that when we die and come back to earth again in a different body, I'll meet you again. And fall in love with you all over again. I also still want to spend the rest of my natural life with you."

Quadiri lips met Nakeita's. As they shared a passionate kiss, he squeezed her as if he were hugging her for dear life.

***

As she watched Nakeita and Quadiri from a distance, the cool, fresh air brushed against Ms. Matty Mae Strong's face and danced through her hair. The beams from the sun toyed with her pupils, as the wise old lady continued to smile.

"They make a beautiful couple. Thank God my grandbaby only went though one bad relationship, before she found her true love. God is good."

"All the time," said Big Johnny, making his presence known. He'd been standing behind Ms. Matty Mae Strong for at least a good ten minutes or so, but she was busy snooping and way to focused on what was going on down by the lake with Nakeita. "Lady, you standing up here all in they business, that you're not paying attention to your surroundings. If I would've been a rattlesnake, I would've bit'cha."

"You too fat to be a rattle snake," Ms. Matty Mae Strong teased, grinning. "But I'm not going to deny the snake comment. I'm sure you have traces of a serpent in your DNA."

Big Johnny laughed.

"Now come on here woman; my Disco Dynamite ready to put some life in you and the people. I promise he'll live up to everyone's expectations."

"You speak mighty highly of this guy."

"Lady, I know my man like the back of my hand."

Ms. Matty Mae Strong mimicked Big Johnny as she continued to chuckle. Once Big Johnny made Ebony aware of his intentions to take Mr. Cain to the barber, she apologized for not being able to be present. She knew she was going to be missing out on lots of fun and laughter, but did agree that Mr. Cain would be good for Ms. Matty Mae Strong's soul.

"Yeah, you can thank me later for bring the party to you, just don't be a party-pooper."

"Ok, I promise," Ms. Matty Mae Strong said, talking like a child. "I watched that fool friend of yours drink a whole bottle of whiskey like it was water. So I know he can't help himself and everything he do or say gotta be funny."

"You know Mr. Cain?"

"I know whiskey and whiskey sho can talk some trash."

"But have you known whisky to sing and dance?" Big Johnny asked, laughing.

"After that frog was dancing and singing on TV with that umbrella, anything is possible."

"Sometimes people can't tell the truth to shame the devil." Big Johnny said, leading the way. When they finally reached the picnic area, Mr. Cain was running off at the mouth as usual. He was sharing corny jokes, and Betty had tears in her eyes from laughing so hard. Silk was laughing just as hard that he had to gag and choke to feed his lungs air.

"This fool can talk some cash shit," Ms. Matty Mae Strong mumbled.

"Mr. Pump ya brakes, slow ya roll." Big Johnny said, joking. "I hope you ain't gav'em everything you have."

"He's not a normal fool, he doesn't believe in savin' nonsense for tomorrow, "Ms. Matty Mae Strong replied.

Mr. Cain held up his second bottle of wine.

"Boss has no fear. I always recharge my battery with this rat here," he took a few swallows then continued. "Rejuvenation! Y'all this to me reenergizes me like Spanish does Popeye."

"Ain't it supposed to be spinach and not Spanish?" Ms. Matty Mae Strong said, still laughing.

"Dem ya words not mines," Mr. Cain smiled. "This is my story and I can tell it like I wanna." He took another swallow from the bottle. Discovering the bottle was almost empty, a tap of fear rushed his face. "This hear is all that Superman needed," Mr. Cain swirled the last couple of swallows of whiskey around in his mouth, then swallowed.

"Yup! He down a couple of bottles a day of this here goody good stuff. Like me, he can say the hell with kryptonite, and damn Lois Lane because he's the lowest, poorest and needs the morest."

"Louise Lane, you smiling dummy,"Ms. Matty Mae Strong corrected.

"Mr. C, what time is it?" asked Big Johnny, speaking in their own private language.

"Showtime," Mr. Cain said, bucking his eyes. In his King of Soul voice, he shouted, "Let me get up and do my thing." Mr. Cain began doing the James Brown dance in the soft, low cut, green grass while repeatedly singing, "Baby,baby,baby."

Big Johnny told Mr. Cain days ahead of time that Ms. Matty Mae Strong was a true die hard James Brown fan and so was Mr. Cain, so he put his heart and soul into giving the best possible performance that he could. As the whiskey oozed from his pores, Ms. Matty Mae Strong's two eyes didn't see Mr. Cain, and her two ears didn't hear the wino voice either. To her, she was live, front and center at a real James Brown concert.

"I'm black and I'm proud," Silk sung along.

"Say it loud," Betty shouted.

Once Mr. Cain looked as if he was running out of gas, Ms.Matty Mae Strong started clapping and singing.

"He's the greatest dancer that I ever seen."

"That's because you ain't seen me yet," Big Johnny said.

He jumped up and began doing the Robot. His jelly roll stomach bounced one way, while his male breast jiggled in another direction. Ms. Matty Mae Strong had a field day laughing, she laughed so hard, she was crying. She covered her mouth with one hand and held her cramping side with the other.

"Oh, help me, my dear God," she cried out.

As Silk, Betty and Mr. Cain begin doing the Robot also, they competed against one another as if they were on America Idol. It was almost like they were leaving the decision up to Ms. Matty Mae Strong. In their eyes, she was the judge. She was going to pick the winner and determine who the greatest dancer out of that group really was.

Nakeita and Quadiri raced up to the group to join in the fun. They could care less about winning; they just wanted to say they had a chance to dance with the best.

Epilogue

Quadiri turned out to be Nakeita's Knight in Shining Armor. Two months after getting better acquainted, he married her and because of her love for him, she named her son after him. Later on down the line, Quadiri's characteristics really unfolded. Nakeita saw him not only as the perfect gentleman, but also as the perfect husband and father. In observing the relationship Quadiri had with her son, she was given the opportunity to see what she'd missed out on with her very own father.

As the years progressed, Quadiri kept Nakeita barefooted and pregnant. And within their time as husband and wife, she gave birth to four of his children.

Betty and Silk stood firm with their uncle and auntie role to all five of her kids. However, the first born was their favorite. Betty nurtured him and Silk aided in grooming and molding Lil' Q into becoming a young man who would have a bright future.

Since Nakeita's first day on earth, Ms. Matty Mae Strong loved and cherished her to death. So from day one, Nakeita's kids thought Ms. Matty Mae Strong was their biological great-grandmother, due to the way she treated them.

Big Johnny remained family connected, as he continued to rule and run Lover's Lane with an iron fist. Also by beefing up security, his two younger brothers helped him keep his club as popular as it was from the time it initially opened.

Lawyer Lance landed in one of society's spider webs. He got a nasty taste of the real cruelty the world had to offer. His oldest daughter became addicted to crack. Sadly, one day he stopped by her apartment to visit and walked in on her while she was in the process of negotiating her body for drugs. Lance lost his sense of direction and murdered her supplier in cold blood. Thankfully, he didn't spend one day behind bars. He escaped the prison term and became a full fledge superior in his group, which was not a secret.

Darrel received another parole setback. His celly had a twelve-inch prison shank that was discovered in their cell, and anything over six inches was a mandatory free world prosecution that carried up to an additional year. Darrel received a total of three years and was transferred to a twenty-three-hour one-man cell in maximum security; because he beat his celly mercilessly for not admitting the shank was his.

Ebony remained faithful to Darrel. She wrote religiously and kept his account full. She continued to visit every first Sunday of the month, and after all those years, she remained faithful to her wedding vows. She loved him and remained with him for better or for worse. Fornication never crossed Ebony's mind for the two and a half decades her husband was incarcerated.

Jazz died of full-blown AIDS. Bell also contracted an incurable disease. Tasha's big brother murdered Kenny for disrespecting her. Life lived up to his name by catching a life sentence for the robbery of a corner store. It was reported in his arrest warrant that he killed both owners for eight dollars and some change.

Tasha and Wonder became roommates once again. And though they were old, they were still going to night school, trying to get their G.E.D. They finally decided their life had purposes and planned on trying to get into the nursing field.

Toni became a nun, claiming she had enough sex, violence and drugs for the rest of life. She too learned as well as Wonder and Tasha, that the words too late were only a figure of speech, because she too finally straightened up and attempted to fly right....

About The Author

I am here for the readers. I wrote A Daughter's Cry, because I believe that we, as a whole, need to treat women with more love and respect. I'm a firm believer that once one knows better, he will do better. That is why I share my knowledge. We don't encounter experiences to take them to the grave with us, we go through things in life to pass on to help others improve their situation.

Basically, what I'm saying is this, I wrote A Daughter's Cry to show other men why it is mandatory for us to stop walking out on or leaving our babies and their mothers. We need to stop making our women feel unappreciated and help them see the value they add to our lives, our children's lives and our homes.

In this novel, I give it to you real and raw. And though it had me very emotional and was one of the hardest stories for me to write, I hope that for many readers, who may be dealing with similar situations, and you've yet to change your circumstances, that you use this story as a wakeup call and do better for yourself.

Thanks

Available Now

Coming Soon

TRANSFORMATION PUBLICATIONS PRESENTS
FEED THE BEAST
THE KING OF BEASTS
PART 1
A. PLAY

TRANSFORMATION PUBLICATIONS PRESENTS
FEED THE BEAST
EATING OUT OF EVERYONE'S PLATE
A. PLAY

TRANSFORMATION PUBLICATIONS PRESENTS
OPPORTUNIST
THE FORBIDDEN WAY OF LIFE
A. PLAY

TRANSFORMATION PUBLICATIONS PRESENTS
OPPORTUNIST
THE EVIL OF GREED
A. PLAY

TRANSFORMATION PUBLICATIONS PRESENTS
TRENDSETTER
THE GAME OF A LIFETIME
A. PLAY

TRANSFORMATION PUBLICATIONS PRESENTS
TRENDSETTER
NOTHING BUT MURDER AND MONEY
PART 2
A. PLAY

TRANSFORMATION PUBLICATIONS PRESENTS
TRENDSETTER
EXECUTING AN IMPECCABLE PLAN
PART 3
A. PLAY

Make **Money Orders** PayableTo:
KBA Publication
PO BOX 2863
Phenix City, AL 36868

QTY	KBA Publications Available	Price
	A Daughter's Cry	$15
	Career Criminal	$15
	Ridaz – Part II of Career Criminal	$15
	Trans-4-ma-tion Part I	$15
	Trans-4-ma-tion Part II	$15
	Atl's Finest Part 1	$15
	Atl's Finest Part II	$15
	Port City Playaz	$15
	Feed the Beast Part I	$15
	Feed the Beast Part II	$15
	Opportunist Part I	$15
	Opportunist Part II	$15
	Trendsetters Part I	$15
	Trendsetters Part II	$15
	Trendsetters Part III	$15

Ship To:

Name: _______________________________________

Address: _____________________________________

City: _______________ State: _____________ Zip: _____________

For Shipping and Handling, Add $6.75 for 1st Book. Add $1.75 for each additional book. All books are also available on Amazon and Kindle.